# THREE NOTCHES OF DESTINY

### By

### Annie Champa

ISBN: 1-4033-1094-7 (E-book)
ISBN: 1-4033-1095-5 (Paperback)
ISBN: 1-4033-1096-3 (Dustjacket)

This book is printed on acid free paper.

1stBooks - rev. 8/22/02

*TO THE MEMORY OF MOM AND DAD*

*AND*

*FOR BERNIE*

**With Love and Thanks**

# TABLE OF CONTENTS

**CHAPTER NO.**    **CHAPTER NAME**

# ACKNOWLEDGMENTS

I would like to thank Nina Keenam, Kay Rettger, Robert Thrower, the Erie Shores Writers' Group, and the Cleveland State University Writers' Group for reading and commenting on early drafts. Also, I would like to thank Molly Watt, Edward and Joan Moore, Bettie Magnusen, and Mary Moore for their support and encouragement.

I am grateful to Beulah Shanks, Irene Glow, and Elizabeth Alder for their astute, insightful edits.

Above all, I would like to thank Bernie for convincing me that I could write this book and for his support and technical assistance throughout the long process of its emergence.

# PROLOGUE

1983

Daniel Zamora was not overjoyed to leave lively campus life at Alabama's Auburn University; but a greater force, passion for his major in forestry, would help him adjust to Andalusia, the small, insular town in southern Alabama, home of Auburn University's Forestry Education Center. The "frat," the sports, and the friends could wait until after he had completed the ten-week stint of day and night instruction in basic forestry studies and skills for which he would earn seventeen credit hours. Besides, he liked the sound of the town's exotic name, and Florida beaches were only "minutes" away.

While on a Sunday afternoon social call to a young woman's Andalusia home, Daniel was awed by a shell crucifix. It hung from a buckskin neck strip that was draped over an open Bible. The Bible rested on the vestibule table. The crucifix looked almost identical to the one his Creek grandfather kept in a box on his dresser back in Oklahoma. As a child, his grandfather had told him stories about the crucifix, stories which had been passed down through generations but were now fuzzy in Daniel's mind. His elderly grandfather was uneducated and valued the stories more than he.

Nevertheless, in the next telephone call to his Oklahoma home, Daniel told his half-Creek father about the crucifix he had seen in the Andalusia home, even how it was displayed. His father, a professional engineer whose education had been made possible through the GI Bill, had kept in close touch with his Creek community. Having always treasured the family stories and now strongly sensing a connection between the two crucifixes, he prevailed upon Daniel to pursue the source and background of the newly discovered Alabama heirloom.

To Daniel's amazement, this pursuit led to ultimately reuniting the two family heirlooms, along with members of both families, many generations removed. Like weavers creating intricate tapestries, they wove their handed-down stories together. Both families surmised the crucifixes were the ones worn by Padre and Genesis on the Indian Ridge trail—that later became the Three Notch Road—when they had traveled from Pensacola to southern Alabama, escaping Andrew Jackson's invasion. The carefully woven story of the heirs is the basis of *Three Notches of Destiny*.

Daniel had not only solved the mystery of the similar crucifixes, but also of the prominent local use of the three-notch symbol. In the process he gained the friendship of the appealing young woman in whose home he had been awestruck by the familiar-looking crucifix, the one that had remained in Alabama.

Another mystery remained. Daniel Zamora wondered if intermarriage between offspring of Genesis Zamora (who had been banished out West) and Big Brother (whose family had earlier taken one of the crucifixes out West) had propagated members of his ancestral roots. One thing was not mysterious. Daniel felt that the epic begun by Padre and Genesis, over a century ago, was still in the becoming stage and that his future just might play a sizeable part in the drama.

# NOTCH

# 1

# CADIZ, SPAIN

1811

The ship would sail from port in only minutes. A Dominican padre walked to the swaying gangplank and stopped. He looked up, down, and all around before taking a tenuous step. Just as he set foot aboard, heavy cargo slammed on the aft deck; the ship rocked; and though the movement was slight, he dropped his satchel and grabbed the rail. This view changed everything. Water. Water everywhere. Water now separated him from the country where he had spent his first twenty-four years. His fingers whitened as he gripped the rail tighter. He was about to leave the land that held the dust of his parents' blood, his brother's, too, spilled by Napoleon's soldiers. The words of his village priest hauntingly returned: "We found the corpses of your family stiffened into postures and gestures revealing the defiance and terror each faced at the moment of death. Stench of rotting flesh, neglected too long in the sun, and bloodstained scythes, their only means of defense, deepened our horror of their needless deaths."

The padre released his cramped fingers when a reflection in the harbor water riveted his attention. It silhouetted a solitary priest, though not an ordinary one. Yes, he stood alone now and yes, he wore an ordinary cassock, but no, he had never been ordinary in every way. Even the ill-defined image in the ripples revealed his humpback deformity. Since early morning his intense excitement of embarking on the long-awaited oceanic voyage had shielded usual concern of strangers glaring at his distorted shape. And he was heedless that soon he would be without the comfort he had been privileged to in his Dominican Order of Preachers, that is, until his

3

reflection mirrored reality and prompted rational thought. He reached inside his satchel of meager worldly possessions for his prayer book, unaware that somewhere on board this vessel the captain agonized about a confession he should make.

This day had held promise of being a golden one for Padre, ever since the moment he took a clandestine look at the brightly dawning day. His soul had so brimmed with the blessings of early mass that he had hardly felt the need for his boiled barley breakfast. Despite all the wavering feelings of the past few minutes and all the obstacles of past months, he knew he had made the right decision to seek assignment at the Spanish mission and garrison in Pensacola.

Having come from a northerly village in *Andalucia*, this port city had brought unparalleled fascination for Padre as well as the two friars who had been ordered to accompany him to Cadiz. When they had edged closer to the quay, wheels of ox carts and mule-drawn wagons, heaped with barrels and casks of last-minute provisions, squealed along the cobblestones and queued up for unloading. Some drivers scurried to retrieve precious bucolic droppings while waiting to discharge their lading. Nearby, a fisherman dumped mounds of shimmering sardines and pilchards from a fishy-smelling net, patched from end to end. Longshoremen's chants, in perfect rhythm with their work motions, carried on the wind along with the deckhands' shouting and swearing while they stowed heavy cargo. A tall, wooden boom, bowing with each weighty load, looked alarming as anything Padre had ever seen. Would it snap any second and spoil this near-perfect, God-given day? Family members and lovers of the seamen and onlookers milled near the quayside. A group of women competing to entertain ship crews laughed and capered while eating caramels. The two women who wore shawls sometimes playfully tossed the tassels decorating their wraps. Spanish chatter hummed in contrast to the shrillness of block and tackle, which resounded louder and louder as it hoisted cargo. Padre had veered toward the brightly-blossomed cannas. Fertilizer of rotting fish heads and guts overpowered their usual subtle sweetness, yet he could not remember ever having seen more vivid scarlet cannas.

Now, as Padre raised his prayer book, the panorama stretched before him in an altogether different perspective. Sudden sensation of being absolutely alone and leaving Spain transformed excitement and anticipation into awe, then trepidation. But before praying about these feelings, he sought sight of the two friars, also members of his beloved Dominican Order of Preachers. They had fulfilled their duty and offered their blessings for the voyage. Padre imagined the friars, steeped in the historically mendicant philosophy of the Order, would minister to the port beggars and offer hope before returning to the monastery. Sure enough, the friars huddled with the destitute and shared their scant supply of bread. They would beg for more as they traveled.

After a short prayer Padre resolutely meditated on his forthcoming foreign mission effort, an effort not completely sanctified by his brethren. Background din smothered energetic footsteps. The approaching figure was unnoticed. Then, startled by the grip of a strong hand on his shoulder, the padre turned to face the stern sea captain.

"Welcome aboard, Padre," a somewhat out-of-breath, though still stalwart, voice said. "Captain Zamora here. It is a pleasure to have a holy one as a passenger for a change. I haven't transported a priest to Florida in several years. It fills my heart with gladness to see a priest headed for Pensacola." He squinted his solitary eye and quickly scanned the rumpled, tobacco-stained ship's manifest in his hand. "I am looking for your name. I saw it earlier. Here, it is—Padre Morales, Juan Adamio Morales to be exact."

Struggling to stifle his startled reaction, Padre said, "Yes, yes. The name is listed correctly. It is, indeed, unfortunate conditions have not been conducive for sending priests to our colonies. I am sure you are aware that the Church and Spain have suffered great financial expenditures in their effort to quell Napoleon's invasion. It was not easy for me to get appointed to St. Michael's Mission in Pensacola."

"People poured into Pensacola after America negotiated the Louisiana Purchase," the captain said. "My shipping business prospered. New settlers needed many supplies. But with war in the homeland, you are right— there's not much left for the colonies." Captain Zamora grimaced toward the sun, swished the sweat from his brow, and said, "I'll have no peace of mind until we're under weigh." He forced a smile. "Important orders must be given. You know. Strike the sails, heave the anchor, but I must first make last minute checks on the crew and cargo." Then he leaned forward in the manner of one conveying a cryptic message and added, "I need to make a confession, a very important one, one that I have put off for years. It had to be God's will to send you on this trip, my last ocean voyage. For one reason or another, I just keep putting off this obligation. It's just never the right time."

"Certainly. On this voyage, I look forward to serving the holy Catholic Church in every way: hearing confessions, ministering to the sick, performing liturgical ministry, or in any other helpful way." Urgency in Captain Zamora's voice immediately intrigued Padre. He had always treated confessions as routine. They usually consisted of predictable and even boring offenses, but this request seemed different. Truth is, he just knew it concerned a different sort of transgression. How? He did not know how, but he knew it. He knew it the same as he knew his fellow Dominican brethren had grown suspicious of him after he pursued an assignment in Pensacola. One by one they had withdrawn from him, even walked away from him whispering after vespers and mealtimes. Despite these odds he had remained obedient to his Order and staunch in his calling.

Padre's attention turned to the blessings being implored from dockside for a safe voyage. At once, he felt glorified as well as exonerated in his decision to make this change. He would serve God on the voyage. Besides, the captain had validated the need for priests in Pensacola.

The windlass work song burst forth in cadence as deckhands wound the line hoisting the anchor. Alas, departure time had arrived. While the ship came about, Padre's flush of elation lay mostly hidden under his dense black beard, which matched his long, wavy hair and added to his apostle-like appearance. He drew in a great breath and gazed out on the sea of early civilization and back again at the fading Cadiz Harbor, its long, rocky shores so new to him. With the lowering sun the ever-diminishing towers of Cadiz's Baroque Cathedral and whitewashed buildings slowly dimmed. So familiar to him was the developing, though short-lived, scene of the ancient *Andalucian* countryside dotted with olive trees. Shepherds peacefully tending flocks, which grazed on the hills, finally faded. Hillside gypsy caves became mere specks. Dark jagged mountains rose in the distant background, then disappeared as if entombed in the infinite ocean.

Captain Zamora finally ceased shouting and issuing orders. His flailing arms now rested alongside his bulging girth as he again approached Padre. Though the captain leaned forward with an air of respect, his voice sounded like a military officer's command as he said, "Padre, do me the honor of dining with me this evening."

"Certainly, thank you," Padre answered, and made a closer visual assessment when the captain pushed his hat backward. The black eye patch over his right eye now showed more conspicuously in the hollow below his protruding forehead.

At dinner Captain Zamora poured wine, cupped his hand around the flowing golden stream in the manner of drawing the fragrance closer, and smacked his lips before he even tasted it. "The nutty aroma is unmatched, fit for any king," he said. "This evening is special, an occasion that merits the best sherry from Jerez de la Frontera's finest vineyards." He passed Padre a tray of bread, along with the sherry, then a *tapas* tray, heaped with anchovies, cuttlefish, olives, dried figs, and other delectables, some of which Padre had seldom tasted.

No sooner had Padre partaken of the savories than his stomach seemed to swing in the same wide arcs as the garlic garlands and the lantern. The oil-reeking flames flickered with the ship's pitch and roll and cast eerie, whirly shadows against the walls and ceiling. A whirling sensation commenced in his head and stomach. A bilious taste welled up in his mouth. He retched. Surely this had been the evening Captain Zamora had chosen to make the confession, but none would be heard this time. Even with all Padre's might, he barely suppressed a second retch and staved off the heave until he reached the rail. The dinner had been for naught. What a pity to forego his priestly duties, the rare delicacies, too.

While Padre sequestered himself in periods of seasickness, scenes of his brethren's rejection haunted, hurting worse than the pain in his distorted back whenever he had pushed himself to physical excess. True, he had been devastated by his family's harsh deaths. But try as hard as he could, he had failed to move his fellow Dominicans to understand that he had not placed his mother and father and brother ahead of the family of God. It just so happened that after French soldiers had slaughtered his parents and older brother, he sensed an urgent calling to Pensacola. After the family deaths his younger brother had gone to sea as a deckhand, never to be heard from again.

Seeking assignment to the mission in Pensacola by no means meant that he needed to escape the homeland, unable to deal with personal family losses. Ever since his ordination, and earlier too, the family of God had always come before anyone else. The angels and saints knew it, knew his heartfelt convictions, though somehow the brethren just would not accept his explanations. Nor could he convince them that he possessed sufficient endurance, regardless of his hunched back and lack of foreign mission training. Padre firmed his posture resolutely. He had taken his stand; he must not fall short, no matter what the future might hold.

Over a period of several days, Padre overcame seasickness to some degree only to discover bedbugs and head lice irritating him. A lice comb, given to him at the monastery, helped in ridding the hungry leeches in his hair and beard, but what could he do about the bed bugs other than scratch and chase the fat-bodied parasites? He loathed the dark, bloody spots on the mattress tick, which bespoke of some of the critters having met their demise. And though he had been forewarned about rats, cockroaches, too, a monstrous cat kept those creatures under control.

Finally, on an unforgettable day, as the ship plied the endless ocean, Padre and the captain arranged a time for the confession:

"I have a son in Pensacola," the captain said haltingly and paused. "He, uh, lives with his mother..."

After the confession and absolution, the captain continued, "I come from the Zamora shipping family and even completed some university studies. It is hard to believe I put myself in this position, and it is harder to believe the boy will be thirteen years of age this year. My lawful *senora* in Cadiz knows nothing about him, nor do my sanctified children and

7

grandchildren. I just drew the curtain on that sin, but I can't tell you how penitent I always felt whenever I thought of him, especially that his mother had to raise him alone. She is a full-blooded Creek Indian, and since you might meet her, I'll tell you her name is Naja. At the time I met her, she did scullery work at the garrison. I had been landlocked in Pensacola during hurricane season. During that time, I ate a lot of oysters on the half shell," he said with a diabolical twinkle gleaming in his solitary eye. "When I sailed away, I never knew she was in a family way. On my next trip to Pensacola, I was a bit surprised. The mission had helped her through her hard times. From the influence there, she named the baby boy Genesis," he said, his last words quivering. "Even though I have always contributed to his support, I am tired, terribly tired of feeling like a runaway renegade."

He quickly swiped a tear, regained composure, and said, "It is with great pride that I tell you this ship carries precious cargo for my Pensacolian son—a white, *Andalucian* stallion. Since this is my last sea voyage, I went to great lengths to bestow a symbol of his *Andalucian* heritage. After all, he is half Spanish; I want him to be proud of it."

"You chose a most appropriate icon of the region, Captain. I grew up in the hills of *Andalucia,* and I admired those horses, even dreamed of riding one. As a matter of fact, my sentiments run so deep that at the monastery I read all I could find about them. The Carthusian monk breeders had opposed crossing heavier foreign breeds with these horses and thanks to them, the ancient, pure line of the *Andalucians*, going back as far as 200 B.C., was preserved."

"I don't know how they came to be," Captain Zamora said, "but I knew for sure as soon as I laid eyes on this big, white one, I wanted him for Genesis. That's the kind that's fit for a prince to ride, wouldn't you say so?"

"Well, yes. You see, the Carthusian monks resisted outside influences and continued their pure breeding in Seville and Cordoba, too, an honored Spanish principle I might add," Padre couldn't resist saying with unabashed pride. Then he looked down. Leaving the monastery had not given him freedom to act self-important, possibly pompous. Kindly rebukes from his superiors, for his repeated tendency to show off his education, sprang to mind. In the future he must take greater care to refrain from repeating this venial sin.

The fine horse increasingly became the most important topic of conversation, next to the weather, during long days of sailing the immense ocean. Captain Zamora took tremendous care while shipping the animal and one day invited Padre to observe its exercising session in the specially prepared cargo hold. From that moment on Padre felt a connection to the noble stallion.

"I have been mulling over a name," the captain said.

"Grand! Grand is the first word that comes to my mind," Padre said as he stroked the thick muscles of the magnificent horse's neck. Perhaps you might consider naming him *Grandeza*."

During the windless afternoon, Padre watched Captain Zamora playing dominoes with the first mate. The captain mopped his wrinkled, weathered forehead. He then lifted the patch over his right eye, wiped perspiration from the scarred socket, and said, "Padre, you probably think this patch covers an old wound made by some buccaneer with a sharp cutlass that poked out my eye."

"Not at all, Captain, though in all honesty, I will concede I am curious as to how you lost your eye."

"During past years, I have been in a number of close encounters, especially with corsairs. Those pirates have the guts of a lion and power, too. They attacked my ship in the Gulf of Mexico time and again, and yes, I lost my right eye last year."

"I offer my deepest sympathy. Eyesight is such a God-given blessing."

"But my eye was not gouged in a pirate attack," the captain said with an air of protest. "It happened in a freak accident while I supervised crewmen who parbuckled flour barrels. You see, I had to make sure they did not waste one. Another group set up the winches and a pulley for unloading, and the rope snapped on the first load. I had been looking up at the pulley when it fell and couldn't get out of the way fast enough. The hook on the pulley ripped out my eyeball."

"What a tragedy, God bless you. You perform your duties well considering the loss."

"In my sprier years, I could draw away from danger faster than any sword-stabbing corsair or any fast-falling pulley. Now that I am sixty years old, it's time to give up the risky life on the seas."

Captain Zamora frowned. He had admitted enough. Why should he mention that during his treacherous years of sea life he had accumulated a small fortune in dealing with hundreds of barrels of contraband flour and other illegal commodities? After the last play of the domino game, he leaned back and said, "Padre, I have decided to accept your suggestion; I have named Genesis' *Andalucian* stallion *Grandeza*."

"Very well," Padre smiled. "The name is quite befitting for its grandeur and nobleness." Padre tipped his head, an unconscious habit similar to a common tic movement. His dark brown eyes glowed, as always, when someone heeded his advice.

Hour upon hour Padre wiled away the days by taking lessons from the sailors in whittling and carving, particularly when the crew was idled by stilled wind. When Padre first attempted to sharpen a knife and carve a wooden spoon, he found carving not only a worthwhile activity but also quite satisfying, one to which he seemed suited in a natural sort of way. He also watched as the crew deftly mended sails as well as their clothing and sewed intricate patches of webbing from seabirds' feet into tobacco pouches. These pursuits finally ended.

Alas, the joyous sight of land came into view. Never, had the brilliant color of green been so welcome. Different intensities of light had brought out subtle shades of the hue in the sea, but never the vibrant verdancy of the pine trees on the distant, gently rolling hills.

"So this is the jewel," Padre murmured. One writing from the seventeenth century, which had filled him with intrigue, read something like, "The finest jewel possessed by His Majesty..." He had read other works that for over a century had praised Pensacola Bay for its depth, spaciousness, protection from wind, and its friendly "Panzacolian" Indians. Many writers reported it to be blessed with a hinterland bounding with game and virgin timbered forest. Ownership of the colony bounced back and forth under control of powerful nations. Agues, hurricanes, fires, and pirates hindered growth of a stronghold. Even with all the troubles that had beset the colony the regal sound of "jewel" lured him. He just knew there was hope for the colony, and a sorely needed mission to be accomplished there beckoned him again and again. Pensacola lacked a church building. He felt eager for the challenge.

An afternoon thunderstorm passed slowly; then, instead of nature's rumble overhead, Captain Zamora's thundering voice blasted on deck. He gave orders for *Grandeza's* entrance into the Pensacola port, a momentous occasion. Padre watched the ofttimes-horrifying maneuver and marveled at the complicated feat. The crewmen hobbled the horse's legs and placed him in a sling. Next they released the bindings on his legs and winched the noble animal from the ship. Two crewmen, one on each side, swam alongside the stallion into port.

The captain shouted, "Hold onto the reins and give the horse plenty of space. He needs to kick his legs to stay afloat!" Captain Zamora's sole eye flashed authoritatively as he yelled again, "Keep his legs moving or he'll sink." His attention remained fixed on *Grandeza* until the stallion stood safely on shore. Then the captain cast a satisfied look at Padre and said, "A ship's arrival always attracts a crowd, but you won't have any trouble picking out my son. You can't mistake him. His hair is the color of cayenne pepper, like mine used to be before it turned gray. And it won't take you long to notice his behavior can be peppery, too. Well, he's at that changing stage. Last time I saw him he would act mannish one minute and the next like a child."

Filled with his own thoughts about the new priests he would meet and wondering what St. Michael's Mission would be like, as well as the garrisoned men and Pensacola's other inhabitants, Padre's overloaded sensory system could barely integrate the captain's informative conversation. Padre saved space for selected thoughts, though. His face lit up, and he basked in the attainment of the first part of his long-sought goal. Then, in a great leap of imagination, he dreamed of perchance becoming a luminary during this mission. Why, he might have been sent to Pensacola by the grace of God to perform a reverently wrought miracle.

# SPANISH PENSACOLA

1811

On hallowed land at last, Padre crossed himself and kissed the sand. Upon arising he wobbled, trying desperately to find his land legs. The crowd witnessing presentation of *Grandeza* to Genesis, though fascinating, thwarted Padre's eagerness to find the priests with whom he would work. The mixture of colorful people called out greetings in French, English, Indian dialects, and, of course, Spanish. Hawkers with baskets of wares peddled them through the gathering. Captain Zamora had understated the description of Genesis, for the lad appeared as worldly-wise as the wharf waifs he had seen in Cadiz. In a bright, blessed moment the captain hugged Genesis and handed him *Grandeza's* reins. How engaging the captain looked as he told his son of the wonderful gift and partook of Genesis' unmistakable awe. Genesis' boyish smile now belied the initial image. The soon-to-be-thirteen-year-old's demeanor transformed into one that would captivate and melt the coldest heart, somewhat like that of an *Andalucian* urchin in front of a confectionary.

In the thick of the crowd, a shrunken gnome of a priest with a pointed, white beard waved his walking cane and called out to the newly arrived one, "I am Padre de Galvez, priest in charge of St. Michael's Mission." His thin, white hair blew in the gulf breeze. He plodded forth guided by a younger priest who held the elderly one's forearm. Up closer Padre de Galvez said, "In the name of God, I extend a heartfelt welcome to the Pensacola garrison and St. Michael's Mission. I thank God for your safe deliverance." He looked toward the priest who supported his arm and said, "At my side is

12

Father Mulvaney, second in charge at the mission. He is one of the priests educated at the Irish College of the University of Salamanca in Spain."

Immediately, Father Mulvaney said, "I also welcome you in the name of the Lord."

Bowing slightly, Padre Morales said, "Thank you. Thank you both. And I thank God for a safe voyage. I am delighted to be here." But amidst all the excitement, he tried to stave off mixed feelings—the tingling and wonderful, though strange sensations of regaining land legs. And why had the brethren in Spain been so opposed to his requesting this assignment? True, he had been trained only for liturgical ministry in the homeland and had not undergone the rigorous training for foreign mission work. Albeit, these beautiful white sandy beaches, cooled by salubrious gulf breezes, looked like a halcyon setting for mission work. Moreover, he already felt safe from Napoleon's army, for from the vantage he had had on the ship's deck, Ft. Barrancas had hugged Pensacola Bay in a strong, protective way.

On the way to their living quarters Padre Morales took stock of the new surroundings, much of it so different from the narrow, cobblestone passageways of towns and trailed hills in Spain. Instead of whitewashed stucco dwellings, Pensacola's sandy streets shouldered rows of wooden houses, mostly one-storied. Fences and porches adorned several, and a brick sidewalk fronted one. After they had passed the residential section Padre de Galvez said, "We will stop here in Plaza Ferdinand, and Father Mulvaney can explain to you how to find your way around Pensacola."

"To begin with," Father Mulvaney said, "the town extends about a mile along the bay and a quarter of a mile inland. Our mission also serves the settlers whose huts dot the miles of yonder hinterland. His forefinger scribed a semicircle in the air toward the north. You will find most of the streets have Spanish names like Zaragoza, which ribbons east and west. On our right, Tarragona, of course, extends north and south." He pointed and said, "Over toward the bay, you can see the late afternoon sunlight angling on the southern end of Tarragona. This block-style layout earmarks the era of English occupation, and you will find that some of the streets still bear English names from that period."

Padre breathed a relieving sigh at the comforting sound of Spanish-named streets. But what about Father Mulvaney? Something about him seemed, in a vague way, rather unleveling. While the foreigner pretended not to stare at his deformed back, Padre caught him taking glances that seemed unfavorably judgmental. One thing for sure, he had never known the likes of an Irish priest.

"It may come as a surprise to you," Father Mulvaney continued, "that in addition to Spaniards, other Europeans, free blacks, slaves, and Indians, as well as many people of mixed blood inhabit this area. They live together harmoniously, some of them with and some of them without—which may shock you—the sacrament of marriage. As we walk on I will tell you more. In the center of Pensacola is the *presidio* or stockade as the English had called it during their rather brief occupation."

"Yes, I saw the walled area from the ship," Padre Morales said.

"One of your duties will be to minister to the incarcerated men of our garrison," Padre de Galvez said. "A few men consume an inordinate amount of *tafia*. The fieriness and rawness of this rum gets them into brawls." He leaned over and whispered, "Some even disorder their robust bodies by engaging in promiscuous intercourse with lewd women." Then in his usual voice he said, "But your assignment for tomorrow afternoon, sure to be a memorable one, is at the hospital, officially called Ft. San Carlos de Barrancas Hospital. You will visit a maroon who has undergone unusual surgery."

"Forgive me for interrupting, Padre de Galvez, but I am not familiar with the term 'maroon.' Will you explain it to me, please?"

"Very well. It is a West Indian word meaning free Negro. This particular maroon was a Negro slave who ran away from his master in the American territory and sought refuge in Pensacola. The doctor who performed the extraordinary operation is a surgeon stationed at the garrison here. While on a visit to New Orleans he purchased a guillotine, which was manufactured in France, and had it shipped it to Pensacola. He thought the contraption performed operations more humanely than doctors operating with knives and saws. Perhaps he is right. A weighted, sharp blade and pulley, and rope, too, on the device, enabled him to lop off the maroon's gangrene-ravaged leg quite efficiently."

Padre Morales grimaced but caught hold of himself and said, "Certainly. I am pleased you asked me to visit the maroon in the name of our Lord."

"In addition to encouraging Indian settlements," Padre de Galvez said, "our Spanish government also encourages fugitive slaves. Indeed, the Spanish border of Florida represents a refuge. Indians and Negroes are valuable to the Crown, for more settlers increase Spanish trade."

Padre de Galvez tapped the arm of this newest member of his group and said, "Tomorrow morning, you will celebrate mass. But first, I must be assured that you know there is no church building in Pensacola. The mission is located in an old *almacen* or warehouse."

"Yes, I was informed, but I wonder how it happened that a warehouse came to be used for a chapel," Padre Morales said.

"A Capuchin," Padre de Galvez answered, "was sent from New Orleans to St. Michael's after the United States purchased Louisiana. Finding no church, he converted an old warehouse into a chapel. It is large enough, but it is shabby and ill-suited for the purpose."

Padre Morales tried to appear unruffled, but the thought of no real church building still seemed deplorable. He said, "One of the main reasons that I asked to be assigned here was to help build a church."

"That is an admirable ideal," Padre de Galvez said, "and much appreciated, I might add. Truth is, I have determined we have an even greater need. I have been saving for a horse and have received permission from Havana headquarters to purchase one. In order to provide Catholic succor for all our people in the surrounding area, a priest must be able to reach them. We need all these people to gain support for a new building. Since you are the youngest, you will spend some days, as soon as we get the horse, ministering to the people in the hinterland. Meanwhile, we must continue using the present chapel."

Jolted, but ever true to his Dominican vows, the obedient Padre Morales said, "Certainly, I respect your decision."

"The bishop wrote me," Padre de Galvez said, "that he had wanted you to go forward with your liturgical service in the homeland. Your gifted baritone voice seemed the most compelling reason. He praised your chanting as the best he has heard amongst the younger priests. I am looking forward to your celebration of mass tomorrow."

Though deluged with the novel aspects of Pensacola and disappointed about his proposed church-building plans, Padre dutifully shared a part of his past. "I feel deeply honored by His Excellency's comment. I always chant as best I know how in the presence of the Holy Virgin's image. At the monastery I learned that chanting has a timeless quality, not old, but everlasting. It is amazing how little has changed since Pope Gregory I codified the rules. I think these rules create the ancient, mystical sound. That sound must be veritably the same now as it was then."

"It is truly the root of our Catholic music," Padre de Galvez said. "It has the spirit of a universal language. The resonance is actually a yearning, a yearning for discovering spirituality."

"Certainly, Padre de Galvez. I was also told while studying at the monastery, 'He who chants, or sings a prayer, prays twice.' The mysterious rise and fall of the song enhances our ability to reach deeper spiritual depths."

Padre's resolve to work ardently at acquainting himself with the new people, new territory, and new cultures filled ensuing days. He learned the names of the officers and men at the garrison as well as other inhabitants of the area, sought out information on the Indians and Negroes, and listened to the people's anecdotal accounts of real and perhaps imaginary happenings in Pensacola. However, he made a special effort to be present at dockside the day Captain Zamora's ship was scheduled to sail for Spain. Understandably, the occasion provoked heart-wrenching unhappiness in

Genesis. He looked like a forlorn waif. Considering their short spans of time together, it seemed remarkable that Genesis still looked up to his father with immense pride.

As the ship faded below the horizon, Genesis asked in a pouting way, "Just what is so special about Spain anyway?"

"For one thing, Spanish people breed those wonderful *Andalucian* horses like *Grandeza*. You did not forget about your birthday present already, did you?" Wishing to comfort Genesis, he continued without waiting for an answer. "I will make a trade with you. I will tell you something about the *Andalucian* Region of Spain, if you will tell me a story about Pensacola."

Genesis pursed his lips and silently searched Padre's eyes in a quizzical manner.

Padre returned the questioning gaze. Would he be able to help the lad let go of his sadness?

In a few moments, Genesis mumbled reluctantly, "All right, my father liked you a lot, so I'll make the trade. You go first."

Without much thought, olives sprang into Padre's mind. He asked, "Have you ever heard of olives?"

Genesis shrugged, "I dunno."

"They are one of the richest gifts of heaven, and Spain is famous for them. Olives are tiny fruit, which grow on trees that dot the landscape throughout the *Andalucian* Region like palmettoes do here. They are green at first. When they turn black they are ripe. Trees are covered with these black spots, lots of them close together, close as pips in a domino bone yard. That came to my mind, because I just remembered seeing you play dominoes with your father yesterday afternoon."

Genesis unleashed a small smile.

"Olives are good to eat, even the green ones, if they are prepared in salt brine to get rid of the bitter taste; but you have to watch for pits. They are just as hard as peach pits, and though much smaller, they can crack a tooth. Spanish people also press olives to make olive oil. My mother warmed the oil and spread it on bread, which she baked in an outdoor oven like the one by the dining hall." Essence of the hot bread started Padre's mouth watering.

Genesis shrieked in childish amusement when he rounded his lips and sounded the *"o"* words. He brushed his fingertips across his lips and said, "That sound tickles my mouth, plays tricks on my ears, too. But I like it. I like different sounds and different words."

Padre smiled. Perhaps the youngster possessed a budding gift for learning new words, one that might develop into an even stronger trait for speaking the different languages heard in Pensacola. He took Genesis to the garrison's kitchen and explained, "In Spain, brick ovens are built outside like this one. Don't you think it looks something like a huge egg, almost an oval shape?"

Genesis grinned widely at the sounding of another "o" word. "I chop wood and stack it for the cooks, but I never thought about that thing looking like a big egg."

"Now, I will show you Spain's lifeblood." Inside the dining hall, he scraped residual oil from the pouring side of an olive oil vessel, rubbed it between his fingers, and displayed it.

"I saw it here lotsa times, but it surefire ain't the color of blood."

"Of course not, but it provides for Spanish people much like your blood does for your body. It is so dear to our hearts. It has fed, provided light, and healed *Andalucians* for centuries. Even in droughts, that sometimes lasted several years, the trees' blessedly long tap roots kept them alive and bearing fruit." It seemed strange that olives, such a commonality to Spanish children, turned out to be such an oddity to Genesis. This first lesson brought biblical joy, surely similar to the kind Jesus Christ, or at least like an apostle, must have felt preaching parables. Without a doubt, time spent teaching had kept Genesis from watching a gambling game or cockfight. Why, angels above, had Captain Zamora not taken more time with his son? He had missed so much of the youngster's life. Padre grimaced and shook his head. Then he forced a quip, "All right Genesis, now it is your turn to tell a story."

Genesis simply folded his arms tightly over his chest and asked, "Do you have a father?"

"My father and mother were killed by French soldiers, my older brother, also. It was a tragedy, since they were only trying to protect their little piece of land. They were poor, humble farmers and had only their scythes for protection."

"What's a scythe?"

"Let's walk over to the sand, and I will draw a picture for you."

Padre scribed the picture and after wiping the sand from his hands, said, "There, that's what it looks like. People keep them sharp for clearing fields and harvesting."

"That's surefire a fearsome kind of knife. I'd like to have one to show to some of them big heads around here that have fathers that live with them." He looked up at Padre and asked, "Do you have any other brothers or sisters?"

"Oh yes, but the only other one that lived was my younger brother who went to work on a ship something like your father's. The ship was lost at sea, probably in a storm."

With unfettered youthfulness, Genesis asked, "Did your brothers have humps on their backs like you?"

Somewhat taken aback, Padre simply shook his head and uttered, "No."

Without any pretense at deception, Genesis asked, "Does that hump hurt?"

"Most of the time, it does not bother me," Padre answered. At this opportune moment, he launched his mission work. "Young man, this is the way I was born. God, the God of the Holy Catholic Church, cares about people equally, no matter how they look. My crooked back has not hindered me from becoming a worthwhile person. I would like you to pay more attention to what I say, and what I do. Then you might forget about the way my back looks. Now, let's return to our agreement. You owe me a story."

Genesis stared in space for a few moments, wiped the back of his hand across his mouth, and said, "I bet you don't know what Red Sticks are."

"I probably do not know about the particular red sticks that you are referring to."

Genesis' dark eyes brightened. "It's a nickname for the Seminole—not all of them—just the ones that like to fight. They got the nickname from painting sticks red."

Padre chuckled.

"Don't laugh. The red sticks are important."

"Painting sticks red seems like a strange thing to do."

"There's surefire nothing strange whenever they leave a bundle of red sticks at a town. It means they declared war. And the number of sticks give the message when it will start."

"Now Genesis, sticks do not talk where I come from." He tipped his head back and with a mirthful laugh, enjoying the fact that he had distracted Genesis from the forlorn mood. He said, "All right, I will sacrifice my honorable status and ask how?" Instantly, he cringed at the resurfaced pompousness of his tone.

Unaware of Padre's recurring problem and his cringing reaction, Genesis said, "Red Sticks' sticks surefire talk in their own way. And it makes plain ole good sense. The number of sticks tells the number of days that will pass before war starts."

"Well, Genesis, you *surefire* know things *Andalucian* children might never hear about."

Genesis tried to restrain an erupting smile.

Indeed, Genesis' explanation of the Red Stick Seminole put many conversations, which Padre heard around Pensacola, in proper perspective in days ahead. Who would have ever guessed them to be warrior-type Seminole? Other exchanges, especially concerning *Grandeza*, cemented their relationship. Many times Genesis looked and acted, in Padre's eyes, like his long lost, younger brother.

Genesis showed genuine sparks of promise and instructing him became a part of Padre's mission in a natural sort of way. It was so easy to teach the eager-to-learn lad. Why, he soaked it in like the sandy beaches soak a summer downpour. The poor half-orphan had no place to learn except in the streets. Pensacola had no schools. Though a gutsy youngster, willing to try learning anything challenging, he still respected the distinguished position of priesthood, and without a doubt, Genesis felt good about acquainting him with life in Pensacola.

Genesis, however, needed direction in harnessing his temper, especially whenever he heard people refer to Creek or Seminole as wild savages. He would get so angry that he would fight like the wildest, young bull in *Andalucia*.

In ministering to him, Padre explained how his brothers and other children had taunted him about his hunchback and how the acolyte helped him when he went to church to pray about it. He said, "The acolyte scolded my brothers whenever he caught them teasing me for praying so long on my knees. He had faith in me and helped me get into the Dominican monastery. I have faith in your abilities, and I intend to help you develop them as the acolyte did for me."

As the weeks and months passed, it became evident that Genesis not only yielded to anger but also to envy. Yet it was hard to hold him solely responsible for all his transgressions, in particular, whenever he envied other young men who had fathers present in the family. Truth told, he needed fundamental instruction in overcoming all the deadly sins, all seven. Consistent hammering of words mastered at the monastery made a difference: "...catch hold of yourself and start all over again; the greatest of people have learned to do it." Without intervention he might have even taken up with the warrior Red Sticks, for altercations between them and Americans at the borderlands had begun increasing in number and violence.

Appalled, Padre heard more and more stories about the way Indians and Americans bandied purloining, exchanged woeful raids of destruction, and massacred each other's people. He had escaped fighting in Spain and never expected to find it in the colony, not yet anyway. And no, he needed not a single reminder of more war atrocities. He yearned to accomplish his mission of building a church.

# SHARP KNIFE'S FIRST FORAY

1814

The severity of each new threat to Pensacola's future had intensified. Rumors now circulated that the American general, Andrew Jackson, intended to invade. Padre had reviewed the orders from Pensacola's governor so many times that he knew them by heart. They had appeared strong. One order demanded all militiamen to muster on a Sunday morning at ten o'clock in front of the Government House for inspection of their weapons and ammunition.

Another order required all militiamen from the Second Company as well as white men and free persons of color, from age fourteen to sixty years who worked in the countryside, to appear in town to perform their share of guard duty. Failure to comply carried an eight-day penalty in the *calabozo* and even included a negligence penalty of four dollars for hiring a substitute guard. Padre tried tirelessly to reconcile the men to the necessity of these strong-sounding public announcements. "Yes," he murmured many times, "I do my part in getting those orders enforced. The military can do the rest."

While en route on one of these outlying missions to motivate the men, he thanked God for the horse and appreciated not only that Padre de Galvez had bought it, but also that he had allowed the horse to be named Captain in honor of Captain Zamora. At the same time he longed for the day when the mission could generate sufficient funds for building a church. Was it to be? Not from all appearances—far from it. Conditions in Pensacola had worsened. The garrison weakened for lack of supplies and funds. Spain's treasury had not recovered from the Napoleonic invasions.

20

Despite weaknesses abounding at the garrison, the bond between Genesis and Padre had endured ever since they met in 1811 in the touching scene after the ship landed. Angel Roundtree, a Creek woman who had married an Anglo and worked at the kitchen, once said, "Padre, you sure have God-given strength of character. Talking with Genesis is not always easy. You are one of the few people he pays attention to. He's come a long way from his job of cutting firewood for the kitchen to working at the tanning yard. His mother told me he learned a lot from you, a lot of book learning. And he's done a good job taking care of that fine, white horse, too. He sure makes a pretty picture riding down on the beach at sunset."

"Yes, indeed," Padre said, stroking his beard, "Genesis can brighten the bleakest of days." How well imprinted in his mind were the times Genesis had galloped up to him on *Grandeza*, the stallion's long, silky mane freely flowing in the gulf breeze. The memorable scenes scrolled in his mind's eye: Genesis' dark skin and clothing, even when dusty and well-worn, contrasted with the white horse. The emerald bay formed a perfect backdrop for the juxtaposition of these lifelike colors against the perspective of the sandy beach. These were not ordinary colors, rather, striking ones of an artistic sentiment and sense of description: Genesis' hair, not cayenne, but burnt sienna; skin, not swarthy, but bronze; clothing, not plain but colored in earthy shades—trousers of umber and shirts of yellow ocher. Padre tipped his head in sanction and said, "The scene would be perfect for the brush strokes of one of Spain's fine artists to capture for posterity. There could be no better composition than that of this mixed-blood son of Pensacola reining up his noble stallion toward the coastal vista of a glorious orange and magenta-streaked sunset." At those times Genesis' youthful, carefree spirit and the intense black irises of his eyes had always reminded him of his long-lost, younger brother.

Genesis' mother, Naja, and sister, Maypearl, had emigrated farther south in Florida to join a small tribe of Seminole. With the threat of an invasion by General Jackson, they preemptively took advantage of an opportunity to get away from the mission and resume tribal life.

Aspiring to place their departure in the most promising perspective for Genesis, Padre said, "I have heard that Creek who have mastered skills and crafts, like your mother and sister, are readily accepted by the Seminole. After all, most of them are of Creek heritage, too, and surely need to increase their clans with members like your mother. Her skillfully woven Creek-style raffia baskets are some of the best I ever saw."

"That ain't all. My mother taught Maypearl how to weave them, too. And she showed Maypearl lotsa other things like how to boil salt. Bet you didn't know it takes a hundred buckets of salt water to boil down a half peck of salt."

21

Not only had Indians, like Naja, abandoned Pensacola, but also civilians and military people. The town's growth, realized after the Louisiana Purchase, had steadily declined. Then suddenly, in November of 1814, Jackson stormed into the vulnerable town, a pushover for the general.

The American takeover was not only demeaning but also mystifying to Padre. He had continued to perform most of his regular duties: interacting with the garrisoned men and civilian population; celebrating masses, marriages, births, christenings; and taking care of the rituals of deaths. All the while he functioned under the faulty impression that the garrison, though in a state of decline, could still protect Pensacola. After all, they had received British aid.

Still feeling totally duped by his naivete, Padre dwelt more and more on the notion of learning details about the takeover, unpalatable as they might be, that enabled Jackson's history-making invasion. One thing was sure. He must not rely entirely on Father Mulvaney's interpretation. His Irish background just might have tainted his view. On many occasions he had talked with Padre de Galvez in an effort to satisfy his curiosity, but he needed laity's perspective, too. Reliable sources were scant, and written accounts trickled in meagerly.

Then the momentous turn back, a miracle of sorts, had taken place. Padre would forever remember his precise location and the accompanying events that had occurred when he learned that the American president had ordered the return of Pensacola to Spain because of Jackson's unauthorized seizure. It had happened one day as Padre pored over a rare *Washington Globe* newspaper. Vibrations of a fast-approaching figure distracted him. It was Genesis. "What's the rush?" Padre asked.

"We won! We won! Pensacola's been turned back to Spain. *Whew!* I'm out of breath—just about broke a leg getting here."

Padre felt his lips move spontaneously in prayerful thanks, followed by the signing of the cross. How pleased he felt owing that obligation of thanksgiving, for he had prayed often that Spain's diligent diplomatic efforts would soon come to fruition.

After basking a few moments in the justice of the return of Spanish power, Padre picked up his newspaper with the intention of joining the other priests right away. Above all else, he wished to relish with them the full savoriness of this blessed news for the Church and the Crown.

Genesis called out, "Padre, can I use your whetstone? I want to carve my initials in my powder horn, but my knife needs honing."

Padre hurriedly fetched the whetstone. He would just have to trust his cherished whetstone to the young blade for a while. Padre silently enjoyed his thoughtful pun.

"Go ahead and get that church stuff over with," Genesis said as he slid, from his shoulder, the buckskin strip attached to the powder horn and started honing his knife.

Genesis inspected his work as Padre returned with his newspaper. The knife's edge seemed to suit Genesis, so he handed the whetstone to Padre and said, "Don't waste your time reading that American stuff. C'mon, I'll get ole man de Ballestre to tell you all about how Jackson took over Pensacola while I carve my initials on my powder horn. He's been commander of San Carlos Fort so long, he claims he knows every grain of sand there, and he surefire likes to talk about it. Besides, he knows the truth of it. He's as Spanish as they come."

Padre, trying to overlook Genesis' need at the ripe age of sixteen to flaunt his maturity, said, "I would like very much to hear the commander's interpretation." As they started walking, he said, "By the way, I noticed you carve with your left hand as well as with your right. That means you are ambidextrous."

"Padre, you surefire thought up a damned ugly-sounding word for such a handy thing."

Upon arrival at the officers' quarters, Padre said, "I will wait while you go inside and get Commander de Ballestre. We might as well sit here on the veranda and take in the gulf breeze while we talk."

"Sounds good to me. The commander surefire shoots out a lot of hot air, a hell of a lot."

Flattered by Padre's interest the commander began his version with, "Oddly, the campaign started in northern Alabama after General Jackson had decimated the Red Stick Creek at Horseshoe Bend. *Humph*, the general, just a backwoods harness maker, found power by using guns against the Creek arrows. In that one-sided battle, over 500 Creek lay dead on the battleground, and over 300 floated like flotsam on the river that curved around the horseshoe-shaped land. The very bend in that horseshoe that they had thought was protection turned into a trap. After the carnage of that battle, you can understand why the Indians always called him 'Sharp Knife.'"

Genesis said, "That's what I started calling him. He don't deserve to be called no general by me."

Commander de Ballestre, though a clever officer, had a habit—Padre thought it was coarsely debased—of noisily sucking air through the wide gap between his two front teeth. He took care of that habit, looked at Padre straight in the eye, and said, "Jackson's brief study of law books, as well as service in the American congress expunged neither his hostile heart nor his uncouth manner. That devil adamantly held his longtime grudge against the

Spanish Crown and our allies no matter what explanations our governor gave."

"You probably have strong opinions countering that grudge—justified opinions, I might add."

"Well, you know Governor Manrique was unable to get men from Spain. There were no men to spare. They were defending the homeland against Napoleon. So the governor had no choice but to reinforce the garrison with runaway slaves and Red Sticks or whatever Indians he could enlist. This infuriated the hot-tempered Sharp Knife, since some of these Red Sticks had escaped from battles in northern Alabama. Besides, Jackson also owned slaves at his farm and bitterly opposed Spain's protection of runaway slaves."

"Bear with me, Commander," Padre said, "but did this merit an invasion of Pensacola?"

"For Sharp Knife, it did. He was especially hot about the three Indian chiefs we protected after they escaped from him at Horseshoe Bend. And he accused Governor Manrique of aiding runaway slaves that settlers needed for farming. Besides he accused the governor of abetting Indians—said that they threatened settlers who wanted to buy Alabama land. And another thing, by the governor's acceptance of the British as allies, Sharp Knife thought the British would get a stronger grip in Florida and infiltrate the states. But he was the one that was infiltrating. After he got nearly all the Creek land in northern Alabama and took Mobile, the greedy Sharp Knife cut his eyes towards Florida."

Genesis looked up from his carving and fidgeted. Anxious to make a contribution, he said, "After Sharp Knife took over here, I heard the head man from the Forbes Tanning Yard talking at the Emerald Tavern. He said that them Inneraritys, with all that power they had with their Forbes Trading Company, favored Americans over the British. He said that John Innerarity even sent a warning to the Americans about the British plan to attack Mobile. That was how come the Americans won there."

"And that still makes my blood boil," the commander said, "because the Inneraritys are supposed to be true Pensacolians." With an air that appeared like a well-rehearsed story, he continued, "While Sharp Knife was still negotiating the victory treaty with the Creek for their land in upper Alabama, he sent a captain and scouting company to Pensacola with a letter. I want to make it clear, that stubborn general was no more than a harness maker with a lot of gall. In that letter he demanded our governor's surrender of the three fugitive Indian chiefs we sheltered *and* an explanation of British proceedings in a Spanish territory or face consequences."

The commander squirmed. Then, like a Shakespearean actor, he said, "Governor Manrique, faithful arm of the Church and Crown that he was, not only gave the American captain a short interview but also refused to withdraw our Spanish protection from the Indian chiefs." de Ballestre slapped his hand on a table with a powerful blow and said, "Nor would the governor back down and acknowledge existence of any British activities as Jackson portrayed them. I'm proud to tell you that he asserted this admirable stand in spite of the infirmities of old age," de Ballestre thundered. He caught a deep breath and said, "You will probably recall that three British men-of-war that Jackson had forced out of Mobile, entered Pensacola Bay and put two hundred royal marines ashore."

"Of course, I remember. I went about my mission duties feeling rather safe after they arrived."

"But the governor was in a quandary. He sensed their presence was an invitation to American aggression, since, among other things, the British had promised slave emancipation. The thought of freeing slaves always brings out the worst in American farmers. But you know, the British generated improvements in Pensacola, partially repairing some of our worn-out installations. They did more. They enlisted Indians, and—as you must have witnessed—armed, and drilled them in the streets for our protection."

Padre nodded.

"But this cooperation which the Spanish received from the British and Indians got to be too much for Sharp Knife to bear. Horseshoe Bend and Mobile victories didn't satisfy him. No, by God. On to Pensacola, he marched, hell-bent with the Devil's work." de Ballestre looked patronizingly at Padre. "He did it without a hint of charity taught by the Holy Catholic Church. And that devil augured his pitchfork even deeper here *without* authority. It was rumored he'd sent a query letter to the American Secretary of War for permission to proceed to Pensacola but then didn't wait for a reply. He gathered a force of three thousand men and marched them just outside Pensacola in only four days." He held up four fingers emphatically.

"I know. I was frightened out of my wits."

"The governor was, too, yet demonstrated Spanish loyalty again by ordering Jackson's flag fired upon," the commander said with an air of admiration.

"I know all so well, Padre answered. "That is when the dreadful invasion began."

"That's right," de Ballestre said and sucked air between his teeth again. "The British evacuated Pensacola like a summer storm taking off toward the gulf, but not before blowing up the forts. The sight of Ft. San Carlos being blown to bits made my heart bleed. I had commanded it ever since I came to Pensacola. I knew every grain of sand there."

Genesis looked up and grinned. "I told you, Padre, he knows every grain of sand there."

The commander half-smiled, then said, "My heart holds it against them, but my head, of course, knows that's what the military is all about."

Lieutenant Muldanado, a younger, dapper-looking officer, mysterious as a minaret, had been observing the banter from a few feet away. He lit up a huge cigar and walked closer. In a snappy manner he asked, "May I add a point or two?"

Commander de Ballestre motioned for him to go ahead.

Talking faster than the commander, the lieutenant said, "According to our intelligence agents, Jackson charged the Spanish government provided arms for Indian raids on white settlements, but influential officers and Spaniards sensed his sole purpose was for land hungry expansionists— eliminating the protection of runaway slaves, too. You know there is money to be made in raising cotton, and Jackson owned human chattels. Cotton prices doubled right after the takeover."

Genesis still carved on his powder horn, enlarging his initials. He looked up occasionally to note Padre's reaction.

Lieutenant Muldanado said emphatically, "But now, President Madison has come to his knees and admitted the unauthorized seizure."

"Yes, thanks be to God, you have confirmed the news. Truth is, I already celebrated the good tidings with the other priests solely upon Genesis' word."

Genesis jumped up and said, "Aw, Padre, have I ever lied to you about such important business?"

"I realize it sounds dramatic," the lieutenant said snappily, "but national and international pressure forced the Americans to return Spanish power. We figured all along that our crown's diplomatic proceedings would compel the Americans to make the turn around."

Padre nodded. He added to the lieutenant's recital by extolling a remark of the prestigious Manuel de Godoy, master of Spanish foreign policy, "You cannot lock up an open field like Pensacola." Then he added, "This is, in no way, meant to diminish our military."

Both officers stared at the floor. Quietness reigned for a few moments before Padre thanked the officers for their explanations, and he and Genesis started walking back.

Genesis asked Padre, "Did you get enough of the military's part in Sharp Knife's invasion?

"Learning a few new facts fails to relieve the deep anguish we suffered here; however, both military men displayed Spanish civility and intelligence."

Genesis chuckled, "If you ask me, them two was in a pretty good pissing contest, and you couldn't keep yourself outta it. Ole man de Ballestre knows a lot, but the lieutenant could beat him by a hell of a long shot. If I was an officer I'd talk just like him."

After Spain had regained control, Genesis continued working at the Forbes Tanning Yard, that is, whenever there was sufficient work to be done. He loved the contact with the Alabama Creek who brought hides there to sell.

Padre continued with his mission activities, but Pensacola was never the same.

In a meeting called by Padre de Galvez to discuss concerns over ominous and ever-shifting winds of change, Father Mulvaney divulged, "Notions are being widely circulated that Spaniards are...well, to quote the exact description, 'lazy.' According to rumors, this is a major cause of Pensacola's decline."

Sharply stung, Padre Morales bounded to his feet and said, "Spaniards are *not* lazy, my brother in God. They may appear, in part, indolent because they tend not to work as soon as they have gained enough to live on for a little while. Still, they have a sense of personal pride which is to be commended rather than condemned."

"That is not the only unfavorable, rampant notion," Father Mulvaney said. "I have also noted concerns about Spaniards' fondness for gambling. And in all honesty, I should bring out the fact they are further criticized for innate cruelty in their fondness for bullfights in the homeland."

Padre Morales frowned and moaned. How deeply this cut into his national pride.

In an effort to maintain cohesion, Padre de Galvez took advantage of his superior status and stated authoritatively, "Spaniards are emotional, but the *aficionado,* or bullfight fan, is appealed to by the skill of the bullfighter and the outrage of the bull, instead of the flow of blood. The keynote to understanding our character lies in an appreciation of the fact that Spaniards, in general, combine their emotional temperament with intellectual matters. It is true, however, that a certain lack of intellectual stamina in Spaniards has been known to prevent them from using the brains with which nature has abundantly endowed them."

Padre Morales obediently abided his cue and smothered an oncoming heated rebuttal to Father Mulvaney. The meeting then moved forward.

After Andrew Jackson's invasion in 1814 and the subsequent return of Spanish power, there was still no peace in Pensacola. The group known as the filibusterers provoked unrest, and the West Florida Rebels threatened.

Predatory American settlers and militiamen as well as Red Stick Indians continued ravaging each other on the Florida borderlands.

Worse yet, Pensacolians heard the explosion that destroyed Negro Fort, 100 miles away on the Apalachicola River. They knew that Andrew Jackson had ordered this Spanish stronghold attacked because it harbored hundreds of runaway slaves and Indians. Of the fort's 320 inhabitants, 270 burned to death. Negro Commander Garcon and a Choctaw chief amazingly survived. Then they were stabbed, shot, and scalped, but not until after they had heard burning dismembered body parts of their men hissing in the river and survivors' writhing moans. Padre needed no further clues that the future portended some sort of disaster for Pensacola.

The irony of escaping Napoleon's war in Spain only to find himself in the midst of more horrifying battles in Florida baffled Padre. Martyrdom had never entered his intentions, nor would it become his legacy, though his enthusiasm had considerably dimmed. Questions languished. Would he live long enough to help build a church? And with battles approaching closer and closer, what would happen to Genesis and the priests and everyone?

# ABANDON PENSACOLA?

Padre cast a second glance, his face turning fearful. The young man heading toward him was definitely Genesis. But no nineteen-year-old would rush like that on an uneventful day unless something drastic had happened.

"Sharp Knife's back in Florida with his army." No time to talk. I have to get back. Another spy may come in with more news." He turned and sped away as fast as he had arrived.

Would the general dare march into Pensacola again with more dire consequences, Padre worried? Fright stirred up the old frustration of how he had allowed himself to be duped into trusting that the garrison would stave off Jackson's invasion of over three years ago. Now, regardless of how awful events might become, he must keep constant vigil. He stepped lively to the Government House, waited around until Lieutenant Muldonado appeared, and asked him, in confidence, "Are you at liberty to tell me about General Jackson's current whereabouts?"

With a grave expression the lieutenant said, "The general has reentered Florida with his army, brutally raiding Spanish settlements and Indian villages along the way, sometimes killing man and beast. But they always pilfered whatever they fancied or occasionally burned everything else in sight. After Governor Masot received reports of these heinous attacks on Spanish soil, he wasted no time ordering strict surveillance by the spies."

Days later, in a meeting with the spies and officers, Genesis heard more dreadful news. Sharp Knife had seized St. Mark's and ousted Spanish Commander Francisco Luengo. Genesis hustled to find Padre and said, "An American major with not just one, but four companies marched into St.

29

Mark's, and can you imagine that them gates was wide open? Our soldiers in the fort, all seventy of 'em, was so surprised they acted like pure fools trying to man the cannon. Sharp Knife's army had no damn trouble stopping them. The officers here at the garrison are all addled, wondering what Sharp Knife's going to do next."

With trepidation, Padre listened.

Genesis inhaled a deep breath. "The head man of the spy posse reported that Sharp Knife ordered his army to hang or the firing squad to shoot every man of the enemy that resisted if found armed. If he's planning on invading here again, I surefire ain't ready to die."

"The down side of your job as Creek interpreter is that it's a highly valued military asset for the enemy." He looked around to make sure no one was listening and said, "In the event of capture, the American general would surely order you into his service. My mission work is in jeopardy, too, great jeopardy. He could place me in some menial job, possibly as a record clerk. My divine calling as a Catholic priest might even be ridiculed by those nonbelievers of the Holy Catholic Word."

"Maybe a rattlesnake will bite a chunk outta him and kill him, but he ought to suffer a whole lot before he draws his last breath."

"I would not wish that on anyone. Besides, the evil general may have as many lives as a cat. One thing is sure. If he does not change, he will burn in everlasting hell one day."

Genesis nodded and with a dreaded sort of expression said, "If he invades again, we'd be dirt dead. Sharp Knife surefire gets meaner all the time. The spies reported that he ordered stripes and lashes for the first two offenses of his soldiers and shot them like dogs or hung them for the third one. They even saw his officers beat some of their men till they was bleeding, beat them half to death, sometimes outright killed them while they was yelling for clemency. Sometimes it was for a little, shitty disobedience." He ran his fingers through his massive red hair, then blurted, "Hell, I'm even thinking about doing what a lot of the others around here have already done—leaving. I ain't going to sit around here like some thumb-sucking baby."

Padre rued the coarse language Genesis had begun using more frequently, but survival now took precedence over appropriate language. The mere thought of leaving his holy service to God and St. Michael's Mission rent his heart. Yet, in utter shame he harbored, in a tiny corner of his heart, a dream of carrying on missionary work in another place, a safer place. At times it dangled before him like a savory during Lent. Still, he had to address another matter: "Do you have any misgivings about…about deserting? You know that if you leave, you would be a deserter."

"Hell no, everything's changing just like my mother said before she left. And I'm a believer now."

"Even though you now have no family ties here, I know you have deep concerns for *Grandeza* in these troubled times. I want to make sure you know I'm just as concerned about your fine stallion."

"Padre, you know lotsa big words and stuff, but just how do you think you know what's it's like to worry about a prized horse like *Grandeza*?"

"I have given the matter much thought. In the event you take *Grandeza* away from this threatening situation, it would not be wise to risk robbers or the American general's guerrilla warfare. The point I am leading up to is this: it may surprise you that the question has crept into my mind about where I would go if I had to leave."

Genesis nodded, nonplussed.

"I certainly would not go west to Mobile or far worse and farther, too, to New Orleans," Padre said. He poked his head forth, like a sea turtle's from its shell, and whispered, "You know those places are under American control now, but there is still too much inherent Frenchness reminiscent of Napoleon." Padre had used discretion when speaking about the French, since learning Padre Vives was expelled from St. Michael's Mission for preaching openly against them. He had been ever mindful in that regard, even though the superior priest had told him that Padre Vives committed other violations, also, like cavorting with unseemly people.

Genesis folded his arms over his chest, propped a hand under his chin. "I'll never forget Sharp Knife's letter that got me the interpreting job, 'cause that letter set everybody at the garrison on fire."

"Refresh my memory. What was so fiery about the message?"

"You remember Sharp Knife's letter that Commander de Ballestre told us about, the one that demanded release of the Indian chiefs we was helping and an explanation why the British was helping us."

"Of course, of course, I remember, but I thought you were going to divulge something new. As time passes, I understand more and more why many men deserted back then."

"Lucky for me the interpreter was one of them that left, and I got my first chance to be in a meeting with everybody important. That letter fired me up, too. I was sixteen and couldn't hardly believe how important I was already."

"I have always thought you possessed talent for the languages."

"After my first meeting with the officers, I told Squeaky Thomas about my job as interpreter, and he called me a liar. I'd about quit fighting so much by then, but he made me so mad I was going to knock his teeth out, that squeak in his voice, too. But he ran like a scalded dog. He's surefire a yellow-headed coward. You probably know his father is British. I never

31

liked him 'cause he was always bragging that his father lives with him, not in a ship on the ocean. Besides, way back he pissed higher than me with that pointed pecker of his. Anyway, that evening when I told Maypearl I got the interpreting job, she stuck out her tongue at me. I grabbed her hair so hard I damn near tore it out, and she screamed like I was just about to slit her throat. Our mother ran in and broke it up before she had a foaming fit. Hell, Padre, nobody but you would believe I got the job interpreting. Well, my mother did, too."

"Getting back to the general," Padre said, "and to the true meaning of *hell*, as soon as General Jackson finished off the British in Mobile, he brought Satan's hell right here in Pensacola."

"Now Padre, don't start that preaching stuff."

Padre forthwith decided to build on an idea that might be helpful in the future. The notion of leaving Pensacola seemed too incomprehensible at this time to put into words, yet Genesis would be the best candidate for a traveling partner if the nigh unthinkable need for leaving ever occurred. So, he reminded Genesis how his father, Captain Zamora, had exchanged stories with *Senor* Colabro years ago when they played cards and drank rum at the Emerald Saloon. Captain Zamora usually talked about the supplies, which his ship transported to Pensacola for *Senor* Colabro's Montezuma Trading Post in the Alabama Territory.

"Ever since I have been here," Padre said, "the *senor* and his Creek helpers have been well known for trading their logs, skins, and furs, and smoked turkey and venison."

"They was floating them timber rafts long before you came here. I've been knowing that they run them rafts all the way down the Conecuh River to the Escambia River and then all the way to the Pensacola Bay ever since I was knee high to…"

"I know. I will finish your sentence—a brown pelican. Back to the subject, have you seen *Senor* Colabro lately?"

"He was here not long ago trading his goods."

"Do they still use the Indian Ridge Trail when they return to the Montezuma Trading Post?"

"There ain't no other way through that giant forest. It's surefire something to see them workers when they leave here with all that rum and flour and tools. Their backs are bent way over. The head man at the tanning yard said they remind him of tender blackberry canes after a heavy rain, the kind that's loaded with heavy, green berries like the ones on the bayou bank. And don't forget, Padre, when I worked at the tanning yard, I saw them many a time when they came in, unloaded skins from the rafts, and then separated the logs so they could be sold for timber."

"I understand the trail borders the rivers from Pensacola northerly all the way to the Montezuma Trading Post. Finding one's way on that trail should not be too difficult."

"If them workers can do it, I surefire can, too. Shoot, I heard them Creek traders say a hundred times that the trail follows close by the rivers. Them rivers have plenty of water for *Grandeza, too*." He smiled. "Traders tell people around Seville Square that the trip takes five days, sometimes six. I heard them say it lotsa times."

"That is my understanding also. Another important detail—I have heard that every stream that cuts across the trail to the river is fordable." Padre felt it rather harmless to act a bit self-serving and swell Genesis up a little more about a possible quick getaway, if need be. He said, "Remember how the *senor* bragged about the Montezuma area? He talked about the rivers and lakes jumping with fish and the forests filled with game, and the friendly Indians. What really intrigued me was when *Senor* Colabro told Captain Zamora how much the Montezuma Trading Post area reminded him of their village in Spain near Villamartin on the Guadalete River." His eyes brightened as he said, "Their village is near the one where I grew up, in the *Andalucian* Region."

"*Humph*, what I like to hear about is that Creek princess up there in the Alabama Territory. I heard she's beautiful. I surefire would like to lay my eyes on her."

Without acknowledging the matter of the princess, Padre continued, "Have you forgotten how proud your father looked when *Senor* Colabro told about naming his trading post in honor of the Mexican Emperor Montezuma?" Surely this bit of nostalgia would excite Genesis.

Why had Genesis not answered? Instead, he had lowered his head and picked at a thumb cuticle in a sulking way.

Suddenly, Genesis cut his eyes in an oblique glance and said, "Now I don't want to hear no more about that naming hogwash. You must have forgot something, too. My father knew *Senor* Colabro way back, way back when the *senor* worked at a trading post in Mexico. My father's ship carried supplies from Spain to that place, too. He was the one that talked the *senor* into opening a trading post in the Alabama Territory. My father had told the *senor* how the Indians brought hides and smoked venison and turkey to trade in Pensacola. That's why the *senor* named the place in Alabama Montezuma in honor of one of them rulers in Mexico. It all happened because of my father. Remember, I do have a real live father, even if he does live in Spain."

Padre studied momentarily and said, "I had no intention of agitating you." He stroked his beard. "I think you are aware of what is in the back of my mind. You are good at sensing things."

"Padre, you are stalling like a rabbit that's scared to move. You're scared of getting killed here in Pensacola and that's why you really want to go with me to the trading post in Alabama."

Padre looked around as if someone might have been listening. "Well, uh," he said, "I must confess, perhaps you have hit upon a...an element of truth, at least about going to the Montezuma Trading Post area with you."

# ANOTHER PERSPECTIVE

Meanwhile, at Ft. Gadsden on the Apalachiocola River, General Andrew Jackson sat obscured inside a dark camp tent. When he re-lit his pipe, the momentary flame revealed his ghostly face, the lingering dull jaundice of malaria. The natural red hair of his younger years now resembled that of an old bobcat, graying with residual chestnut-red streaks. Despite his rundown condition from chronic dysentery, the iron-willed general roiled in mind and body on this day, May 5, 1818. Pensacola had possessed his best faculties and had ever since he marched his army there and whipped the greasy faced Spanish almost four years ago, only to see President Madison return it to those Indian lovers and slave snatchers.

Yes, the Spanish again played their same old tricks of denial and cover-up. They aided and abetted the Creek and Seminole and, worst of all, the warrior Red Sticks, enabling them to kill and raid white settlers. As long as these atrocities continued, how could the newly sovereign United States and its territories attract settlers? And why should American farmers be denied their much-needed slaves? Furthermore, the Spanish violated their so-called neutral status by conspiring with the British. It had been rumored that the British had provided a whopping 20,000 muskets for Red Sticks and other Indians taking refuge in Florida. British traders, like Royal Marines Edward Nicholls and George Woodbine, continued to incite every Indian and runaway slave they could persuade.

This evening Jackson overheard Sergeant Stover, a medic, talking with his guard outside the tent. Sergeant Stover's lisp was distinctive on beginning "s" sounds.

35

"*Thir (Sir)*, has the general mentioned *thending* for me? He looked more peaked than usual this morning. I told him that a mullien poultice might help draw the pus out of his carbuncle."

"He hasn't mentioned it to me. Maybe he just needs to get some of the worry off his chest, especially about the British."

"*Yethiree*. Them British are enough to torment Jesus Christ."

"I've been guarding the general a long time. Ever since Nicholls recruited them 800 or 900 Indians to reclaim the land at Horseshoe Bend, everything's come down hard on the general. Nicholls knew damn well the general had good reasons to put them Creek down, and the first one was to pay back for their massacre at Ft. Mims. Red Eagle just plain ole out and out butchered the whites there."

"*Yethir*. What's more, Nicholls don't even understand the meaning of justice. Them Creek marked their *X's*, rightfully *theded* that land in northern Alabama to the United *Thates*."

"Stover, you got that right. Nicholls brayed like a pea-brained donkey, putting out his own interpretation on that treaty that ended the war (1812) with the Redcoats. Incited them Indians like he was getting paid for it. Sometimes, I think putting out just one eye was too good for him. We'd be better off if we had taken care of his other one, too, at Mobile. Then he couldn't have seen fit to make so much more trouble. I heard another officer say that he had that one eye aimed at getting assigned as Indian Superintendent for Britain for the whole state of Florida. Said the job has a lot of perquisites. Imagine the nerve."

"*Theaking* of nerve," Stover said, "his buddy Woodbine takes the prize, in my way of looking at it, offering $100 for every white *thalp*. There's no way the Army would *thit* on its haunches and let him get by with that. We'll get rid of them British, all of 'em, just like when our *thide* fought for independence from them double-taxing cheaters."

"Amen. I've been guarding the general since them British started up war again in 1812. Just about everybody called it the Second Revolutionary War. Seemed like we had to prove all over again the country was independent. There's not a doubt, no damned doubt, our men are dead right when they say we're fighting the third revolution, but some high and mighty people call it a Seminole War. After the treaty (for War of 1812) was signed, I was ready to get mustered out and go back to Tennessee and buy some land. But here we are, still fighting."

"*Yethir*, there's plenty of blame to go around. You'd think all of them foreigners and Indians woulda learned a lesson by now."

Only a few days earlier, Jackson's army had overthrown St. Mark's Fort on the Apalachicola River. Then the arrogant General Andrew Jackson triumphantly entered that defeated fort. During the War of 1812 he had been military commander for United States Southern Division. Since British, Spanish, and Indian infractions had continued, he had retained that title, even after the Treaty of Ghent supposedly ended the fighting.

Conquering St. Mark's had deliciously whetted Jackson's appetite for further recompense, but he knew he must wait to feast on Pensacola for the second time. He had taken the pleasure of personally lowering the Spanish flag at St. Mark's, for it symbolized conspiracy with British and Indians. After hoisting the American Stars and Stripes and watching the flag mightily slicing into the breeze, the general handed the vanquished red and gold one to the crestfallen Commandant Francisco Luengo. Luengo solemnly furled the cherished Spanish flag.

Lieutenant Ham Heath, an aide for Jackson at the flag ceremony, had walked alongside his formidable superior to the field tent. Heath's youthful air exuded. His neatly buttoned jacket, and well-developed chest, swelled like a ripe ear of corn. In contrast, the general's opened coat, well-worn and faded-blue, revealed his emaciated chest, and his wide-topped boots flopped loosely around his corn stalk legs.

Heath had finally achieved his goal of personally attending the general on a triumphant occasion and to boot had never seen the general in a more cheerful mood. Providence was on his side today. He would take a risk. The nascent lieutenant's ambition hastily spawned a plan:

"Sir, I have a jug of backwoods 'corn' in my tent. Fine vintage claret would be my first choice to offer you, but having none, I'm hoping you might be of a mind to sample a slug of home brew. If it's to your liking, we can quaff a few. This blaze of glory is an occasion for celebration."

The general had liked the way Heath had handled the men during the recent measles epidemic as well as his fairness in rationing provisions. He had grit, determination, and stood stalwart while thinking on his feet. He would make a good field captain. Feeling a tinge of magnanimity, Jackson said, "Bring the jug to my tent directly. We'll have a go at it. I'll tell my guard I'm expecting you."

Jackson had two tin cups waiting. He rubbed his rough fingers along the dents of one as Lieutenant Heath poured. The lieutenant looked away from his general's dirt-filled nails and welcomed the tang of the whiskey. It settled his stomach, neutralized the close, musty tent air and sweaty odors.

"I always wanted to tell you that you're a hero with my folks, Americans everywhere for that matter," Heath said. "Major Pierce told me about the critical battles he's fought in with you, how you led and won. Wish I woulda been in all of 'em, all three of 'em..."

The general raised his hand and cut him off. "You're talking about the last three, but there've actually been four major battles, starting with Horseshoe Bend. You were just a shaveling then."

"That *was* several years ago, wasn't it?" Heath asked patronizingly as he took the initiative and poured refills.

"Almost four years ago, and all four battles occurred in the year 1814. After we quelled the savages there in northern Alabama, the reprehensible Redcoats swarmed into Washington and burned it in August. Very thought of those blazes set me afire, sent me recruiting. Tennesseans volunteered from every holler and settlement. I enlisted Cherokee by the dozen, Creek too. We rode the river to Mobile and ran the lion hearts out of that portal. From Mobile, some British ships took off to Pensacola. Had to clear them out of that port, too, and set the Spanish on their heels. Can you imagine what liberties they would have taken if they controlled the important ports— Mobile or New Orleans or Pensacola? Why those British would have clawed their way through the whole country." He drank, slammed his cup on the table, and helped himself to more whiskey. "It took a lot of fighting."

"That Pensacola battle, sir, that's the one that Major Pierce made sure I understood. He said that there's where you showed the entire world you're a first-class tactician."

"Never had any formal military training, but I was determined to get even with the British after the suffering they caused my family and me in the Revolution."

"Yes sir, I felt bad when I heard about the loss of your widowed mother and your brothers in the Revolutionary War. Don't know how you managed all alone after that, being just fourteen years old."

"Managed by vowing to get even, or else I was going to die trying. Tactics come to me more natural than a hunch comes to a gambler." Jackson recounted his arrival in Pensacola back in 1814 when he had discovered the British ships still anchored in the harbor and the Union Jack flying in tandem with the Spanish flag at the garrison. "As soon as we arrived in Pensacola, they gutted the very forts that they had repaired and fled, leaving the castrated coastal town stranded like a starving capon. The place looked like hell."

Jackson leaned back. "That's when we made the move that would have astonished even Shakespeare's creative mind. My scouts learned that the Spanish and British had planned to meet our attack from the west along the wide, sandy beach." Jackson smiled wryly. "I marched my men from the narrow eastern approach. Led them myself and circled the town, quietly, before dawn.

"But," he chuckled, "I sent 500 men in from the west as a diversion. By sunrise it was too late for the bullies to change their defense. We had them trapped. I gave the signal and my men moved in three columns, one on the beach and two above it. They fought through artillery fire from an infantry battery and volleyed small arms from street corners and rooftops. Wasn't long before old man Manrique scurried around with a white flag trying to find me. He was in feeble shape to be a Governor. Anyway, I made arrangements to meet him at the Government House for surrender."

"Wish I coulda been there. Makes the hair rise on the back of my neck when I think about it."

"You'll get your chance. I've got plans.

"How's that, Sir?"

Jackson drank and smacked his lips. "We have a job to do in Pensacola."

"Amazing," the lieutenant said, his tongue beginning to thicken, and the mildew and tallowy smell sickening him. All of a sudden feeling hopelessly inebriated, he muttered a nigh unintelligible amenity, offered a semblance of a military protocol salute, and staggered out.

Jackson had sat back, thumbs pushing his suspenders away from his skinny chest, and indulged in his feats. Damn right, he was a first-class tactician and more, too. His eyes slowly closed. A mosquito bit his cheek and whirred away. He had slapped his face to no avail except that it impelled him to grope, as one who is besot, to his cot.

On this evening, he had enjoyed reminiscing. It mattered not a whit what his guard and Sergeant Stover had been discussing outside his tent. Nothing mattered a hoot now except reinforcing his Pensacola plans. In Jackson's mind, the door to Pensacola had been left open for other countries. It summoned to be closed again just as the flap on his drawers demanded to be buttoned. And, by God, now was the time. Nothing would interfere, not international diplomacy, not the Secretary of War, and for damned sure not Florida's greasy governor.

# SPANISH SPIES

1818

Pensacola's sunbaked stockade nestled sleepily as always in the center of the thirty-acre open-fronted plaza facing the emerald bay, but unfortunate changes had taken place. Lately, pine planked stronghouses at the corners betrayed their name. By sheer will Padre avoided noticing them, particularly the sagging one at the northeast corner.

Today, as thirty-one-year-old Padre climbed the steps to the second floor of the shabby barracks, an even more important issue consumed the greater part of his faculties. He joined Genesis, who watched with unusual diligence from a north window, awaiting the return of the garrison's spy posse. Standing at the best viewing angle, the two men kept their covert vigil in the dilapidated, desolate, and ghostly place on this fateful day. A goodly number of men had deserted.

In grim single mindedness Padre soon lapsed into shallow breathing in anticipation the spies' return, the crucial outcome. Earlier, he had taken special notice of the remaining men. Many sat staring blankly, as was their usual way, midst the trappers, traders, and Indians who peddled their wares around Seville Square. Others cajoled with women, French Creole, mulatto, and Canary Islanders, though the number of women, as always, was disproportionately small to the number of men. As was customary, settlers, too, seemed to enjoy the warm, lazy day on Seville Square. Why should they bother themselves about the possibility of the American general invading again? Most of them had never even bothered with agricultural ventures, or timber, or cattle enterprises.

Ubiquitous card games scattered throughout the gatherings of these diverse people. Prohibition of the import of playing cards had failed, and not a day passed when one did not see at least a few men playing whist. Some men, no doubt, were driving cue balls. Nearly every man had shot billiards at one time or another. Looking back, the elite governor and officers had often engaged in this pastime of equality, even amongst coarse-mannered scalawags and adventurers, but not on this day. Today they would gather for a meeting as soon as the spies returned. Padre and Genesis, unlike the majority of Pensacolians, worried about the future. Now, they stood on watch.

"Them ole worn-out boots piled in the corner surefire stink," Genesis said. "That mold is thicker than rat fur. And look at that moth-eaten blanket next to them. The whole pile reminds me of a woolly ole goat that's all scrunched up and dead to the world."

"This is not the time to use that morbid word."

"What word?"

"Under these dire circumstances, I'm not comfortable with your using the word 'dead' carelessly."

"Well, you know you didn't have to come up here. I just thought you wanted to know that the governor ordered top-rank officers to meet as soon as the spies return. They just might come back any minute."

"Genesis, you are egging me on. You know as well as I that the spies' message is what's compelling me to wait up here."

"Padre, if it makes you feel any better, remember Governor Masot's waiting, too, just like us."

"I am quite aware. I particularly noted the way he entered the Government Building, a manner so unlike his usual Castilian air."

"*Humph*, he looked about the same to me."

"Oh no. His brisk walk, though still in a rhythmic cadence, seemed to harbinger disaster. His head favored the weighty side of his body where, on this day, his largest saber swung."

"Uh hm, that's the big, curved one with the cordovan scabbard. It makes him look mighty powerful. I'd surefire like to look powerful like that."

"I agree it is impressive, the way his strong fingers usually cup the top of that enormous basket-like guard. But not today. Today, his fingertips nervously ran along those handsome silver-filigreed arches that rib the basket shape."

Padre, though wearing flat leather sandals, stood as tall as his humpback permitted. He had always thought he would have been at least five feet nine inches tall if he had not been born with the blemish, which had lowered his height by two inches. His dark brown eyes, unusually intense, pierced the

41

sun's rays. A fine layer of sweat shimmered over his olive skin, contrasted with his drab clerical robe. Rather than being merely a successor to an apostle, he appeared, despite the deformity, as if he were one of Jesus Christ's original twelve, preserved for posterity and transported through the centuries.

A crucifix, which Padre had hand carved from a conch shell, rested against his cassock-covered chest. Many times he had admired it, not only for his craftsmanship but also the crucifix's holy symbolic meaning. A long, narrow strip of buckskin circled his neck and looped at the center of the crucifix, in a way that held it securely. As he waited, he shifted his weight from the right leg to the left, watching in extreme uneasiness. Unbeknownst to him, this back and forth movement generated the flickering of sun-fed highlights in his shell crucifix. These luminous specks flitted back and forth from the creamy streaks to the rich coral ones. Even if Padre had been aware of the natural beauty glowing, it would not have mattered at this time. He was not even aware of some of his own actions, let alone the sun's. As was his habit, he alternately stroked his black, curly beard and mustache. To-and-fro he repeated the monotonous action, gazing and wondering if the American general would dare invade Pensacola again.

"You're watching like a paid sentry," Genesis said and slumped down on an old flat-topped wooden trunk. His long and lean, though muscular, body dwarfed the dusty discard. He pulled a titi shrub twig from his pocket and chewed on it. Frowning, he twirled the twig around with his tanned fingertips and studied the end, which had become fibrous from chewing. He reminisced. "My mother told me our people learned to clean their teeth this way from our ancestors."

Padre quickly shaded his eyes from the early-afternoon sun and said, "I think I see something moving down Red Hill. Could that be the spies?" His heart thumped.

Genesis sprang upward. "I see three somethings. That's them. That's them. All three of them galloping down the hill."

As soon as the leader approached within viewing range of the garrison's opened gate, he spurred his horse to a bounding pace. In an effort to keep up, the other two men goaded their horses, seemingly to their limits.

"They're mighty tough," Genesis said with admiration.

"But they're prodding the animals relentlessly. My goodness, foam is flying from the horses' mouths, thick as a wild gulf wave."

"Hell, forget the foam and think about what's important, Padre. Look at the leader. That's Slick Walters. Looks like a rowdy, but just watch how he directs signals. He's surefire a military man."

Weathered cypress stakes, about ten feet tall, outlining the gloomy-gray stockade, shook when one of the horses bumped the fence. If a stake had fallen, surely the brittle wood would have crumbled into dust. In the quietness, that bump amplified the rusty-iron gate hinges creaking for oil. A frozen stillness in the warm afternoon of that May 20 had been interrupted. A bevy of curious gulls swooped down to eye level, oddly noiseless for the moment, but nothing else moved except the horses dragging their laggard hooves through the sandy street. White sand stuck to the dark hair covering the lower joints of their legs. Bearing their sleuthing riders, the horses trudged on past two napping sailors who had found a shaded bench.

As the commandant's posse rode past the storehouse and barracks, Genesis said, "Nope. Nobody would ever guess they're spies. They look for the world like three roughnecks."

"Ah, but they are stiff necked as a trio of tin soldiers. They have really pushed themselves. Just look at the salt crusts marking the sweat-soaked areas of their clothing, a real contrast with the dark colors. They have pushed the animals, too. The horses' mouths are still frothed, hanging limp."

The burly leader signaled a turn at the three-story, wooden Government House and led on past it. Surrounded on all sides by verandas and neglected flower gardens, now nigh filled with knee-high weeds, its decrepit condition was deplorable, and everyone knew that only the brick paving on the first floor had remained in good condition. They stopped at the next building, the commanding officer's quarters. It was also a three-storied, wooden building, though smaller. It, too, had fallen into disrepair.

The spies leapt from the weary horses and with a flick and tie of the reins had them tethered to the rickety hitching post in no time at all. Hastily, the leader cranked up the wooden bucket of water from the well.

"They're surefire gulping, gulping like big-mouthed bass," Genesis said.

The first two passed the communal dipper back and forth until they had slaked their thirsts. After they splashed their faces, the leader yelled to the youngest rider, "Let them cool off before you water them. We can't afford to lose a horse to colic." Then they dashed into the officers' quarters. The youngest rider fetched water for himself and later for the thirsty horses. On his way to the door he reached down and stroked the head of a lean, gray-tabby cat that had scampered up and licked scattered water droplets from the scrubby grass.

Though it seemed ridiculous, Padre's mind flashed back to March and the amusing patgoe in the Holy Week Festival parade. "I feel akin to it somehow," he had said to Padre de Galvez who stood beside him during the Fat Tuesday celebration.

"Why? I find it strange to hear that from you." Padre de Galvez laughed. "You don't mind letting people know that you do not have a wooden brain. Furthermore, I thought you were quite satisfied wearing your plain cassock and all it represents."

"I surely would never ever be decorated in festive ribbon plumage, contributed by beaux-hunting women, like that mythical patgoe. But…but I could be shot at. Not by the beaux's competing fowling pieces but by real gunnery, American gunnery."

"Oh ye of little faith," Padre de Galvez said. "Trust in the Lord God Almighty and do not worry. We do not know precisely what General Jackson has in mind since he moved his army over the Florida line. After nearly starving himself, and his men and horses in the Georgia swamps, perhaps he will not take the chance of traveling all the way to Pensacola."

The elderly Padre de Galvez's patrimonial treatment seemed rather superficial, too superficial so the younger padre thought. The danger *was* real. Suddenly, the people clapped when one of the competing beaux "killed" the patgoe with his fowling piece.

Padre cleared his throat and returned his thoughts to the present. There won't be any winning beaux around to be proclaimed King of the ball next year nor any to pay for it, as was the custom, if the general marches back to Pensacola and invades again. Something worse could happen. He feared he might have to pay…pay with his life like the wooden patgoe.

Abruptly, Padre's attention turned to Governor Masot's aide as he emerged from the meeting. His heart skipped.

Genesis jumped up saying, "He's coming for me."

"Yes, the aide is on his way to summon you. They probably need you to translate some Creek words that the spies heard."

Genesis had already turned on his heel. He ran across the gritty floor, bounced down two steps at a time, unmindful of all the loose boards and ragweed poking through the cracks. Then, true to his "Arrow" nickname, he sprinted straight ahead and met the aide midway of the veranda. Before the second syllable of his name sounded, he blurted, "I'm here, I waited. Watched. I'm ready." The aide turned and led the way. They quickly disappeared beyond the entrance to the commandant's quarters.

Padre's heart beat faster. He murmured, "There is no doubt. The spies have news and from all appearances, it's forbidding. This is one time I wish I could eavesdrop—if only I could just be a fly on the wall." He bowed his head and softly prayed, "God help us." Afterwards, he crossed himself and hastened toward the mission chapel, which was still located in the old warehouse.

On the way to the chapel, vivid images flashed across his mind, images that pieced together how his relationship with Genesis had developed. It was one he had often marveled at, for it defied conventional boundaries. In some ways Genesis seemed like a kindred soul, in others not a shred of kinship existed. Much faster than Padre planted steps, even faster than his eyes blinked, events in the courses of their lives unfolded. Genesis had changed so much since meeting him over six years ago. But no doubt about it, Genesis' company had brought balance, sometimes sparking dull routine with a story he'd heard about Creek lore or some wild tale about a river monster or forest thieves. Would the young man have come so far in his development without *my* help, Padre wondered? No doubt, *I'm* the one who had the greatest influence on his growth ever since his father sailed back to Spain. The first years of remolding the toughened brat in him had challenged every virtue. For a moment Padre felt a flush of exhilaration, the familiar kind that used to exude along with thoughts of his virtuous deeds. He did not always feel contrite about *thinking* of self-importance. It, somehow, was not as sinful as spoken words.

Angel Roundtree, long time supporter of Genesis and a friend of his mother, had noticed Padre's earlier corrective measures. She recently remarked that the young man had grown into a fine person and was one of the handsomest blends of Creek and Spanish features she had ever seen. But was she aware that with all the problems which had followed the 1814 invasion, Genesis had gradually lost his childhood innocence and increasingly taken to vulgar talk, even unchaste behavior? Nevertheless, Padre felt that early ties to Genesis had remained intact for the most part.

At once Padre's reflections ended as he entered the dingy warehouse, shocked he'd arrived at the chapel without paying an iota of attention to direction. Though it was a perfect place to put soul-destroying anguish into perspective, his heart pounded as he let go of his reminiscing and faced the grimness of his superior. Padre de Galvez awaited with a saint's sanctimonious stare.

# A HOLY MANDATE

In a halting manner, the shrunkened, shriveled Padre de Galvez said, "I am anxious...I am terribly anxious to hear the spies' report."

"There is no word yet, Padre de Galvez. Genesis is meeting with them and the officers as we speak. It must be God's divine intervention that you are here. I need to tell you..." His insides turned jittery. He hesitated for a moment and then said, "I must confess about the talks I have had with Genesis recently."

"You may proceed," the elder priest said as he sat, bent forward, and gathered his limbs so as to snug them to his frail body, even in the warmth of May.

His small, elderly, almost oval-shaped form, colored in shades of gray, looked strangely like a newly-birthed lamb. Padre had seen plenty of them in his shepherding days on *Andalucian* hills. On second thought, and even stranger, his saintly superior seemed more like a sanctified soul about to enter the womb of the Holy Heavens. Unable to begin directly at the most poignant part of the confession, the subordinate priest said, "You are aware, Padre, I am haunted by the way my family lost their lives to Napoleon's hideous war crimes in Spain." His normally resonant voice pinched each word, and his mouth tightened, tight as the stubbornest oyster shell he had ever tried to open.

"Napoleon is unquestionably the root of our dilemma here," Padre de Galvez said softly in a way of easing the tension. "The despot's unceasing war with His Majesty on the mainland has emptied the Treasury and stripped our manpower. Every day it gets more galling to see the garrison's decline and vulnerability."

"That tyrant has trapped us here in Pensacola, too," the subordinate priest said. "Genesis began talking about leaving Pensacola's perilous situation after General Jackson reentered Florida and seized St. Mark's. Ever since he ousted Commander Luengo there, Genesis is possessed by the general's mania. He refers to him only as Sharp Knife." Suddenly the younger priest felt a pang of pity. He adjusted his shoulders to a more upright posture and said, "I fear I am imposing too weighty a matter on you by asking you to hear my confession now."

"There is no need for a confession."

Padre Morales sat silently, stunned at the leniency of his superior's indulgence in this critical matter. Had his perceptive nature already suspicioned that he had been conspiring with Genesis to leave Pensacola?

Padre de Galvez continued, now in a subdued manner as if talking through the protection of a caul, "Though my health has been in great decline as of late, I would have no peace if I did not hear you out. God will spare me the strength to share your concerns. It is despicable what the sharp-knifed general and his army have done to the honorable Commander Francisco Caso y Luengo, one of our most revered Spanish military figures. Holy Mary, Mother of Jesus, knows the American general rightfully deserves his unfavorable moniker ever since his army killed so many people in their raids on Spanish and Indian settlements." He started coughing, then wheezing. After recovering, he said, "It is incomprehensible how he crossed over the Florida line, killed Spaniards and Indians and burned and pilfered their villages along his way." Then the elder padre hawked severely and held his hand over his mouth. The younger padre led him to the door where he spit a mass of phlegm big as a bay oyster. After being reseated he paused a moment and then said, "You may proceed with confidences you and Genesis shared."

Padre still feared for the superior priest's physical condition, but marveled that the elderly one seemed to have already perceived the point of this talk, yet had not admonished him. On the contrary, Padre de Galvez seemed so amenable about the conversations he had engaged in with Genesis. Why?

After relating the particulars about *Senor* Colabro, the Montezuma Trading Post, and the possibility of taking the Indian Ridge Trail there, the younger priest said, "I told Genesis, that place may resemble my homeland village." Then he shot a questioning look at his superior and said, "I have told you everything, Padre." He exhaled a relieving breath and said, "I truly regret that I did not get permission, beforehand, to talk about these matters with Genesis." He bowed his head.

A visionary, in the truest sense, Padre de Galvez said, "Look at me. By the grace of God I am in my seventy-fourth year. I have given much

47

prayerful thought to the weak defensive position of Pensacola in the face of another possible attack by General Jackson. You can plainly see that my health has failed along with the deterioration of the garrison. There are times when I can hardly catch my breath. So, I have just this morning met with Father Mulvaney and placed him in charge here, since he is next in line. Now...now I *order* you to leave Pensacola with Genesis if the spies report that the general is approaching. In that case, you are not to place your life at risk. Spanish priesthood is much too precious."

Padre Morales sat stultified, still feeling guilty. He had never left a flock, not a single time in the *Andalucian* hills, and certainly not a church flock.

Padre de Galvez continued, "You will take the horse and leave immediately upon hearing of an imminent attack. May God go with you. My prayers will ever intercede for you." He turned grim again and held up his hand with an air of the advantaged privilege of his position. He had always done this whenever he had given his final word and there would be no rebuttal. Then feebly he arose and found his way to the altar.

In shock and disbelief, Padre Morales followed, stuttering, "Thank you for your compassion. Thank you in the name of our Lord Jesus Christ and Blessed Virgin Mary, but I, uh...I..."

Padre de Galvez again raised his hand in protest. He had given his final words.

The mind-numbing, bitter finality of the incredulous order hit Padre Morales' ears like an exploding cannonball. How he needed to douse his head with a bucket of water and how he needed to pray, but he could hardly wait to hear the spies' report. Would he have to leave the beleaguered St. Michael's Mission right away? Was danger lurking near this very moment? The thought of traveling the Indian Ridge Trail no longer seemed like a vague dream or adventure, rather it loomed over his head, like a "twelve-pounder" falling in slow motion, despite common-knowledge rumors which described the trail as easy to follow.

Kneeling beside his small, saintly superior, he prayed as earnestly as he ever had in his entire life: "Merciful Mary, Mother of Jesus, may your faithful mercy intercede and strengthen my will to obediently follow my fateful orders in the event Satan has his way with the American general."

When the door of the officers' quarters eventually reopened, everyone, except Governor Masot, filed out. Genesis stood agog as the officers sallied forth resolutely to rally the forces, such as they were. The spies' lips looked as if they were sealed tight as kegs of gunpowder. The broad shouldered leader led the other two toward the Emerald Saloon on Seville Square, undoubtedly for grog and grub. Of the nine taverns, the Emerald stood closest and offered all sorts of entertainment, including ladies of the night. Fortuitously, the spies had just picked up their pay.

Genesis watched the spies' sorely troubled faces brighten after they had stashed their pay in their pockets. He speculated that after they ate, they might dare to eke out time for gambling, rum, or even women, before returning to duty. How he wished he could accompany them, hang around, and possibly hear stories that might spark the afternoon. Instead, he stepped lively to the mission chapel where he felt sure Padre Morales would be praying.

Fearful, Genesis genuflected in a hurried sort of way and made the sign of the cross as soon as he entered the chapel, not even wondering why he had gone through these religious motions. He was certainly not in the habit of practicing them. Before he risked attracting Padre Morales' attention, he made sure that Padre de Galvez was in deep prayer. Genesis said nothing even though he knew the elderly priest was partially deaf. He simply stepped forward, nudged Padre Morales, and whispered, "Meeting is over. Spies went to eat. We need to talk on the beach. Right away."

Before Genesis left, he took a second look at the holy water vessel. So apprehensive, he decided it might help to bless himself with holy water, and for good measure he would even make the sign of the cross. He respected the Catholic Church; however, his deepest spiritual feelings remained staunchly grounded in the Breath Maker. He and his mother and sister had never embraced Catholicism. This in no way diminished his gratefulness that the Catholic Mission had helped, at times, to care for him and his mother, before his birth as well as during his early years. And though he had listened to Padre's efforts of conversion, his Creek mother had long ago instilled in him devout faith in Breath Maker. Walking from the chapel door, her departing words rang clearly in his mind: "I trust, my son, you will keep the teachings of our ancestors in your heart always."

Padre's eagerness to hear Genesis' news spurred him onward. Still, he had taken care to face the altar as he backed away. He kept his head bowed and his hands in prayerful form until he reached the holy water vessel. There, he blessed himself, made the sign of the cross, and even said one more prayer, a brief one, before departing. In deep sadness, he looked back. The sight of Padre de Galvez made him even sadder. Saddest of all, would they ever see each other again? No one knew but the Lord.

# UNCERTAINTIES

Making a conscious effort to walk slowly and act in his customary way Padre reverently looped his rosary over his right hand and headed toward the beach. As he passed the *calabozo*, or jail as the British called it during their short occupation before the turn of the century, he lowered his head. He wished he were on a mission to speak with the incarcerated ones about their transgressions, rather than meeting with Genesis about the spies' report. Nevertheless, he merely stared at the red and yellow ochre bricks that paved a short stretch of the sidewalk. A giant teardrop of gray, scraggly Spanish moss almost touched his head as he made his usual turn at the sprawling-old, live oak tree. Prayerfully, he entered the pathway edged with cabbage palmettos, his eyes remaining at the level of the cabbage palmettoes which dotted the landscape as far as his vision reached.

Soon the surface under his feet began fluctuating with his footsteps. Sand. Near the tide marks he stripped off his sandals and clutched the straps. The breeze over the bay water wafted the usual fishy scent toward him. Sun, salty sea breeze, and vast bay boded as such wonderful forces of nature yet on this day rendered little solace. If only they could share the burden of the probable perils facing Pensacola's future.

Sandpipers chattered while feeding. As sure as the colossal orange of sun would set and rise tomorrow, sandpipers would routinely perform their rituals. They raced up on the beach whenever a wave swished toward shore. Then the handsome birds kept just ahead of each breaker, chasing after the surf and feeding on the tiny stranded marine life, stranded like himself. The sting of feeling trapped provoked the painful notion of taking stock. How had this vexing situation developed? How could he, an ordained priest with scholarly training, so obedient, and acting as God's ambassador on earth, be diminished to this disconsolate level? He had practiced the four cardinal virtues faithfully. He had abstained from the cardinal sins, daily, all seven—except...well, a few times he had slipped, and had been granted absolution.

In meditation, Padre stroked the crucifix, which rested on his chest. Today, this gesture evoked some sentiments about its origin. After General Jackson's history-defying invasion of almost four years ago, the crucifix on the mission altar had disappeared. So distressed, Padre had taken the one he wore, the cherished one he had gotten at the Dominican Monastery, and placed it on the chapel altar. Right away he started carving a conch shell crucifix for himself. Padre remembered that invasion as if it had happened yesterday. A quirky incident of that fiasco sprang into his mind, the rumor that the officer in charge of the garrison had sent his favorite concubine to safety; because there was not enough gunpowder for defense, not even enough to fire a salute. Another more sobering memory flashed: The sinking feeling of watching Spain's glorious gold and crimson flag being lowered. It still sent shivers down his spine, shivers that were incredibly touching even underneath his warm, sunbathed cassock.

With the same swiftness that the unbidden memories had darted forth, Padre tried to sink them into obscurity. Still, the aggravation of Jackson persisted. Padre de Galvez's order felt as strong as the seashell Padre had just glided over. It was a Rising Sun, burnished so smooth the tapered golden streaks shone like beacons, contrasting vividly against the white background. In need of a good omen, he wiped away the sand and put it in his pocket.

Despite finding the shell, the malleable sand under his feet turned into a bed of needles. No matter how grievous leaving might be, he must obey Padre de Galvez's orders. His finger grips tightened on the sandal straps in one hand and his rosary in the other.

To the east and then to the west, he scoured the beach for Genesis, but he was nowhere to be found. Suddenly the flap of wings came so close that he felt the breeze they created. At the same time he felt something else—a warm, slippery substance between his toes. At once it oozed. What was it? The light color gave away its identification. Gull dung.

He shook his rosary-festooned hand at the bird, now soaring over the bay, and blared in frustration, "You and that, that greedy general are both full of shit." Then he looked around surreptitiously to see if anyone had heard. Seeing no one close by, he yelled, "Maybe Genesis is full of *shee-it*, too." Indignation forced him into a vigorous gait to the water's edge to clean his foot. A crab popped up on its haunches as if glaring a disgusting look.

51

Two familiar people loomed into view. The peg-legged maroon who worked at the Ft. San Carlos de Barrancas Hospital and his Seminole wife waded under the distant wharf, netting crabs. Their mixed-blood children played at the water's edge. Padre put his sandals back on with obvious vengeance. He smothered his shame by recalling his very first assignment in Pensacola—to visit that very same maroon at the Ft. San Carlos de Barrancas Hospital after his leg was amputated with a guillotine. The doctor who performed the extraordinary operation should see the former patient now, peg legging through the gulf water, harvesting a meal, and apparently experiencing only minor difficulty maneuvering over the sandy bottom. This sight brought a much-needed feeling of fulfillment. Counseling them as well as others had made a difference. Angel Roundtree had often praised his work with the maroons and passed on their favorable remarks.

Ordinarily, he might have walked over and visited with the couple, but feeling too distraught, he quickly threw that inclination to the sea breeze. The only future for Pensacola might have already passed. He sensed Spain's possession slipping away like a slow-motioned nightmare.

What had detained Genesis since he left the chapel? Padre wiped his clammy hands on his robe, careful all the while to protect his rosary. Then he winced, the edginess growing unbearable. What if Governor Masot had ordered Genesis on duty already?

With utmost effort, Padre walked along the water's edge, his body as inflexible as the ship mast in the distance. He hurried away from his reflection in the water, for it reminded him of the one he had seen in the Cadiz Harbor. Looking back, the anguish created by that image of his deformed back had been quickly overcome by his dream of building a church. But would he ever get the chance? The conundrum—risk facing another invasion vis-a-vis attempting escape—had turned over in his mind again and again for days, but was now a moot issue. He must honor his superior's orders.

At once Padre's mind erupted with "what ifs." What if Genesis had been order on duty; what if he were spreading the spies' news? Or God forbid, what if he had panicked and fled the garrison already? His stomach, at first unsettled, now churned. Vaguely aware of the "Kip-kip-kip-killick, kip-kip-killick" of the least terns, a fast-moving shadow caught his attention. Could it be Genesis, finally? A rush of expectancy swept through his body. As the shadow quickly advanced, a familiar call, "Padre," interrupted the least terns' prattle. An inciting element in Genesis' voice sliced through Padre, knifelike. He clutched his abdomen. Genesis' news, Padre just knew, was sinister.

Though now almost face to face, Genesis called out again, "Padre, the spies said Sharp Knife's on his way with more'n a thousand men!" His voice carried a primordial ring.

Padre stopped still as a mythical patgoe bird. Urgency for the news had already roiled into vexation. "And you've been withholding this dreadful news while the sand under my feet turns to needles? Where in the world have you been?"

Genesis merely challenged, "When are we leaving? Sharp Knife's men are breathing down our necks. And they've got plenty of howitzers, eight-inchers, nine-pound guns, too." He panted, heat radiating from his body as hot as the blood-tinged sun and flared again, "Spies saw 'em on the bank of the Escambia, seven or eight leagues north, resting up for attack." Catching a deep breath and swiping his furrowed brow, he said, "Spies said the whole army, Red Sticks and other Indians that Sharp Knife hired, will strike the garrison. Right up to the time the bastards bivouacked, they was still slaughtering every Creek and Seminole in their path, stealing everything they wanted from the villages, and burning the rest like your fires of hell."

"God forfend. A thousand?"

"You heard me. Sharp Knife didn't send nary one back home. Should I tell you the rest?"

In his most serious mien, Padre said, "I'm in no frame of mind to tolerate any foolery."

"I was just putting a flea in your ear and giving you a second to scratch it. You see, attack's coming tonight or tomorrow morning." The governor's letter to Sharp Knife didn't help no more'n teats on a bull. Spies said old Sharp Knife just laughed when he read it."

Padre winced at— "...attack's coming tonight or tomorrow morning," yet he said, "Our governor is filled with Spanish sensibility, proffering his best explanations for His Majesty and the Church."

"But Pensacola's about naked as that spot on the governor's head. Last muster, they counted only 175 men guarding this whole town and countryside. We've got no more of a chance than a mullet fighting a starved barracuda. Their bayonets'll rip out guts, or else they'll blow us out in the bay."

Powerless to stop the reaction, Padre's shoulders stiffened up to his ears. He wrung his hands and moaned, "Wars, wars, wars. But thank God the governor's spies have kept us abreast." The foreboding feeling that had grappled him during the Holy Week celebration, nebulous at that time, now returned more direct and intense. It had felt absurd to identify with the mythical patgoe bird dangling from a stick at the Fat Tuesday celebration. Yet today, he felt every bit as vulnerable as that wooden bird. As in previous years, it had been bedecked in ribbons contributed by eligible women and was to be "killed" by beaux competing with fowling pieces. Though not being carried through the street by a slave in a festival, Padre felt that he dangled at the general's whims like a patgoe dangling from a stick.

# OVERLOOKED OBSTACLES

Genesis frowned. "It don't take much brains to make a fast getaway. *Whew,* can't hardly get my breath." He rubbed his throat. "Everything's happening so fast, it's raised a lump in my craw bigger than a goose egg. Governor didn't waste no time, ordered the gates closed and every sentry box manned. Muster before sunrise, too. Said Pensacola wasn't going to be open-gated like Commandant Luengo let St. Mark's go, open for disguised American officers to roam and gather intelligence."

Padre stared at Genesis straight in the eyes. "I've been waiting for this crucial news like an unfledged bird in the nest, just as helpless. The posse left the commandant's quarters long ago. For the love of God, where on earth did you go after speaking to me in the chapel?"

"I went..."

"You went? Knowing the slaughterers are so close to the garrison? Dear God, where?"

Before Genesis answered, the embroiled padre lashed out, "I interrupted my prayers at the chapel and scurried down here to meet you. I looked up and down this beach. You knew I was nigh dying to hear what the spies had to say."

"Padre, if you'll just listen. *Humph*, I never thought you could be so pigheaded. And another thing, you should see yourself standing there wringing your hands like some feeble granny. Don't you think more than a thousand soldiers marching to attack scares me too? Well, it scares hell outta me."

"My...my brother in God," Padre relented stroking his beard and mustache. "Calm down, and I'd thank you to watch your language. I just don't understand you sometimes."

Genesis snatched hold of Padre's arm. *"Some times* I don't understand you either. That's just it. *Time.* Time's running out. We need to tuck tail and get outta here before the sentries go on duty, or else we might get turned back or worse yet get our chests full of American grape." He caught his stomach. "Feel like puking right here. Can't hardly stand thinking about Sharp Knife's army, with all that butchering, burning, and beating, too, they've done to my mother's people."

Distraught, Padre looked at his feet sinking into the white sand and felt his heart sinking, too.

Genesis slapped his hands to his hips with both elbows angling out offensively, set his chin in determination and hurled, "Dammit, I'll just go it alone."

Padre jerked out of his mulling mood. "Oh, so now you are ready for a fast getaway?"

"I took a few minutes, only a few minutes," Genesis said and whisked his brow again. "I wasn't exactly sure if you would leave the chapel right away, so I uh, stopped in at the Emerald Tavern."

"Emerald Tavern?" Padre scowled.

"Well it wasn't like I was entertaining myself. Didn't stay long."

"Thank the Lord for your smallest of favors."

"Padre, will you let me explain?"

"Of course. Proceed."

Genesis' back stiffened. "Point is, I thought I could overhear the spies say something offhand at the tavern that they wouldn't say in Governor Masot's meeting."

"So, make haste; get on with your story. Did your errant trip shed any more light?"

"The spies didn't say much, just kinda grunted between bites and swilling. Put it down like hungry alligators. When I saw 'em this time, I got a strange feeling, like one of them sickening nightmares. One of 'em said them Tennessee bastards was sitting on the banks of the Escambia cracking jokes. Said they looked big enough to charge the gates of hell."

Genesis quailed in a lower voice, "Besides, three girls from Madam Maria's house came in. And Cleo, she's the one I go to, her real name's Cleopatra. She winked at me. I uh...it got to me," he said with a semblance of shame, "but when I walked over to her, she snarled, 'Begone with ye, sonny. Slick and his men doubled the ante if we'd take care of 'em right away.' So I got the hell outta there."

"Cleopatra?" Padre exclaimed in disgust. "What a disgrace! You were watching a whore wink at you in the Emerald Tavern, and I'm down here on the beach awaiting the spies' news like a...like a starving man waiting for a piece of bread." For a moment he wanted to shake Genesis to the ground.

Genesis recoiled. Nervously, he scratched the back of his neck, raising red welts, and squinted when the salty sweat smarted. Jutting his chin forward, he said, "Maybe I shouldn't have told you the whole truth. Now listen Padre, we better get going and mighty fast, too."

Padre swallowed hard. "Well, what's already done; let it be. But you should know that in the midst of this life-threatening quandary my destiny has *not* been left to chance." He unwittingly wrung his hands. "Padre de Galvez ordered me to leave if the spies reported an imminent attack. I will obey." He cast an oblique glance and admonished, "*And* get you away from that sin-infested Madam Maria's house, too."

"Orders?" Genesis asked in disbelief.

Padre massaged his throat and said, "Yes, you heard correctly. I shall not explain at this dire time. A lump, like a lead ball, comes in my throat, too, or craw as you call it, when I think of leaving." He paused, prayer-like, long enough to reverently kiss the rosary dangling from his hand. "Sharp Knife's really complicated the situation, stuck us right in the throes of far greater jeopardy. For days, we thought he'd be coming from the Apalachicola direction." He looked toward the sky and said, "Dear God, can you hear me? The general is heading straight south. Will that devil's demon point his guns right in our faces if we head north?"

"Don't worry. Don'tcha think I could figure out what to do about that? Coulda even figured it out when I was knee-high to a..." Without finishing his thought or waiting for an answer to his question, he chuckled in a ridiculing sort of way. "We can stay east of him. It's easy if we just take the easterly trail up Red Hill. And I don't believe a word of that tale about old Sharp Knife marching south straight as buckshot. He's surefire gonna be curving around them nooks and bends, staying close to the Escambia no matter how meandering it is. He's not gonna risk getting his army lost again."

"I suppose you're right, and God willing, we will get to the Indian Ridge Trail before encountering his evil soldiers or scouts. Then, I'd feel better about our chances of making it all the way to the Montezuma Trading Post." Padre dug his fingers into his forearms, frowning. At last he admitted, "You know, it frightens the life out of me to think about traveling that trail to the north, but I know I must."

Tolerance of Padre's tired rhetoric had worn thin. Unable to bear his cant any longer Genesis said, "I don't wanna hear no more whining and

preaching, and I sure as hell don't wanna get my guts slit with a bayonet."
He turned to leave.

# THE CEMETERY

Padre yelled, "Wait," and grabbed Genesis' arm, jerking it with the passion of a steeple bell ringer jerking the rope. With a fresh start, as if new life had been breathed into his body, Padre's countenance brightened. "You know I have high regard for your scouting abilities, or else I wouldn't be in this covert meeting making these rash plans. He shuddered. "Flesh-creeping plans. I'll do whatever is necessary to fulfill my duty."

Genesis *hmm, hmmed*, clearing his throat. Again he cleared his throat and droned, "Oh shit. I, I guess have to tell you what's really on my mind." He paused wondering if Padre would flare up again.

"Merciful heavens, now what?"

"Well, I have to take *Grandeza* to the smithy—but just for one hoof. This morning when I fed him, I noticed he'd lost a shoe. I surefire forgot when we were in the barracks watching for the spies."

Padre scowled, "Genesis, you will be my nemesis yet." He looked up at the sky, wrung his hands, and implored, "My, my, dear God, what to do?"

Genesis tugged at a loose thread on his shirt pocket.

"No question about it, you'll have to get *Grandeza* shod, but there's not a second for you to hang around the spies again, much less the harlots. Remember, the path just over Red Hill that cuts a straight line westerly down to the smithy's place is where we'll have to keep a sharp lookout for devilish American scouting parties. Our very lives'll be at stake, more so for you with that musket."

"Worry about yourself."

"I'll meet you there," Padre said. "It's best if we don't leave the garrison together."

Genesis' eyes snapped. "My saddlebags are ready. Been like that ever since the spies found out Sharp Knife was on the move. If a sentry stops me, I'll show him how *Grandeza* needs a new shoe. They know I always take my gun when I ride outside the garrison, so there ain't nothing suspicious about me leaving with the gun."

"Have you gone mad, Genesis? Don't let this trip into Creek country numb your faculties. You know today's not an ordinary sort of day. *Of course* there could be suspicions."

Genesis shot a repugnant look.

Padre switched to a patronizing tone and said, "Don't tarry. Just fetch your belongings. I do want you to make it safely to the Montezuma Trading Post, so you can meet that beautiful Indian princess. But before we start this formidable venture, if you can just hold still a few more seconds, I have something for you."

Hurriedly, Padre fetched an object from his pocket and handed it to Genesis. "I carved this crucifix for you. I had searched until I found a conch shell with the same vivid coral as mine. I'd like you to wear this as a symbol sealing our pact that together we'll reach the Montezuma Trading Post. I don't want you to let anyone talk you into becoming a scout and leave me stranded in some wilderness."

Genesis twisted the crucifix around, admiring the way the sun highlighted its contrasting colors. So anxious to get away from the potential invasion, he said, "I'll honor your God and ancestors for our trip," while he looped the buckskin strip over his head and centered the crucifix on his chest. Then poised on the balls of his feet and with arms outstretched, and eyes uplifted, he implored, "Great Breath Maker, be with us. Guide us." He turned and dashed away with Padre's words echoing, "Go and God be with you."

In disbelief, Padre gaped at the slant of the sun's rays, now glinting on a deserted frigate's remaindered mast. Rays beveled only a few feet lower than when he had first arrived at the beach. Befuddled, he cast another look at the cant of the sun's rays. Had only minutes passed since he had come to the beach? He must get hold of himself, put elapsed time in true perspective. Yes, mercifully, the long length of time had been an illusion. Yes, thank God, time spent here had been only a matter of minutes. And yes, the conversation with Genesis had seemed interminable but had miraculously flowed like an uncontrollable, rushing river.

Though burning with a sudden sense of urgency to move on, Padre, instead, strolled in strained steps for a couple minutes, giving Genesis ample lead time. Hopefully, Genesis, in his youthful exuberance, would not make some careless mistake and blunder their plans or be ordered on duty, or encounter overlooked obstacles. Padre had never broken his Dominican vow of obedience and chafed to get moving. Padre de Galvez would be praying for him.

This extraordinary relationship with Genesis had developed into a partnership for an uncertain journey, a journey fraught with endless dangers, and, ironically, a journey promising potential. Just how would his leaving Pensacola affect their lives? And dear God...the outcome? What would that be?

As Genesis veered around the bend and out of sight, Padre's gait grew faster. He refused, steadfastly, to walk close to the water. Seeing his reflection would be unbearably reminiscent of the day he had sailed from Cadiz. But now it was not humiliation of his humpback, but the unfulfilled desire to build a church for St. Michael's Mission that grievously bothered him. There was nothing he could do about his deformed back, but he surely had cherished hope for building a befitting church. The endless, white-sandy beach sparkled with a brilliance that reflected his sharply contrasting shadow. Curiously, he accepted his sand shadow with less difficulty than his shadow in the water.

The ofttimes amusing teeter tail sandpipers, with well-plumed rears incessantly bobbing, failed to lighten his burden of this fateful day. Farther on, sounds of laughing gulls that had been noisily eating their newly found meal, now languished from hearing range. "Nothing's funny, not the slightest bit funny," Padre said half aloud. The gulls' low chuckling sounds, he knew, were simply instinctive and not directed at his plight; yet he would take the opportunity to voice frustration, for precious seconds were blowing away on the sea breeze. He pondered whether he would he have to confront Father Mulvaney and get involved in explanations, but Padre de Galvez would take care of that. More disturbing was whether he could be ever mindful and cautious of the least iota of potential danger and escape the garrison posthaste and unnoticed. Never had prudence been more important.

Silence, the silence of death permeated his stark, old abode. The other priests were probably at the chapel. While looking around, he suddenly lurched with a poignant sense of exposure. It was only the mere scurrying of a mouse that had usurped more of his precious fleeting seconds.

Hastily, he changed to his well-worn leather boots, the ones he'd brought from Spain. Two or three years ago, a shoemaker had helped preserve them with new heels and soles. He slipped his leather sandals into his buckskin shoulder bag. Unable to resist, he slid his hand to the bottom, reassuring himself that his hatchet and knife still topped some old letters. A precious bar of Castile soap was still wedged into one corner. He had to also make sure that his container of holy healing oil was properly corked. In another corner of the bag, on top of the old vermin comb, rested the little metal box for storing his rosary and crucifix. Impulsively, he pulled it out, popped the lid on the empty box, and basked for a moment at the etching on the lid's inside surface— "*Andalucia*, Spain." Why that comforted him, he was unsure. About eight years ago, he'd wanted so desperately to get away from that very place. After taking stock of the wafers, unconsecrated remainders from outlying missions, he straightened the folds of his spare cassock and rearranged it on top of the other clothing.

A flaming impulse, the likes of which he had never known existed, forced quick movements. The news of Jackson's approach would surely soon travel throughout the garrison. He grabbed the frayed brown blanket he used in place of a saddle. At no time had there been a chance for a fine Spanish-leather saddle like Genesis' rich cordovan one. He was fortunate just to have Captain. He slung the strap of the buckskin bag over his left shoulder and tossed the blanket over his left arm, its frayed ends dangling. He clutched his breviary in the other hand and departed, not glancing back, not even once.

Mustering up every kernel of courage, he set forth to fetch Captain, his heart thumping wildly. At the ramshackle horse barn, he went about his business, willing with all his might to squelch the need to dart looks around the place. But he just had to take a look for *Grandeza*. The stall was empty and without thinking he sighed, "Oh thank God." He caught himself and vowed to be more careful. If anyone were to see him, he must appear to be bridling Captain for a customary mercy mission. Mounting, he tried his best to appear at ease, but as they rounded the bend from the barn, what would he find? He stole a quick look at Captain's profile as they made the turn, searching for some sort of comradeship, even for strength of character.

Riding past the old plank and brick dining hall and kitchen, Padre swallowed hard. The little, old kitchen had provided meal service for the entire garrison, though only about ten by twenty-five feet. The outdoor ovens loomed up, the ones he'd taken Genesis to see when he explained about the outdoor ovens in the *Andalucian* Region of Spain.

At the well in back of the Government House, he feared that someone might see him and warn him to stay at the garrison. He *must* take the risk, possibly die if he couldn't. Unable to stave off his anxiousness, he halted Captain and looked around. Seeing no one at the moment, he dismounted. With utmost swiftness, he rolled the wooden bucket down, vigorously cranked up the bucketful of water, and dumped it in the trough for Captain. He drew another and drank a dipperful, refilling the dipper two more times before pouring the remaining water in the trough.

Mindfully, he replaced the dented tin dipper on the old nail sticking out from a board that supported the well's roof. As he looped the curved handle onto the aged nail, corroded with salt-air rust, he felt keenly touched about leaving the timeworn dipper behind.

Padre made only one more stop—to purchase hardtack and meat, and a flask of wine for sacramental use. After tethering Captain, he merely nodded respectfully to greetings and spurts of Spanish conversations spoken amongst street spectators and quickly passed them.

He entered the shop, hoping his fright would not show through. The air thickened with the pungent odor of sauerkraut emanating from a newly opened crock. When he stepped forward, other smells mixed. Though he had no appetite at all, the rich aromas of smoked turkey and venison complemented the wafting of the sauerkraut.

Always jolly, the massive chested *tendero* laid his knife on the butcher block. He wiped his hands across the apron girdling his bulk, adding grease streaks to the already grimy marks of unknown origin. When he greeted Padre, his *senora* looked up and quickly replaced the lid on a barrel of dried garbanzo beans over which she hovered near the rear of the shop. She grabbed a tin cup, probably containing larvae she'd been picking out of the bean barrel, and disappeared.

Still making an effort to conceal his apprehension, Padre gave his order and watched the *tendero* wrap the salt pork and smoked turkey, separately, in brown paper while intermittently fanning black flies. Just as Padre sighed with relief of his successful ruse, he noticed the *tendero* smiling through his heavy, dark mustache and heard him say, "The larder at the kitchen must be getting empty."

At this point, Padre had a curious sense that he was becoming a suspect. He had already begun opening his little leather money pouch. He pretended to count out money and nonchalently asked, "Why? Have you had more customers today than usual?" He basked in his brilliance at tossing the issue back to the shopkeeper in these crucial moments.

"Oh, I don't know about that, Padre." The shopkeeper accepted the dulled silver coins and said, "I thank you for trading with me," without raising any more suspicions.

Had the shopkeeper known more than he divulged, Padre wondered?

After that experience, he would get away from the corner of Zaragoza and Adams Streets as soon as possible. Moreover, he would take the least traveled route, the one with least risk of being questioned further.

As he mounted Captain an overwhelming sensation possessed him that something terrible might happen. Trying as hard as he could to behave in an ordinary manner, would his efforts be sufficient for getting out of the town without being restrained or thwarted? And how had Genesis fared in his escape? Unanswered questions swelled the sweat on Padre's face and increased the motion in his stomach. Instead of just a noticeable aggravation, his insides now churned. Nevertheless, he forced himself onward. He mustn't weaken now.

The mixture of people around Seville Square seemed about the same as it had in recent weeks, though no laughter sounded anywhere. Rather than risk initiating any conversations, he simply bobbed his head with politeness and kept moving. If anyone stopped him, he could always say he needed to respond to an emergency.

It had always been impossible to fully understand Pensacolians. Why more of them had not taken advantage of the fertile soil, for extensive agriculture, as well as the timbered land and its related commodities, he could not fully fathom. They appeared satisfied taking life easy and mostly purchasing imported goods and supplies from the Forbes Company. The two sawmills and a brickyard, along with a few farmers, seemed a mere pittance of commerce for such a community.

Padre figured the least noticeable route away from Seville Square was Alcaniz, the street bordering St. Michael's Cemetery. In better times he had presided over funeral processions in that very street with the acolytes and the funerary retinue following him to St. Michael's Cemetery. Maybe no one would be visiting the cemetery at this time of day. He looked about warily as he continued on.

The elderly Siguera couple sat on their front porch, leisurely fanning themselves with what looked like finely woven raffia fans, large ones peddled by the Indians. *Dear God, I'm really being heedful, paying attention to the smallest details.* The Sigueras seemed satisfied with a passing greeting.

As he passed another house, an old-timer, barebacked and suntanned, poked around in his garden with a hoe but seemed not to notice the passer-by. Padre wouldn't have had much to say to him anyway. He was an Anglo, a leftover resident from the British occupation of Pensacola, and pretty much kept to himself.

Soon, a group of excited children, with tangled hair and dirt-beaded necks, ran up to pet Captain. They were followed by two barking dogs. How he loved talking to children, and ordinarily barking dogs would not be so bothersome. However, on this day, delays rived his patience. "The dogs may upset the horse, children," Padre said. "You'll have to run along this time so no one gets hurt." The children turned their disappointed faces and walked away.

The distance to the cemetery passed in no time at all. Oval-shaped tombs, looking much like Spanish ovens, suddenly struck him with a new meaning, a sinister one. A mound of dirt, over which he had recently offered prayers for the dead, still looked fairly fresh. Pensacola's soil always dried quickly after the almost daily, afternoon thundershowers, leaving little or no trace of rain. Occasional hard downpours were another matter, but no torrential rain had fallen since that burial.

On this fateful day Padre would not stop to console the woman standing beside a grave. Up closer he recognized her, the beloved Angel Roundtree, now widowed. She had, indeed, been like an angel during his years at the garrison. True as ever to her moniker she visited her recently-deceased, Irish husband's grave daily. Padre waved but could not risk speaking with her for fear of being detained.

The sobering sights of both the widow and St. Michael's Cemetery provoked a profound sense of mortality. Now eerily wracked with uncertainty about this frightful journey, more questions issued forth, haunting ones. What else in the world might he encounter? Bullets? Beasts? Bandits? And just why, why had he been so brave, almost defiant, of the archbishop's warnings back in *Andalucia?*

# FT. GADSDEN, FLORIDA

May 5, 1818

In this Florida campaign, General Jackson's orders had been restricted to taking defense against menacing Seminole, yet he felt he'd waited too long for a second conquest of Spanish Florida to begin, especially to drive the remaining British bastards out for good. They kept popping up like forest cankerworms.

Secretary of War William Crawford had not ordered an attack; but inasmuch as he was Jackson's bitter political rival for the presidential candidacy, their mutual hatred had festered worse than Jackson's carbuncles and hampered communication between them. Nor had the chronically indecisive President Monroe granted permission for any of the previous invasions against Spanish Florida, not a single one, although when Monroe was president-elect, he had revealed in one of their private conversations the inevitability of Florida's occupation by the United States.

This evening Old Hickory massaged his hickory stick, the backwoods badge of his very being, and exhilarated in his position as an arm of central government. Hell, he'd been empowered to act for the protection of the country. Jackson found himself planning strategy as instinctively as one would take a drink of water to slake his thirst.

He had rested the army for two days and reconnoitered. Now he would initiate his strategy, for history must not play out helter-skelter. He groaned as he lifted himself from a rawhide-bottomed chair, his tall, lanky body, gaunt and ravaged by dysentery and arthritis. "Send for Gaines," he snorted to the guard.

When Jackson reached down to yank up his boot, a spasm of pain gripped his guts. Boots reminded him of the humiliation suffered in his early years while under capture of a Revolutionary War British Major. At that time, the young, envenomed Jackson suffered a saber slash when he refused the officer's order to clean his boots. This painful memory was enough to bring on diarrhea that had plagued him recently as he marched his army through Georgia and Florida swamps without sufficient food, leaving them no choice but to eat only bitter acorns in the wilderness.

"Tell Gaines I want see him right away," Jackson ordered the guard. After all, subordinates served to accommodate their superiors rather than as convenience permitted.

Brevet Brigadier General Edmund Pendleton Gaines, second in command, had already earned a hero's reputation in the War of 1812. Besides, Jackson knew he could count on him ever since Gaines had ordered the Fowltown attack. Most recently, the brigadier "took care" of other Indians, too, as he marched his army into Florida. Both men shared an unusual trait, the habit of making policy regardless of the War Department's orders.

As soon as Gaines appeared, Jackson pushed his crop aside on the table and poured two tin cups brimful, one for Gaines and a refill for himself. Spirits soothed the discomfort of his diarrhea. He handed the rum to Gaines, and after they clinked the cups in a toast, Jackson pointed to an empty chair. As soon as the brigadier sat, Jackson thundered, "Now that we got the two hellish British banditti taken care of, it's time to forge ahead."

"Yessir," Gaines said in strong support. "They pulled off all their underhanded work while they carried on their trading, really swindled the Indians. I wasn't about to turn soft like the rest of the court, Sir, especially not on the duplicity of Arbuthnot nor Ambrister."

Jackson rubbed his fingers over the scar on his face and interjected, "Arbuthnot, *humph*, the sly old villian had that noose a'cracking his neck coming to him. Getting the job done on the yardarm of his ship, full of trading goods, rightfully finished him off. It was justice for the old geezer I couldn't have hoped for." He looked to Gaines for confirmation. Gaines had preemptively lifted his cup to celebrate the remark.

"Inciting the savages to beat the band," Jackson ranted on. "Spying sure as hell. And the nerve of that runty Ambrister, just a young'un. Only a young'un would think he could get away with joining Chief Bowlegs to train runaway slaves and Indians for British warfare. The way I see it, he wasn't even worth the firing squad's powder."

"Yessir, we had the goods on 'em in court—that letter Armbrister blundered into camp with. Of all Arbuthnot's duplicitous dealings, the worst was that warning to Bowlegs of your advance. It's nothing but comical now." Gaines smiled.

"Hell yes. Not only warning of my approach but also offering gunpowder, ten kegs." Jackson gulped a goodly portion of the rum without a wince and raved on, "Way I see it, we had to crush the two fancy-talking British, damnedest opportunists on the face of the earth." Court martial of Arbuthnot and Ambrister in the Florida wilderness, without precise observance of legal detail, would not keep him awake at night. No siree! Deep in the cockles of Old Hickory's heart, he reckoned the British had caused the hardships in the Revolution that killed his widowed mother and brothers, leaving him alone when he was only fourteen. It had tortured him throughout the years. Now his vowed revenge had a redeeming quality.

He ran his hand through his matted hair, not bothering to smooth the wiry tufts, which extended outward from the back of his ears. The reddish tufts resembled those of the wildest bobcats in Tennessee. His eyes glowed in the dimness with the same wild fierceness. In a backwoods drawl that matched his looks, he said, "Hell, there's no two ways about it. I have to finish off Pensacola, and by God I'll get the job done." He poured refills.

"Sir, I don't think Governor Masot is any Luengo. And Pensacola is no St. Mark's."

"*Humph*," Jackson countered, coughed, and caught his chest at the spot that was a daily reminder he'd taken a shot in the Dickinson duel. The plaguing wound was a mixed blessing, though gratification of killing Dickinson more than outweighed the pain. Ever since that duel, his pistol was ready for draw at anyone else who scandalized Rachel's virtues. He had believed with all his heart that her divorce had already been finalized when he took her, the love of his life, as his wife. As far as he was concerned the issue had been straightened out. If not, he would kill all of them that disagreed. And now, come hell or high water, he would "take care of the savages as well as the greasers," their British friends, too.

"Uh, not that it matters a hill 'o beans to me, sir," Gaines caviled, "but since we last spoke, have you received orders from Washington to take Pensacola?"

Threat of diarrhea had subsided, so Jackson's voice grew stronger. "One man with courage for his country makes a majority."

Gaines nodded in mutual understanding of the cryptic statement. From all appearances, they were two of a kind. Besides, in an audacious manner, Old Hickory had, months earlier, established his modus operandi when he slapped his hand over his pistol handle and snapped at his officers, "I'm the first and last link of chain of command regardless of orders from the War Department."

"I am in complete accord with you. I've had a hankering to get even with that oily-faced Masot ever since he levied custom duties on goods and rations for my men at Ft. Crawford. A strike on Pensacola would be a hell of a chance to get even."

"Damn right. But, I'll take care of Florida's western side. I need you and sufficient troops to secure the area east of the Apalachicola. First, you'll appoint an officer and all other available forces to march with me to Pensacola."

Gaines listened attentively.

Jackson further ordered. "In the event of our enemies fleeing to or receiving succor from a Spanish garrison, they are to be viewed as war enemies and treated accordingly." His voice grew more authoritative, "We'll march in two days—May 7." He waved his arm toward the door in dismissal.

"Very well, sir."

As soon as Gaines left, Jackson grabbed his hickory stick. He pounded it and yelled to the guard, "Send for Young." Captain Hugh Young served as topographical engineer.

Upon Young's arrival and without asking him to be seated, Jackson commanded, "Prepare a report outlining the best approaches to the Spanish fortifications at Pensacola. On second thought, I want you to include these approaches on an enlarged map of western Florida." Though Young drew his maps with precision, his limited knowledge of Florida's topography left doubts.

After Young left, the general impatiently thumped the table with his hickory stick. The rum was wearing off, but his diarrhea remained subdued, for the time being anyway. So he reveled in his plans to bring Florida under the eagle's wings. Later that evening Jackson wrote two letters: To the Secretary of War he stated, without equivocation, that he had ordered the army to march to Pensacola precisely for taking command there. He reported that 400-500 Indian warriors, armed by the Spanish, roamed the area to assail whites in southern states and western Florida.

He explained further that the Innerarity brothers, of the famous Forbes Trading Company in Pensacola, had told him of their vexing problems. The Spanish had not only blocked their Escambia River supply route to Ft. Crawford, a fort crucial to protecting Alabama Territory borderland, but also abetted nefarious Indians who greatly hampered their trade.

Jackson sharpened his quill and wrote to Rachel that he would bring Spain's Most Holy Catholic Majesty to the ground in Pensacola. With the impending invasion on his mind, he asked that she kiss, for him, their adopted son Lincoyer as well as her two nephews under their care. He loved the boys as if they had been his own flesh and blood. As he wrote he could still picture Lincoyer, a young, full-blooded Creek, orphaned by the Battle of Horseshoe Bend, clinging to his dead mother's bosom. He wrote, "Lincoyer is so much like myself I feel unusual sympathy for him…" Then Jackson promised Rachel he would bring home the finest cow he could find after seizing the greasers in Pensacola. The ache of loneliness, which he knew so well, overshadowed him. Echoes of her voice embraced his ears. How he needed her.

As Jackson's army readied its gear at Ft. Gadsden, on the day before the journey westward, a messenger rushed into camp, bringing an express letter from Brigadier General Glascock of the Georgia militia. The letter contained news of a deplorable incident, which had taken place at Chewhaw Village. Only two months earlier, Chehaw Village's Chief Tiger King had provided Jackson's starving army, on their way to Florida, with a generous supply of food and forty warriors. Now, the letter has informed Jackson that the entire village has been destroyed by the overzealous Georgia militia.

The messenger then told the story as he had heard it. It sounded to Jackson like mayhem, for they had shot Chief Tiger King as he held a white flag and his wife as she tried to shield her dead son's body. Still, they hacked the son to death anyway. The messenger said that militiamen tore Tiger King's earrings from his corpse. Even Old Hickory sighed, aghast at the grisly souvenirs the Georgians thieved for themselves.

Jackson's face, usually pallid as a breathing cadaver, was now reddened with rum. He tore into one of his infamous rages, his nostrils flaring. The same invisible force, which had bolstered his unrelenting obsessions and galvanized resentments and vengeance, erupted into outrage. Yet this time was different. Instead of being enraged because Indians had raided whites, it was because whites had victimized the Chehaw. And the Chehaw had recently befriended his army. Baffled by the massacre, he fired letters to the Georgia Governor and General Obed Wright of the Georgia militia, condemning the atrocity as malicious and indefensible.

Old Hickory was well aware the incident might fire up Pensacola Governor Masot to write another letter to Washington condemning the U. S. Government for permitting breach of distinctions between friendly and hostile Indians. Since April these attacks on Indian villages as well as Jackson's activities on the Apalachicola River had been under surveillance by Governor Masot's informants and spies. Jackson would come down harder on his men to capture Masot's scouts and spies, but he would be the one who would have the pleasure of seeing to it that the sleuthing greasers got the hangings they deserved.

When Jackson rode out of Ft. Gadsden on May 7, he had in his hand a map, prepared by Captain Young, for his campaign against Spain. But after crossing the river at Ochechee Bluff, the army got lost in the Florida wilderness and swamps with few clues and even less hope. Governor Masot's posse lost track of them. During this blunder Jackson and his army slashed and sloshed for days until they came to a lake near the Alabama Territory. There, they rested and fished. Then while marching south they chanced upon a river which Jackson's scouts traced to a point within sight of Pensacola. They knew they had found the Escambia River.

Governor Masot's spy posse had discovered those American scouts and followed them back to their camp on the river eight to ten leagues north of Pensacola. It was the return of these spies that Genesis and Padre had waited for in the barracks window at the garrison. And it was to this camp that Governor Masot had sent a letter in which he explained that shipments of supplies to Ft. Crawford could pass without any kind of tariff being levied, and no Indians hostile to the United States had been harbored in Pensacola. He also wrote about the eighty-seven Indians who had tried reaching Ft. Crawford to surrender, only to be accosted by Governor Bibb's Alabama militia. But as Genesis had earlier indicated to Padre, Jackson's only reply to Masot's letter was a hearty chuckle.

On the banks of the river, Jackson bivouacked the weary army and waited for provisions from Mobile to feed the starving men and the starving horses, so ill-suited for travel in the swamps. Food for the men had run out long ago, and there'd been insufficient forage for the horses. The animals must be fed, and his army must have more than fish. They must have beef in their bellies before marching southward to seize Pensacola. Jackson would not wait for beeves on hoof. Salt beef delivered by cart from Mobile would suffice.

Francisco Luengo, former commandant at St. Mark's, wondered just how soon General Jackson would end bivouac and advance on Pensacola? Luengo had experienced defeat firsthand with his surrender to Sharp Knife at St. Mark's. Though Luengo knew that Masot's letter was futile, he could not bring himself to become the messenger that the governor should prepare to surrender his beloved saber along with His Royal Majesty's garrison at Pensacola.

# THE ARCHANGEL?

Padre noticed Captain's steady gait gradually slackening as they ascended Red Hill's hardened-clay path. Heat and humidity intensified the trudge. The weather, about as unpleasantly humid as he had ever experienced during May, and the disturbing motion, which had rotated in his stomach ever since leaving the *tendero's* place, added to his misery. The turbulence just wouldn't subside, but what could he do about it? Take a look back at Pensacola? Wrong. Absolutely wrong. It would be too painful. His mission to build a church in honor of St. Michael had not been completed.

Yet about halfway up the hill he halted Captain, hesitated, and before he knew it, his apprehensive face had turned southward and sneaked a glance. After another filched glimpse he gave in and surveyed the entire landscape, circumspect and grim. His line of vision jumped over clumps of palmettoes, through layers of palm fronds, and snaked around live oaks, all the way to the harbor. Ft. Barrancas had been repaired after the British blew it up prior to their escaping General Jackson's last invasion. Once powerful and a source of pride, the fort still dominated the harbor, while Santa Rosa Island looked like only a speck. These thoughts began overshadowing his discomfort.

He could not remember ever purposely appraising Pensacola from this vantage point. Without a doubt, the surrounding countryside revealed more dots of clearings, where new settlers had established themselves, than he had seen when he first entered the Pensacola port. At this moment the entire settlement seemed peaceful; yet he shuddered and rued the flaws that had rendered the town vulnerable, let alone thoughts about what tomorrow might bring.

When his gaze met the old warehouse, another sort of deeply disturbing, but unidentifiable, sensation rekindled his distressed condition. It had nothing at all to do with the warehouse, that is, not the warehouse itself. Rather, it concerned St. Michael's Chapel in some sort of dreaded way. A daunting detail of uncertainty? He was unsure, but one thing he knew for certain. The poignancy of this matter reached deeper than the level of some triviality. If only he could put his finger on it.

Mindlessly he stroked the shell crucifix that rested against his cassock, and like a jolt, it came to him. His head jerked upwards; his eyes blinked rapidly. "Crucifix," he gasped and grabbed his cramping stomach. That was it, the one from the monastery, his beloved crucifix, which he had placed on the bare altar at St. Michael's as a gift, his ultimate sacrifice. After Jackson invaded four years ago, he had put it there, since the one that belonged to the chapel altar was missing after the fighting had ended.

Then he had carved a crucifix of shell, which he now wore. Angels above, with a second invasion imminent, his precious offering to the mission altar could become just another unaccountable object. Why had he not realized this possibility prior to his departure from the garrison, only minutes before, and at least made peace with the idea? He shook his head in incredulous disbelief.

If he were to return to the chapel, he would never get to the blacksmith's place before dark. Even if he returned, would he *really* want to retrieve the beloved crucifix? No. A gift is a gift. He must not turn back. Too many things could go wrong. Besides, he might weaken and be tempted to disobey Padre de Galvez's orders. Instead, he gritted his teeth, reluctantly shunted his attention northward, and in a wavering voice commanded Captain to continue.

What a difference from the day his ship had sailed into the harbor, the day he had seen Pensacola for the first time. Not the view, the sentiments differed. This disparity could not have been caused by the mere indulgence in a nostalgic final look at the old town, and there certainly was more to it than his visceral churning. Something else, far worse, had encroached. "Holy God, what is wrong?" he muttered and clutched his cramping stomach. An oppressive veil of humid air closed in over him bringing a strange sort of sickening feeling.

Nausea, then weakness gripped him. Bitterness, like bile of influenza, rose in his throat, and his bowels roiled, sending a cold trickle down his back. Would the flux afflict him? Might he even faint? God forfend. He could slide off Captain and hold onto a palm tree, but he had never resorted to anything of the like in his life. "Hmm," he groaned through his clenched teeth to stifle the sound.  Instinctively, he released the grip of his teeth and gasped through his open mouth for more air.  Never had breath been more blessed.  Besides, out here in the open without a soul in sight, there was no harm in groaning.

Late afternoon shadows grew grotesque, distorting his image as well as Captain's into bizarre caricatures.  Unrelenting mugginess added aggravation.  He wiped his brow and the scruff of his neck.  The predicament now seemed unmanageable.  His shoulders slumped forward. He retched and then leaned aside and vomited.  Captain jerked at the heaving noise though, blessedly, his coat had not been soiled.  Somewhat relieved, Padre dabbed his sleeve to his mouth.

Quietness of the desolate hill, instead of providing solace, intensified his forlornness.  It kept silent except for faint clops of Captain's hooves and an occasional, gentle rustling of palmettoes, urged by stray, southerly breezes. When the air lay motionless even the swish of Captain's tail, fending flies, resounded.

Overhead, gulls flapped their wings whenever there was no sea breeze to ride.  Padre was oblivious to their behavior as well as their squawky raucousness.  He had placed their celestial companionship below the threshold of consciousness since the feces-dropping insult on the beach.  No other animal life came in sight other than the ubiquitous mosquitoes and flies and clouds and clouds of gnats, which scattered as far as he could see.

Fading Pensacola would be curtained off by the hill as soon as he descended on the other side.  He needed to take another look, a *final,* final one.  Yet he did not feel up to it.  Numb, unable to think in a rational way, he merely muddled.  With a limp hold on the reins, his body gradually bent forward, legs dangled, and his head wobbled as Captain lumbered laboriously on the steepest part of the uphill path.  "God help me," he sighed and crossed himself in an ill-defined way.

The cresting of the hill heightened Padre's awareness.  With clammy hands on the reins, he halted Captain.  Unsteady and meek, he turned for his last view of the panorama that had been his home for more than seven years. The gray garrison shadowed against the horizon, scarcely a shade darker than the grayish sky and bay.  Only a few green-topped trees and the gold and crimson Spanish flag contrasted with the overall grayness.  As the flag, once majestic and defiant, rippled northerly, it waved a silent *hasta la vista.* Through quivering lips he offered his best, "God be with you," and bowed his head.  Then he faced the north again and flicked the reins.  Captain clumped forward, straining against the downward slanting slope.

Ahead, vast vistas of silence closed in on the path and enveloped the despairing padre.  Stickiness hung heavier in the air on the backside of the hill.  His throat tightened.  The reality of leaving was now absolute and palpable. Having to labor for short breaths brought on a fear of choking out here by himself. Even scarier, if Jackson's men were to come into sight, he would not have the wits or stamina to evade them. "Oh Lord," he gasped as a terrible wrenching afflicted him. Like a sea monster, it clawed inch by inch, coiled, and twisted. Massaging did not help. Is this my punishment, he wondered? Doubt begat doubt. "Merciful Mary, please intercede with St. Michael for favors," he prayed.

After his outburst subsided, unbidden dreamlike visions of De Soto's ghost, then of Don Quixote, floated through his mind. Fleeing to the Alabama Territory must have come to him from some of the same adventuresome Spanish blood strain that had flowed through De Soto or Spain's wanderlust-like, legendary Don Quixote? But no. He was not like the gold seeking De Soto or the foolish Quixote lancing with windmills. He was obediently obeying orders for the love of God and Spain.

His entire life passed before him like a huge scroll being unfurled:

    I.   Years at the monastery;
    II.  Loss of family;
    III. The call by Divine Providence to Pensacola's St. Michaell's Mission;
    IV. Deterioration of the Spanish garrison;
    V.  The American general's invasion four years ago;
    VI. The need to now evade capture, or possibly death.

The word *invasion* struck his senses like a clap of thunder and triggered a reaction more powerful than the clawing sea monster. *Breathe deeply.* He took a deep breath and exhaled ever so slowly, then again and again. Blessed relief trickled through his body, freeing the confined tightness inside. His hands and feet tingled. Along with better circulation of blood, confidence began rebounding. A mystical, but wonderful, phenomenon soon flowed throughout his being like a soothing, healing calmness. He savored and basked in the comfort but wondered at its amazing appearance. What in the world brought this gift? Had none other than the patron saint of St. Michael's Mission heard his supplications to the Blessed Mother? Perhaps St. Michael wished to reward him, for he had always given his best efforts for the archangel's namesake mission. The patron saint surely had sent one of his favorite angels to guide him.

In affirmation, Padre bobbed his head with the usual tic-like motion. Indeed, another very definite energy, though weightless and invisible, had entered the space at his right shoulder—a guardian angel? Yes. Yes, without a doubt, a nurturing presence had evolved from heaven. It hovered with consummate care. In a fading voice, Padre said, "I'm not alone. Thanks be to St. Michael for the divine guide."

In this time of mystically divine beauty, blessings throbbed throughout his entire being, better than any dream. Though unable to completely comprehend the moments, they were precious, golden, energizing. He could not help offering the "Hail Mary" prayer over and over until his throat became so dry, he struggled to swallow, and his voice dropped to a whisper.

As Captain moved onward in a laggard sort of way, the crickets' staccato chirping, though somewhat monotonous, brought a welcomed evening greeting. When the air staled, Padre cast a serious gaze at the expanse of heavier growth. These hawthorn thickets marked the area where he must soon direct Captain to a sharp turn westward to Blacksmith Gunter's place.

The trail sloping down to the stream valley looked formidable. Stretches of it lay hidden by overgrowth, likely cover for Sharp Knife's cunning scouts. Shadows of palmettoes pointed like sharp knives. Though he had been riddled with agony during his gut-wrenching spells on Red Hill, he had been rescued and blessed by a heavenly presence. He wished for that presence again to help him reach the smithy without encountering enemies. He worried about Genesis and *Grandeza*: how they had fared on the trip, and how *Herr* Gunter would receive all of them.

# GIFT OF RESIN

Padre gathered his strength and reined his unbridled concerns under control. Stealthily guiding Captain down the footpath, he viewed, through the last fading sunlight over the lowland, smoke plumes spiraling. That had to be the smithy's place.

The remaining path downward narrowed to a mere knife's slice of space for squeezing through. Grooves carved by erosion made it tedious for Captain to negotiate, and overgrown thickets now shut out most of the setting sun's faint light. Pesky mosquitoes started buzzing and biting more fiercely. Delicate swaying sounds of tall palms floated down in confused, small sounds, sending shivers down his back. Who or what lurked ahead? In the dim distance, a heart-stopping, ghostly, white blob, about as shocking as anything Padre had ever seen, appeared against the barn. He blinked and looked harder. A weird feeling came over him, as if he were witnessing, of all gruesome things, his very own ghost.

He cleared his throat and collected his wits. Captain would have reacted if any danger threatened. The thought of Captain in turn brought *Grandeza* to mind, and was followed by a silly feeling of self-deception, the kind Padre would never divulge to laity. No need to worry. Of course, the ghostly, white blob transformed into a horse, and it had to be *Grandeza*. Padre's eyes fixed in a steadfast stare on the silver white shape until *Grandeza*'s form loomed unmistakably. What a joyous sight! Tang of smoldering hardwood embers wafted from the forge area, warming his heart. Though repulsive residuals still reeled, from the long, difficult trek over Red Hill, he thanked the Lord. But were they all really safe so far?

*Grandeza* stood tethered near the barn, enjoying a meal of freshly picked vines. Padre exhaled an audible sigh of relief as he entered the barn. *Herr* Gunter was proudly showing Genesis his new bellows, so new he had not yet used them. "I made dem," he boasted, "from de deer skins bartered from de Alabama Indians." Since Genesis had alerted the blacksmith that he expected his friend to arrive before sundown, *Herr* Gunter stepped forward and beckoned for Padre to enter. The smithy's friendly face was flanked with frizzled side whiskers. His buckskin apron covered, but did not conceal, his portly paunch; and, despite his stoutness, he glided about almost effortlessly in his buckskin moccasins. Black burn marks of the smithy's trade dotted the moccasins and matched those on his apron. His arms, also, bore what appeared to be burn scars. He greeted Padre warmly as if expecting his arrival.

Lo, further strokes of good luck befell. Genesis and *Grandeza* had arrived shortly before *Herr* Gunter banked the forge up for the evening, so *Grandeza's* shoe, surprisingly, had already been replaced. And Genesis' shrewdness had surfaced. He had already made arrangements with *Herr* Gunter for the night's stay. Padre admired another resourceful deed. Earlier Genesis had gathered vines and provided water for Captain's arrival. Maybe he would work out very well as a traveling partner. Now, Padre could hardly wait to find water for himself.

"Umm, smells good and it's still warm. Thank you, thank you, God bless you," Padre emoted as *Frau* Gunter handed him a bowl of rabbit stew with cornmeal dumplings. *Frau* Gunter, a full blooded Seminole smiled at her husband, at least two decades her senior, and cradled her pregnant abdomen when he affectionately said, "Mein *frau* cooks the best rabbit stew."

As Genesis accepted his bowl, also with thanks, he suggested, "We can sit here on the log."

Padre crossed himself and gave thanks for the food before eating.

While sating their hunger, they watched mixed-breed chickens lazily clucking and pecking through nearby weeds and then ambling onward to roost in the trees. Behind them came nearly invisible guinea fowl, their slaty plumage the color of the evening, their white speckles almost invisible. With only a sliver of sunlight left, their footprints and droppings barely showed in the shadowy sand.

"I have not yet built a chicken coop," *Herr* Gunter said and then called attention to the piggin which he had just placed on a chop block near the cabin door. "I vent to the spring house," he said, "and fetched fresh, cool vater for you." The visitors thanked him and later drank, in turn, from a communal, gourd dipper.

After spreading their blankets on pine needles, which they'd piled in the nearest corner of the barn, Genesis and Padre settled into their makeshift sleeping quarters. The surroundings reminded Padre of his days growing up on a farm, and Genesis took right to it.

Now sensing it was safe to talk without being overheard, Padre asked, "Did you have any problems leaving the garrison?"

"Hell, no. Didn't look at nobody in the eye. Just went straight about my business like I knew what I was doing, all the way out of town and on to Red Hill. Why? Did you?"

"Well, when I bought provisions, just some hardtack and smoked meat, a flask of wine, too, for sacraments, the shopkeeper asked me if they were running low on food at the garrison kitchen. I think he was suspicious."

"That ain't no surprise. The commandant said in the meeting with the spies that they had stores for only twelve days. Could the news travel that fast to the shopkeeper?"

"It might have."

Genesis said, "You didn't have to preach to me about forgetting *Grandeza* needing a shoe. The blacksmith sells supplies and you outta know we need more'n what you bought. Anyways, I been thinking I better disguise our plans to go to the Montezuma Trading Post when we talk with *Herr* Gunter in the morning." In the darkness of the barn, he silently studied the matter. Suddenly, he propped himself on his elbow and said, "I know what to do. I'll ask *Herr* Gunter how to get on the westerly trail, the one to Mobile. That trick should cover up our plans."

"You mean he didn't ask already where we're going?"

"Hell, no. We was too busy. He's real fast with the shoeing, that is, once the iron got red-hot. And he was so good and gentle with *Grandeza*. Handled him just like I do. I like that smithy, wouldn't mind learning how to be a blacksmith myself. Still, we better cover our tracks."

Padre neither addressed the issue nor divulged the intensely emotional dipping and peaking experiences he had undergone on Red Hill. One thing he would get off his chest by telling it to Genesis was, "That trip over Red Hill today was the longest I ever made. And dear God, my leaving Pensacola means I have to give up my status. After all, my importance was well recognized by Lieutenant Muldanado and Governor Masot and all the high-ranking officials at the garrison—all the Spanish-speaking people in St. Michael's Parish, too, even the most distinguished statesmen like Jose Noriega. He had told me only last week he's certain he'll be appointed *alcalde*." Padre did not see Genesis scrunch up his face when he said the "importance" word. Padre simply turned his back and changed the subject by adding, "Now I have a new appreciation for Mary and Joseph for spending the night in the stable when there was no room at the inn. This barn surely looks a lot like the ones in the Nativity scenes, same crudely hewn posts and thatched roof."

Genesis stayed within his own thoughts, answering only, "Uh hm."

Raising on one elbow, Padre said, "*Herr* Gunter was smart to locate his forge under the stream ledge. This place would blaze like a tinderbox if a stray spark floated in here."

"Uhm hum," Genesis replied as he yawned.

"Well, time for prayers," Padre said. "We've been blessed, bountifully blessed, so far, but only God knows what the days ahead will bring." In silence, Padre confessed that he had overdone calling on God and the heavenly hosts, all up and down Red Hill and all the way to the blacksmith's place. He repented for calling on them too often and for asking too many favors on the trip today. In a way it was very selfish, but never in his life had he felt so needy. Then with smiling satisfaction Padre wished deep rest for the Heavenly Father and the same for Blessed Mary, St. Michael, and all the angels, especially the one who guided him.

Padre awakened before the first crowing of the rooster. The whereabouts of Jackson and his army popped into his mind immediately. At Genesis' first stirring, Padre asked, "Did you hear any kind of gunfire during the night?"

"Didn't hear nothing but the bullfrogs and owls and something else, maybe like some rats here in the barn, and just hoped they'd be scared to death of us. I guess ole Sharp Knife didn't get close enough to the garrison yet. Probably still waiting for the beef."

Just then the cow lowed, apparently anxious to be milked and get her morning rations, and the rooster crowed lustily again. As they fed and watered their horses, they felt the chill in the air from the heavy dew and dampness. Afterwards, they watched *Herr* Gunter bustling about his morning chores. Then he invited them inside the cabin as he carried the milk bucket, over half full with warm, foaming milk. After placing the milk bucket on the table, he replenished the fireplace wood.

Standing by the open fireplace, Padre welcomed the warmth and beauty of the blue-edged, orange flames, along with their soft roar, and even enjoyed the staccato popping and uneven crackling of the wood. While trampling around outside, the dampness had cut clear through to his bones.

*Frau* Gunter, though bulky, moved with an air of pride in her baggy, calico frock as she prepared breakfast. She flipped flour cakes that cooked on a spider skillet. In a long-handled frying pan, salt pork sputtered in its hot, rendered grease. She stacked the browned pieces on the side and broke eggs into the bubbling fat. They bubbled and crystallized around the edges. The aroma of steeping sassafras tea mixed with that of the browning pork. *Herr* Gunter, sat on a three legged, split log stool at her side, poking the wood, which had burned gray and thin in the center, and rearranging it in the coals while his *frau* confidently demonstrated her cooking skills. His eyes glowed like the fire when he called attention to the andirons he had wrought. "Forged the tripod, and the poker, too. Vrought all the iron pieces," he said.

Cooking odors tantalized the wayfarers' taste buds in the fresh, early dawn. However, even with Padre's fiercely whetted appetite, he remembered to ask if he could say a blessing. While they shared the morning meal, Genesis lobbed questions about the route west to Mobile: "Would you tell us how to get on the trail to Mobile? Have any American soldiers been seen coming from that direction? How's the mood with the Chickasaw Indians lately?"

To Padre, Genesis appeared pleased with himself as he carried out his strategy of feigned questions, though his voice had sounded rather tense. Perhaps the Gunters would not know the difference. Understandably, Genesis had thought the move necessary for their protection, even though Governor Masot's officers did not have sufficient men to have him followed.

*Herr* Gunter maintained his enterprising discretion throughout the questioning session. Were the visitors completely unaware of the blacksmith's penchant for turning a silver coin?

After breakfast the visitors praised *Frau* Gunter for the unusually good food. Padre called special attention to, "...the wonderful butter on the flour cakes." But he dared not mention the black specks in the cakes. In this subtropical climate, he, like the rest of the people, commonly accepted bugs, without complaints, in the precious, imported flour.

Then Genesis told *Herr* Gunter, "We need to buy supplies for the journey. Really need corn for horses," he stated with the firmness of a master journeyman.

Padre suggested, "Some sweet potatoes and parched corn are what the two of us need."

When *Herr* Gunter placed two squares of homespun muslin on the table, Padre grimaced and quickly looked away to conceal it. He couldn't help thinking how much the whitish squares reminded him of surrender flags.

*Herr* Gunter carefully measured five handfuls of parched corn onto each piece of fabric. He gathered up the corners, two at a time, brought them upward to a point, and tied each into a sort of pouch, with a rawhide strip. He placed shriveled sweet potatoes, with their already budding eyes, into a palmetto basket woven by his wife.

"Das's all of last year's sweet potato crop...been keepin' in de spring house. No vorry...garden brings in fresh vegetables for us."

Next, they went to the barn for the horses' corn. When they looked into the barrel of corn, no one emoted over the usual beetles scurrying about.

After *Herr* Gunter filled the baskets with ears of corn, Genesis said, "Me and *Grandeza* will take these baskets. They're big, but I know what to do about that. *Herr* Gunter, you know, too." Genesis winked and said, "But just let me explain to Padre."

The blacksmith smiled and returned the wink.

Genesis continued, "We can join the baskets with raffia rope, and I'll just swing the rope over my folded blanket..."

Padre said, "Oh yes, you plan to let *Grandeza's* withers draw the load."

"Hold up, Padre. I'm handling this. Now will you let me finish? A basket'll hang down on each side. And Padre, you can manage the sweet potatoes and parched corn. They're small."

Mindlessly scratching his whiskers, *Herr* Gunter erased his amused expression and said, "Before you leave, I have something else for you, a snuffbox of resin." He handed it to Genesis. "No charge for good customers like you two. In case de horses get scratched in de thickets, cut a vood chip and spread de resin ower de vound. Vill keep de flies avay, and dank Gott, keep out infections. Believe me, I see many a need for dis vhen de trawelers come through here."

After expressing thanks for the resin and tucking away their supplies, Genesis and Padre took out their small buckskin money pouches, loosened the strings, and came up with enough money to pay *Herr* Gunter. Each prudently eyed the remaining silver coins in their respective pouches, heads tipping up and down as they silently counted the pieces. Before mounting their horses, Genesis and Padre exchanged brief, but sincere, amenities with the Gunters.

It passed through Padre's mind that his heart would have to serve as the chapel for his morning devotions this day, a tensile test of his flexibility mantle. He bobbed his head, in the habitual way, his face reflecting satisfaction that fine training at the monastery had provided his mind with a storehouse of resourceful information.

Slowly, the two horses bearing their masters began their tread toward the path while *Herr* Gunter and his *frau* waved them off. The two men rode in silence as if concentration on keeping the horses on the narrow path took priority, as if the long, sharp spines of overgrown hawthorn thickets might injure the horses, as if the horses' unfamiliarity with the earth's uneven surface added to their apprehension.

Genesis fought back doubts about traveling with the fancy-talking priest. A lot had changed since Padre used to daze him with big words. But, since Sharp Knife's army was waiting only until casks of salt beef arrived by wagon from Mobile, he'd put up with some of the fancy talking.

Padre whispered prayers. This journey in search of safety had commenced. How would destiny unfold with this journey's potential to end their lives, its potential to change their lives—infinity, too?

# INDIAN RIDGE TRAIL

Sensing the path's crest, Genesis said, "Stop, look up yonder. I think that's it, the main trail. Wait here. I'll walk up and check it out." He slid off *Grandeza*, tossed the reins to Padre, and in passing stroked his horse's luxuriant mane.

"Remember caution is the very essence of our existence now. We must be ever duteous, heedful." Padre's whispered words faded as Genesis set forth. While watching him, Padre speculated about the soldiers' response to the officers' grim announcement of General Jackson's huge army being nearby on the Escambia. The ordering of a high alert status would be nothing more than an unlaughable joke. More crucial, had the officers noticed Genesis' absence yet?

Genesis dashed back. "It's the north-south trail all right, has to be the Indian Ridge Trail. Not no sound or sign of nothing near the crossing but can't see very far, 'cause it's foggy. We still have to be careful. Anything could happen." Frowning, he said, "We better walk alongside the horses in case we hafta to hide in the bushes in a hurry. *Grandeza*'s white coat makes him real easy to spot."

Padre dismounted and followed, not bothering to correct Genesis at this crucial time. Of course, one would not have to be a scholar to know that *Grandeza*'s white coat could not be easily seen in the fog.

With their reins in tow, the men's heads rotated in sweeps, from one side to the other, their wary eyes in search of possible danger. Both were sorely aware that unknown trouble could lurk anywhere.

Moments before entering the main trail intersection, they scrunched their heads down, lower and lower into their chests, like frightened turtles escaping into their shells. Then they paused. Both men checked toward the south, then toward the north and south again. Slowly, their heads emerged. Their necks stretched.

"Here Padre, hold the reins. I think we are at the highest point on the trail. If I climb this tallest pine, I think I can see over the hill. I want to see what's going on at the garrison."

Before Padre could protest, Genesis had already begun scaling the tree.

Padre reflected on what had happened to Pensacola when Sharp Knife's strategic tactics had tricked the Spanish militia in the invasion four years ago. The Sharp Knife had feinted with his Mississippi Dragoons on the western beaches, where the Spanish officers had expected him, but had directed General Coffee's Brigade, the main force, to the eastern side of Pensacola. The Dragoons inflicted damage with a two-cannon battery until a bayonet charge silenced them momentarily. But Coffee's Brigade charged from the eastern side. After the American troops poured in from the east as well as the west, Governor Manrique's soldiers, unable to keep them at bay, asked for terms of surrender. And Sharp Knife quickly occupied Pensacola, though his unauthorized seizure turned out to be an empty victory. Padre knew this story so well.

Meanwhile, Genesis took a good look from his perch high in the tree. Then he slid down, walked toward Padre and said, "I could just barely make out the garrison banking against the bay. It's just a shade darker than the milky fog."

"Watch out, Genesis, you're about to step on an ant hill."

"That's funny you mention an ant hill. That's what the garrison looked like. And the men looked like ants running around."

Padre shook his head and moaned, "If only the garrison had the manpower comparable to the ant colony." He chose to ignore the disparity of work ethics between ants and the local people.

Before mounting, the two men stood silently. They were humble and respectful as feudal serfs, as if paying homage to the doomed, old fort.

A wave of comfort enlivened Padre when he brushed alongside *Grandeza*, such a majestic icon of the *Andalucian* Region. Captain, though of a more lowly status, brought some consolation as well. Padre felt stronger, standing amidst these sources of strength. The subtle shuttle of life had finely interwoven his life with Genesis' and bridged the two countries of their heritages. Would fate preserve these nexuses? An elbow nudged.

"We can't stay here forever," Genesis said. "This ain't no time to lose yourself in prayer or whatever you're thinking about. Them big Tennessee bastards may be in spitting range of the garrison. We got to go."

"Yes," Padre said as they hoisted themselves onto the horses, "but I want you to know that your instinctive cunning, combined with your understanding of the Indian languages and customs, should get us out of any dangerous encounters, even with the Alabama militia. And there's at least one favorable condition we'll have today, an important one—daylight. If the murderers advance, we can see them coming."

Side by side they plodded for the main trail was wider. All morning, they rode in silence. Their eyes orbited, with the intensity of Pensacola Bay red snappers evading hungry sharks, as they watched for danger—ambush, snakes, or whatever perils might befall.

Easily recognizable spoon-shaped leaves of hawthorn thickets crowded along both sides of the path. Genesis took to heart *Herr* Gunter's warning about consequences of the long, sharp spines and always looked out for low, overhanging branches. Whenever necessary he jumped down, threw his reins to Padre, and held the branches back for *Grandeza* and Captain to pass.

"By the blessings of Holy Mary and the angels," Padre said, "our morning has been uneventful." Usual hardships of sweating, dust, and mosquitoes, he unmindfully accepted.

When the sun blazed directly overhead, Genesis announced, "Better take a siesta. We'll be safe. Sharp Knife's men ain't going to do nothing in the heat of the day." It was easy finding a sprawling, moss-laden live oak. Genesis, in taut, youthful form, sprang off *Grandeza*.

Thirty-one-year-old Padre alighted cautiously and straightened his body in stages. After stretching, he sat with his back against the cool, gray-lichen-covered tree trunk and rubbed his tense neck muscles. Genesis had already plunked himself down on the ground, flattened out on his back, and sprawled his long legs and arms. Silent heat of midday overcame his defenses. At once he fell asleep. Both horses rested in the coolness of the giant tree's shade.

In the quietness, Padre heard the horses' tails swishing flies. Occasionally he caught the sound of Genesis' gasping a deep breath and knew he must keep a watchful eye on the horses. Soon they began grazing, free-reined. In his line of vision, Padre scrutinized a gnarl on an ancient tree limb hanging overhead. Two eyes bulged; an off-centered, jagged nose pointed at him. A deep mouth cavity sank into the gnarl. Long, gray moss hanging in the background formed a scraggly, old beard. Altogether, the features bore a likeness to a wise prophet of a past era. "If only it could speak to me," he whispered, "tell me what's happening in Pensacola...tell me what this journey will bring, and what it's like at the Montezuma area."

Noticing that the horses had grazed to the bend in the trail and the sun's rays had slanted, Padre eased up to a standing position. He was about to prod Genesis' shoulder when he realized the young blade had already awakened. Padre took advantage of *his* chance to say, "We better get started on our way."

They picked up the bridle lines and walked alongside the horses. Soon, the calmness and bobbing repetitions of the horses, grazing along, spellbound their masters. Pent-up fear, like being clamped in the jaws of vises, which had forced the wayfarers' visions into constant surveillance, had finally begun loosening.

With newly sensed relief, Padre considered Genesis' youthful outlook, how it paralleled his own dreams and ideals at that age. Hopefully, the young man would have a better experience in the Alabama Territory than fate had dealt his mission in Pensacola. When he reached down and idly plucked a blade of grass, the wine he'd bought gurgled in its flask. It revived hope, hope of celebrating the Eucharist with new converts. His scholarly training and obedience to the Word and his superiors would surely bring blessings in due time; and if he saved enough "heathen" Indians, God might even grant him extraordinary blessings.

After they'd led their horses for about an hour, Genesis sighed, "Water. We surefire need water."

"Yes, it can't come any too soon."

"I've been watching for signs of it," Genesis said, "and that valley down there with the big trees," he pointed, "looks promising, like it may have a stream."

Lo and behold, Genesis' observation proved right. At the bottom of the slight hill, they came upon a stream that was edged with large trees. Padre thought perhaps survival instincts from centuries past, flowing latently in Genesis' blood, had come to life.

"Look," Genesis said, "it's got a sandy bottom." Paying closer attention to details, he added, "Plants along side hold junk. Chief Opayahola told me that plants by streams keep the water clear."

Padre crossed himself and gave thanks. They let the horses drink first and then while they grazed, Genesis took the drinking gourd hanging from his saddle pack and gestured for Padre to walk upstream. There, they enjoyed the cool, clear water. Refills followed before they splashed their faces. Refreshed, they picked up the trail again.

Their morning of watchful silence was followed by an entire afternoon of the same. Padre could not get a certain sound out of his head—the twelve-pounder blast that set off Jackson's first invasion nearly four years ago. Time had not dulled the roar of that thunderbolt a bit.

Late in the day Genesis broke the spell. Pointing toward the west, he said, "See the sun? It's setting on the end of day. We might have to camp without water. I've been looking, looking real hard for a sign of a spring or stream. Nothing's in sight," he said, unmistakably disappointed.

At once, Genesis turned and shot an inquisitive glance at Captain, then ahead to *Grandeza*. Again he looked back and forth at the horses. "Watch!" Genesis exclaimed, "they're chafing at the bit."

"They seem unduly agitated," Padre answered, exchanging a puzzled look with Genesis. "You're right. Something's amiss. They are snorting, rearing their heads awfully high."

"Something's surefire wrong. Now they're tucking their asses, kicking up dust...really upset..." In a blink, Genesis signaled a stop and reined *Grandeza*, all in one continuous motion. He cupped his ear toward the west. "People are coming. I hear more than one." Looking frantic, he blurted, "We gotta hide. C'mon before we get robbed or killed."

Just then, they heard bells tinkling. Captain and *Grandeza* reared and stomped and whinnied.

Genesis swung down and whispered, "Gotta find a hiding place. Now!"

Padre dismounted hastily and at the same time watched for directions.

Genesis bent a bough back and ducked his head into the dreaded hawthorn thickets, Padre following. Each time, Padre caught hold of the branches before Genesis let them loose. Quickly, they forged their way into the dense growth. Up and up the ridge they thrashed through the tangled mass of thicket limbs. Hawthorn spines jabbed and scratched, man as well as beast, yet they climbed onward as fast as they could.

Unlike when they were riding, their hands were now too busy to fight fiendish mosquitoes that always seemed larger and pierced like the devil's pitchfork near the end of day. Farther into the thickets their panicked rushing and fear stimulated more sweat in the already saturated air. Creeping dimness was a blessed concealment as well as a hardship.

At last, Padre felt the ridge top might be attainable and had managed thus far to avoid any disastrous gashes. Just as he was about to taste victory, his shoulder bag was yanked backwards, hopelessly pierced by a long spine. After freeing the shoulder bag, he was unable to catch the next branch which Genesis let loose. That branch banged against padre's cheek, and he cried out, "Ohh my!" Captain whinnied. Genesis let out a quick, "Shhhh!"

Still out of rhythm and catching the branches haphazardly, the next one, a hefty limb with longer thorns as fate would have it, scratched Padre's cheek. And once more, just as he was about to be thankful that he'd stifled his lament this time, disaster struck. A monstrous thorn snared his cassock, and as he tilted forward, he lost his balance. At the very same time, there came a ri-ri-rrriping sound, all the way down the middle of his chest. The sharp tearing sound continued until he was flat on his punctured belly. The overlapping edge of his cassock had torn, stopped only by the tension of his cord belt.

In righting himself, miseries compounded. He inadvertently rolled onto the torn strip of cloth, and another rip sounded out. As soon as he heard that final rip, he reached down and grabbed the strip, now completely severed from the cassock, and crammed it in his pocket, at once regretting that the nearly threadbare fabric was weak like most everything else at the Pensacola garrison. He wouldn't take time to salvage a scrap, which the hawthorns still claimed.

"Oh Mary, Mother of God," he murmured, as salty sweat smarted the abrasions. Then he caught himself and silently contained the remainder of his suffering. His cassock was ruined. All the while he'd struggled forward with Captain in tow, he feared foremost that the horses would become alarmed by a spine. Hapless fate had harbored and dealt this unexpected blow but worst of all, he could have prevented the tearing of his cassock. If his faculties had not been so dimmed by apprehension, he would have been content to pack his robe and ride the deserted trail in his knee britches.

Genesis had glanced back anxiously, but increased darkness prevented Padre from realizing the token consideration. Padre doubted that Genesis cared for anything other than his own safety and that of *Grandeza's*. So this was how Genesis reacted when faced with danger? Five or six days on the trail with this kind of inconsiderate treatment would be too much. And heavens above, what had they been hiding from? Even if they survived this ordeal, only God knew what might happen next in the threatening, gaping maw of the unknown. Could the general's invasion have been worse than this?

When Padre looked up, silhouettes of none other than Genesis and *Grandeza* loomed in view. So, with some remorse he realized that Genesis had waited for him to catch up, after all. However, Padre's contrition was fleeting. Indeed, Genesis had given the impression of acting flagrantly inconsiderate.

Now reunited, their forging continued. Padre could see that Genesis was leading them toward the protective arms of a large tree that grew on the ridge's peak. But, before they reached refuge underneath that long-sought tree, bells tinkled louder. The strange voices grew stronger.

# VARMINTS

From the ridge top Padre and Genesis watched as large blurs advanced along the path. Right away, they recognized double yokes of oxen, oxen with bells around their necks. The beasts pulled what seemed to be a heavily loaded cart, its wheels creaking. Beyond the lead yoke of oxen, a man led with a bullwhip outstretched in his right hand. Two shadow-like men followed at the cart's rear, one at each end. All three carried walking sticks as tall as their shoulders. While the spectacle moved along, they noticed the travelers leaned toward their walking sticks, which leveraged each step trudged.

"Beef, salt-beef, wagon from Mobile for Sharp Knife's army," Genesis said after the procession had passed. "When the wind blew this way, I cupped my ear toward them. Heard something like '*Penzacola manana.*'"

"You're right. Undoubtedly, that's the salt beef General Jackson ordered for his troops. What a pity for the garrison's militia, His Majesty's treasury has no funds for beef."

"Have to stay here tonight," Genesis said in exasperation, "too dark now to move."

"*Whew,*" Padre sighed, "I'm so thankful for safety, I won't even complain that we have no water. But just look here," he turned toward the moonlight, ran his hand down his chest, and complained, "a whole strip ripped from the front of my cassock."

"I'm not surprised, I heard something tearing."

"You did?"

"Sure. I wondered what was going on, but the most important thing was for us to get up here under this tree."

"I've got the missing piece in my pocket. Well, that is, I got most of it. A little piece is still stuck on the hawthorns down there."

"Padre, I can't waste time talking about a little piece of torn robe. I gotta inspect *Grandeza*. You better look at Captain, too. Need to see if they got any deep scratches. We just might have to use that sap *Herr* Gunter gave us."

They tethered the horses and, by the light of the moon, grazed their hands over the horses' bodies, checking for the wetness of bleeding. "*Grandeza*'s not in too bad shape. Has some scratches. I'll cut a chip and cover them. How's Captain?"

"He has one nasty gash. I thought the longest spine in the world caught me, but its twin must have jabbed him. Remember when he whinnied?"

"Don't worry," Genesis said. "I'll take care of it."

They pulled enough Spanish moss from overhead to sleep on. Next, even though ferociously thirsty, they gnawed on small pieces of smoked turkey and hardtack, taking long rests between bites. Their dry mouths became drier and drier.

"I'm glad we gave the horses some corn back at the stream," Padre said. "I wouldn't risk giving them corn now. They need water more than we."

"Tomorrow," Genesis said, struggling to swallow, "We find water and stop before dark." He coughed. "This hardtack turns to powder on my tongue."

Later, while on self-appointed sentinel duty, Genesis listened to the steady, ritualistic mumble of Padre's prayers. Soon he became completely immersed in the earthy smells and woodsy atmosphere, so different from the sandy beach and sea odors of the Pensacola Bay. Even with an overpowering thirst, the raw, natural setting exhilarated his body and soul. He liked the feel of the earth underneath his rear and the open sky overhead. The scent of dank moss mixing with fresh, aromatic pine needles seemed so right. He sensed a belonging to everything in the woods: the stillness, the darkness, and the nighttime animal calls. To relieve his thirst, he chewed succulent live oak leaves, draining their moisture.

A hooting owl snuffed out the faint sounds of Padre's light snoring. Later, bull alligators bellowed mating calls in the far distance. Genesis liked the rise and fall of forest sounds. His breathing caught their cadence whenever they amplified on the occasional southerly breezes, then died away with them in the stillness. As the night wore on, the sounds began echoing eerily, haunting him into wakefulness for hours of watch, his musket ready for draw at the throat of beast or man that dare approach their camp.

Off and on, Padre had scratched fitfully. It would cease, only to start again with greater agitation. Suddenly he groaned and opened his eyes.

"Something's biting the blood out of me. I'm itching and scratching like a man possessed with demons."

Genesis smiled wryly. "I'd be scratching too if I was lying down on that moss. You know what's biting. Don't you?"

"What?"

"I said you know what's biting. Don't you?"

"I heard you. I want to know what it is."

"It's most likely bugs in the moss, them little, red-chigger bugs. They're tiny, but they bore in like an auger and suck blood till they get their fill. I guess that excitement over the meat cart dimmed my wits. I didn't think about them shrewd little varmints when we pulled the moss for padding."

Padre scratched more vigorously but felt too tired and drowsy to make a change. "In the future I'll take a chance on pine straw," he said as his voice trailed into a yawn.

Some time during the wee hours, an extraordinarily luminous shooting star blazed across the northern sky. It not only caught Genesis' attention but also beset him with wonder. Its brightness surefire meant something. Maybe it signaled a special lighting of the way for the trip in that direction. Aroused by an urgency to get on with the journey, he shuffled his position. He could only wait for dawn. He drew his close-in-hand gun only once during the night. Then he let go, imagining a field rat or some other small animal caused the rustle. Simply holding his trusty musket gave him a comforting feeling of what it was capable of doing. Finally he dozed.

At the breaking of day Padre slowly pushed up on his stiff legs. After breathlessly scanning all around for predators, both man and beast, he glanced over at Genesis, then down at his torn cassock. Yet, he felt touched, profoundly so, and grateful that they were still alive and that Captain and the precious *Andalucian* stallion were, too. Straightway he recoiled with a tinge of guilt, regrouping his priorities. He would put the torn robe inside his shoulder bag and be content to ride in his knee britches, as he should have been doing all along. Besides, he was thankful that rogues had not stolen their provisions.

He diverted his attention from the hawthorn spine mishap by whispering the "Hail Mary" prayer over and over. There was one thing he'd keep secret. Genesis must not know how his thighs burned and how sore his legs and back felt from yesterday's ride. He stretched out some kinks in his neck and legs and then walked about twenty feet away, relieved himself, and said his morning devotions. There, he discovered his arms mottled with ugly whelps where the red bugs had perched and leeched till he scratched them away. The ropey scars on his arm, from a childhood accident on the farm, appeared to be as relishing for the bugs as his unscarred skin.

At Padre's slightest movement, Genesis had sprung to wakefulness. He jumped up, while at the same time he reached for his gun. Carefully, he searched through the scrub and trees for any danger, turned completely around, and searched even more thoroughly the second time. Finally he allowed himself a yawn, in the midst of which he hurried to inspect the horses. "Just what I expected," he said and rubbed his still sleepy eyes. "I covered nearly all your scratches last night," he said to *Grandeza.* "Now I'll finish the job." He fetched the resin can from his saddlebag and cut a fresh chip of wood for applying it. Meanwhile, the gladness of his heart went out to *Herr* Gunter for giving the stuff to him. Carefully, he moved alongside *Grandeza*'s body from head to tail, inspecting every inch. As he covered each scratch with the pine resin, the animal's flesh crawled. He repeated the process on the other side, all the while enjoying the hopefulness brought by the bright shooting star last night. Then he examined Captain. While he squatted taking care of a scratch on one of Captain's legs, Padre walked up.

"If it had not been for my beard, I would have needed some of that tar on my face." He smiled, but it vanished quickly. He said, "Just look at my cassock," and held it up.

"Don't worry about it," Genesis said, without looking up. "I heard Chief Opayhola say that them robes don't make you no better than the rest of us, 'cause you sleep at night and shit in the morning same as us."

Padre endeavored to come up with a short-term reply to Genesis' rebellious attitude. This was not the appropriate time for a serious discussion. He would be patient to let further trust gather before attempting to dissuade Genesis from enjoying his flagrant vulgarity. Yes, indeed, a heedless reply was not what Padre wished to receive, but he would abide for the present. *I have always thought since his boyhood days, and always will, that he does have a good heart. I will not give up on him.*

93

# RUMBLE OF HOWITZERS

After riding along the trail only minutes, Genesis and Padre approached the intersection of the western trail to Mobile. At this crucial point they proceeded as stealthily as hunters stalking a pack of wolves.

Genesis released his tight grip on the gun, which had provided immeasurable comfort. He pointed down, not to the center of the weedy crest on which the horses stood, but to the flanking sandy strips. Cloven hoof prints and human footprints, along with ruts in the sand, clearly belonged to the ox cart outfit, which turned onto the north-south trail the previous evening.

Padre nodded, saying, "I see."

They turned to the north and rode on. Within an hour they spotted a narrow stream ahead. Moving closer they peered in unified gazes at a second stream in the distance, also a narrow one. Both streams meandered across the gently sloping land toward the river. The horses sped as if sensing the nearby water. Not only did both the horses chafe to drink, but also the men.

"The water is too shallow here," Genesis said and disappointedly led the way to the second stream. He looked up and down for a deep spot. There was none, though he spotted a fallen tree downstream, its bare roots upturned like tousled hair of a mythical forest giant. "There should be a hole alongside the stream," Genesis said, "where those roots grew. Let's go." And he was right. The cavity turned out to be plenty deep enough for the horses to drink all they wanted.

In the opposite direction, slightly uphill, clear water trickled over a small rock outcropping. Genesis pointed to it with ever-enlarging eyes.

They could hardly wait to tether the horses, and drink their fill of cool water. Cupping their hands, rather than waiting to fill their gourds, they guzzled greedily. After quenching their ferocious thirsts, they fed ears of corn to the horses. Both men relished munching on their hardtack and smoked turkey, and again, the riders and their mounts enjoyed water.

In the quietness, Genesis asked, "Do you hear that mewing sound?"

"Yes. It sounds like a small animal," Padre said. "Perhaps it is in distress?"

Genesis looked no farther than a few feet when he found, not the exact spot of the mewing sound, rather a possum, its neck and back shredded and partially eaten. The blood was a fairly fresh, red color. Upon examining the carcass he found baby possums, their eyes still unopened, inside the mother's pouch, one at each teat. He said, "Looks like telltale bobcat hair hanging from the possum's mouth."

"The bobcat must have caught the poor possum from the rear," Padre said, "when she tried to get one last drink of water, possibly just before daybreak."

"That possum surefire didn't have much of a chance, 'cause it was attacked at the neck," Genesis said. "I still hear that mewing, but I got to get them little possums out of their misery, hafta do it fast. You never know how hungry them wild cats are, especially a mama with mewing kits to feed, too, or some big ole tom. We'd probably see more than one pair of fiery, green eyes staring at us from the bush if it was still dark. They was probably still gnawing on the possum when we walked up." He placed the hairless, but warm, babies on a rock, one by one, and quickly crushed their heads with a heavy rock and threw them near the carcass of their mother.

While waiting for the grisly act to end, Padre winced and wrung his hands anxiously. "Sometimes," he said, "a man has to do what he thinks is right, no matter how distasteful the job. The little ones probably suffered less by instant death than if they had been eaten alive."

They headed toward the horses, the distinctive sound of mewing kits hastening their ever-elongating strides.

"Let's get outta here fast," Genesis said. "Faster, Padre. That mama cat's surefire got babies. She might be stalking us right now. She can fight it out with the buzzards."

After remounting, Padre took a deep breath, looked back at the first stream, and said, "If only we could have gotten to these streams last night, what a difference the water would have made."

At midday, in the stillness of siesta time, Genesis bounced up. "Did you hear that rumble? Howitzer, sure as hell."

"I heard it, too, but I thought that it was thunder in the distance."

"Hear that? There it goes again—far to the south, and Padre, face it. That came from the land—surefire not from the sky."

"You're right. As much as I hate to admit it, I suppose the worst has actually happened."

"Uggh, there goes a damn howitzer again. Betcha Sharp Knife ordered an attack just as soon as his men got their bellies full of beef. That cart that scared the fool outta me last night must have unloaded about the time them chiggers started biting you. We surefire got outta Pensacola not one second too soon. All hell's probably broke loose."

Padre quietly intoned a prayer to the venerable St. Dominique and crossed himself. He always saved the most pressing prayers for the beloved founder of the Dominican Order.

Later, traveling along a swath of flat terrain, Padre felt the afternoon lasting for an eternity. Every woodchuck and grouse as well as all the other living creatures seemed to be hiding from the fetid heat, though the bugs never retreated for a moment. The fresh greenery of springtime was still vibrant in the palm fronds and live oaks, scrub trees, too, though some grass and weeds already looked sun-scorched. In sandy spots, where the horses kicked up dust, Padre tilted his head upward for fresh breath.

In the loneliness of these surroundings, a euphoric sensation, so unfamiliar that his faculties seemed untrained to handle its full meaning, sprang within. His first righteous notion was to reject this gift of well being. He did not deserve to enjoy being alive, considering what might have happened at St. Michael's Mission. But the feeling persistently revisited him, overwhelmed him. Despite the fate of all he had to leave behind in Pensacola, this satisfying sense dominated. When he tried to feel remorseful about leaving the parishioners at St. Michael's and the men garrisoned at Pensacola, the primal pleasure of still being alive prevailed. He tried to pull back from indulging in this invigorating buoyancy, especially since Pensacolians might have been killed, yet the bliss spilled over unstoppably.

He pondered whether he should do penance. During this introspection, a grace evolved, slowly like the sun emerging out of fog. No war, nothing in the world, neither natural nor man made, could change God's love, nor his love for God. Will to live, while others may have died, *was* acceptable. Many times, in counseling survivors, he had said so. He would cherish life and go forward to fulfill his orders. His initial selfish desire, weeks ago, to leave the danger of an invasion had surely been redeemed by Padre de Galvez's forgiveness and his order to leave. Now, his own faith had been revitalized. He would press onward and do God's work. Surely, Padre de Galvez's prayers had been answered by St. Michael. Always...forever he would care deeply for everyone in St. Michael Parish—including the very

Irish Father Mulvaney—and especially His Majesty's troops even though he could not be with them physically.

As the evening sun softened, differences in the environment nudged at Genesis' awareness. He stretched his shoulders, sat more erect, and broke the silence. "More large trees on trail now, not many palms. Not much sand now either."

"I noticed, too," Padre said, "pines now dominate, but plenty of palmettoes still prevail, and passels of mosquitoes reign. He fanned his face. Then he swept his line of vision across the sky and said, "I caught sight of a hawk gliding underneath stationary puffs of clouds, but there aren't many gulls flying around here. Alas, we must be getting near the big forest of the Alabama Territory."

"Look," Genesis shouted in sheer delight. "Look at that ridge to the west? Over toward the setting sun, there's a rocky ridge. Has to be a spring somewhere in there."

"May the Lord direct you to the spring, if it exists," Padre said. "It's getting late. Let's not let the sun disappear without our reaching water."

"Don't worry. I'll surefire find some over there," Genesis said while handing the reins to Padre. "We'll camp here this night, you'll see." Then he traipsed off to investigate.

He bounded back. "I'm right. I'm right. I told you I'd find water. There's water dripping from cracks in them rocks. Just follow me."

Observing Genesis' returning trot and cheerful face, Padre had preemptively surmised the finding. These were moments for rejoicing. Albeit, Padre would not join in Genesis' full sense of the moment, not because he was oblivious to Genesis' thrill over unleashing another newly discovered power of observation, which came as naturally as breathing. Rather it was Padre's need for water that simply overpowered all else.

Through tall broom grass, they walked the horses toward the crumbly ridge of gray shale until Genesis yelled, "Stop, I warn you to watch where you step. There's a hell of a gopher hole around here some place. Almost stepped in it myself when I came over here the first time."

Padre then walked with greater care, but suddenly commanded, "Now Genesis, *you* stop. Look at this snake skin."

"Don't worry about no snake skin. Can't hurt you."

"But it is the second one I have seen within a few feet of each other."

"Aw, c'mon. I'll show you the water. See over there. Clear water dripping slow. Betcha it's nice and cool, but it'll take time to catch it."

"Dear Lord above, here's another snake skin."

Genesis ignored the remark and looked up at a pile of fox-dense, leafless limbs on top of the ridge. Suddenly the pile started moving, then separating. He stepped back, flushed excitement turning to horror. "Damn, that ain't no pile of brush. That's…that's snakes. Surefire lots of 'em."

Padre cringed back in terror and whispered, "Hear that dry rattling sound? Can't mistake their identity."

Without answering, Genesis watched the rattlesnakes as they denned.

As soon as the last snake had disappeared, the appalled padre said, "Let's get away from here." Overcome with consternation as well fear, he could not help saying, "I knew those shed skins were a warning, and you would not listen. You must be aware that snakes like to bask on a sun-warmed rocky ledge."

"But that's the damdest thing I ever saw," Genesis said. "Couldn't believe my eyes. Surefire never heard tell of a stack of rattlesnakes. The men at the garrison would never believe this. Never. They'd flat out call me a liar. Now Padre, just give yourself a minute to calm down. That's what I'm doing. You see they smelled us and when they felt us gettin' closer, they just wanted to get away." He took a deep breath and pointed to the bottom of the slight hill where water had trickled down and collected in a low spot. "See down there. Place for horses to drink, in that pool that spills into the gully. Soon as we all get watered, we'll find another place to camp."

Then both men, with well-practiced wariness, succumbed to the patience of collecting the trickling water and quickly quaffing it.

Genesis rubbed his palms together. His eyes brightened in a crafty way and he said, "We'll keep going till I find a camping spot, and when dark comes, I'll rub flint, surefire make fire. We'll have warm, roasted sweet potatoes, and we can try some roasted pheasant eggs."

"Just make sure we get away from the rattlers," Padre said. And though he had no will to even water the horses and certainly no appetite whatsoever at the moment, he asked, "Where will we get pheasant eggs?"

"Don't worry. When I first walked through here, you probably saw that flock of pheasant flying away. They looked so good, I got a hell of a craving to taste one of them fine birds. Chief Opayahola—he told me lots of things while we was hiding him from Sharp Knife at the garrison. He said that's the sweetest fowl on Mother Earth. Since the birds got away I thought I'd look for eggs. I found a clutch, at least two dozen of 'em, but they ain't no bigger than the end of your thumb. It wouldn't hurt to take a few for us before some fox or snake sucks them dry."

"I can hardly wait," Padre said, "to find a safe place. Then I'll think about watching you perform your surefire wizardry with flint and even trying roasted pheasant eggs. One thing is sure. I will not agree to stop by any rocky ledges dripping with water or anywhere I see all sorts of snake skins around."

That evening, while poking the fire, Genesis said, "Chief Opayahola told me he knowed of a man that killed a rattlesnake with a stick. Then later he scratched his hand on the stick and died."

"Its enough to bring on nightmares," Padre said. "I prefer thinking about how tasty and filling those little sweet potatoes are going to be. They're mighty little, but they're smelling sweet and hearty."

Genesis seemed mesmerized by the flames. He sat cross legged, then cupped his hands under his chin and said, "River Raven liked to tell the men at the Emerald Saloon about that Indian princess at his tribe. She's the chief's daughter. You know I already told you about her. Her tribe is the one that's close to the Montezuma Trading Post."

"Yes, but who is River Raven?"

"Oh, you've seen him. Couldn't miss him. He's *Senor* Colabro's head man, head of the Creek helpers that raft to Pensacola."

"I probably saw him, but can't place him at the moment. Do you think his information is reliable?"

"Hell yes. Everybody pays attention to what he says. He bosses the whole rafting crew. He said the Princess is named Blue Heron, and she wears a special headdress of blue heron feathers. Said she's very beautiful."

"Wouldn't there be complications for you to try associating with a princess? There are probably traditions she has to abide by."

Genesis shrugged, "We'll see."

Padre gently stretched his paining back and moaned.

"Looks like your back is bothering you."

"Yesss," Padre moaned again, "it's because my collarbone and shoulder blades formed into distorted positions which can cause pain in the backbone. All this horseback riding is aggravating it. When it bothers me, I am always reminded of what a seasoned sailor on your father's ship told me about humpback whales while we were on our way to Pensacola."

"So what kind of a tale did he tell you?"

"First of all, he said they can grow as long as fifty feet. Comparing my size to that would be contrary to reason, but it seems I do have something in common with the humpback whales. Though the fish is not at all humpbacked except when it arches its back as it rolls over to vocalize sounds, our common trait seems to be the ability to sing. You see, most people believe the sounds made by this whale are actually songs."

"Well," Genesis said as he picked some immature burs from his pants, "you surely can sing."

"Mostly, I chant, but while the ship plied the ocean, I kept hoping I would see one of those humpbacks. The old sailor said he had seen them jump clear of the water with straight-up springs, halfway of the mast, and fall back with enormous splashes."

Padre discerned, in the dim light of the small flames, a faraway look in Genesis' eyes and decided that he better change the subject. "There's something I think I should tell you." He hesitated until he caught Genesis looking at him straight in the eye. "Your mother told me firsthand that she knew her 'Arrow' had already pierced his place in the great circle of life."

Genesis groaned, "Aweee, she called me that nickname only when I was little, before I was knee-high to a brown pelican."

"Hear me out, Genesis. I strongly feel I should tell you. She was proud you had established yourself as an interpreter at the garrison. In her wisdom, she realized that you shared the best of two worlds in Pensacola— the Creek culture, which she had instilled in your childhood and the Spanish culture which you learned from the garrison and mission."

Genesis turned sideways and swiped a tear.

A breeze rekindled a whitened ember into a curling orange flame. The warmth of the glow matched Padre's warm feelings. He said, "Tonight we are blessed. We had time to gather pine needles for padding underneath the blankets. There'll be no scary ox cart, no devilish hawthorn spines, no suffering thirst, and maybe, just maybe, no biting chiggers or rattlesnakes. Thanks be to God." Then he crossed himself. Genesis' roasted sweet potatoes had turned out fine, and he might, after all, turn out just as fine as a traveling companion.

The following day, Padre's sentiments kept shifting to St. Michael's Mission, each time bringing a sharp pain that cut through his conscience with the force of a scythe slicing through fodder grass. Though he hurt deeply, he must not falter now. A countering voice convinced him to remember the grace he had received yesterday and the better times of the past.

Soon, in the subtropical heat of the afternoon, the sky darkened. When web-like lightning flashed through the trees, Genesis said, between jostles of *Grandeza*'s gait, "There was a red sunrise this morning. I surefire knew there wouldn't be no usual light shower 'cause I used to listen to the sailors in Pensacola, so I knew heavier rain comes this day."

Thunderbolts shot around them. When crashing thunder disturbed the horses, Genesis and Padre dismounted and attended them with comforting pats and calm stroking. Shortly, light refreshing rain commenced. Layers and layers of leaves overhead absorbed the heaviest part of the rain.

Padre noticed that Captain's worst lesion—it had to have been slit by the most monstrous of all hawthorn spikes—still had some resin on it. "The tar surely kept the flies away from the injuries, Genesis, you did a fine job doctoring the horses."

"See," Genesis said, "I don't have to use big words to be smart."

As soon as the thunder and lightning passed, they remounted and resumed the journey, drying out along the way. Forthwith, they came upon a stand of short trees with lush green leaves. Captain and *Grandeza* struggled against the reins with gusto to taste them.

"We have very good luck," Genesis chortled. "These are horse-sugar trees. We can let the horses eat all the sweet leaves they want."

While the animals greedily devoured the tasty foliage, Padre stood back, cogitating. He'd show the smart, younger talker he could assess the new environment and make some astute comments, also. "These short trees," he said, "appear to be the first story of this multistoried forest."

"I ain't making no fancy speeches," Genesis said, "but I surefire know them short trunks make it easy for the horses to reach. They're having a feast."

Refusing to be intimidated, Padre said, "All this moisture in the valley has helped make the leaves extra succulent." Then he examined the unripe fruit.

"It has five teeth," Genesis said. "All five, sort of come to a point. You can plainly see, too, that the fruit rounds out a little bit but won't round out as much as oranges." As he ran his finger around the green specimen, he said, "Turns brown in fall. Then it's ripe."

Later, the full-bellied horses lumbered along, expelling gas. First, Captain let loose, followed by *Grandeza*. The men looked at each other. Padre forced restraint of a smile, not allowing his teeth to show, while Genesis mischievously grinned from ear to ear.

Suddenly, both horses cut loose at the same time, multiple-noted but with different cadences. The cacaphony continued. Spontaneous eruptions fired one after another and billowed lewd and potent as yellow clouds of sulphur.

"*Grandeza* is surefire winning over Captain. You hafta admit he's louder and stinkier. Sorry Captain's not the winner of this farting contest, Padre."

"Why for goodness sake, it's only an audible report on the sugar tree feast. This just proves that you have had a dearth of amusement lately. The last time I recall our having been amused was when we last listened to one of the raconteurs spin stories on Plaza Ferdinand. Fortunately we're in open air. And thank the Lord, I have the patience to bear with your youthful commentary."

"You think you're better'n me?"

"I have lived longer, and my experience gives me a different perspective. What else can I say?"

"I can say something else. You surefire ain't perfect. Sometimes you're stubborn as a barnacle."

"And I might as well try to pull up one of those monstrous pines by its tap root as to try to pull you up from your unrefined remarks. Most living creatures, as in the case of the horses, become afflicted at one time or another, even the holiest. I must relate to you an experience which might somehow lead you to understand how awkward situations can be coped with in a refined manner."

Genesis merely looked ahead with a stoic expression.

"It happened when I met with the archbishop to appeal for assignment at the Pensacola mission." He looked upward and mumbled indistinctly, "Dear God, help me as I try to guide this young man."

Padre would, of course, spare Genesis the details of the first part of the story that dealt with that meeting back in Spain. But he permitted flashes through his mind of how the archbishop, after he had just finished celebrating mass, entered the sacristy using his crozier to lead his unsteady steps rather than the flock. His white hair hung loosely from under the miter, touching the top of his distinguished chasuble. Unfortunately, he'd seemed in no hurry to announce his decision about whether Padre could be assigned to the Pensacola mission. The more the prelate procrastinated—rearranging his outdoor cloak and picking lint from it, brushing mice droppings from an ancient manuscript with the feathered end of a quill—the more fearful Padre became. Would his request be denied? His vision followed the ecclesiastical head as he walked to the window, his feet moving softly, with a long habit of reverence, across the creaky floor. Then he stood looking out the window, as if he could see through the translucent stained glass.

At this point of the recollection, Padre said, "The archbishop had reached down and nervously slapped the dust from the edge of his soutane. It was difficult to determine whether the dust caused him to cough, or the bending motions, or both. I'm almost certain that he broke wind, but not noticeably. It was incredible how fast he jerked himself upright. Again he coughed. This time it seemed as if on purpose for distraction, and as he did so, I was almost sure, again, that he expelled a little more gas."

"What did he say about all that farting?" Genesis asked with a diabolical gleam in his eyes.

Padre mumbled indistinctly, "Dear God, grant me strength to bear these outbursts as I counsel this young man." In a stronger voice, he asked, "How could you talk like that when I'm speaking of one of my holiest superiors? I am trying to cultivate in you a sense for a more refined outlook on everyday life."

"Padre, you don't have to act so high and mighty. It's just the two of us out here on this trail."

"I shall not permit you to distract me. I must tell you. The archbishop would have made anybody proud of him. He merely stood in stark silence with an unreadable expression. Then he looked at the wrinkled tops of his hands and rubbed them. A mouse, a timid, gray mouse, peered from an opening in a stack of timeworn manuscripts as if checking out the situation."

"Just like Chief Opayahola told me," Genesis said, "you all ain't no different from the rest of us."

Padre rested his case. His memories of the archbishop were too precious to try imparting more understanding for Genesis at the moment, for it had just passed through Padre's mind how he had wiggled in his seat, straightened his torso, and stared at a crucifix, the only ornament on the barren sacristy walls. He had fixed his gaze on the crucifix, Jesus, nailed to the cross. Certainly, as his representative on earth, the very least he could do was to show compassion and respect for the venerable superior.

Padre remembered vividly how the archbishop had swallowed hard, then regained his pious air, and blessedly started afresh as he said, "I must make sure you're aware that St. Michael's Mission is not very large, though it is now growing." He picked up a piece of paper from a table. "I dug out this old report on the mission when it was still named San Miguel. Auxiliary Bishop Cirilo de Barcelona made the report after his pastoral visit around 1791, after the British occupation of Pensacola. He reported a large number of the 572 settlers were Protestants." The archbishop turned the paper sideways. "You can see I underlined the numbers to get them right. Our Crown tolerated the foreigners, because settlers were needed for trade."

Padre relived every moment of how he had sat silent and rigid, divining what he could from the timbre of the archbishop's voice. He hoped with all his heart that the disruptions were over and that the prowling mouse would stay under cover. More distractions could utterly ruin his chances of obtaining the Pensacola assignment. At last the archbishop sat, easing down with great care. With a relaxed expression he said, "I see that nothing seems to discourage you." He interlaced his crippled fingers and paused.

Padre had bent his head so low, he heard his heart thumping. His eyes briefly met the pulsing of his cassock-covered chest, then the rough-hewn boards of the dark floor.

By and by, the Holy One looked into the seeking eyes of this humble-appearing supplicant and said, "I won't hold you back, since I know your reasons for wanting to go. Priests are needed in Pensacola. The town has grown since the Americans made the Louisiana Purchase. Many of our Spanish people relocated there. I'll intercede on your behalf with his Eminence, Cardinal Alvarado. May God ever be in your presence during this appointment."

103

Today on the trail, Padre saw the long-ago action so clearly in his mind that he almost said aloud, "Thank you, thank you, your Excellence, and thanks be to God," just as he had said it to the archbishop. In unison, they had reverently bowed their heads to each other. Padre would cherish his meeting with the esteemed archbishop, forever. It held a place in his heart with the best memories of his entire life, even though he was now in the throes of escaping Pensacola.

Genesis had settled down and stayed within his own thoughts as they rode onward.

Padre straightened his posture, wondering what quirky circumstance might be encountered next. Or might he experience another grace? Or another baffling conundrum? Or was even greater danger lurking in the days ahead? Surely, soon they would enter the vast maw of the great forest. A chill ran down his spine. His unsettled mind leapt with rampant thoughts of cryptic things that the immense, old forest might conceal.

# THE PRIMEVAL FOREST

"I can't help wondering," Genesis said as they plodded along the trail, "if Sharp Knife's army...well, you know...if they killed anybody, especially anybody I know, or if they wiped out the garrison. Them howitzers surefire boomed away at something."

"My hunch is that after Jackson provided his army with their fill of beef, he feigned, perhaps by directing them to fire just enough to alarm the Governor. They probably were not even within range of the garrison when we heard the howitzers."

"Oh hell, Padre, we might as well stop our sweet talking and just admit Sharp Knife's beat the shit outta Pensacola by now."

"Genesis, if that is true, it's as much a part of history as growth rings in a tree trunk. It cannot be changed. And I'll remind you again that I'd appreciate it if you would mind your vulgar language, not only because of my own personal distaste, but also because a habit can be manifest at a most importune time. For instance, when you get a chance to speak with that princess, or God forbid, her father who is chief."

Genesis cast a carping glance at Padre.

As the two wayfarers pressed ahead, they began exchanging quizzical glimpses. The path became nearly invisible at times. Would they find their way through the great forest or get hopelessly lost in the unending trees with nothing to help them keep their bearings. Beaches and bay were now mere memories as was sea-scented, salt air. Earthy tang of rotted and decayed leaves, cones, and limbs filled the closeness. Hour by hour their eyes bulged, like roving orbs, as they searched for distinctive markings to make

105

sure they were still on the Ridge Trail. At times it seemed nigh imperceptible.

A haunting dove called from the summit of one of the lichen laden giants. The sound attracted Padre's attention to the upturned limbs, which had sought their share of sunlight and, in turn, had swelled into an unbelievable, majestic emerald crown. "Those massive arms must hold a world of surprises up there," he said. Then his vision plummeted, along with the descending dove, to the lower limbs. They were as big around as his waist and swept downward in great, graceful arcs.

Genesis swayed with *Grandeza*'s gait and said, "Just think. We don't have to worry about sun or rain for…about three days…thick forest shuts it out. You want to know something? I like this forest, I like it a hell of a lot…more than I ever dreamed."

"Just as I'd already surmised," Padre said in a pompous way. "But heavy canopy of these ancient trees shuts out direct sunlight, so that nothing much grows near the ground. And that is a blessing. Scantiness of ground growth helps us somewhat in staying on the trail." Soon dimness grew dimmer. Unbeknownst to him, his forehead furrowed like the shadowy bark on an aged walnut tree, which they passed. Why, he was a mere speck in the immensity of these forest trees of endless age, unfathomable enormity. He said, "Fading daylight is only a glint from the west now. There's not much time left to look for a camp site."

The next morning, Padre's eyelids blinked rapidly. "Where am I?" he murmured, blinking again. Awakening in a great primeval forest for the first time in his life, he looked around in fear. Was anyone watching from a hideout? Through the infinite shades of green and the trunks' tawniness, nothing looked suspicious. Freshened by sleep, he took a deep breath and gazed upward. The pungent, resinous growth from above met his nostrils. When he lowered his head to pick up his prayer book, he met the merging rich aroma of decaying needles, branches, and cones on the forest floor. It seemed as if he were in a vast, natural enclosure with unspoiled massiveness and minutia unified. Never had he experienced such pristine surroundings. At his first stirring, Genesis had groaned and turned over.

Still gaping in disbelief Padre searched again for possible danger and then stepped humbly and in an uncoordinated gait from his pine needle bed to the trail for morning devotions. Thin forest fog seemed so different from usual, dense seashore fog.

Inspired by the ancient forest's tranquility and magnificence, he burst aloud, "Oh my! Holy Mary Mother of God, it's…why this forest is a cathedral, a great one. Just what I need, a cathedral. It's a great cathedral," he said and kissed his rosary. Looking straight ahead he imagined the trail as an endless nave. Then, peering upward he envisioned the high, multistoried limbs as strong, flying buttresses and the giant tree trunks as solemn support columns. "It's a wondrous place," he murmured, "as wondrous as the great ocean I crossed but oh so different, too."

He would just have to chant. It seemed so long ago since he'd tried, but he felt it coming on, unstoppably. After warming up and finding his finest baritone voice, he chanted until his heart filled with contentment. Between his favorite selections he rested his voice and listened to myriad musicians—red ones, yellow-bellied, blue, and speckled ones, too. Some swooped, others perched, while still others pecked rhythmically. "A natural aviary," he mumbled. In the north a beam of sunlight canted through a stand of dead trees, riveting his attention. "It...why it unmistakably hails heavenly presence," he whispered in reverence and stood meditating for a while. "It's a good omen...I need it...I'll take it. Thanks be to God," he said aloud and crossed himself. *It's the most touching spiritual experience I've been privileged to in a long, long time. It's like...a little bit of heaven on earth.* Then he chanted once more, concluding with the awesome crescendo, "For only God knows how long." For this momentous occasion he prayed one of his favorite prayers from St. Thomas Aquinas:

> "Your pleasure, merciful God—
>> grant that I may
>> desire it ardently,
>> learn it carefully,
>> recognize it truly,
>> fulfill it perfectly,
>> to the praise and glory of your name.
> Lord my God, give me
>> an understanding that knows you,
>> a diligence that seeks you,
>> a wisdom that finds you,
>> a way of life that pleases you,
>> a steadfastness that waits for you,
>> and a confidence that shall at last embrace you."

A spiritual feeling stirred within, a phenomenal one, which touched him deeply. Could it be that the vastness of the forest was a symbol for the enormity of possibilities lying ahead?

Back at the campsite Genesis was clearly chafing at the bit to travel. However, moved by the priest's plaintive haunting chants, he said, "I heard your singing while I fed and watered the horses. Sometimes the sounds reminded me a little bit of my mother's chants." He immediately caught a trace of sentimentality in his voice and straightaway changed the subject. He said firmly, "We better be on our way."

Padre hastily shook his musty blanket and then drank the gourd of water which Genesis had waiting for him. He would eat his few bites of hardtack and smoked venison after they got on the trail. He mustn't delay their progress.

As they approached the opening in the forest that Padre had seen while chanting, he looked out on a swath of lightning-scarred tree trunks whose tops must have been snapped by wind. He watched Genesis, apparently unmoved by the scene, swaying comfortably to *Grandeza's* rhythm. Genesis looked full of himself sitting on the handsome leather saddle from Spain. A saddle, any kind of a saddle would be nice, for it would make the jostling along on Captain much more comfortable for his crippled back. Nevertheless, the hypnotic movement along with his awe of nature's forces combined to conjure up nostalgia of Spain. In a drowsy sort of way, Padre said, "I've been thinking about the letter I received from Padre Ontiveros. You might not remember, but he's the priest in Spain that I told you entered the monastery with me. The letter came...let me think when...it came around the time that the American president had ordered Pensacola returned to Spain's control, back in 1814 after General Jackson made the unauthorized seizure."

"Um hm," Genesis said.

"In that letter Padre Ontiveros wrote about a painting he'd seen in Madrid, painted by one of Spain's famous artists, Francisco de Goya. He said the artist named it *The Third of May 1808*, for it depicted how Napoleon's firing squad executed civilians in Madrid on that day. My fellow Dominican described it as a very powerful painting." Padre swallowed hard and swiped his furrowed brow. "In that one scene, he said *Senor* Goya captured the essence of the entire horrifying story of Napoleon's war in Spain."

Latent sorrow surfaced. After clearing his throat, of no obvious necessity, he continued in a strengthened tone, "It happened after Spanish troops had murdered some French troops, but our soldiers were completely justified. You see, that previous day the French had massacred twelve hundred Spaniards, wounded thousands. Streets flowed with blood. Oh Lord, it must have been awful. My parents and older brother were killed while fighting guerrilla-style, perhaps identical to that portrayed in the painting. Like so many others, they were just untrained peasants, defending themselves with whatever they could find—cudgels, barrel staves, kitchen knives, scythes." *Whew*," he sighed, "Wars, wars, wars. That's why I am on this trail now."

Genesis appeared to listen, giving an occasional nod without comment.

As they rode Padre prayed he'd left the evils of war behind, first in Spain and more recently in Pensacola. He vowed to think a positive thought, perhaps about something he'd read during his extensive education at the monastery. Yes, he had received rigorous instruction in theology, mathematics, and humanistic studies. Instead, he commenced admiring the horses.

Hour by hour progressing along the trail, Padre's eyes became familiar with every inch and movement of Captain and the majestic *Grandeza*. In this wilderness how could he relate this scene to his distinguished education? He needed to recall some of his readings lest he forget. It wasn't long until his head jerked at a recollection, a fine one, something he'd read a long time ago. That's it—the way Genesis rides *Grandeza*. Why he looks as if he's Alexander the Great on his beloved horse, Bucephalus. He smiled at remembering the detail of that horse's name. When Genesis was just a youngster he had taught *Grandeza* to kneel whenever he wished to mount, the same as Alexander had done with Bucephalus. He and *Grandeza* seemed to have a mutual understanding, the same type that Alexander and Bucephalus had.

One thing about the comparison bothered Padre. Bucephalus had carried his master on long journeys, through fierce battles. Would this hold true for Genesis and *Grandeza*? Why had that thought never come to mind before this day? He could do nothing about it now. The feeling finally faded into more positive comparisons.

Even though Padre had always enjoyed the comfort of having an edge on Genesis in education, it was not difficult to own up to the fact that Genesis possessed some of Alexander's admirable qualities, especially courage, tenacity, too. Perhaps Genesis possessed even finer horsemanship. Looking back to the days when he had galloped along the Pensacola Beach with such naturalness, he looked more like a centaur than any rider Padre had ever seen. Now, could he dare give the young man his ultimate due? Leadership ability? Well...yes, he'd have to admit he'd noticed the gradual emergence of leadership qualities. Moreover, Padre recognized the fact that the physical characteristics of the two young men, who lived centuries apart, might have some commonality. Genesis' thick hair, lean, muscular body, strong hands, and keen eyes, too, just might closely resemble the great Greek's features.

The comparison rang so true that it stretched into yet another realm, the realm where Padre reigned supreme. He rightfully envisaged himself as Genesis' mentor, much akin to Aristotle's teaching Alexander to love Greek art and literature. After all, he had spent many hours, during early evening walks on the Pensacola Beach, instructing Genesis. What a pleasure, revisiting memories of how much he'd taught him in those early years of their association. It felt as satisfying as finding a lost lamb when he shepherded on the hills of *Andalucia*. Well...it was satisfying back when the lad would listen. He hoped these teachings would soon reappear in the young man's speech and values. Regardless of Genesis' taking to earthy talk and behavior in recent times, Padre realized he had made a difference in the scion's tendency toward impulsiveness and brooding moods in his early teen years. In affirmation of his godliness in directing Genesis' life, he tipped his head and basked in the glory.

Smiling to himself, and unbeknownst to Genesis, this pleasant mood conjured up an amusing story, which Padre kept private. It was the one about the despotic Emperor Napoleon's having, of all things, experienced disappointments. It had been reported the Emperor fantasized about the notorious Queen of Spain. Napoleon, in his imaginary skirt-chasing notions, had pictured her with a well-endowed bust and a tempting rump. He dreamed of a secret rendezvous with her, but his meeting with her revealed a gross truth. She was ugly, displayed ill temper, and had sickly skin. Furthermore, her low-cut neckline revealed drooping, flabby breasts. Matters like this were not discussed openly at the monastery. Padre had overheard this story during the trip when he appealed to the Bishop for the Pensacola assignment.

Genesis looked back to check on Padre and Captain.

Stricken with embarrassment, Padre urgently cleared his throat and said, "You know, I really enjoyed playing dominoes with your father on the ship. After he learned that I was reared in the *Andalucian* region, we played nights after dinner whenever there was enough moonlight, sometimes by lantern. During that time I first heard about *Senor* Colabro and his Montezuma Trading Post. It's really hard to believe we're headed for that very place. I would never, never have imagined things would work out this way."

Still, Genesis refrained from commenting. Engrossed in his own dream world, he faintly nodded in acknowledgment. Padre's lips moved in prayer, silent prayer, that Genesis' increasing aloofness had no sinister meaning. He also prayed that he would be able to convert the heathens in the Alabama Territory to the holy Catholic way.

With ever-heightening awareness that Genesis had begun distancing himself, Padre speculated that Genesis, because of his long bloodline of Creek heritage, now identified with the great forest, its myriad animals and vegetation. He sensed that this was part of Genesis' birthright. Native inheritance, eons of it, probably had been passed on and now flowed through the young man's veins.

In Pensacola, Chief Opayahola, one of the three Alabama Creek Chiefs being protected from Sharp Knife by the Spanish, had taken a strong liking

110

to Genesis and shared his knowledge with the half orphan. Genesis had also listened to many other Creek from the Georgia and Alabama Territories. In his work of interpreting Creek language, as well as in his social life on Seville Square, he sought every opportunity to learn about his people and squirreled it away, the good as well as the questionable gleanings. But considering Genesis' increased aloofness, had his loyalty diminished?

Padre now recognized his own blindness to forest dangers, a concern he wished to keep to himself. He related to the primeval forest in light of his Spanish upbringing. There had never been a primeval forest in his background—not a single area he had known in *Andalucia* had come close to it. True, he'd been a peasant in his childhood, albeit he had never been exposed to the heathen elements of natives who challenged the perils of old-growth forests. Besides, he had overcome most of his peasantry with cultural and spiritual training at the monastery. He still cared deeply for nature, though he lacked the most important traits which men linked to it possessed—the desire to hunt and fish and the will to kill. Genesis' detachment brought on deep concern for the future.

The following afternoon Padre asked, "If I sharpen a river cane for a harpoon, would you be willing to spear a fish down at the river? Today is a fasting day."

"I'll surefire give it a try. A fresh fish sounds mighty good to me."

They left the Ridge Trail and began winding their way downward to the river, hacking and maneuvering the horses through massive vine growth. Some of the vines looked as big around as a man's arm.

Suddenly Genesis stopped, raised his hand, halted Padre, and in a low voice, asked, "See the black snake coiled up at the root of that vine? Up there on that bump of a hill."

Padre naturally turned to the right.

"Not there. Look up to the left."

"Uhm hmm," Padre answered, agape.

"His tail. Listen," Genesis said. "Hear the vibration?"

"Uhm, hmm." Is it...?" Padre lost his voice momentarily, then whispered, "A rattlesnake?"

"Nope. Don't think so. I'll check."

"Sounds like one to me," Padre said softly.

Gingerly, Genesis crept closer to it. He stopped.

"From here," Genesis said in a near whispered voice, "the tail looks like a whip, a braided whip. I think that's a coachwhip snake."

"Is that right? Oh Lord above, look at the fangs!" Padre gasped. "Must be...a killer. Oh, now its head's swaying. Tongue's flicking out of his big mouth. In and out...fangs look sharp as the devil's pitchfork and that tongue's nearly as long. It's ready to strike! What in heaven's name are we going to do? That serpent's big as a rattlesnake."

"First thing, Padre, don't make any fast moves. There's no rattles. That braided tail tells, surefire, it's a coachwhip. Fastest snake. Better just wait a few seconds. Maybe it'll leave."

# CHICANERY

Genesis slipped backwards. He had intended to reach for his Spanish flintlock and powder horn. Instead, seized by the sudden sense of a deadly fall, he scuffled for balance, hung onto a sapling. Would the coachwhip feel the commotion or worse yet see him? Sure enough, two black eyes, like those on an unlucky die deuce, rose upwards. The snake swayed its head backwards, and in a blink leveraged the remainder of its body forward, uncoiled, and whipped onto Genesis' leg. Instinctively he bashed, barehanded, the stout, shiny body; whereupon, it flipped and whorled itself around his other leg. Before it imbedded its fangs, he walloped its girth again and at the same time took the most precipitous leap of faith in his life, knocking Padre to the ground. In the confusion and disorder, the horses squealed and reared their heads wildly.

Over and above heart-stopping terror, Genesis vaulted up in time to see the rustling vines swaying progressively toward the west, the snake invisible as it tore through the tangled masses.

Padre clambered to all fours and righted himself, his cavernous mouth now closed. He said, "I thought the monster would surely kill you, then me. That serpent moved faster than any devilish French Dragoon in Napoleon's army. But the ironic thing is that *you* are the one that nearly killed me. Why, you knocked the wind right out of me. But your bravery is phenomenal and probably unprecedented. I've never in all my life heard of any person retaliating barehanded against a serpent."

"My bare hand was all I had to fight with, Padre. What else could I do?" Then Genesis silently watched the snake's escape through the swaying vines until they settled. He wiped his brow, and said, "I was scared to death, it was goin' to whup the daylights outta me. It's out of our way now. Let's go."

"Hold up! I don't need fish that badly now. I could even fast altogether."

"The horses need water though," Genesis said.

"But...let's not...uh, go to the river now. We can go later. We have plenty of time."

"Padre, we've already come this far. And if we wait for another watering place, or even go to the river later, we're liable to run into something worse. Calm down. Your eyes are bulging like you're looking for the world to come to an end." Genesis started forward.

Padre felt it was too much for a man to bear, but he had no alternative other than to follow along. Hesitantly, he let go of each step and then only with greatest difficulty. *Thank the Lord,* he thought, Genesis is weaving through the twining vines cautiously.

Closer to the river, Padre felt his feet slipping while trying to plant them on a slope, slick with damp moss. He reached upward to steady himself with a lopping "vine."

As Providence would have it, the men were now side by side on the slope, for Genesis called out in a low-pitched, primal cry, "No, nooo, don't touch that." And with sure instinct, he instantly jerked Padre's upper arm, snatched him sideways, and steadied him.

Still wobbly, Padre looked up, his face filled with horror. A swaying, black head with a long, wavering tongue thrust intermittently in his direction. Two round, shiny-black eyes stared at him straight on.

"Stay still," Genesis whispered. Padre was already numbed, like a statue, with terror. The horses had been paces behind and had not become startled, though their ears were pinned back.

"Now we'll back away," Genesis said in his softest voice, "very, very slowly." Edging away, their eyes remained locked on the huge, black snake.

The serpent remained perched on the bend of a huge vine. With a deadly look steadfast in its beady eyes, the creature raised its head and body about a foot, dangled the long, black coachwhip of a tail, and switched it about. It looked ever so ready to lunge.

At a safer distance, Genesis said, "That's the same damn snake that already nigh flattened me out to nothing but a layer of dirt."

Sweat trickled down Padre's frozen face as the "vine" vibrated its tail, abruptly propelled itself into an arc, and with an incredible burst of speed thrust away from them. It alternately squeezed its body into shortened lengths and then arced as it tendriled from one vine to the next, real vines, until it disappeared, fortunately, toward the south.

"I warned you," Padre said through his clenched teeth and shook his pointing finger at Genesis, "and you refused to take heed."

"Now Padre, I warned you, too, another killer, man or beast, could be waiting for us at any other watering place. This forest is home for the animals, even if some of 'em are mighty dangerous. Anything could surefire happen." Genesis' wooden expression came alive. He asked, "Didja shit your britches?"

"You deserve prickly sweetgum balls under your blanket tonight for that ignoble remark, at least a few dozen of the largest, prickliest ones I can find."

"Oh heck, if you can't take a tease, I'll get serious. That snake has a hell of a bite."

"How did you come to know so much about it?"

"Ramie Ramirez—you know, that hellava hunter I told you about—killed one on a hunting trip. Ramie is about the best hunter in Pensacola. He brought the snake back in a croker (burlap) sack and hung 'em from a tree limb in Seville Square, so everybody could take a good look at the tail. It's braided like a whip. That thing stayed there till it started stinking. Ramie called it a coachwhip. He said it's not poisonous like a rattler, but it can do a devil of a job if it bites. It don't just puncture wounds with its fangs. It sinks its teeth and then yanks away, making jagged gashes in your skin. Besides, he told me there's a saying that a coachwhip whips whoever it attacks till the sun sets, and where it likes to whip is right in your face."

Padre stared, wordless.

"C'mon," Genesis said, "let's get going."

"Young man, if you want me to offer kind words about you when you meet that beautiful Indian princess, you better start heeding my advice."

Carefully, very carefully thenceforth, they descended to the river and pushed northward along the riverbank until Padre mustered the courage to agree to let the horses drink. Suddenly Padre jumped.

"Look across at the other bank," Padre said. "Is that the white of a...?"

"That ain't no cottonmouth moccasin, Padre. It ain't nothing but a trout lily. Just a very nice, little ole, white trout lily like grows on the bayous close to Pensacola. There's probably more of 'em in the bushes."

Genesis studied the lay of the land and spied a rivulet suitable for their drinking water.

While carving a river cane harpoon to a sharp point, Padre had constantly turned his head and darted apprehensive looks toward the south. This world, fraught with hidden dangers, felt so different, so vastly different from any he'd known. He felt so ill-suited. Would that devil of a snake dare turn back and torment them again, possibly debilitate them into wilderness victims?

Genesis scouted for a favorable fishing spot. A small clearing revealed a crescent in the riverbank that looked promising. In no time at all he harpooned a magnificent fish. Upon examination, it turned out he had gored a large-mouthed bass. After Genesis had wrestled its thrashing body still, he said, "See, the mouth is about big enough for me to poke my fist in." In the river clearing, he scaled and cleaned it and then roasted it in wetted mullein leaves.

Famished, the men at first pulled large pieces of the succulent fish from the bones, and ate. Then they started taking one pinch at a time. Only the shiny skeleton and tail remained.

Back on the trail, they progressed until the scant light faded. Padre, early on, had relied on Genesis' intuition for selecting their campsites. Genesis seemed especially adept at taking precautions against snakes, since the infamous incidents with them. Having gone through encounters with two different species of snakes, what other dangerous creature would they confront next?

At Genesis' bidding, they swung away from the trail, stopped, and cleared a campsite. They picked up pinecones and threw them out of the way, piled up pine needles, and settled in for the night. But neither Padre not Genesis slept well.

The next morning, Padre rubbed the crick in his neck so he could straighten his head. How it pained. With pontifical certainty his lips moved, "Dominicans do what they have to do." And he did. He rode all that day, in pain, his head favoring the left side.

Hence forward, Padre depended upon Genesis to trap the game and cook it, since they had depleted every morsel of their rations. Without malice Padre assumed other work detail. Not waiting to be prompted, he dutifully gathered stones to circle the fires. He cobbled roasting frames by cutting straight limbs for hand-turning spits and forked limbs to cradle them. Becoming the helper and follower now seemed the right role to accept. While cutting firewood, he sneaked looks at Genesis snaring the squirrel or rabbit most suitable for roasting. Squirrels scampered everywhere. Rabbits romped everywhere. Wild animals, though plentiful, were still wary.

"Shoot," Genesis said, "no need to waste gunpowder. I think I can trap one of them rabbits that ran scared from us. See them two dead logs laying crisscrossed?"

"Of course, of course."

"I know at least one of them rabbits hid in one of 'em," Genesis said. "Take your hatchet and when I say 'ready' I want you to give the log a hell of a whack on the end where the roots grew. I'll be sitting at the other end ready to cover it with my blanket as soon as I see fur."

It would have taken the wisdom of King Solomon to judge which one was more surprised when the plan finally flushed a rabbit. It happened only after Genesis yelled a number of times, "Harder, hit it harder."

The next evening held the promise of a roasted turkey, for Genesis had taken his turkey caller from his bag after they had come upon a drove of turkeys. These turkeys, at least twenty, had slowly pecked along, heading away from the trail. When the riders came closer, the birds escaped and alighted in the distance. In a low voice, Genesis began practicing, "keouk, keouk, keouk." His imitative sounds gradually grew better and better. That evening, they stopped earlier than usual and set up camp.

Genesis eagerly wound his way through a scarf of tall grass and bushes, which had taken on the amber glow of the lowering sun. He squatted behind a tree and made the imitative sounds, louder and louder. Patiently he persisted until a curious gobbler answered from afar. As they exchanged calls, the gobbler sounded nearer and nearer. At last he came running, with his head low, a whole flock of hens and poults trailing behind.

"Claim your power," Padre said softly.

While the flock strutted on their way, Genesis pushed his luck by returning yet another call, from his hideout, to a call deeper in the forest. Whereupon, from that direction the inquisitive gobbler winged overhead, alighted on the ground, and commenced a majestic strut. He was a larger one with a great, red wattle and a beard hanging from his chest about a foot long. The huge tom looked ready to prove his two-inch spurs would crown him king of the forest. His fully fanned feathers glistened with a golden, bronze-green sheen.

Padre shielded his eyes and observed intently. Genesis thrived on thrill-taking chances. Again, as if cheering for him, Padre whispered, "Claim your power, young man! I'm supporting you."

The gobblers met with no fear. Instantly, their claws clenched and unclenched. When a passel of disturbed hens scudded past the tree shielding Genesis, he reached with both hands. The first hen slipped through his hands, even her tail feathers. Not to be outdone, he quickly stretched his arms out farther and snapped up the next one as it tried to turn away from danger, his bare hands clutching the wings tightly. The racket and uproar reverberated through the pines as both gobblers and the remainder of the flock chaotically flew away.

To Padre, the echo resounded with notes of betrayal. Nevertheless, Genesis returned with a wide smile, holding the hen as far away from his body as possible.

"These feathers are duller than the gobblers'," Genesis said, "but she may be sweeter."

"I see you're keeping it a respectful distance," Padre said.

"Uh hm, she's a nice hen, but I broke up what could have been a hell of a cock fight."

Padre's stomach growled, prompting him to say, "Your rendition of the gobbling sound attracted a drove in quite a respectable time; and it, indeed, looks as if you caught one of the plumpest hens. My mouth's already watering." Yet Padre turned his back when Genesis grabbed the turkey's neck, flung it away from his body, and spun the turkey in circles. Padre felt a shiver when he heard the neck bones crack.

"What's the matter, Padre? I thought you was raised on a farm."

"Yes, I was. I have seen my mother use the same method, but it has been a while."

"Well, I saw my mother kill and clean a chicken many a time," Genesis said.

While drippings sputtered on the embers, the turkey turned crusty brown, and gave off a sumptuous odor. They took turns rotating the spit, barely able to wait for the blessed feast. Padre said, "I'd like to take a look at your turkey caller."

Genesis fetched it, handed it to Padre, and said, "It ain't nothing fancy. Just a flat bone, you know, the second joint of a turkey wing. Ramie showed me how to make it. He knows everything about hunting. But there ain't nothing much to a turkey caller except carving some holes. The hard part is learning how to blow on it to make the right sound, and he surefire helped me learn. He said you have to practice turkey calling till you can do it right, 'cause if you make the wrong sound, they know the difference right away and won't come. But I figured Ramie ain't no smarter than me. Shoot, we breathe the same kind of air, even if he did have more practice learning how to make the right sound."

Padre marveled at Genesis' turkey caller. He even tried to make the sounds, though he had no interest in actually using it to attract a turkey.

At last, Genesis slipped the blackened turkey hen off the spit and onto a flat rock. The legs and wings easily pulled away from the carcass. The men crunched the charred edges and savored the succulent, meaty parts. Then they pulled strips from the breast and ate until the bones were bare. They even gnawed the bones.

Though white-tailed deer abounded in the great forest, Genesis had refused to consider killing one, for he remembered his mother's words, "Our people take from the land only as much as they need."

Chinkapins and other full-bodied nuts, scrounged from the fall crop, as well as tangy wild berries, added some variety and nourishment to their meals of game. Occasionally they munched on fresh, green shoots of smooth sumac. Since they had eaten so much fish and other seafood at the

Pensacola garrison, they preferred game to the plentiful fish, in the nearby river, except for Padre's fasting day.

Sometimes they ate white-capped mushrooms that popped from rotting logs, smooth and shiny and big as a man's palm. Once while plucking mushrooms from a log, downed by lightning or wind, Genesis poked his knife into the rotten pulp and wedged an opening. Beetles scurried and larvae tumbled. "That's just a sampling of how much life is in it," he said. "These logs give off a lot of food for all kinds of little critters." As he walked away Genesis turned back and said, "Just look how fast them birds moved in for a meal."

"Yes, and now *you* look at that long lizard soaking in the sun. It's like a rounded strip of green velvet ribbon. Watch. Its throat's expanding. Why it expanded into a rosy bubble. What a sight! Uh oh, the beautiful bubble has collapsed and disappeared. That lizard snapped up a meal, too, on the run to the bushes."

Padre would take his meager knowledge about the forest further. *Humph*, if Genesis knew how he was flaunting himself. *I taught him so much. I'll show him.* Padre piped up, "There's another benefit of the logs which you failed to mention. Eventually they decay into the soil, giving nourishment back to the earth. That, in turn, provides for new growth," he said, not trying to conceal his loftiness. He felt no reason to add that he'd learned that from farming the land when he was only a child.

Unfazed by Padre's occasional need to show off, Genesis said, "Uhm hm, there's even some goodness in trunks of dead trees that are still standing. River Raven told me they're just as sacred as live trees 'cause animals nest in 'em, 'specially in the hollows and crotches. He said that he had a hard time keeping *Senor* Colabro's white workers from burning them snags. Said if they was meant to be burned, the lightning that struck them woulda burned 'em all the way down in the first place."

Whenever Genesis reverted to his introspective mood, Padre, though becoming weary from the ordeals of trekking and camping in the seemingly endless forest, sought companionship in the surroundings. Once he stretched his neck so far upward, he almost toppled backwards, marveling at the trees' heights. But it was worth the risk. It was like being in a world, which one could only have imagined in one's dreams. Though the understory of shade-tolerant trees looked as tall as any he had ever seen heretofore, the canopy trees of pine and hardwood towered much higher and had trunks and limbs of gargantuan girth. By a stretch of imagination, he had earlier characterized them as topped with crowns of emerald. These spectacular crowns topped pines and three hardwood species that he could identify—oak, hickory, and ash.

119

Not having been privy to information about these giant trees, he was unaware that they were of 100, 200, 300 year-old, virgin vintage. Neither did he know about layers of lichen and debris, which had turned into soil in many places on their multicentury limbs; nor did he know that these habitats hosted a great diversity of other plant and animal life.

Nevertheless, Padre wished to share his awe of great forest's wonders with Genesis. Instead, he kept a respectful silence. He attempted to keep time with the staccato percussion of woodpeckers by wiggling his toes or tapping a finger on the reins, and he tried to keep track of the frolicsome, flying squirrels. But there was no way for his fingers and eyes to compete with the God-given speed of either set of creatures.

Later, darkness brought not only different forest sounds but also magnified them. Dominant bull alligators in the distance bellowed for mates as they had all along, but now the sound rang out primordially in a flesh crawling way. Hooting of owls echoed eerily, bouncing from tree to tree. Occasionally, bobcats, in a fray or mating, added their cries to the mix, screaming in high pitches and alternating low growls.

Padre noticed that Genesis' eyes were losing their luster; his intrepidness was vanishing. Padre was also growing weary and hungry. How he wished for a piece of bread.

On the sixth morning, morale of the two Pensacola fugitives sagged to lower levels. Supplies had long ago been exhausted. Having entered the swampy area, the men and horses languished wearier. While slitting the sixth notch in his time stick, Genesis also sliced through the silence barrier. With his eyes focused on the knife and time stick, he hesitatingly began. "I...uh...last night I felt like somebody was around us. Then it seemed like more than one. Like several people."

"Real people?"

"That's what I said. Real people."

"Maybe it was some other kind of animal? You know some bobcats had a fight or were mating or something. Sounded like mayhem."

"No! No animals, no bobcats," Genesis said looking up. "It was after the bobcat fight." He scratched his nose and said, "I smelled them, too. Bear grease. Whoever it was."

"Your instincts are most always accurate. I, I believe you. But who could it be? Robbers? American scouts? Your people?"

"Don't know," Genesis answered, his eyes intense and fearful expression intensifying. "But I have an idea. And like that's not enough to worry about, just look at *Grandeza* and Captain. You must have noticed that they are starting to look pitiful. You can almost see their ribs. They really need corn."

"Of course, I realize the horses are looking more gaunt and angular. We are, too. I can feel it. All four of us must be a dreadful sight. I did not want to complain about pickings being so slim in the spongy area we just went through. Nothing, absolutely nothing, seemed to flourish there except those insect-eating plants. Now, these swamp conditions are even worse. We couldn't cook anything here even if we found something suitable. Angels above, if we only had a little more hardtack and corn. But dear God, safety's more important than food. I always pray for safety; just think, we've come a long way. And we are safe so far." Somehow he managed to summon a mischievous look and said, "Even if our bodies grow moss as long as what's on the cypresses, we'll get you to that Indian princess yet. You know, this is probably the last part of the traveling now that we are in the swamp. But I am concerned, deeply concerned. Someone may, indeed, be trailing us. Forest rogues really bother me now. No matter how our horses look, they are still valuable. I promise you, I'll look and listen, even more carefully than ever. You'll have to admit I've been very diligent in my prayers for us."

"Don't worry," Genesis quipped with a pouting face, "I always keep plenty watch for us during the day. And at night your snoring keeps me plenty wide-awake."

After they had passed over the spongy, boggy capsules and entered the swamp, they came upon numerous holes, which had turned muddy and slimy. Then the trail grew even more swampy and was studded with cypress trees. Each step they took in the rich, black mud, released the tang of decay and rot. Slipping and sliding over the gnarly cypress roots made balance more difficult to maintain, especially as they grew hungrier.

In a struggle to keep his mental attitude above the onerous conditions, Padre used some valuable energy to say, "That scant breeze whiffed the sweet scent of swamp magnolia blossoms our way. I inhaled a deep breath and filled my lungs with their smell, like pleasant perfume. It was very nice." At once, he realized he might as well have kept his thoughts to himself. But it was all right for Genesis to act withdrawn. So be it, if only the swamp could part like the Red Sea and let them pass.

Little did the men know of what it would be like to spend a day sloshing through a swamp, which sucked on every hoof and foot every step of the way, and maneuvering over swamp cypresses that splayed their roots into lethal obstacles. Their bellies and guts were so empty, the bitterness of bile hung in their throats. There was no forage for the horses.

"Horses are tired," Genesis said, "we need to take it real easy. And I hafta say—I keep thinking about last night—I'm sure men hid close by during the night. They might be evil ones. And it's not just my imagination about forest devils. I surefire know people was somewhere around us. I felt it."

With a ponderous expression, Padre stroked his scraggly beard, his sight fixed on an eerie light, like the will-of-the wisp, which hung faintly ahead in the swampy forest. A premonition struck him that surely something terrible awaited. Gooseflesh popped out on his arms, yet he would not burden Genesis with another bleak thought.

The gait of the hungry horses and men became slower and slower. Wordlessly, they passed the skeleton of a deer. Carrion, lingering underneath the bones, reeked malodorously and oozed with shiny-white maggots, full-bellied. Padre grimaced. The sight intensified the bitter bile taste in his mouth. They passed it, heads hanging low, as mud splattered with each step, caking layer upon layer, on all legs of beast and man, adding troublesome weight to their already overburdened bodies.

At last, an awareness of faint light caused the men to lift their heads upwards. A long-awaited shaft of dim light shone through an opening in the far distance, meagerly, albeit mercifully. Padre quoted a favorite Bible scripture: "Let there be light." Perhaps they might, after all, get out of the swamp of the great forest without further disasters. Before reaching that opening of light, they came upon a pond and as they approached, longed to relieve themselves of some unwanted weight by scrubbing off some of the mud. First of all, they, as well as the horses, drank the sorely needed water.

At the pond's edge, an unfamiliar bird, larger than a sandpiper but smaller than a heron, barely caught Padre's fuzzy awareness in the forest's dimness. Yet the bird's bursts of energy somehow pervaded his fuzziness and stimulated his attention. He watched its long-stemmed legs hopping from one water lily to the next, leaving the lilies to bounce in the water. Padre, in his condition of dulled sensibility, turned from the bird's direction and blindly thrust a leg toward a "log" which lay at the pond's edge. He had intended to leverage part of his weight on the log while he washed himself.

Genesis leaped intuitively and grabbed Padre's forearm before he had stepped his full weight onto it, and just in time. Padre rocked backwards toward Genesis' righting arm. Simultaneously, the end of the "log" opened into an incredible, scarlet cavern lined with jagged, pearly teeth. At once more mouths in the pond opened; some growled and thrashed tails, terrifying both men beyond belief.

Padre gasped. He had every reason to be scared to death—the enormity of the primal beasts. When their upper jaws raised open, they formed angles well nigh perpendicular to the lower jaws. The pond turned from a sea of floating logs to a sea of gaping maws and dozens of eyes glowing like oranges in a Florida orange grove. Padre looked urgently toward the horses. Already in a weakened condition, could he outrun the alligators?

Slowly, they eased backward, first Genesis and Padre followed. Then they fled with all their suffering might, not daring to look back. When Padre could run no longer, he caught a hefty breath. Genesis slowed his pace and let him catch up. They reached the horses, took the reins in hand, and walked alongside their mounts.

Genesis rubbed the back of his sweated neck and said,"I wonder why the hell that monster you almost stepped on, why it didn't come after us and attack us. Must have been stuck too deep in mud...or maybe the size of the horses had something to do with it. That 'gator had probably never seen any horses."

"Who in this wide, wide world," Padre said, as he felt his knees still wobbling, "would ever believe that an alligator could grow to that size? A behemoth! Why that beast had to be at least twenty feet long. Holy Mary, that alligator would have snapped me in half, backbone included, with one bite."

"Scared the bejabers outta me, too. Just about pissed my pants myself. But Padre, remember this is a old, old forest swamp. You know alligators surefire mess around most any water's edge."

"I know that. One of the first warnings I received from Padre de Galvez at the mission was that an alligator will investigate any potential meal. But it truly looked like a log, the earthen color. It lay perfectly still, too. And its cracked skin looked exactly like the bark of an old tree."

"Uh hm, that mossy-looking stuff on top of him," Genesis said, "was just old water plants he'd swum through."

Revitalized to some extent by surviving the cyclopean encounter, Padre pontificated, "Some writings by monks centuries ago described alligators as beasts that could have crept out of the catalog of devilish bestiaries. Now I am a believer."

Still muddy, they walked. Padre heeded a respectful distance for the pond, staying on the side of Genesis, which was farthest from the pond. Padre darted sporadic glances backwards as if he expected an alligator to attack at any moment. He tried to ignore the hollow in the pit of his stomach. A meal from the garrison kitchen would taste like a feast now. Those years spent at the Pensacola garrison were only memories, memories that didn't seem so bad now, especially memories of the food. Though the garrison kitchen was lacking in some respects, a portion of nourishment of some description had always awaited him there.

Finally, after trudging an attentive distance, Padre gained enough confidence to look upward at the blessed bright spot ahead. Although drained of energy, the increasing brightness invigorated him enough to do some talking. "Those beautiful blue herons back there surely knew which side of the pond to stay on. You saw they stalked the shallow rim on the far side, away from the alligators."

"Heck, they can just fly away if a hungry mouth opens. One thing I can't do. I surefire can't fly. Aggravates the daylight outta me. But sometimes I dream I can fly. I take off, real nice, like an eagle. My wings are long as my arms. And when I go up real high and look down, I ain't scared. Nary bit. I just flap and float like an eagle right by itself. And I *always* land on my feet. I just shiver inside when I think about it."

Padre was still amazed at Genesis' delivering him from jaws of the colossal reptile. Genesis' loyalty had not diminished, after all. Padre shuddered. He felt he could never, as long as he lived, be thankful enough to Genesis for snatching him from those ravening jaws. His lips moved in thankful prayer. Then on the other hand, Padre thought of himself as no different from any other white man with pure blood. Only an Indian or half-Indian, like Genesis, would be able to distinguish an alligator from a real log.

Pine trees now outnumbered the swamp cypress. Genesis and Padre welcomed the scent of tangy sap seeping from the sun-warmed pines. Soon, space between the trees became greater, making it necessary for the fugitives, as well as their horses, to begin adjusting to sunlight. Time after time, the men alternately shaded the glare and rubbed their stinging eyes. The horses reacted to the light, also, shaking their heads from side to side with sniveling dismissiveness.

No sooner had they adjusted to the light, than they found themselves again traveling through a darkened swath inhabited by a large stand of trees. As they limped along with their horses on these last leagues of the journey, hunger, tired muscles, bones, too, now shrouded the weary travelers into strange, dreamlike trances. In need of the clearest vision they could muster up, they instinctively paused and massaged their eyes to readjust to the darkened area.

As Genesis stroked his eyes, he noticed in his peripheral vision at the left, a fleeting brown cloud. The stroking stopped, his hand hanging aimlessly near his face. The dark cloud darted, disappearing behind a tree. Again it moved. No, it was not a brown cloud. It was…it was a dark form…a ghostly form.

# APPARITIONS

A brown flash, fast as greased lightning, jolted Genesis into keener awareness. Abruptly, he jerked to full attention.

Padre did likewise, and at the same time his line of vision followed Genesis' gaze toward the west. The next streaking apparition was barely discernible through the eerie swamp fog. His eyes widened. Had the wraith of De Soto finally found them? Had De Soto been embodied and resurrected? In his better judgment, these bizarre speculations struck him as downright silly. His weakened condition could have precipitated a phantomlike, imaginary vision. Albeit, some forest creature, in the end, might outwit him. He leaned toward Genesis and said softly, "It might be another vicious animal stalking us."

Genesis sniffed noticeably, in different directions, and said under his breath, "Nope, it ain't no animal. It's the same scent as last night, bear grease. I told you somebody's around."

Padre caught a whiff of the strange, unpleasant odor. Neither ghosts nor phantoms ever smelled of bear grease. *Upps.* There it went again. The ill-boding blur darted from behind one tree to another. Closer. Padre held his breath.

Genesis froze for a moment, then whispered, "Listen! Hear that?"

Another mud-sucking step resonated louder.

"Maybe...," Padre began.

Genesis interrupted with, "Shhh."

A dark, scary silhouette leaped forward and hid behind another tree, which stood even nearer. The ill-defined figure now resembled the shape of a person.

Shocked into helplessness, Padre still sensed imminent danger, his vision holding steadfast on that tree. He blinked and blinked, sharpening his vague focus. Who on earth lurked there? And why the mysterious behavior?

A cloudy object began emerging. Unable to distinguish the sinister entity, Padre's heart pounded. Mouth tightened. He felt wooden as the trees. Thankfully the horses had not reacted. Perhaps they were too weary.

The mystic form waxed clearer. No. It was no illusion. Without a sound, a single-feathered headdress advanced outward from the tree trunk. A chestnut-colored face peered. The body moved upward from a crouched position and evolved into a fully formed being, a native. Sure, but dreaded, identification loomed. This man embodied the stark fierceness of a Red Stick warrior. Worst of all, he held a huge bow with arrow notched, ready for draw. Silence of death enveloped Padre. He shivered an involuntary shudder. An icy tremor shot down his spine.

Genesis squinted in the direction of his Spanish flintlock, hanging from the saddle horn, when the native, his monstrous bow now tautly drawn, edged closer. How long could the native resist the force in the bow? Now nearer, the sharp tip of the arrowhead shone so brightly, its gloss pierced through the swamp fog. Beyond the arrowhead the native's fierce, black eyes gleamed straight on with only darted looks toward Padre. He surefire couldn't hold the powerfully drawn tension much longer. Would he shoot the arrow before the next heartbeat?

Spellbound by the deadly weapon thrust in his face, Genesis' clammy hands wilted, unable to reach for the gun. Then his wellspring for survival flowed forth just in time and dominated. He squeezed his limp hold on the reins tighter. His head jerked involuntarily from the right to the left in rapid motion, searching for a way of escape.

There was none.

His forehead beaded. His heart pounded faster than ever in his entire life.

In seconds, the torment worsened.

A larger brown cloud of motion sprang forth. Moving blurs developed into a swarm of weapon-bearing natives. One after another they came closer. Their faces bore formidable expressions, unrelenting formidable expressions. At least two were painted red, as if ready for war. Inch-by-inch, they eased nearer. Genesis' went numb, save for his eyes cutting oblique glances at Padre.

As more of them appeared, Padre's shoulders sagged lower. Would they become Genesis' nemesis? Why couldn't his inherent native intuitiveness issue forth, handle this confrontation, and rescue both of them now?

Genesis, overwhelmed in the presence of such grim adversaries, let the perspiration drip from his forehead, too afraid to move his hands. In a helpless daze, he watched the natives. He'd seen plenty of them around Pensacola, barefoot, long black hair braided or bound in tails, clad only in loincloths; but never had he witnessed the likes of this hostile-looking group. Now, with a bow drawn in his face and his life at stake, this was a different world, terrifying as a nightmare that drains every bit of power and leaves your body unmovable, unable to utter a sound.

Gesturing toward Padre and Genesis, the native leader ordered, "Hold your hands up. High." When they obeyed, he released his drawn bow and caught a breath.

As soon as Genesis heard the pinging release of the bowstring, he exhaled a breath, but still stoically pondered his fate.

Padre breathed shallowly, praying for their lives with incredible raptness, which a few minutes ago he never would have believed possible. Yet he was too afraid to make the sign of the cross. Though only seconds had elapsed, it seemed time had stood endlessly still. The stench of bear grease lay in the already muggy air. A drink of water would help. They would've had more water hours ago if that behemoth of an alligator hadn't thwarted their efforts. Suddenly awareness struck him like a blow on the head—not water. Water can wait. Our lives are still at stake! His eyes rolled upward. His body wavered sidewards. He teetered and fell forward, stumbling over the ragged end of a deadfall, and landed flat on his face. In a fuzzy state of consciousness, he wondered what the natives would do with him now? How he itched to rub his eyes, but he realized he should keep his arms still. Wetness dripping from his nose distracted his attention. On the ground he saw dark red spots. Blood.

Genesis spontaneously bent down to help Padre to his feet. The native leader seized this opportunity, approached Genesis even closer, and redrew his bow. At once sensing his mistake, Genesis looked in the direction of the movement. As the leader drew the bowstring, his knotty arm muscles grew larger. An arrowhead loomed, pointing so near that Genesis' eyes turned inward. At no time in his life had a lethal weapon ever been pointed in his face like this. The native's physical might, coupled with the powerful killer intensity in his gaze, was too much. Genesis cowered like a dog being beaten, casting only a mere fleeting glance upward.

The tall leader looked downright, damned vicious. A bird's claw, a large, rancid one, with the longest talons Genesis had ever seen in his life, decorated his bare chest. It dangled from a braided buckskin strip encircling his neck. Taut, scarred skin stretched over prominent ribs, ribs prominent enough to count if he'd been in a counting mood. The overbearing presence unmistakably conveyed power, absolute power.

127

When the native released the bow's tension, Genesis' frantic inner voice cried, *try to make friends! But how?* Even in a state of desperation, it dawned on him that he'd have to force himself to get up the nerve to say something aloud. Utter surprise registered on the leader's face as Genesis, after finding a timid voice, humbly offered a Creek greeting. It didn't help an iota, for the leader's expression grew stern, again glaring into Genesis' face.

"Gun on horse," the leader said, as he offensively repositioned his bow with a quick jerk. Though his arrow was already nocked, he did not draw the bowstring. Sharpening his gaze with rapid eye blinks, the leader continued, "The gun. We take. Our chief knows whites kill."

A wolf cried out over and over, as daunting as their predicament, and Padre's nose continued dripping. Blowflies swarmed on the blood. Mosquitoes hovered and bit fiercely, but nary one lit upon a bear-greased native.

"We come in peace," Genesis pleaded. He flinched and shrank with defeated eyes when the native moved the point of the arrowhead closer. Without looking up Genesis said, "It's, it's all right. You can take the gun." Immediately astonished at his own words, relinquishing his beloved gun, his next words, "The powder horn, too," faded. Though he had not cried since he couldn't remember when, his lips quivered and his eyes welled up. Gathering all his might, he tightened his mouth. He must plead his case and try to win over the leader. "We're, um, from Pensacola garrison," he said meekly. "We look for safety from the white warrior general. He makes war on Pensacola again."

The leader's eyes moved back and forth, from Genesis to the gun, studying, without a hint of compassion. His line of vision soon shifted to the group of natives, sifting among them. He ordered, "Big Brother, take the white horse. Big Turtle Trapper, take the brown one."

Genesis' heart sank. His beloved *Andalucian* stallion in the clutches of strangers? He couldn't bear the sight. Never, since his father brought the horse to Pensacola, had *Grandeza* been under another person's control, not even once. He cringed and bit his lip when Big Brother snatched the reins.

The natives celebrated in whoops and rhythmic monotones while raising their weapons up and down and stomping their feet.

Damn them, Genesis wailed inside. Damn them all! He was madder than hell. Yet, an inner spirit, greater than those words, arose. It steadied him in the closeness of the mighty bow and arrow.

"Quiet!" the leader shouted. "Their hands must be tied! Wild Buck Fighter! Hatchet Thrower!" he snapped. "Take out the wahoo ropes. Tie their hands. Search them. Take everything."

Wild Buck Fighter and Hatchet Thrower, the two painted like Red Sticks, released their aggressive grips on their tomahawk handles. They quickly complied with the orders, tying the travelers' hands in back of their bodies and seizing the gun and powder horn. At once, Wild Buck Fighter grabbed the padre's shoulder bag and his money pouch and rosary while Hatchet Thrower stripped Genesis' bag and pouch. They handed the booty to the leader. The other natives raised their weapons, chanted, and cheered wildly.

Padre, his nose bleeding profusely, slumped forward into blackness. As it turned out, he'd fallen into only momentary unconsciousness. When he fell, the blood had rushed to his lowered head and revived him. Using all the leverage he could command, he braced himself against the deadfall, which his head had narrowly missed when he toppled over, and struggled upright, even with bound hands. No one offered to assist him.

Prisoners and possessions having been secured, the leader nodded and said, "Yah, the warrior general killed hundreds of our people, like they was mad dogs. We call him Sharp Knife."

Genesis said, "We call him that, too."

Without acknowledging Genesis' remark, the leader said, "Sharp Knife said that our people are children. *Humph*," he scorned, "I hate him. Killed most of our people in the North, drove the rest from their Mother Earth at Horseshoe Bend. Not just Red Stick warriors' Mother Earth, but took Mother Earth belonging to peaceful tribes, too. Mother Earth is part of our people." The leader shook his head, "We do not trust whites with guns."

"But that's the one, that's the same general we're escaping from," Genesis pleaded. "Spies said he comes soon to capture Pensacola again with a great army, thousands of soldiers and hired Indians. We feared for our lives."

The leader ignored Genesis' plea for understanding.

"Take the gun and powder horn to the chief," the leader commanded Wingfoot. "And Swamp Hunter, you're fast. You go, too. Give message that we return with the white men and their horses from Pensacola. The men say they wish to escape Sharp Knife's war in Pensacola."

After the gun had been confiscated, the leader had placed the previously nocked arrow in his quiver among a bouquet of other colorfully-fletched arrows and looped the bowstring over his shoulder. Anxiously, he looked inside the money pouches and smiled gleefully at the contents, rattling the coins. Before he placed the money pouches in Padre's shoulder bag, he inspected the bag's contents with great satisfaction. First, he pulled out the flask of wine. As soon as he uncorked it he let out a whoop, which drew the other natives' attention, but he would have the pleasure of taking charge of the shoulder bag. He dangled the rosary, inspecting the beads with great admiration before tucking them in the bag. All the while, he and the natives had acted as if they were unaware that Padre's nose still dripped blood.

Padre, also, ignored his bloody nose. It paled in comparison to being deprived of his precious prayer book and rosary, cassocks, healing oil, and letters, too. He would have willingly given them the hatchet and knife, but he needed the holy belongings, especially the wafers and wine which he had intended to consecrate for celebrating the Eucharist.

Genesis watched Padre's reaction to giving up the shoulder bag, but he had his own problems. He felt a chunk of his body had left with his gun, leaving a big hole right in the middle of his stomach. And how he itched to scratch his mosquito bites and stinging eyes. He tried dabbing his eyes to his shoulder but couldn't make the reach easily even though his shoulders rounded like the binding, which restrained his hands. Too afraid to make a more noticeable motion, he attempted to blow the mosquitoes away but was too thirsty. Eyelid blinks gave no relief.

Youthful bravado in Genesis began to stir again and he said, "We uh..." He shifted his weight to bolster his courage and started anew, "My name's Genesis, Genesis Zamora. My friend is Padre, Padre Morales. He's a missionary. We look for the Montezuma Trading Post and *Senor* Colabro. We've known the *senor* a long time." Genesis inhaled a deep breath. "And besides, I know River Raven. I talked with him every time he ran rafts to Pensacola for the *senor*."

The leader stood wordless, seemingly giving Genesis permission to continue.

"My father was a Spanish sea captain." He brought me the white horse on his ship from Spain, the same ship the padre came on, from across the wide ocean. He brought many other shiploads of supplies for *Senor* Colabro's trading post." Genesis, his energy waning, caught another breath before saying, "*Senor* Colabro came to the Alabama Territory because of my father. My father told him how the friendly Indians bring trade to Pensacola. The Montezuma Trading Post is supposed to be near here, where two rivers meet." He wished he had free hands to make the sign for intersecting rivers.

"Aaah," the leader responded, nodding his head. He and his native party studied and examined the weary travelers in silent awe. Whites, with their strange clothing and belongings, seemed a rarity to some of these wilderness men. Other than when they had celebrated confiscation of the gun and horses, the entire group had maintained silence, holding true to their reputation that they kept the spoken word as sacred in most circumstances. Soon the natives gathered around *Grandeza*. So overcome with a sort of reverence for his white coat and shod hooves, which they found in spite of the mud, they broke their usual silence and sounded out in "whoops" and "ahs." Two natives offered chants for his sacred white coat.

"My friend," Genesis said and motioned his head toward Padre, "is a special missionary, a priest. He comes from same region in Spain where my father and *Senor* Colabro are from, called *Andalucia*, far, far, beyond the water that is much greater than the Father of Water."

The word *Andalucia* drew a mirthful laugh from the leader. The rest of the natives turned away from *Grandeza* and laughed uproariously. Then they tried saying the strange word, succeeding only in getting sounds like "Analoos" or "Adalozsa," snickering with each try. Even Genesis smiled faintly at the sound of laughter. The leader "sshed" the sportive natives.

Padre straightened his posture upward, trying to think in a priestly vein. Had common ground been found at last? He had noted the leader's laughter, a commonality that could bridge the culture gap. Might this commonality be sufficient to mitigate their plight? Or was something ominous still in store for the future?

As the natives laughed, Padre, although fatigued and sorely in need of water and nourishment, noticed their decayed and worn down teeth. Many had teeth in various stages of decay, some had only rotted snags. Would he have to give a lesson on caring for teeth? Forget the bad teeth, he shuddered and grimaced. More dire worries loomed—saving his very life, getting released, and regaining, he hoped, his holy possessions. Only then could he think of saving the heathens' souls, much less their teeth or anything else.

After the natives settled down, the leader, with a puzzled expression, asked Genesis, "How do you know our people's language?"

"My mother is Creek, full-blooded, now lives with Seminole in Florida. My sister, Maypearl, went with her."

In the meantime, though his nose had stopped bleeding, Padre still felt light headed and weak as if he might faint again. He moved, unsteadily, and leaned against the rough bark of a nearby hickory tree. Old doubts returned. Had Padre de Galvez made the wrong decision by ordering him to leave Pensacola? It was too late now. All he could do was pray that Genesis' heritage might soften the hearts of these savage natives.

Genesis swallowed hard. Directing his eyes toward the leader, he said, "I want in the worst way to learn more about my mother's people. I spent much time talking with them when they came to trade in Pensacola. Some men in your village know me."

With that, the leader let down his guard and said, "I am Owl Claw. Our hunting party comes from the Owl Clan. We are Muskogee people."

"I thought you were called Creek," Genesis said, trying to remember if his mother had ever mentioned Muskogees.

"Ah, only whites call us Creek because we've always lived by the creeks. Ancestors said whites didn't know how to say all the old Muskogee tribe names like Alibamos and Hitchitis. There are many tribes; but they speak one language, our Muskogean language. Whites didn't even know difference. They just called all of us Creek." Owl Claw pushed his bow further back and said, "We followed you in our swamp hunting grounds and into the night. I sent Wingfoot and Swamp Hunter to our chief with the message that we found two white men with horses and a gun. Our chief sent them back with braves to help us. Now we take you to our people for a council meeting."

"Council meeting?"

"That's right."

"What's wrong? We didn't do nothing wrong." Genesis caught himself and added gently, "We want to make friends with you."

"Wise council members and Shaman Skytalker and Chief Wahoo are our most wise elders. They lead our clan and make all decisions. Now our elders prepare for the meeting. They must first drink the black drink to cleanse bodies. Makes thinking clear. They will make the right decision."

Genesis had heard of the drink (an elixir of holly) and how it caused heaving, vomiting, and set one's guts aquiver, emptying them. He clamped his teeth together, remembering how his mother had told him of warriors using the black drink to purge themselves before battle. She'd said it brought out their fierceness. His arms turned to gooseflesh. Hair on the nape of his neck stood up. If he were not so hungry, he'd try like hell to figure out how to fight for freedom.

Adding to Padre's dreadful condition, mosquito and black fly bites had swelled into welts, big as corn kernels, on his cheeks and arms. If only he had a few sips of water. He had been leaning, unsteadily, against the rough hickory tree trunk. He mustn't faint. Not again. He dug his shoulders into the tree trunk, its unevenness reassuring him of reality. Lacking sufficient strength for rapt prayer, Padre had no choice but to servilely count on Genesis' half-Creek heritage to soften the hearts of these savage natives.

"We go to the village now," Owl Claw said.

In a glance, Genesis noticed that when Padre tried to swallow, his lips trembled, his body shivered. Genesis' eyebrows met as he tried to sort out whether Padre's weakness and shivers were caused by deprivation during the last part of the journey or from just plain fear. Would Padre be able to travel at the natives' pace? To hell with the padre for the time being. He had himself to think about.

# THE TRIBUNAL

The band of natives crept nearer, hovering like vultures over carrion, as Padre and Genesis trudged, rigid with dread about the council meeting. Minutes seemed to stretch into unmercifully long hours. Onward they persevered, hypnotic, unmindful that the swamp was behind them. The horses, as if in trances of their own, had not reacted negatively to the natives during the capture, not even a neigh had sounded. However, wolves howled again. This time the howls came from the direction in which they were traveling.

Light, which projected from a clearing in the north, penetrated Padre's trance-like state. Increasing sunlight sharpened images and revealed a lessening of the natives' body tension. Their movements gradually became rhythmic, even though their mouths remained as tightly closed as hickory nuts. Some swayed their sharp-tipped cane spears from side to side while others swung their forbidding bows back and forth. If placed in an upright position, these bows would certainly tower above their tall, lean bodies. The fletched arrows protruded ominously from their buckskin quivers. Surely, the two natives, who carried tomahawks and whose faces had been painted red, hailed from one of the dreaded Red Stick warrior clans. Padre trusted that the others in the group belonged to a white or peaceful, clan. Ironically, the desire to escape Andrew Jackson's second invasion in Pensacola now placed him in yet another life-threatening predicament much like the one from which he had endeavored to escape. Confrontation with Jackson's scouts and ambush by rogues on the trail or displaced, hostile natives roaming the border, had been possibilities all along. However, until this encounter he had totally trusted hearsay of friendly Indians near the Montezuma Trading Post.

Open spaces overhead, which were now filled with sunlight, no longer seemed promising. Besides, Padre dared not look directly into the piercing brightness yet. At the ground level of vision, bright daisies in every sunny spot now replaced waist-high ferns and greenery that had been dappled with luminous fungus spots. It would take more than daisies to lift his spirits. Padre's spirits, again, slowly dwindled into a dreamlike condition, except for the pinch of hunger. Even fresher air failed to awaken full awareness. Neither the odor of dry earth nor the feel of dry air penetrated his forlorn senses. However, the bramble bushes, now loaded with green berries, might have attracted his interest if they had been ripe.

One thing Genesis now noticed. The natives' gait had become faster. Accompanying the change, they wore triumphant, victorious expressions. Suddenly, a native sounded wolf howls and received like howls in return. Was it a signal of some sort, perhaps that the group was getting closer to the village? And the previous wolf howls, had they been messages or real wolves?

Padre barely found energy to put one foot in front of the other. A sinister word entered his thoughts. Scalp. Not just any scalp, rather his own as a trophy of the natives' accomplishment? Perish the thought. He had never contemplated any notion of martyrdom, not yet. Abiding faith in St. Michael comforted him; and, thankfully, the natives possessed no power to confiscate it. The potential of a miracle from the archangel offered hope and sustained him though this ominous threat.

Finally, they came to a narrow stream. Owl Claw ordered, "We stop for water."

Wonderful, clear water flowed over the white, sandy bottom. With scorched throats, Genesis and Padre watched the natives enjoy drinking from their free, cupped hands. Then they watered the horses. Lastly, the prisoners were allowed to drink. They lowered themselves to the ground; and, on their bellies like serpents, they drank.

Padre cut an oblique glance at Genesis. He, too, had endured the same abysmal humiliation with each sip that their captors had swallowed. Would the natives keep their hands bound forever? Soon after resuming travel, tawny forms in the distance took on the shape of huts and houses. This, no doubt, was the Owl Clan Village. More and more Creek dwellers appeared—all ages, scantily-clad and barefoot. Little children toddled about completely naked. The curious crowd clustered, all eyes at first drawn to the crucifixes. Older boys who had been playing on the ball field, which centered the village, ran nearer, still clinging to their lacrosse racquets. They thronged around, though at a safe distance, snickering as they pointed first to his long beard then at Genesis' red beard, which had grown bushy on the journey.

Girls gathered, gushing giggles. They came closer, mocked, and taunted while jutting their heads forward and clasping their hands in back of their bodies. They then abruptly flung their free hands forward, flaunting them before the hostages' faces. Some of the frizzed-gray-haired elderly had eased nearer, gaping. Still, they always carefully positioned themselves behind the younger members.

Near nakedness of the natives appalled Padre. The women's bare breasts begat utter disgrace. What missionary would be up to the daunting task of saving such a wild, naked, or partially naked, bunch of savages from their pagan ways? Even with his extensive education and holy training, the notion paralyzed his innards.

Genesis frowned at the young men's affectionate attention to *Grandeza*. They were more fascinated with *Grandeza* and his silvery coat than with the white strangers. They took turns stroking it, and chanted that the white horse had spirit power, like an albino deer. Many people in Pensacola had admired his *Andalucian* stallion, and that had been all right. Here, it struck him like an insulting blow, for they'd seized his horse. Had he outwitted himself, instead of Sharp Knife, by deserting the garrison? And would this nightmare ever end? How?

All the while, Genesis and Padre plodded, unaware they had reached the center of the village, the area that the Muskogee called the square ground.

When Owl Claw asked them to sit cross-legged on the grass, Padre felt stricken with impropriety. A cassock, even the torn one, would have improved his sense of dignity. Would the natives return the robes in his shoulder bag? A conical-shaped building ahead intrigued him and diverted his attention.

Owl Claw ordered, "Big Brother, Big Turtle Trapper, tie the horses and bring maize for them." Then he asked a woman to bring food and drink to the white men. Most important, Owl Claw finally cut the ropes binding their wrists. While he stood watch over them, he pointed to the conical-shaped building and said, "That's the council house. Muskogee call it *chakofa*. Council members are inside. They make ready for the meeting."

An oncoming aroma set their mouths watering. Precious food arrived. A stew, in clay pots, with green beans, yellow squash, and corn dumplings touched their taste buds like a royal treat. Never had food felt so soothing. Sassafras tea sweetened with honey tasted wonderful, a surprising treat. Unidentifiable meat in the stew mattered not a whit to their growling stomachs. The wayfarers had no inclination to question it. Although the men's worn-out condition slowed their eating, it, nevertheless, gave them a chance to look around.

Padre peered more warily than Genesis. If a scalp pole abounded, he'd rather not see it. Albeit, he could not help wondering if one existed. Most importantly, his scalp mustn't be added to some grisly collection. "I never," Padre said quietly, "in all my imagination thought we'd have to go through something like this. I had dreamed of riding into the village triumphantly. Now, they're putting us on trial." His expression tightened. Ill-prepared to subsist in this wilderness, he asked, "What do you think they'll do with us?"

"My mother told me it's our people's custom. Council of Elders and the chief and shaman are elected by the people. She liked very much that the council represents will of the majority. Always, it's been that way. I worry, too, but you know everybody in Pensacola said that they're friendly. Maybe…maybe I understand how they feel about my flintlock. I guess they had a right to fear what I might do with it." If he had stayed at the garrison, it might not have been necessary to relinquish the gun to the Americans. Nevertheless, while enjoying the nourishment of the food, wild, wonderful times in Pensacola came to mind—trysts with Cleo, billiards games, even gambling.

After Genesis and Padre finished eating, the enthralled group of villagers, which had surrounded *Grandeza,* stopped their soft chattering and chanting and integrated into the semicircle near the prisoners. An air of respect permeated throughout the gathering when Shaman Skytalker appeared. He stood about fifteen feet away from the fugitives, wearing an antler headdress and an albino deerskin cape, his white hair closely matching the albino deer fur. In a way, he looked like a part of an old cypress tree under the flowing cape, with fingers like gnarled branches and feet like gnarly old roots.

To Padre, the shaman's wrinkled face had an ancient appearance, the patina of a crinkled-copper pot lid. His ceremonial prayer stick, adorned with owl feathers, doubled as a walking stick. He planted it and lifted his face toward the crowd. Unable to read the shaman's expressionless face, Padre became interested in the old man's anomalous thumbs, twin thumbs, on both hands.

Genesis figured it out and unobtrusively told Padre. "The number four is sacred for our people." Bit-by-bit, he explained how it represents not only basic elements of earth, fire, water, and air, but also the four directions, north, south, east, and west. "I betcha his four thumbs are very sacred," Genesis said and gazed forward slack-faced.

Next came council elders, who looked to be in their late thirties, each bearing an unusual physical trait. They stood in a line beside the shaman. The first one, Arrowhead Maker, had scars in the shape of an arrowhead on each cheek. The next one, an extremely tall, bony man, Tall Cane Walker, held a towering bamboo cane. The last man, short, and stocky, Turtle Shell

Dancer, held his rounded face high. Turtle shells, filled with rattling stones, were tied to his bowed legs, which bowed as much as the warriors' bows.

After a respectful lapse of time, Chief Wahoo Rope Maker appeared. Though he no longer made the rope supply, he still taught rope-making skills to young men and knew the locations of choice wahoo shrubs and trees. In addition to a huge headdress of owl feathers, he wore a series of his finest ropes in graduating sizes and lengths. These encircled his neck as well as his waist. The smallest ones, close to his neck, were finely woven from bear grass. His fingernails, long as hawthorn spines but curved at the ends, served as tools in his rope making.

Very solemnly, the chief raised his face and stretched his arms to the sun for a few moments in silence. After slowly lowering them, he looked at Owl Claw and said, "It is time for you to tell about finding the strangers and horses in the swamp forest with a gun."

Owl Claw stood straighter and explained the entire episode. "Hunters found these two white men and their horses…Wise chief sent braves to help us."

Owl Claw turned and pointed to Genesis. "The younger man said his mother is a full-blooded Muskogean. Now lives with Seminole in Florida. She taught him our Muskogean language." He looked at Genesis and commanded, "Tell our honored elders about yourself and why you come here with gun."

Genesis swallowed hard, and explained everything as he had to Owl Claw in the swamp. As he spoke he looked straight ahead at the elders, unaware that some of the village women concealed their surprised expressions with their hands when they heard he was half Creek.

Then Owl Claw turned sideways, pointed to the padre, and told how he and Genesis and had come to know each other and how in Pensacola Padre had worked for the white god religion and given help to Creek and Seminole.

Padre looked down. Embarrassed that he did not have the dignity of his cassock, he scraped at the mud on his boots.

Owl Claw said, "They make no trouble, so far."

When Owl Claw completed his presentation, the shaman nodded to the other council members and pointed his prayer stick toward the entrance of the *chakofa*. Both captives sat in rigid restraint under the watchful eyes of Owl Claw.

Padre's heart fluttered in his throat like a hummingbird, when the councilmen followed the shaman and chief inside the *chakofa* for their deliberations. He knew, painfully clear, that their lives depended on the council's decision. *Truth is I had hoped and prayed that the governor's letter to the murderous Sharp Knife would work a saving miracle. Yet,*

137

*prudence had tapped at my heart and with the grace of that powerful virtue, I prepared myself for the worst, just in case.*

Genesis strained to hear what the councilmen were saying but had no luck.

The conical-shaped structure, containing the words of their fate, mesmerized Padre. It appeared to be about thirty feet tall, with a base about fifty feet in diameter. Its support poles, bound together at the top and fanned into a circle at the bottom, had been thatched with bark, which was most probably held in place with clay mud. The shaman and chief sat within sight, beyond the entrance, and faced the ceremonial fire centering the square ground.

Genesis noticed that the shaman pointed to an eagle soaring overhead and said something to the chief like, "Our brother watches us." The eagle winged toward the horizon but made a wide loop, returned overhead, and floated, its distinctive white head shimmering in the sun. Genesis tried to remember what his mother had told him about eagles bringing messages in times of great decisions. He wished he'd paid better attention to what she had said, for now he couldn't remember just how it went.

# NOTCH

# 11

# THE VERDICT

The shaman began the meeting by holding his hands up and wiggling his four thumbs back and forth. He called on the council members to speak, one at a time, beginning with Arrowhead Maker, next Tall Cane Walker, and then Turtleshell Dancer. Finally, the chief spoke.

Other than his jaw muscles tightening, Genesis sat motionless. Soon his eyes roved, seeking any sign that could be interpreted as favorable; he strained to hear but never could distinguish enough to make sense of it. By the time the chief spoke, he noticed that Padre glared like a man waiting to be burned at the stake.

Padre's chin quivered, even in the warmth of the late afternoon sun. From within, his abiding faith cried out not to weaken now. If they would only spare his life and return his holy possessions, they could have the hatchet and knife. He would even forego the sacramental wine. It probably had been consumed already. But dear God, how he wanted his prayer book and rosary, that is, if they did not kill him. His priesthood training behooved him to lend levity to the tension. Instead, he found himself regressing, whisking his sweated brow with an unsteady hand and quietly asking Genesis, "What do you think they're going to do with us? I never dreamed we would be captured by the Creek, never would have dared dream we would be brought to trial, a trial that could mean the end for us."

"I told you. It's our people's custom. Decisions have always been made by..." he stopped in the middle of his statement. "I just thought of something. I got me a idea, a damn good idea," he said as he straightened his torso upward to a taller position. "Don't worry. I think my idea will work. If I get a chance to talk, you'll understand my plan. You know I

141

learned some cunning tricks playing cards in Pensacola. Besides, you know, they had a right to be afraid of my gun after some of the things that happened to the Creek. They might need me to show them how to use it. And they really like *Grandeza*," he said as a painful pang coursed through his guts.

Owl Claw's eyebrows furrowed with a questioning look. He came closer to the fugitives, listening intently.

Genesis paused and nervously worked his upper teeth back and forth over his lower lip. Then he said, "We'll hear soon…what they decide." He studied his newly-thought-of strategy. Might it help win *Grandeza* back? He couldn't bear to completely let go of his cherished horse.

When the chief walked forth from the *chakofa* with the demeanor of one contemplating a serious act, Padre could take little more. Still he anxiously tried his best to read something more promising into the chief's intent.

The chief summoned, "Owl Claw, bring the white men inside. The shaman will examine them for disease. We have lost too many Muskogee to white man's diseases."

All the villagers whooped and clapped.

After the examinations the chief, shaman, and council members emerged, followed by Genesis and Padre. The shaman directed Owl Claw to guide the visitors to one of the four square ground structures. There, they all sat on benches. Villagers followed.

With the comfort of having passed the physical examinations, along with the food and tea nourishing his body and soul, Padre sighed with relief. The blessed relief was like the time he had found a lost lamb, a highly prized one, in his shepherding days on the hills of *Andalucia*. Now he could look around and take further stock of the Creek Village. Buildings were located at each of the four cardinal directions of the square ground. The other three were identical to this fourth one in which they now sat; all were roofed and rectangular and appeared about sixteen feet long by eight feet wide with open fronts. The Creek had located this aptly named square ground area adjacent to the ball court. As far as Padre's eyesight reached, he saw family huts and storage huts surrounding the area. The natives had constructed their family structures with poles, mud, bark, and palmetto thatch, like the *chakofa*, but as far as he could see, only the *chakofa* bore the conical shape. "The village is so organized," Padre said, almost in a whisper. "I never envisioned such an orderly layout in this wilderness."

Genesis did not respond. He had caught a glimpse of an eagle overhead as it circled, fixed-wing and silent against the clear blue sky. The eagle cut out of its circle and angled southward, flapping its wings against the southern breeze. Again he wished he had listened more carefully to what his mother had said about the importance of eagles' messages. Had the same one returned to reiterate some mystical message? If so, what in the world might it be, especially since the eagle headed in the direction of Pensacola.

After everyone had sat on the crudely hewn benches, Shaman Skytalker arose and commanded, "Owl Claw, have the prisoners stand before the council."

Padre's stomach churned as they moved and stood a second time before the Council of Elders. *Again? What is about to take place now?* A chill shot down his spine. He hoped with all his heart that he wouldn't get that weak feeling, the kind that he had in the swamp.

Shaman Skytalker pointed his prayer stick at Genesis and asked, "Do you have anything else to say?"

Momentarily, Genesis studied. No doubt about it, the time had come when he must...he must play his trump. He'd seen men do it with real card playing in Pensacola. Now was the time. So he began: "My mother taught me about Breath Maker, taught me the language, and ways of our people. All my life I have honored Breath Maker." Now enlivened, Genesis felt like talking louder and with more authority like the officers at the garrison. He said, "My Creek blood flows strong. My greatest wish is to be accepted by my mother's people and learn more of their ways. I pray for Breath Maker to bring many blessings on the Owl Clan village. And I pray it is Breath Maker's will to let us stay here." He looked for the shaman's reaction, then the people's. Their faces mimicked the shaman's solemn response. Had his trump overridden? Would anything else hinder their acceptance?

"We can make barter," Skytalker said. "Ancestors taught us to share. We honor Breath Maker by helping visitors. But you must prove yourselves. Owl Clan gives you shelter and food. You give us the gun forever. You," he pointed to Genesis with his prayer stick, "must show us how to shoot gun. Horses and money belong to village. You may speak now."

All Padre wanted at the moment was to get away from there alive, so when Genesis shot a questioning look at him, he nodded.

Genesis had known that in the Creek tradition most goods and property are never personally owned. Why had he not thought of this earlier, and more importantly, what it could have meant in losses to him? Could he have made peace with the idea? Since he wanted so much to be approved by the people, he knew he must make a very difficult decision immediately. Was he up to it? It seemed too hard to give up so much. But he could not stand here thinking. He *must* do the right thing to get their approval. He must do it now.

Carefully measuring his words, he proceeded: "We honor your decisions," the empty spots already deepening for his treasured horse and gun.

"Come. We sit on the ground in a circle," Shaman Skytalker said. As soon as they were seated, he packed the long-stemmed medicine pipe, walked over to the sacred fire, and lit it. He took a few draws and handed it to Chief Wahoo. The chief smoked and passed it on. Each council member took a few puffs. At last Padre and Genesis were invited to participate, though the pipe had to be re-lit twice for the novices. By the time Shaman Skytalker readied the ceremonial drink of persimmon wine and offered ritual blessings, intoned petitions as well, the former captives had begun relaxing. And after the council members had sipped the wine, Shaman Skytalker invited the visitors to drink from the same vessel.

Chief Wahoo stood and waited for silence before he spoke to the gathered villagers. In a most eloquent manner he announced, "Muskogee follow teachings of ancestors. We are sharing people. We do not wish to anger Breath Maker. Our village gives food and shelter to white men as long as they prove worthy. May the Owl Clan always have many blessings." He nodded to the shaman.

Shaman Skytalker stood and with arms outstretched and the prayer stick pointed toward the setting sun said, "We have asked Breath Maker for the right vision on these white men. We have smoked the pipe lit with the fire of our Breath Maker. We obey ancestors. Our half-brother of blood," he pointed his gnarled, double-thumbed hand at Genesis, "speaks now."

The villagers looked at each other and nodded to the leaders.

Genesis returned the nod, while struggling to shield his sense of loss. The empty hole in his heart bled for *Grandeza*, but he must...he had to speak to the people. "We agree to wise Chief Wahoo's barter," he said. "We thank you." A goose egg of a lump in his craw hardened when he tried to swallow.

The people cheered and chanted. Some danced while wildly whooping.

Intensely relieved that the long process was over and saddened at the same time, Padre crossed himself and said a prayer. How could he live without his prayer book and rosary? There must be some way to negotiate the return of his beloved possessions. How he ached to ask for them but was not up to it now. With his fine education, surely he could figure out some method.

Meanwhile, Genesis ached to impress the elders. It might make a difference. He briefly raised his hands and face to Breath Maker and in a humble way gave thanks while still stifling his emptiness of spirit. Without his musket and horse he felt...incomplete...like parts of himself were missing. It stole the ground from under him, came between him and his people. Dispossessed and discouraged, what else could he do now but watch as a group of men gathered around *Grandeza*. Again, they stroked and clamored over the white spirit horse, paying little attention to Captain. One young man, after cleaning mud from one of *Grandeza's* legs, placed his lucky, silvery rock against the stallion's coat, comparing the colors. Genesis turned his head. It was too damned hurtful to watch, but in his brief prayer to Breath Maker he had done his best to impress the elders.

Several women, carrying babies on baby boards strapped to their backs, had walked away, the crying of one of the infants still ringing out. Other villagers began dispersing. Elderly men and women followed the retreat, carefully staying behind the younger people.

Genesis shielded the sunlight from his eyes with his hand, squinted, and searched. So where was the beautiful Indian princess? She ought to be somewhere in the crowd. After a diligent, full-circled sweep, he gave up. He'd seen no blue-feathered headdress anywhere. Had River Raven taken one snort of rum too many when he told the men about her at the Emerald Tavern?

A group of young women still hung around covering their mouths and snickering shyly. They mimed the visitors' beards and pointed to Genesis' saying something about the red color. When a newcomer joined them, they immediately called her attention to Genesis and started the commotion afresh.

Padre observed in surprise, whereas Genesis seemed to like the attention rather than consider it an insult.

After the council meeting Owl Claw had sent his son to fetch loincloths for the visitors. As soon as the son returned, Owl Claw said, "Visitors must cleanse themselves. We will now go to the bathing creek." Both men's crucifixes paled with the smeared mud, and their clothes were splattered with caked-on mud as well.

On the way to the creek Genesis caught sight of the shadowy image of a feathered headdress protruding from behind a pine tree. He blinked. Apparitions again? No. His stomach felt full, and the area had no eeriness about it. There! Again it appeared. For real. No dream. A woman with a blue-feathered headdress dashed elusively behind the cover of another tree, a closer one. He stood still, his mouth agape. The headdress looked as though it might belong to a princess. He asked Padre, "Did you see the blue-feathered headdress darting from tree-to-tree, following us?"

Puzzled, Padre looked around.

"To the left, Padre," Genesis whispered.

"Oh yes, I caught a glimpse. She may be the fabled princess?"

"Surefire looks like it."

When they came to the creek, Padre asked, "How on earth can a priest be expected to disrobe with a Creek princess hiding behind a tree, stealing looks?"

Before Genesis could answer, the young woman lilted out of hiding and, surprisingly, approached the padre with her eyes cast downward and handed him a square, woven object. Dumfounded, Padre accepted it. She looked up, smiled shyly, then flitted away graceful as a butterfly, completely ignoring Genesis.

Owl Claw explained: "She gave you a raffia wash mat. Women weave them. These mats do a good job of cleaning."

Genesis, astonished, put his hands to his hips and said, "Can you beat that? Hell, she didn't even look at me. But you wanna know something? I don't give a hoot." Yet he asked Owl Claw, "Was the woman a princess by any chance?"

"Yes. Yes. That's Princess Blue Heron, daughter of our chief. She always wears blue heron feathers in her headdress, the largest, bluest ones."

"I'm sure the princess doesn't understand I'm a priest, a celibate priest." Instantly Padre handed the mat to Genesis as if it were contaminated and said, "Here, take the wash mat."

Genesis refused it with unmistakable steadfastness, quickly stripped off his clothes, and waded into the creek, a strange look filling his face. But no one needed to know of his disappointment in the princess.

Although astonished by the young woman's bare breasts, Padre would have explained to her about his exalted priesthood if she had given him a chance. He froze in place while Genesis began washing himself. After moments of consideration, Padre's mind settled. She was not the only problem. All the village women wore nothing above the waist. Just how could he ever bring himself to the daunting task of teaching the Holy Word and saving these half-naked women?

He squeezed the raffia mat. It was supple. The princess must have woven it herself. She had looked up only long enough to see if he had accepted it, albeit he had forthwith sensed sadness as well as beauty in her soulful eyes.

Padre shed his muddy boots and headed for the water. He waded into the creek up to his waist, then took off his clothes, threw them ashore, and put on the loincloth, which had been provided for him. The cleansing, hair and beard included, was delicious. He couldn't get enough of the luxury. And the raffia mat worked wonderfully. The loincloth was an entirely different matter. Never had he felt so debased as when he tied the article of so-called clothing around his private area. The only good thing about it was that it was much better than sheer nakedness.

146

After bathing, he and Genesis began washing their clothes. Padre kept looking around to see if anyone might be watching how he looked in his heathen strip of covering. He asked Genesis, "Why did you refuse the wash mat? I want you to have it."

"Oh no. I don't want it. She's not 'xactly what I expected in a princess."

"But she's really beautiful."

"Hell yes, but she's older than I ever imagined. Must be as old as me. And after I thought about it, it seemed like she's got that...I dunno know...she's got that faraway look in her eyes, like she's surefire sad or something. I like the looks of them younger girls. And they seemed happy, too."

Something unforgettable about Princess Blue Heron's face grappled Padre viscerally. While he washed his clothing, her expression still haunted him. It was so...undefinable. Oh Mary, Holy Mother of Jesus, wearing this worldly loincloth and enduring this wilderness trauma...why it's a sacrilege, blocking my precious words of learning. But, blessedly, his plan to stretch time spent at the creek had worked so far. Creeping darkness already partially masked the uncovered parts of his body; with any luck at all he would dawdle with the cleaning of his boots until full darkness and then return to the village wearing the loincloth, unscathed by any onlookers.

That look in the eyes of the princess persisted in his thoughts without his being able to really identify it. So...imploring perhaps? Maybe. No, he was not quite sure. Yet, he trivialized that notion in comparison to the indecent exposure of her breasts. How could he tolerate this half-nakedness? One thing he resolved with finality. He must try to find a way to convert her from her heathen life to the Holy Catholic Word.

# BREATH MAKER

To the surprise of Padre and Genesis, the *chakofa* served not only as a meeting place for the Creek Council, but it also housed visitors. Upon entering the place, they commenced looking for the sources of reeking, alien odors, which they had noted when the shaman examined them earlier. Their sniffing led them to easily identifiable, rancid body parts of animals, baskets of herbs, and musty animal skins. From a shallow, rectangular basket of snake skins, rattles, talons, teeth, and small bones, Genesis picked out the longest set of rattlesnake rattles and counted seventeen rattles on it. Moving through the quasi-darkened surroundings, they peered at erratically shaped burls, dried mushrooms, and other strangely colored fungi, all the while maintaining a respectful distance. Genesis had no trouble identifying ceremonial dance sticks decorated with tethered fur tails, nor dried gourds and pottery inscribed with spiritual markings, nor drums; but some articles were entirely mysterious.

Padre waxed spiritually. "I have a strange feeling that these relics possess some kind of spiritual quality. It seems their power is even monitoring our integrity as we explore." Cautiously, he investigated farther. He just knew scalps lurked somewhere. Sure enough, a grisly scalp stick stood against the far wall. He covered his eyes and groaned, "That's what I feared."

"What's the matter with you, Padre? That thing's old. Hell, it looks old as the hills. The Creek around here don't do no scalping. That must have come from some other tribe. I'm going to sleep. Everything in here is dead as them snake skins."

148

Regardless of whether Genesis was right, fatigue overcame Padre's uneasiness as soon as he lay down for the night. Remaining strength carried him through only a portion of his prayers.

At first light of day he emerged from exhausted sleep. At once startled, he blinked in wonder of his whereabouts. The strange environment jogged his memory. Yes, he was in the council's meeting house. Although struck anew by its strangeness, the first night of sleeping under a roof, since leaving Pensacola, deepened his appreciation for shelter more than he could have ever imagined. What a contrast to camping outside every night and contending with the threat of venomous snakes, alligators, and other forest predators. Genesis' even breathing attested to his peaceful sleep, but he opened his eyes as usual when Padre stirred. Then he rolled over.

Still clinging to the dullness of his own drowsiness, Padre slipped into his boots and peeked outside. He searched around and only when he was sure no one was looking at him, he walked for a discreet distance and relieved himself amongst the bushes. There was no sound of a crowing rooster; instead, a beautiful, crested red bird perched on a nearby bush and sang a wake-up song. Padre listened for a few moments but could hardly wait to check his clothing, which he'd washed last evening and draped over pine saplings. Dewy spiderwebs surrounding the shirt sparkled, telling the story before he squeezed a sleeve. The heavy dew had prevented the clothing from completely drying. He looked down at his body, bare except for the heathen loincloth, and shook his head. No doubt about it, he would not only don the dewy body linen but would do it with greatest alacrity, riding breeches and shirt, too. Damp, but dignified, he gingerly walked through the dewdrop-covered grass and into a stand of trees. After meditating for a while, he decided to chant softly amidst the songbirds. For this morning's devotion, he chose a melodic plainsong of special thanksgiving.

When he returned to the council house, Owl Claw stood talking with Genesis. It was amazing how pleased Padre felt to see the man who only yesterday had ordered his hands bound and taken him prisoner.

Owl Claw had just taken the third gourd bowl from his carrying basket. He said, "I will make *sofkee* warm with the sacred fire."

"Wait!" Genesis said, "You can't heat it in gourds."

"No worry, watch me." He started forth.

"Wait. Here are the bowls," Genesis said, "you forgot the bowls."

"No, no. I didn't forget."

"But the bowls are here. The fire's out there. I don't understand."

"Shhh. Be quiet. Do not hurry your mind. You will see."

Using two sticks, Owl Claw plucked three small stones, one at a time, from the ceremonial fire, which centered the square ground. Into the gourd bowls, he placed the hot stones. The *sofkee* sizzled, and Owl Claw removed the stones.

"My mother's people surefire can't be beat for using common sense," Genesis quipped, his chest swelling with pride.

"It is amazing," Padre said. "I've never in my life seen anything cooked that way."

"Muscogee are curious. We try different ways. Learn what works," Owl Claw said. "Owl Clan ancestors passed on what they learn."

Padre and Genesis slurped the maize meal gruel from the sides of the gourd bowls just as Owl Claw had done. Then they followed his lead, scraping the sides and bottoms of the bowls with their fingers and licking them.

After they had finished eating Owl Claw said, "Today I will help chop down a tree for a new crossing log over the gully. You can watch our people as they work during this busy time. It's all right for you to walk around the village." He returned the stones to the ceremonial fire and gave thanks. In a sudden burst of energy, he gathered the bowls, tossed them into the basket, and hustled away.

"First thing I surefire want to do," Genesis said, "is check on *Grandeza*."

"Splendid idea. I heard you calling out his name in your sleep."

"I did?"

"More than once. Let's go. I'd like to give Captain a few kindly strokes, also."

Their bellies now comforted with warm gruel, they walked taller than they had for days. The visit with the horses would feed their souls. Both stallions affectionately nudged noses at Genesis and Padre. Though the men did not speak openly about it, the memories of shared companionship and endurance of the horses on the trail added another dimension of comfort on this morning.

Abruptly Genesis said, "C'mon. We better go."

The visitors proceeded to satisfy their curiosity about the Creek village.

In a low voice, Genesis asked, "Didja see Hatchet Thrower sneaking behind the trees when we came by the horses? He tested the sharp edge of his hatchet with his fingers while he watched every move we made when we was stroking the horses."

"No, but I'm not surprised. I just assumed that the elders would appoint someone to spy on us."

"Uh hm, they're probably tracking us every minute." Yet Genesis willed to have nothing bother him this day. He reveled in watching the villagers, soaked in every detail. He took great pleasure in the attention paid to him by village women who went about their chores and could not get enough of their inquisitive glances. He even enjoyed the curious children who tagged along, always keeping a safe distance.

Padre basked in the refuge of the village. Fresh air, warm breakfast, and a new start came together and added to the already perfect morning. Sunshine penetrated the dew crystals on the grass blades, filled them with the fire of opals. Little by little, heat of the sun's rays devoured these delicate jewels and at the same time dried his clammy clothing. The village looked marvelous today. Nothing threatened, not even the usual afternoon, summer showers indigenous to the subtropical climate. Here, they would be inconsequential even if thunder and lightning accompanied them.

Padre soon sensed cockiness developing in Genesis demeanor. With his bare feet and tanned chest he looked very much like a native, that is, except for his reddish hair and the beard, both of which had grown bushy as they journeyed from Pensacola. If he only knew he strutted like a peaco...No, not a majestic, fully feathered peacock, but one plucked bare, except for that loincloth and wild hair. When they encountered two nice-looking, young women carrying baskets, Padre noted that Genesis took a deep breath and projected his chest, flaunting his prowess more than ever.

"Their baskets were empty," Genesis said nonchalantly. "They're probably on their way to gather vegetables or fruit."

Padre struggled against a soaring impulse to let him know a thing or two about his own gallantry but resolved to stay regally above such a fray. He had never discussed his most personal feelings with laity and certainly would not start doing so just because he was in the wilderness.

As the visitors sauntered beyond the ball field, a bothersome sensation stirred, then mushroomed full-blown within Padre, a feeling of not belonging, as if he possessed not even a thread of relevance to the village. So vexed, he could not keep it subdued. This wilderness had isolated him. There was not another soul around whose blood was free of heathenism. The half-naked women were shocking. How could a priest perform mission work here? Surely the merciful Mother of God would show a way to overcome the savage barriers. He turned to Genesis and with a scrutinizing expression said, "You act as if the loin cloth is second nature, but I...I really have no desire to look like a native." He cleared his throat and said, "Under all circumstances, I must dignify my priesthood."

"You'll get accustomed to my people's ways," Genesis said in a cocky way. "You'd surefire look better if you'd take off your shirt and get your chest tanned. Shoot, it's surefire pale as a plucked goose." Then he squared his shoulders and whistled, carefree.

A fork in the path diverted Padre's attention from this scurrilous sting. Genesis turned to the right into the narrower trail, Padre following and the children, too, not far behind. Soon they spotted, underneath a live oak, two

151

women bent over on their knees with their hands busily engaged in some strange activity. In no time at all they saw that the women worked with hides. The visitors' cautious steps begged permission to approach and observe. Sensing it acceptable they eased forward, close enough to discern that the women held stone scrapers, which fit in their hands almost perfectly, high at the stone's center held in the palm and sloping to thin sharp edges underneath their fingers. They scraped fur from the hides with these granite stones, moving side to side and forward and backward, never bumping into one another.

Although Genesis knew they were people of few words, he asked, "How do you make the scrapers?"

"Mine was passed on to me by my mother," the elderly woman said proudly. "Anybody can make one. You pound a special rock against another one, a bigger one. Magic part, you must break it at right place," she said and smiled. "Then you must sharpen it."

The women gathered all the animal hair they had scraped off the hide and placed it into a basket. "We give this part back to Mother Earth," the older one said. "We bury it with proper rituals and ask for forgiveness for killing the deer, so no evil spirit haunts. Nothing is wasted."

The women turned the hides over, scraped away small bits of residual meat, and tossed them. Salivating dogs snapped the tidbits of carrion before they hit the ground. The smell of decaying flesh would have been obnoxious, had it not been for the open-air surroundings. Whenever an occasional southern breeze stirred, Padre took a deep breath.

The younger woman, and stronger looking of the two, split the buck's head with a tomahawk. With one sharp smack, it cracked. With a second hit, it split open. The women chirped with delight while harvesting the brains, the part of the deer that had always worked magic for them. With their hands, they scooped out the brains, dropped them into a vessel of water, and squished them. When the mixture turned a pale strawberry color, the old leader nodded. In collective glee, as if it were no chore at all, they doused the hide in the concoction. Each seemed to anticipate the other's move, always working together with incredible fluidity.

"The hide comes soft before the sun moves overhead," the elderly woman said.

"What happens after that?" Genesis asked.

The woman reached her arms outward from her side as far as they would go and said, "We stretch and stretch it." She laughed so heartily her bare breasts jiggled, and said, "And we stretch it some more...till we're very tired." Her shoulders drooped in pantomime, and her breasts hung below her waist.

Overwhelmed with modesty, Padre closed his eyes. Until this moment, he had carefully maintained his focus on the women's faces. This sight was too shameful for a priest to face. When he opened his eyes he clutched his crucifix and steadied his eyes no lower than the women's faces, while glancing from one to the other.

The younger woman had puckered up her mouth several times, apparently to say something but never got around to it. Eventually, she mustered up her courage and said shyly, "Sometimes we soak the hide in water with bark, a secret kind, and then smoke it very slowly. When it turns brown, no water will pass through. Then the hide is good for making moccasins."

Genesis thanked them for their patience and goodwill in their explanations. Padre smiled, pointed to his heart, and said, "Me, too. I thank you."

The group of curious children, that had been following them, watched for a while. They seemed to grow bored and soon departed in different directions.

Back on the path Padre craned his neck inquisitively toward what looked like a blue-feathered headdress in the distance. Unknowingly his pace had quickened, but he right away sensed awareness that Genesis had noted a difference and had cast a questioning glare at him. Padre glanced down and noticed his shadow. His face felt flush. Without the dignity of his cassock, could he approach a bare-breasted young woman and admonish her to forsake her nakedness? Nevertheless, his concern was short-lived. The young woman disappeared into the woods.

Genesis grinned and said, "You really walked fast when you saw them blue feathers."

"I did?"

"Um hm."

"Well, I'd really like to convert her to the Holy Word. How do you think I should approach her?"

Genesis shrugged. "I don't know. But I'd surefire guess she was in a hurry, or else she didn't want to talk to us."

Farther down the trail Genesis and Padre came upon pottery makers, working near the creek. Since they wore skirts, the visitors assumed they were women. Not so. Closer looks revealed that these individuals wore women's necklaces on their flat chests.

*And no,* Padre said to God silently, *I did not intentionally look for breasts.* But with deliberate intention, he looked for Genesis' reaction and then feasted momentarily on the young blade's astonishment. It was about time his cockiness cooled down. He wasn't the only man in the village wearing a loincloth. Nor could a loincloth provide enlightenment. Once again Padre delighted in the education he received at the monastery, for Brother Franco's lesson on diversity now served him well in understanding the potters' differences as contrasted with the sameness of other clan members. Genesis probably had some worldly word for this type of diversity, but maybe he would keep it in abeyance and not spoil the moment. There was so much to see and learn.

Careful not to stare at the potters, Padre admired decorative etchings of animals and plants gracing the special pottery creations, which baked in the sun. Utilitarian pieces, with mostly plain, smooth surfaces, looked good, too. The potters worked without uttering a word. All was quiet except muffled voices echoed from somewhere up creek, and a nearby mockingbird trilled one of its sweet imitations.

Greater interest in their tools led Genesis to examine a basket that was filled with bone blades of assorted sizes, bone picks, even maize cobs, as well as other design tools.

Fascinated, Padre and Genesis observed as one artisan deftly molded a stack of red clay coils until they blended into a vessel of his satisfaction, while the other's nimble fingers inscribed cryptic designs on a very, very small bowl.

"They make the trade look downright easy," Genesis said.

As the visitors walked away, an elder who had been witnessing them followed. He caught up to them, and said, "I taught the potters all about clay, where to find the best clay and where to find different colors. If you are wondering why they wear skirts, I can tell you about the rules they must follow."

"Rules?' Genesis asked.

"Yes, there are rules. If a Muskogee boy does not want to bathe in the creek on coldest winter days or to kill a deer by his twelfth *Poskita*, he cannot receive the blood of a buck's testicles on his face." The elder stretched out an arm and fanned out his hand for emphasis. Then he commenced pointing into the air with each succeeding statement: "They must keep their childish names and wear women's clothes. They live as couples but are never allowed to do men's work or share in braves' ball games or footraces."

"Some people treat diversity such as this with intolerance," Padre said. "Are they treated all right here?"

"Oh yes, yes. They possess special, secret gifts. They make very good pottery and draw sacred spirit messages on every piece."

As they walked on they passed a young woman pounding acorns with mortar and pestle of stone. When the elder noticed the visitors' interest, he said, "Acorns are boiled long, long time. Gets rid of bitter taste. Takes much time to gather them. Takes much more time to shell and pound them, too." Saliva drooled from the corner of his mouth. He swallowed and added, "Acorn cakes made with goose eggs and honey are very special."

"You are an excellent guide," Padre said. The elder flashed a look of pure joy.

Farther on, the elder's conversation returned to the potters. "The pottery makers are also very good at painting designs on buckskin. And you will see them, one day, sewing buckskin with bone awls and sinew."

"Perhaps I should visit them some time and see if they can help me sew my robe, that is, when it is returned to me. I should explain that on our way here, it got torn in the hawthorn bushes when we hid from strangers on the trail."

The elder nodded.

"So many people are busy. Is it always like this?" Padre asked.

As if speaking with the wisdom of his years, the elder answered, "Spring moons bring good time for work, before it gets too hot."

"The people work together well," Padre added, "one anticipating the other's move, without a word being spoken."

"We are people of few words. Words are sacred. It is the Muskogee way. Today I talk more to help Pensacola visitors. We always obey council decisions. We honor our Father of Breath."

Genesis nodded with knowing satisfaction.

Stopping underneath a large sweet gum tree, Padre said, "Let's sit for a rest." He cast a level gaze at the elderly Muskogee and said, "Now tell me about your Father of Breath."

"Well, sometimes we call Father of Breath another name—Breath Maker. Look up in the sky. There," he pointed, "shining brightly. There is the Father of Breath."

Padre frowned and said, "Oh, that's not a father of breath, that's the sun."

The elder gaped in shock and quickly masked his mouth with his hand.

"I would like to tell you about the true God," Padre said. "I worship the one and only true God. The true God is in the heavenly sky, too, but the true God is not the sun, nor fire. Seems you worship fire, too. That's idol worshiping. Idol worshiping is a sin."

Genesis narrowed his glaring stare at Padre.

"White man is wrong, wrong," the Muskogee said in a raised voice. "Muskogee have one God. Muskogee know that fire respresents God on Mother Earth. Fire is sacred, not an idol."

"What we see up there is the sun," Padre repeated. *"That is not God."*

Genesis groaned, lowered his head, and ran his fingers nervously through his hair.

"No, no," the Muskogee said. "Breath Maker will be angry and send evil spirits. I must tell Shaman Skytalker about this."

Padre noticed that Genesis was shaking his head with a look of dismay.

"Oh, I do not wish to upset you," Padre told the elderly Muskogee. "I had no intention of being insensitive or sounding rude. Far from that. I just needed to tell you about the true God. That is my work. That is what a missionary does. Uh, by the way, my name is Padre Morales. 'Padre' means I represent the heavenly Padre, here on earth. My mission is to tell people about God in a courteous way. I want to be your friend. Will you tell me your name?"

The elder looked bewildered but answered, "Blue Clay from the Carrier family."

"Blue Clay, I just needed to explain to you about the holy God. The one and only holy God loves you."

Blue Clay pondered and finally answered, "I need no other God. I leave before Breath Maker gets angry."

Padre glanced at Genesis and sensed rage developing. He had seen the signs in the past. He must change the course of action and change it fast.

"Please do not be upset, Blue Clay. I beg this of you. Uh, wait! I talk to you in the spirit of respect and consideration. I ask for forgiveness for any hard feelings. I would like for us to be friends."

Blue Clay did not answer as he got up to leave.

"Peace be with you. May we talk again in brotherly love?" Padre asked.

Without answering, Blue Clay lowered his head and left.

Genesis squinted directly at Padre and lashed out, "You got us in big trouble." He balled his fists, projected his head forward and said, "Now I have to talk with Shaman Skytalker. Try to make peace." He spit. "Everything was going all right after the chief got my gun and *Grandeza*. Now you make problems. And I have to try to make peace."

Padre woefully uttered, "I am truly sorry, forgive me." Then he lifted his hands in prayerful form and implored, "Holy Mother of God, what is a priest to do here? I humbly ask that you guide me out of this mire. I only tried to perform my mission." He made the sign of the cross.

Genesis glared.

Padre recoiled. Only minutes ago he had felt the pulse of excitement over the activities he had observed and the things he had learned in this Creek village. Now he worried about his status with Genesis and the clan. Would he be banished? God forbid. He was ill-prepared to subsist in the stark wilderness alone. Only a flickering promise remained. He remembered the young woman with the blue-feathered headdress, a promising candidate for conversion and certainly a reason for his being here.

156

He needed to reach her soul with the Holy Word.  Hope sustained him.  That look of searching, which her eyes certainly transmitted, was inscribed in his heart, bidding him to save her from the heathenism here.

# SHAMAN'S WISDOM

Without uttering a sound, Genesis flouted an angry expression and stomping gait until he and Padre returned to the council house. Inside, he jerked his hands upwards, braced them on his hips in an unmistakably offensive stance, and blasted out, "Why in hell didja make Blue Clay mad? *Humph*," he huffed, "you and your mission work really piss me off! When we agreed on this trip, I never expected you to make this kinda trouble for us with your God."

"Hmmm," Padre cleared his throat. "I tried to correct Blue Clay, because you know that is exactly what a missionary is supposed to do." Padre dared not speak the "heathen" word. He had seen Genesis in the akimbo posture a few times and deemed it best not to challenge him at this moment. He just watched as Genesis rapidly raked his fingers through his bushy hair, his black eyes livid.

"Don'cha understand? You surefire better understand, we don't need your God."

"But I'm here to convert to the *true* God."

"Breath Maker's been my people's God...our only God," his voice quivered with hurtful anger, "since many ancestors ago."

Padre stroked his beard in a contemplative way. "I regret that my zeal caused you such anguish, believe me. It's most regrettable." No one needed to know that in his heart he tenaciously held onto his original sentiment about dedication to mission work; so he simply said, "I am sorry to see you upset."

"I'm not upset. I'm hot as *Herr* Gunter's forging coals! Hotter than your hell. I'm hottest 'cause I have to try to make peace with Shaman

Skytalker. Everything went all right after they took my gun. They gave us a safe place to stay and food, too. Now you make this trouble." He slumped down, sat cross legged on a deerskin, and slapped his palms on his thighs. Then he heaved a deep breath of disgust and hung his head. The slap and the sigh resonated in the stark silence.

"My urge to speak my mission came naturally. I was so eager. Why, I spoke in pure spontaneity."

"Hell, take your sponta…your big word, somewhere else," Genesis said, not looking up, "like to the Montezuma Trading Post."

"Well, I had that in my mind all along. I'd like very much to go there." Padre cringed at the swearing and thought it best to bide his time for correcting the vulgar language, though it seemed he had lost all control of Genesis' behavior. He might have better results with his efforts at the Montezuma Trading Post. He said, "*Senor* Colabro might even have some news about Pensacola."

"Oh no, nooo," Genesis jerked his head up, looked at him straight in the eyes. "We won't go there now. There's something I want to get done first." He stared into space, his anger calming as he plummeted into deep thought.

Padre shot inquisitive glances and asked, "What? Uh, pardon me, did I hear correctly?" Then he watched as Genesis rubbed his hands together, his eyes brightening.

"You heard all right. I've decided I'd be more like a Creek if I had a bow, one of them real tall ones, and some arrows. Then I could go hunting, maybe with the best hunters and prove myself to the council. After that, maybe they would let me ride *Grandeza*. I'd surefire learn how to be the best hunter. You know my people share their food with us. We need to help them."

"Of course. I need to make a contribution. Perhaps I can teach some of the young people."

"Uggh. There you go again. Only if my people wish. Understand?"

"Surely, surely. Only if they wish," Padre yielded. Crestfallen and worried about his future in the Alabama wilderness, he hung his head and pondered.

Suddenly Genesis leaped up. "I have to find Shaman Skytalker. I'll try to explain you don't want to make trouble for the Owl Clan." He flexed his arm muscles and said, "Now I got me a good idea, a surefire good one," as he headed for the door.

Padre looked up in bewilderment, wondering what Genesis was up to now? Had he not only failed to interest Blue Clay in the true God, but also incited irreversible trouble with the Creek? In a conciliatory manner he said, "That meat roasting on the spits smelled awfully good as we walked back to the council house, but there'll be no food for me tonight. I'll do

159

penance—fast this evening, and pray for guidance." Wafts of the roasting meat again tantalized Padre when he stood in the doorway and peered as Genesis departed. Emptiness in the pit of his stomach started his mouth salivating, forcing him to reconsider his last statement. He needed the nourishment of at least one more meal before any fasting.

Genesis eased down on a fur skin and looked up at the shaman. He crossed his hands over his chest to conceal his pounding heart.

The old, wise one sat on a crude bench that centered a dais. With folded arms, he stared gravely as an executioner before motioning permission for Genesis to speak.

Genesis said, "I, I honor you, Shaman Skytalker," and swallowed hard. "I want to explain something. I want to explain about the missionary's mistake. You see, he'd asked Blue Clay about Breath Maker. Uh...but this is hard for me to say." His forehead furrowed. "Before I tell you all about it, I'd like to ask you about something else. I've come to you for help for myself. Um, I need advice. I want to look more like a brave and learn how to be a true brave. I'd like to make a bow and some arrows...want to make them just like Owl Claw's. I, I need to learn how. I wish to make them just right. And there's one other thing I want to tell you." He caught a deep breath, hoping to find his most suitable voice, and said, "I really need a Cree...or I mean a Muskogee name." Then his pounding heart sank at the sight of the shaman's cold stare.

Motionless and wordless, the shaman still gazed with a faraway stare. Finally, he wiggled his gnarly, twin thumbs, adjusted his sitting position, and said, "Young man, the council decided that you must prove yourself to the Owl Clan. And, you must be studied in order to earn a fitting Muskogee name. This takes time. We are patient people."

"Sure, sure," Genesis nodded while trying to conceal his fear. He said, "I will try hard to prove myself."

Then he felt his chances might be improving. The shaman seemed to be giving a silent message for him to continue speaking. He said, "I am ready to learn. Is it all right to ask if the Owl Clan will teach me? I want my Muskogee blood to flow true and brave."

"Owl Clan braves make bows and arrows the honorable way," Shaman Skytalker said. "Young men use weapons of braves until they prove themselves. They must kill a fox or a bobcat. Bobcats' guts are strongest for bowstring, but you have a better chance of finding fox." He cleared his throat and raised a set of his double thumbs, pondering. Then he said, "Kits were born about two moons ago...already weaned by now. But it's not the right time for you to make a bow and arrow. Muskogee are in no hurry. First, we learn about you. We watch."

Genesis listened intensely, and though his high expectations tumbled, he would try another angle. He said, "There's something else. My beard...it's not right." Stroking it he said, "It grew longer than a wild hog's snout while we traveled from Pensacola. Needs to be shaved. I need some bear grease for my hair, too. And if it's not too much to ask, could I get my hair braided like the braves? And um, there's just one more thing. Will you, wise Shaman...will you help me and ask for Breath Maker's blessings, so I can learn to be a brave?"

The shaman smiled a scant smile and cogitated. Something about Genesis pleased him. Finally, he nodded. "We can help you cut your beard and grease and braid your hair." At once, he sent a messenger for Arrrowhead Maker as well as Owl Claw and his sons.

Now Genesis had to own up to the worst part of his mission. How he wished to just skip over it, but he had to get the job accomplished. While waiting the arrival of the braves, Genesis haltingly explained the padre's challenge to Blue Clay about Breath Maker not being the true God.

The old, wise one listened as if compassionate, appearing to take a genuine pleasure in Genesis. Yet, he said, "Muskogee must not act in haste. Time will tell what is in the missionary's heart and what is in your heart." Then he scrutinized Genesis and deliberated for what seemed like an awful long time. Eventually, he said, "You came to our village only yesterday. We cannot help you make a weapon yet." He raised his arms, wiggled his four thumbs, and added, "Ahh, since you are our half-brother in blood, we'll let you practice with one of Owl Claw's bows and his arrows. And if Owl Claw and Arrowhead Maker approve you, you may use their weapons but only to hunt for your fox and only under their watchful eyes."

By the time the Owl Clan members finished with the barbering and grooming, Genesis knew that he not only looked more like a Muskogee brave but surefire smelled more like one. The changes felt so right. The sentiment swelled and his chest expanded when Owl Claw promised to one day show him a fox lair in the gallberry thickets.

Shaman Skytalker sent Owl Claw's sons for food. Roasted turkey and corn cakes along with a gourd of cold water filled Genesis' growling stomach. His passion for clan acceptance sharpened more acutely than ever.

After eating they went outside. Genesis practiced with Owl Claw's bow and arrows until daylight dimmed. Owl Claw helped him keep his left arm straight and his right one pulled back, arrow, tight against the guts, ready to sing and fly. Genesis tried with all his heart to perform exactly as he was mentored. Never would he admit how strained his arm muscles had become from drawing the powerful tension in the bow but savored relief when darkness prevented further practice.

161

By the scant light of the high-hanging stars and a slice of the moon, Shaman Skytalker listened as the group planned a fox hunt for the following morning. Then he joined them in spinning hunting tales. After a while he yawned and stood, signaling the end of the stories.

"When the right time comes," Arrowhead Maker said, "I'll teach you how to make the sharpest arrowheads of all the Muskogee clans."

To Genesis' surprise, the shaman said, "The braves can take their half-brother on the hunting trip tomorrow morning." Genesis couldn't have been happier. Before they departed for the evening, Skytalker performed a short ritual blessing for a lucky hunt.

As Genesis approached the council house the following morning, Padre perceived him to be in a terribly disgruntled mood and asked, "What's wrong?"

"Early this morning the braves took me on a fox hunt. Owl Claw showed me the gallberry bushes where a red fox hides. I was crouched just like Owl Claw showed me with my weight on my right knee and my left one upright for balance. When twigs rustled, two wild eyes glared, and I just knew this was the fox for me. The critter curled its mouth, and I jerked the bowstring. Just when I let the arrow fly, he snarled; his mouthful of sharp, shiny teeth snapped. And believe me, that little devil looked like he laughed at me, a real mean laugh, and jumped in mid air with all four legs drawn together. That fox bolted away so fast, all I saw was a furry red streak. The arrow stuck in the damn empty nest. Hell, I couldn't even look at Owl Claw."

From the moment Padre had first glanced, strangeness of Genesis' new appearance struck, preempting his tale of woe. Padre attempted to mask his startled reaction to the clean-shaven face and braided hair, which shone and emanated the stink of rancid bear grease. Since Genesis had returned in the darkness the previous evening and left in the early morning for the hunt, Padre had not been unaware of any changes save for the foul smell.

Heavens above, only a person with heathen blood would want to look and smell like Genesis. Though the villagers seemed to think of a priest as a bit odd, he preferred carrying that sort of label rather than having any remote connection to savagery. With an air of self-satisfaction, he clasped his hands and awaited the unfolding of Genesis' story. He had suffered enough since Genesis had gone to visit the shaman the previous afternoon, worrying what the outcome of that meeting would be and even what his fate would be after the episode with Blue Clay.

Genesis kicked up a cloud of dust. Then he suddenly slumped beside the council house and muttered, "I'm disgraced. Owl Claw has to take me hunting again tomorrow." He spit, the spittle carrying a generous eight feet.

But he would not admit to his aching arm, nor that even before today's hunt his arm had ached from the previous evening's practice.

Padre strained to show an expression of compassion. After all, the sooner Genesis killed a fox and crafted his bow and arrows, the sooner they could go to the Montezuma Trading Post. So, he listened attentively.

"Owl Claw told me that my spirit has to feel the fox's spirit. The spirit will guide my sense to the direction where I think the fox will run. And my arrow must aim more toward that direction, not to where the fox is when I first see 'em. Learning how to gauge that distance for moving my arrow, that's the part where the brave proves himself."

"You'll learn that skill. You just have to practice. Already, you look as brave as any Creek. I smelled that bear grease the minute you crept in last night." Smiling, he said, "Just think, only two days ago that odor scared the wits out of us."

At that moment, he remembered something else—not from the recent past, rather from the distant past—Genesis' first stubble of beard and the accompanying change in his voice. "Don't worry," Padre said, "You're doing a lot of things right. Today, Shaman Skytalker spoke with me in a friendly way when I explained to him about my conversation with Blue Clay."

"I have to tell you that *I'm* the one that did a lot of explaining to the shaman about the trouble you made with Blue Clay." Genesis sat upright and said smugly, "And maybe I'm not flat-out disgraced. People treat me like I'm important when I'm around *Grandeza*. He's really sacred to the people."

In a flash, his expression shifted and he said, "But something else is sticking in my craw. My gun, I mean it *was* my gun. Owl Claw told me that today when the sun moves toward the west, I must show the council members how to shoot it. And it's the worst day, since the fox made a fool of me this morning. I wonder what the braves think about me." He hung his head. "The chief and shaman will watch, and you know how their eyes gore right through a person, sharp as a bulls' horns." He looked up at Padre, squinted through the sun's rays, and said, "You can come with me. I'm having a hell of a day. Maybe if you come along, I'll get the gun loaded without getting addled. Shoot, in muster practice at the garrison, I got to where I could surefire load my flintlock as fast as any soldier."

"Genesis, it seems you are striving for happiness without thinking how important challenges are for self improvement. Facing and struggling with challenges brings satisfaction of accomplishment or at least the feeling of having given your best effort. Feeling good about yourself is like the growth of any good thing. It is not just a seed. It is the fruit of the seed after all the work of cultivation."

163

"Well, c'mon, watch me surefire try to do some cultivating."
Padre followed.

# WHISTLING ACORN

Earlier, the council had agreed on a location, beyond the cornfields, for the musket-shooting demonstration. There, the elders quietly assembled. The chief held the gun. The chief and the shaman were shielded by council members who huddled on each side. Chief Wahoo summoned Genesis. When Shaman Skytalker held up his hands and wiggled his twin thumbs, Chief Wahoo handed the gun and powder horn to Arrowhead Maker and said, "We will face south, away from the village." After Arrowhead Maker aimed the Spanish flintlock toward the south, Genesis slowly loaded it. Owl Claw hovered over Genesis' right side and Tall Cane Walker over the left.

With his most sincere earnestness, Genesis called up the surefire loading power he had achieved while drilling at the garrison. It would be a whole lot easier if he were holding the gun in his own hands. Chief Wahoo, Shaman Skytalker, and council members clustered closer, gleaning each nuance as he poured the powder into the barrel. His sweaty fingers mustn't slip. Still, he foolishly dropped the ball. With a quick grab, he retrieved it and slid the ramrod into the barrel as smoothly as poking a bear-greased finger into his hair. Somewhat relieved he said, "It is very important to hold the gun very tight against the shoulder." In an effort to demonstrate the form for the best shot he said, "I will show you first by using a stick." He picked up a stout stick and substituted it for the gun in his mock demonstration. Stems of dried-up milkwort crunched as Genesis planted his feet securely, snugged the stick to his shoulder, and with a firm grasp mimed the correct shooting stance.

Then he punched the end of the stick into the ground and leaned toward it for support. "I must warn you," he said, "the blast will be very loud and there'll be lots of smoke." He watched carefully as Arrowhead Maker raised the long rifle and braced it against his shoulder. Genesis insides quivered, but he would keep that weakness hidden. He couldn't bear another mistake, not two of them in one day. He fiercely wanted the flint to be true and to prove his cleverness in surefire loading. If only he had a lucky piece of some sort to help. He had never felt this shaky at the Pensacola garrison.

Finally, the blast thundered, amplifying in the still air like lightning crashing against a monstrous tree. Orange flames and sparks flared. Black-bellied clouds of smoke billowed. The air smelled like one big outhouse. A passel of cawing crows squawked madly and flapped away from the site. Squirrels scampered for cover. Rabbits darted fitfully. Although the Creek men barely flinched, women's primal screams and wild wails echoed from the village.

Arrowhead Maker handed the flintlock to Chief Wahoo and said, "I'd like to shoot it again, but gunpowder is too scarce."

Genesis breathed with relief, still clutching onto the stick as if he needed it for support. He imagined he'd gained in favor with the council when the flintlock fired on the first try. Yet gnawing pains, of his failure to kill the cunning fox, returned in his stomach. He clinched the stick. Aha, it was lucky. He would keep it by his bed, squeeze it tight, while he formed the image in his head of his arrow killing the fox.

Padre had seen enough. Realization that these villagers were among the most insular, unprogressive members of the Creek nation had now been further substantiated. His woes worsened. Genesis had achieved some degree of fulfillment and success with the Creek by simply demonstrating the firing of the gun and changing to a tribal-like appearance. Padre felt the sharp contrast. He was nonachieving, dormant as a peach tree in winter. True, Princess Blue Heron might be of a disposition to listen to his teachings, but he had not been able to get within earshot of her. Perhaps he, too, should visit the shaman for advice.

The following day, unable to face even Padre, Genesis hid in thickets near the *chakofa*. News had probably already circulated among all the clansmen that even though he had loaded the gun for sure firing yesterday, he had again failed to kill the fox this morning. A cloud of shame still surrounded him. He chewed on a pine needle, studied, and finally set his mind in its strongest will. *I'm surefire more cunning than the slyest fox in the Alabama Territory. And I surefire have Creek blood flowing in my veins, plenty of Creek spirit, too.*

166

Later in the afternoon, Big Brother, a compassionate individual by natural inclinations, found Genesis sitting amongst the scrub pine thickets, scratching his head with a twig. Big Brother sensed his pain and talked with him about ways, which would help in killing a fox. "If you get many yellow jacket stings, as many as you can take without showing a sign of suffering, it strengthens your spirit," Big Brother said. "The more stings you can bear, the stronger your spirit gets. If you are willing, I will take you to a nest."

Genesis wanted to talk about his dream, tell Big Brother it'd appeared so plainly in his dream last night how his arrow had hit a fox exactly at the place where he'd felt it would run. Instead, he decided that might sound like only weak talk, like he was trying to delay the yellow jacket stings. He knew he must answer bravely; so he said, "I'll surefire go."

On the way to the yellow jacket nest, Big Brother stopped at a sassafras tree and harvested a thickly leafed limb. When they came to the nest, Big Brother walloped it with the limb and vaulted away. A cloud of yellow jackets swarmed.

Genesis gritted his teeth. The loincloth gave very little protection. He hoped his tightening jaw muscles did not show cowardice as he suffered sting after sting. He willed himself to stand still…just to endure one more sting…then another…and the next one, too. The piercing pricks came quicker and quicker and pained more and more. Could he hold his feet for another second? Or would he have to dash away? Before he gave up, Big Brother said, "Now, your spirit is stronger. Come here."

Shivers of relief ran through Genesis when Big Brother fanned away the yellow jackets with the leafy sassafras limb as they hastily moved farther away from the nest.

"I will take you to a hole where cold spring water runs. It will make you feel better."

After Genesis soaked in the soothing coolness, Big Brother said, "Take some of these sacred leaves from this sassafras limb. Crush them and rub them on the bites. Makes swelling go down."

The moisture from the leaves felt comforting and smelled lemony.

Before returning to the village, Big Brother said, "Here's my magic rock." Handing it to Genesis he said, "It has spirit powers. Before you leave for the next hunting trip, face the east, turn the point toward Breath Maker, and rub all four slick places. Then pray for ancestors' spirits to help you kill a fox."

Genesis accepted it and stared in awe at the thin blue stone that fit perfectly in the center of his palm. It felt…sacred. It would surely help him. So proud he had withstood the yellow jacket stings to Big Brother's satisfaction, he believed that the lending of the lucky stone was further proof of the brave's favorable feelings toward him. He thanked Big Brother in his most honest way, for he seemed like a true brother.

Over and over, Genesis massaged the magic rock, seeking its powers. He prayed to the ancestors as Big Brother had instructed. On the next hunting trip, he felt ever so ready. His feet glided along the trail as smoothly as his fingers swept over the magic rock. The round, spring moon sparkled through the branches. And he felt as brave as any hunter, lean and hungry, hungry for the makings for a bow. All he had to do was prove that he could outfox the fox. Suddenly, Owl Claw signaled for the hunters to stop. An owl had flown across the path. Owl Claw said, "The sacred owl warns us of bad luck. We must go back to the village." Genesis walked close to Owl Claw as they returned to the village to gain even more bravery.

One lucky morning Genesis finally slew a fox, an exceptionally fine one with a healthy coat of red fur. It would make a fine pelt. Owl Claw taught him how to use all parts of the fox, wasting nothing and warning that the ritual of asking forgiveness for killing the animal must receive foremost importance. It had to be performed correctly, so that the spirit of the fox would not haunt the hunter.

The rendering process took days. After the fox hide, entrails, bones, and all other parts had been preserved, Genesis told Owl Claw, "Now I'm ready to chop a small tree for a bow, maybe one of these pine saplings close by."

"Nooo, no," Owl Claw said. "You must use strong wood. Oak is strongest, and canes are best for very straight arrows. I will show you where the best canes grow."

Meanwhile, Padre yearned for some type of holy symbol. Every precious Catholic belonging, except his shell crucifix, was in the satchel that the natives had seized. When Genesis felled the small oak tree for his bow, a strong desire possessed Padre to make a cross. Showing his willingness to honor the tradition of not wasting anything, he said, "If there is any wood left over from the tree, I'd like to use it for a cross."

While Genesis crafted his bow and arrows, Padre worked on his project. Using the straightest, leftover limbs of the young oak, which Genesis had harvested, Padre made a cross about five feet tall. He slashed notches in two limbs to form the joint for the cross and bound them at that point with buckskin strips. This sacred symbol brought a much-needed sense of accomplishment to Padre, as well as great spiritual comfort.

A full cycle of the moon had passed swiftly since Genesis and Padre had arrived at the Creek village. Increasingly warmer days forced them to speak with Owl Claw about the possibility of finding cooler living quarters. The council house simply did not have enough ventilation. And Padre silently yearned for an appropriate place for his wooden cross.

"I know where there's a vacant summerhouse." Owl Claw said. "Maybe you could use it for a while, at least during the hottest weather."

"Why," Padre asked, "is the house vacant?"

Owl Claw hesitated for a few moments. "Well, one day," he said, "Whistling Acorn's wife threw all his belongings out on the ground."

Padre and Genesis looked puzzled.

"Do you know what that means?"

"Haven't ever heard of such a thing happening," Padre answered.

"Not me either," Genesis said.

"All right, I will tell you." He spit and swiped his hand over his mouth before saying, "It means she divorced him."

Padre couldn't help asking, "Did he commit something really evil?"

"In Muskogee tradition," Owl Claw faintly smiled, "wife's family is boss. Whistling Acorn did not fit into her family's way. And he failed to change. They banished him without an ear of maize. He has to live alone in the woods unless another tribe lets him join."

Genesis grinned.

Padre grimmaced thinking how close he might have come to banishment in his encounter with Blue Clay.

Forthwith, Owl Claw made arrangements with Whistling Acorn's former mother-in-law for the visitors to move, temporarily, into the vacant summerhouse. How they welcomed the relief of fresh air! At the new location, Padre chose a tree upon which he rested his cross. He carefully selected, not the closest one, rather one a few yards away for privacy in worshiping. Yet he made sure the cross was close enough, so he could see it from the house.

On the first morning that he went to the cross for devotions, he caught sight of blue feathers, familiar ones. No, not small ones of a jay bird jutting toward the sky, but large, lucent ones belonging to the elusive princess. He clearly saw the feathers as she eased from around a tree. His heartbeat quickened. The cross must have intrigued her. How fortuitous that he had thought of making it and placing it a short distance from the summerhouse; surely, it drew her presence. What an excellent opportunity to explain his mission. He motioned for her to come hence, but the notion had come to him too late. She had already fled.

After Genesis finished his bow, he ran his hand over the entire length, admiring it one more time, proudly, very proudly, before he handed it over to Owl Claw. He had scraped it with a sharpened shoulder bone of the fox until it shone. Then he attached the bowstring of the dried fox guts just as Owl Claw had shown him. For the time being it must be kept by the council. And as promised, Arrowhead Maker began teaching him how to make the finest arrows as well as sharpest arrowheads. Genesis swallowed the hurt each time Owl Claw turned one over to the council for safekeeping. When would they approve of him, so he could get his bow and arrows back?

Padre noticed Genesis' dejected mood and said, "For some time I've wanted to tell you something you might not be aware of."

Genesis stared at him inquisitively.

"Your life hasn't been all that bad. As a matter of fact, you have reaped many benefits from the two distinctly different cultures of your heritage. Right over there," Padre pointed, "Your leather boots from Spain—heavens above, you used to keep those boots blackened, black as the pupils of your eyes. Now look at the dust on them, layers of it."

"Uh hm, you might as well go ahead and remind me that my Pensacola clothes, like my breeches and shirts, came from the Forbes Trading Post. My mother did some preaching, too. What was it that she always said? It was something like our people always wore buckskin, but you haven't worn much of it in your life. She'd shake her head and keep on about how times have changed. She said that when you need clothes, you don't go hunting for deer. She felt real bad that I never saw how our people cure the skin. My mother should see me now. She'd be real proud that I wear a buckskin loincloth and how I've learned to live like a Creek. I look a whole lot like a full-blooded one, too."

Padre tipped his head in his usual way and said, "You're right, except for your auburn hair. It's the identical color of the streaks in your father's gray hair."

"Dammit, I wish you hadn't mentioned my father and mother in the same breath."

"And why on earth...?"

"Never took a hankering to talking about it. But...well...now that I'm nineteen I can come right out and tell you. Lotsa times I felt like no more'n a piece of rotten meat when I'd think about not having a father around. If I woulda had a father around, I coulda bragged about him like Squeaky Thomas used to brag about his father. But remember, we was speaking of my mother. And I don't like thinking about the time I yelled at my mother when she talked about my store-bought clothes."

"You make a valid point that you had no reason to yell at her. However, the old axiom we have discussed so many times still holds true: We learn by making mistakes."

"Hold up. I'm surefire not ready for no preaching."

"I do not wish to belabor the issue, but it is beyond my understanding why you are being so hard on yourself. That incident with your mother seems like a rather normal part of growing up."

"Well, I ain't no jellyfish, no kind of way. I'll match my backbone with anybody. But I still feel terrible 'cause that's when she first said she'd been thinking about going south with her friend Wahola and another Seminole to Chief Penawa's Tribe. Said times was changing too fast around Pensacola. They was planning to take a runaway slave with them. Wasn't long till she and my sister left with them."

"Your mother is probably very content in her surroundings closer to nature. And you are finding family-like contentment here at the Owl Clan." Padre couldn't help wondering what this realization about Genesis boded for him.

# MONTEZUMA TRADING POST

"Now will you agree to go to the Montezuma Trading Post with me?" Padre asked as soon as Genesis completed his weaponry.

"I'll surefire make good on *my* word. I know you really want to go there. Wouldn't mind going there myself to see the *senor*, the trading post, too, but I have to find out if we can get permission."

The council agreed for Owl Claw to escort them to the long-awaited destination.

What a grand reunion Genesis would have actually riding *Grandeza*. Until now, he could only stroke the prized stallion. On the appointed day of departure to the trading post, freshness of the early morning air added to his anticipation. Captain and *Grandeza* had been well fed and groomed by the young braves of the village. Genesis' heart warmed as he talked to his beloved *Grandeza*, and the horse nudged his head against Genesis' chest with obvious familiarity and affection. But soon the warmth of his heart cooled and humiliation set in. Riding double, he had to take second position on the horse, behind Owl Claw. He was not alone in his lowly status. Padre, too, rode in second position with Owl Claw's eldest son taking charge of Captain's reins.

Beyond the wooded trails they reached the top of a roughly flattened ridge. Blackberry bushes, loaded with berries in all stages of maturation— small green ones, medium-size red ones, as well as some large black ones— flourished along the sunny trail. Padre impulsively reached for a perfect specimen and narrowly missed. Again he reached and again missed his lush-looking target, which brought to mind Genesis' missing the fox on his earliest hunting trips. "Can we stop for a minute and taste the berries?"

Padre asked. "These are the plumpest, purplest blackberries I have ever seen."

The entire riding party began relishing berries. Padre briefly staved off a stirring clash, between his heart's hasty bidding him to the trading post and his wish to savor a few more berries, by darting glances intermittently down at the village and saying, "What a marvelous view of the entire village." His berry craving won out for a few added minutes by making further small talk. "There are more houses in the village," he said, "than I ever imagined."

"Each family," Owl Claw said, "has a summer house like the one you are living in."

"I've noticed that," Padre said, "but from here you can see how they are all neatly arranged in groups of four that surround the fire in the center ground. "Is it really necessary for each family to have four huts?"

"Yes. We need them. You already found the need for a summerhouse. Then for cold weather each family has a winter lodge with a cooking place, a maize crib, and a storehouse."

"You are right. I surely found out why a summer house is needed," Padre said. "However, our summer house stands alone."

"Whistling Acorn and his wife did not live together long enough to build the others."

Padre looked out over the verdant vistas. Then he pointed with his berry stained finger and said, "From my viewpoint, when I am inside the village, I would have never known about all those outlying gardens and fields." The berries tasted so sweet, he had to maintain conversation until he could eat a just few more, even at the expense of sounding like a simpleton. "What are the objects hanging from the tree limbs by the gardens?" he asked.

"Babies are in leather pouches. Their mothers bind them to cradleboards and put them in pouches while they work in gardens," Owl Claw answered.

Padre smiled a purple-toothed smile. It might be beneficial to flatter Owl Claw. Padre popped a another berry and said, "Muskogee are bright people. I keep thinking about the way they run the clan. It's really fair, with the people electing all the leaders." An even stronger thought came to his mind, the ultimate compliment. "Some of your ways, especially like curing hides, are tried and proved. We call this method scientific."

"Yah, we learn by trying out different ways. We are very curious. We learn what works best."

"You didn't mention about our people's respect for the earth," Genesis said, directing his attention to Padre before hurling a handful of berries into his mouth.

"Oh yes. I'm really impressed with that, too, all your reusing of materials and all your giving back to the earth. It's truly amazing."

Owl Claw seemed pleased and answered, "Muskogee always look ahead for future generations."

Genesis' impertinence of breaking into every conversation lately, always adding a remark, bragging about his Creek heritage, aroused Padre's ire. If the young blade only knew that he was behaving like a...a footlicking sycophant for the Creek people. However, Padre would not allow these displays to spoil this long-awaited day.

As they jostled along, Padre's memories of the pact, which he'd made with Genesis to reach the trading post together, now came alive. He looked over proudly at the crucifix he had carved for Genesis as a symbol to seal their pact. His spirits soared. Owl Claw had just said the trading post would soon come into viewing range. Though Padre wished he had his cassock, he would not let that frustration interfere with the satisfaction of accomplishing his goal today. He lifted his own shell crucifix and kissed it in anticipation of future mission work at the Montezuma Trading Post.

"Yee hah! Hear that, Padre?" Genesis asked. "We're getting close."

"Sounds like sweet music to my ears," Padre said, allowing himself a smile of exultation for the nearness of their destination. Water rushing over the giant boulders at the river's falls resounded in the air. The river's roar over the falls set his blood rushing as well. Soon, they rounded another river bend, and the trading post loomed into view. Though it stood a few hundred feet south of the river's waterfalls, the roaring sound swept full force through the open river path toward them without diminishing a whit.

After they dismounted, Padre's excited heart pounded as Owl Claw and his son tethered the horses. First, he absorbed the panoramic view of the trading post nestled on the river's edge. Then he focused on the thatched-roof, log structure, which peacefully centered a sand scallop by the river. In a spirit of gratefulness, Padre crossed himself and stroked his shell crucifix. His eyes glided to the clear blue sky and abundant sunshine overhead, then moved downward toward the pine warbler calls which filled the air. However, not a single green or yellowish feather could be distinguished amidst the dense, long-leafed pine needles.

Padre chose to become familiar with the area while the other three men took a walk. He was unsure whether just one or all of them needed relief, but as for himself, he was pleased he had not eaten one more of the sumptuous berries. Nature's diversity in this area of the Alabama Territory amazed him. Pine-covered, red clay hills gently sloped down to the river valley and met contrasting flat swathes of white sand. Patches of river cane thickly edged the banks as far as he could see, save for one sparse space through which he viewed a doe swimming to the far shore and then prancing into obscurity. Into this sparsely spaced canebrake he walked and impulsively grabbed a monstrous cane. It was so large that he felt an urge to test whether his hand might reach around it. Then he heard the voices of the returning men, so he rejoined them.

"Much cane grows along the banks," Owl Claw said. "Ancestors called this part of Mother Earth *Econneka*. It means land of canes. Whites' way of saying it is 'Conecuh.' They call this river the Conecuh River. Muscogee call it the River of Cane."

"Oh, I coulda told you that a long time ago," Genesis said, with a telltale grin that revealed the blackberry feast. "C'mon, *Senor* Colabro's surefire going to be surprised when we walk in. It always seemed like he was kin to me in a way."

As they strode toward the open doorway, warm sand sifted through Padre's cracked boots. Momentary nostalgia brought a twinging pang for the Pensacola Beach. Owl Claw led the way to the log building and peered inside the doorway. A familiar sound of loud snoring wafted. Just as the three of them entered the post, Genesis yelled, "Look, there's the *senor*."

The snoring stopped. *Senor* Colabro snapped shut his wide-open mouth, fast as the behemoth alligator in the swamp. He shook his head, stirred out of his catnap position, and stuttered intermittently, "Well...well, lookee here. I, I'll be a donkey's do da, 'cause I know I'm...I'm dreaming. My eyes...they play tricks on me."

"No dreams. No tricks," Genesis beamed.

The *senor* levered himself against a barrel and scuffled to his feet. With both arms outstretched, he met and embraced Genesis, then Padre. The three of them quickly stepped back and studied each other. Owl Claw and his son observed silently.

The *senor* smiled, his tobacco-stained teeth showing and said, "I'm mighty glad to see you all."

"Have you had any news from Pensacola?" Padre hastily inquired. "I've been wondering if the American general invaded again or what happened? He was headed there with over a thousand men to invade again. That's the reason we left the garrison."

"Good Lord Almighty, is that right? I'm awfully sorry I can't help you out about the news. Haven't run a raft to Pensacola for...at least two months. Get more money for skins in Mobile. Maybe we can fetch news for you pretty soon. I wouldn't mind running my next raft to Pensacola and seeing for myself what happened. If the Americans took over, we could get good prices for our goods, especially the logs. First, we need to cut many more logs. You can see. The workers were sleeping. They want siestas when the sun is so hot overhead."

175

"I have prayed every day for the safety of the people at the Pensacola garrison and for St. Michael's parishioners," Padre said. "I worry about dear old Padre de Galvez and Father Mulvaney, too. I am anxious, very, very anxious, to hear what happened."

While the *senor* questioned them, satisfying his curiosity about how they had left the garrison, and journeyed through the great forest, Padre looked around for candidates for missionary work. What an incredulous sight of miserably slim pickings! The motley white crew, comprised of three rugged roughnecks, sounded rowdy as they awoke. Now completely aroused out of their sleep, they uncorked rum jugs, in full view, and started gambling with three Creek men who appeared to be hired workers. From all directions, tobacco juice fired into the once white sand.

River Raven, the Creek, with whom Genesis had talked while in Pensacola, had aroused from his nap first and readily recognized Genesis. He jumped up and dashed over to join the greetings. Padre took a second look at him, sizing up his credibility, since he was the individual who told Genesis about Princess Blue Heron.

Odors of rancid, musty hides with foul-smelling residual carrion intermingled with rum and snuff. The smells prompted Padre to edge toward the breeze that he felt coming through the rear exit. To avoid stepping into tobacco spit, he jumped this way and that, dodging most of the spots that desecrated the natural floor of white sand. Padre swallowed hard trying to deal with the shock of seeing neither goods nor any person favorable, other than *Senor* Colabro and River Raven. Even if he had his silver coins, there were no wafers nor wine to purchase for celebrating the Eucharist. For distraction against his disappointment in the Montezuma Trading Post, he tried to count the hides and in desperation attempted to count the burs on the sand-loving weeds (sandspurs) along the edges. They had snuck their heads inside, from under the lowest logs, and had grown much paler green than those outside.

When Padre looked out the back exit, other surprises jolted his senses. A Creek woman stirred a cooking pot. Odors inside the trading post had completely overpowered the pleasant cooking smell. Closer to the riverbank, three sturdy-looking Creek women were in the process of tanning hides in the shade of a huge, live oak tree. At the edge of the river, two more native women, younger ones, sat talking and giggling softly while combing their long black hair. Apparently they had just bathed themselves.

"Up yo ass ya holy one. Don't be taking a fancy to the womenfolk," the tallest of the rowdies said. "Them women belong to us."

"I'm a priest, so don't worry. My only interest is in saving their souls."

When the man scudded to his feet, Padre hurried back toward *Senor* Colabro and the group, his eyes fixed on the vile trading post workers. They had turned the *senor*'s welcome into a disgusting situation. The youngest-appearing of the white men, probably in his early twenties and already missing his front teeth, very likely from a drunken brawl, pointed to Padre. He cracked, "Didja have ya balls cut off?" Then he stood, stamped his feet, and roared with laughter.

The stout, pock-faced one, with snuff drools at each corner of his mouth, slapped his thighs and laughed. Then he said something lewd about the praying fool faking virginity. That remark roused the other two into uproarious laughter.

Padre recoiled. Had he entered the jaws of Hell? Surely a name like Sodom and Gomorrah would be more appropriate for this trading post.

Owl Claw and his son watched with amusement. Padre took a second glance at the Creek worker whose fingers were minus the final digits. Owl Claw whispered, "The penalty for sleeping with another brave's wife." Padre surmised that the other two natives might have, also, been banished from their clans for some transgression.

Apologetically, the *senor* said, "It's hard to get workers in the backwoods of this territory." He twined his mustache and added in a low voice, "They can outswear, outdrink, outfight any saloon bawdies in Pensacola. Try to overlook their bad manners. I've not got much control over them. But I need their help to run the trading post." He paced back and forth a few steps, rubbing the nape of his neck and swearing under his breath.

Bitter disappointment over the prospects for missionary work at the trading post area sent Padre's high spirits tumbling into utter despair. He asked the *senor*, "Are there any white settlers nearby?"

"You might find a few squatters here and there piddling around, trying to eke out a living selling hides, but you could count every one of 'em on the fingers of your hands. Market for hides is good in England, but a feller has to have gunpowder and guts to harvest them here in this wild territory."

Padre pushed his boots into the sand, bracing himself. Genesis' renewal of his acquaintance with *Senor* Colabro had paid off handsomely. River Raven talked up the possibility for Genesis to help run the next raft to Gull Point and on to Pensacola. *Senor* Colabro's long association with Captain Zamora had stood Genesis in good stead, even though at this particular time the captain's unsanctified son had not concerned himself with the daunting detail of how he would be treated if he returned to Pensacola. Yes, he had deserted. But no, no one knew if General Jackson had, indeed, invaded Pensacola, or what was going on at the garrison. Precisely what the sound of the howitzers had meant, one could only speculate. Nevertheless, the promise of Genesis' job was sealed in no time at all, since it would free *Senor* Colabro to remain at the trading post to supervise the workers.

"When we get a good load of skins, and raft of logs," the *senor* said, twining his mustache, "we'll be looking for a good rainy spell to bring the water level up to the mark on the old oak tree out there. Then you can help us run the trip," he reassured Genesis and whacked him on the back. As the visitors turned to leave, he added in a louder voice, "I will send a runner to the village to let you know when the time is right for rafting."

Back at the village Padre, still overcome with disappointment and beset with doubt, wondered if he would ever get a chance to perform mission work in the Alabama Territory? Yet, hope returned at devotions the very next morning. Princess Blue Heron lingered at slightly closer range, sneaking peeks while he performed his rituals at the cross. Surely her interest had grown. Her potential candidacy gratified him more than any thing since...well, he couldn't remember when.

# WILLOW TRAP WEAVER

Genesis kept Padre apprised of progress as he dried all the fox bones and honed them into fine scrapers, hole punchers, and needles. After finishing the tools he asked the elders for permission to begin work on a dugout even though Owl Claw had told him that it sometimes takes more than twelve full moons to finish one. Padre saw less and less of Genesis after he decided to hollow out a log for his canoe. The young man had changed so much, now essentially living the Creek life and looking like a Creek, except for the reddishness of his hair.

As soon as Genesis received permission to make a dugout, Owl Claw explained that the Owl Clan favored using, for many of their activities, a sacred section of the river of cane near the bend. There, the flowing waters had rounded double oxbows into Mother Earth's banks. Near the water was the best place to work on the dugout since burning most of the log's center would save time in carving. Also, this is where he would launch the dugout and keep it tied when it was not in use. Owl Claw said, "I'll help you find the right tree and lend you a hatchet, but you must chop it down by yourself. First, you put wet mud around the tree, but above where you want to cut it." He pushed his hand into the air and repeated, "*Above*. Then you burn a ring all the way around the trunk below the wet mud, so you will not have to chop so much." He pushed his hand lower and emphasized, "*Below*."

"Your idea about the wet mud surefire makes a whole lot of sense."

"That's right and when the tree cracks, giving up its standing spirit and its branches whistle to the ground, I will show you how to ask forgiveness for cutting it."

Genesis heaved a great sigh when the giant gave in and toppled. Then he heaved an even greater sigh after the ceremony of forgiveness.

The next day, though his hands had blistered and reddened, he could hardly wait to chop a cavity into the log for the first burning. Then he would outline the space with wet mud before lighting a fire. In spite of keeping the hatchet honed to a sharp edge and occasionally switching his chopping hand, his palms stung like pallets of yellow jacket stabs, as he chopped and chopped and chopped. Near the end of the day, he sat astride the fallen tree trunk, alternately admiring his work and inspecting huge water-filled blisters in his palms, and just resting. Soon he caught sight of a young woman lilting down the path, which led to the river. As she passed, Genesis tried to figure out what the strange bundle was that she carried. She glanced at Genesis and smiled shyly. He scrambled to his feet and, at a careful distance, followed her. Thoughts of his blistered hands and handsome log left his mind, and his head filled with thoughts of her. As she waded into the water with her bundle, at the oxbow farthest upstream, he watched. Unable to figure out her mission, his eyes fastened firmly on her actions. She began unfurling her bundle with one arm while swimming with the other one to the opposite side of the oxbow. It soon became clear that she was setting up a weir to trap fish. Amazed at her aptness in getting the job done, he edged closer with the hope of speaking to her.

When she came out of the water, he took a step back, awestruck at her sweet face and shapely body. By the time she came within better hearing range he said, "I watched you set the fish trap. Is it as easy as you make it look?"

Her face lit up. She sauntered closer and said, "Most of the time, I have no trouble."

"When will you come back for the fish?"

She stopped. He felt the hair rise on his arms when he saw the water droplets on her shiny, bronze skin. As her face slowly ascended to meet his eyes, a surge, the one so familiar to him in his past, coursed unstoppably.

"Near sunset tomorrow, I will bring baskets for carrying the fish to the village."

"I'll be here working on my dugout. I can wait for you and help."

She smiled and nodded as she walked away, squeezing water from the ends of her two braids of hair. After she faded from sight, Genesis looked at his hands. He honed the hatchet again, punctured the blisters with the sharpest end point, and squeezed them flat.

Unable to work fast at sizing his log the following day, with his hands sore and swollen, Genesis looked up again and again hoping the sun would hurry and lower itself. Time passed slowly. By and by a lilting figure, carrying a basket in each hand, appeared on the river path. With sure recognition, Genesis stood. As she approached she nodded and smiled. He followed her.

Before entering the water she said, "You must be very quiet and stay still, while I untie one end of the trap from the cypress roots and draw it in closer on the fish."

"Sure, sure. Don't worry about me making noise, nary a bit."

Agog, he watched as she scooped a basketful of bluegills, then another. He stood close to the wiggling baskets while the young woman reattached one end of the weir to the roots, still amazed at her learned hands and skill. Afterwards, she disappeared under a ledge. Genesis waited and waited. Had she encountered trouble? Should he look for her? He couldn't leave the thrashing fish.

She reappeared with a pleasant look on her face. He asked impatiently, "What happened to you?"

"I visited my sacred space."

She seemed secretive about it, and though burning with curiosity, he respected her privacy. He merely said, "I'll help you take the baskets back to the village."

As they walked up the river path he said, "You know my name is Genesis and that I come from Pensacola. I'd like to know your name."

"Willow Trap Weaver. My mother, Singing Basket Weaver, and I weave willow branches for the fish weirs, and baskets, many kinds of baskets."

At the fork of the river and village paths, Willow Trap Weaver said, "I will now take both baskets." A questioning expression filled Genesis' face as he reluctantly placed his basket on top of the one she carried. She departed. He gazed at the backside of her fine willowy form until she faded from sight, for even that side was a beautiful sight to behold. It energized him.

The next morning on his way to the twin oxbows, Genesis found his feet leading him first to the Weaver home site. His heart beat with a hard, fast pounding when he saw Willow Trap Weaver and her mother weaving baskets. They sat near racks loaded with small fish that were drying in the sun. Willow Trap Weaver jumped up and with a stick shooed a flock of birds from the fish. Her smile of recognition brought sweet relief to Genesis. A young girl who seemed to have an unusual presence sat nearby, pounding expressionless on a drum. Was she helping to scare away the scavengers? Not wanting to interfere, Genesis walked onward.

*That's her, that's her*, Genesis thought as the figure lilted down the path during late afternoon. She looks just like her name, just like a walking willow tree, a young one filled with easy moving limbs and fresh, young leaves. But who was the little person following her today?

181

"That's the little girl," Genesis said when they came closer, "I saw at your place beating the drum this morning." Her face was round and flat as the moon, her eyes mere slits, and she was short and stout and walked wiggly like a groundhog.

"She is my little sister. Cloverleaf is her name, for the face is like a cloverleaf. Only eleven *Poskitas* she has seen, and already she has earned another name, Honey Cloverleaf, for she is sweet as honey. I am her cradleboard mother."

Genesis gaped with a questioning look and asked, "Three mothers?"

"Yes. We have three mothers: Mother Earth, mother of birth, and cradleboard mother. I have been cradleboard mother while our mother weaves. Honey Cloverleaf grows larger every *Poskita* while her mind stays like a very young child."

They angled to the river. On the sandy shoal of the oxbow, Honey Cloverleaf headed directly for what Genesis later learned was a small chamber under the ledge. In a wild display, she tore away the brush concealing the entrance and ran inside before Willow Trap Weaver could stop her. Genesis followed them. Honey Cloverleaf snatched an object and handed it to Genesis. The shiny, white skeleton was a thing of interest; he tried to hide the fact that it stung his sore hands. Carefully, he held it toward the light for a better look. What was this thing?

"It was a giant fish," Willow Trap Weaver said. "The largest fish bones I ever found."

"I see. I would like to look around," Genesis said.

"This place is a secret you must keep."

"Don't worry, I won't tell, not to a single soul."

The little haven was replete with relics from nature's midden. Genesis' eyes followed the rows of bone sculptures. Some had been cobbled into mysterious objects by shaping or simply juxtaposing bones of an animal or fish. Multiple animal and fish bones were combined in others. In the darkness of this opening in the earth, shimmering bones and skeletons seemed as eerie to Genesis as the forest fox fire in the swamp. Did at least a few of these pieces belong to ancestors of long, long ago?

"This is a strange place for a weaver to have," Genesis said.

"I am first a weaver. A place of the heart is this little cave. Sacredness in these bones lives, a spirit in each one. Lives of animals' spirits speak, speak the way once they were, in these bones' beauty, their bare beauty. They bring me together with Mother Earth."

These words, both natural and momentary, sent an exciting ripple through his stomach. Strange, how they affected him this way, yet even stranger, they brought on spiritual moments such as he had never experienced in his lifetime. He surefire felt a change coming over him, a change in the way he looked at the world, women, too? A lasting one? Might be. Willow Trap Weaver's reverence for the bones' beauty seemed as deep and everlasting as the river's water that he heard gently rushing. Her innocent spirit grabbed hold of his mind and burrowed, quick as a rabbit, into his heart. Yes, he sensed this would have strong staying power. Ancestral kinship. Something like his mother had tried to explain years ago. Never had he heard a young woman speak with such true feelings about Mother Earth. The Owl Clan Village was surefire the right place for him, and Willow Trap Weaver might be the right woman for him.

Initial attraction to Willow Trap Weaver's beauty and willowy carriage expanded and deepened into more caring feelings every day that Genesis saw her. He learned something new each time they were together. She knew the ancestral teaching of how the turtle got its shell. She knew which plants had mouths for snatching bugs to eat. She understood that her mother and many Creek used their teeth too often as tools, causing them to break and rot and the shaman to spend much time passing out toothache grass for pain. She agreed with the chief that the people must continue honoring Breath Maker to hold the tribes together, to live with the Mother Earth, wasting not. Her wisdom filled the gaps of his yearning to know about his Creek background and fitted into his being like an acorn into its cap.

Willow Trap Weaver, while returning to the village, nourished new warmth in her heart. The spirits of the fish and animal bones in her secret space were pleased with her. Their spirits gave feelings as wonderful as honeysuckle blossoms opening in spring. They brought blessings of Genesis' attention. So few braves were left. Many who fought Sharp Knife were either killed or ran off to Florida.

Wishing to share a special meeting with Genesis, she would fulfill a plan. During early morning of the following day, she prepared acorn cakes with goose eggs. She wanted, very much, to be with Genesis for once in the sweetness of the morning before the sun came overhead. She wanted for once to leave the fish baskets at home. And she wanted for once to leave Honey Cloverleaf to play with her cousins. After her mother granted permission, Willow Trap Weaver lined a small basket with fresh, live oak leaves, placed the acorn cakes on top of them, and drizzled honey over them, her mouth watering before she finished.

Upon her arrival at the double oxbows, time had passed so fast that the sun was already high in the sky. Shyly, she presented the basket to Genesis. He wiped the perspiration from his forehead, looked inside the basket, and said, "Uhmm, the cakes smell delicious. They'll taste a lot better if we first swim in the river and cool off." With a vine, he tied the basket onto a tree limb, and they dashed into the water, splashing each other. After the swim they sat on the sandy shoal facing the west and ate the acorn cakes, licking honey that ran between their fingers. Genesis savored the last sweetness of the delicacies by licking his fingertips. His eyes shot up and down from her pink lips to her toes and then to her pink palms, pink as that of his Pensacola Beach, conch shell crucifix. He reached for her hand and gently rubbed it against his cheek.

Willow Trap Weaver giggled softly and ran to the river. She rinsed her sticky fingers, loosened her wet braids, and combed them out with a tortoise shell comb, which had been secured into one braid. Between strokes she rubbed her fingers over the comb's teeth, indulging in the spirit beauty of the shell as well as her careful handwork, the fine honing of the shell. As she sat on the sand, the fringe on her buckskin skirt flared in a semicircle over her shiny, bronze thighs. Genesis moved closer and sat beside her. Her fingertips were still wrinkled, and her nipples hardened like sun-dried grapes. Her eyes shone, and she smelled fresh as the river. Just as Genesis started to ask her if she would like to take a walk, he noticed an approaching shadow.

Owl Claw said, "I have come to check on the dugout." Genesis jumped up and hurried to the dugout. Owl Claw followed and inspected the work. But Genesis did not like the way Owl Claw lingered, much longer than usual. Nor did Genesis like the suspicious look in his eyes.

Willow Trap Weaver showed no sign of distrusting Owl Claw. When she caught sight of the blue feathered headdress loping through the woods near them, she walked up to Genesis and said, "Princess Blue Heron goes there near the trail. Every day she goes to the burial ground."

Owl Claw said, "I must join my son at a special hunting ground." He quietly disappeared.

Relieved that Owl Claw had left, Genesis asked, "Is visiting the burial ground part of the princess' duty?"

"She visits her son's grave."

"She's married?"

"Her husband, Brave Thrower, was killed at Sharp Knife's battle in Horseshoe Bend. She has been a widow for four *Poskitas*. By rules of the clan, she had married a member of a different tribe, the bravest fighter—Red Stick Brave Thrower. He went to Red Eagle's town to help fight for Mother Earth there."

"The Owl Clan must be very proud of his courage."

"Yes, yes. Brave Thrower gave his life in honor. He lived not long enough to see his little son walk on Mother Earth."

"Another son?"

"No, only one."

"And he died?"

"Yes. He saw only four *Poskitas*. She visits his grave. What I remember most about her son was his chin. He had a long chin with a crease in the middle just like his father's brave chin."

"I am sorry to hear about the death of her young son. When did it happen?"

"About a half moon before you and the missionary came to the village."

"I feel so sorry for her," Genesis said.

"For Princess Blue Heron, you need not feel sorry. Chief Wahoo is her father. And Golden Maize Grower is her mother. They watch over her."

"Every time I see the princess, she seems to vanish on purpose. Now I understand the reason for her sad eyes."

"When I look at her, I do not see sad eyes. I see eyes of a good heart. She does not trust white people. White men killed her husband."

Genesis worked on the dugout while Willow Trap Weaver watched. On Princess Blue Heron's return from the burial ground, Willow Trap Weaver called to her and motioned for her to come hence. To Genesis' astonishment, over to them she loped.

"We talked about your son," Willow Trap Weaver said. "Genesis would like to know more about him."

Since Willow Trap Weaver had earlier confided her feelings about Genesis to Princess Blue Heron, the Princess spoke willingly. "First I will tell you his name was Tupelo. I gave this special name to him before he was born. It happened one day when I gathered sphagnum moss for my baby and washed away the sand."

Genesis rubbed the nape of his neck in the manner of one who is ill at ease and shot a questioning look at Willow Trap Weaver. He whispered, "Sphagnum moss, do babies eat that?"

Blue Heron had heard every word and laughed. "My people, from ancestors of long ago, know sphagnum moss holds many times its size in water. Holds other waste, too. Muscogee are smart. They try out different things to see how they work."

"Uhm, I won't say more," for at once he did not wish to hear any more "woman talk." Even so, he did not want to belittle Willow Trap Weaver's friend. He said, "I will not ask questions, I will just listen." Understanding the function of the moss and feeling embarrassed at the revelation, he would not risk delving a bit further into matters concerning motherly duties.

"I had already gathered the moss in my basket when I came upon a tupelo tree, one that stood out from any other I had ever seen. I must have passed it many times. But this day it struck me as the most spirit-filled tree ever I saw. I stood and looked and looked. Then I started chanting, 'Breath Maker, if I have a son he will be Tu-pe-lo, Tu-pe-lo, Tu-pe-lo.' The sounds rang in my head every day till he was born."

185

"Was he very sick before he died?" Genesis asked.

"No, no. The river of cane carried him away." Her look saddened.

"Oh, I'm sorry. He must have drowned."

Surprisingly, she continued, "In the first warm weather of the May Song Moon, Tupelo had followed the older boys, his Grower cousins, on their fishing trip. They had waited so long for the first fishing trip of the springtime, to a sacred place. It is a special place, where the river falls over great rocks."

"You are talking about the falls near the Montezuma Trading Post?" Genesis asked.

"Yes."

"The creek has plenty of fish. I am surprised they went there."

"The bravest ones fish with their hands. They catch the fish when they jump over the rocks where the river rushes and falls. Takes much practice. Must be very fast."

"That's a long way to walk. When me and Padre went there, we rode the horses. And the roaring falls look dangerous."

"Ahh, but you do not know. His future had been decided. He was to have become brave and strong. My brothers and their sons taught him the brave ways of the Owl Clan. And my brothers and my mother and I, too, scratched him whenever he did wrong things like children do, so he would grow up to be honorable."

"Your brothers scratched your son, for punishment?"

"That is our way. For Creek, the wife's family is head of the house."

Genesis said, "I understand now. I won't bother you with more questions while you are explaining."

Princess Blue Heron said, "While the older boys practiced hand-catching the fish that swam through the rushing waters and over the great rocks, my young Tupelo tried to be like them. The older boys have strong legs and could jump from rock to rock. The bottoms of their feet and their toes grab onto the slick rocks." She curved her fingers, showing how deftly the older boys' feet and toes molded onto the rocks.

"While they tried to catch the fish, Tupelo fell. I wonder about it nearly every day. I wonder if Tupelo's young legs and feet lost their hold on a slippery, moss-covered rock when he tried to keep up the big boys. I wonder if his head hit a rock. The rushing river water is loud at the falls. The Grower cousins could not hear if my son forgot to be brave and cried out."

Princess Blue Heron swallowed hard and paused. Genesis noted the pain in her eyes.

"The roaring water swallowed my son's young body and pulled it very fast down the long, long river, never to see him again." She gazed ahead, proud she had kept her suffering inside. Then she said, "I am very thirsty. I will go and drink cool, spring water on the way home." She loped away.

Back and forth between the two young women, Genesis had cut his eyes trying to read Willow Trap Weaver's thoughts as Princess Blue Heron had spoken.

"Where is the burial ground?" Genesis asked as soon as Blue Heron left.

"Come," Willow Trap Weaver said, "I will show you."

# BLUE POND SANCTUARY

Unforeseen obstacles catapulted Padre from one disappointment to another keeping him off-balance. Stymied by the lack of settlers; thwarted by his first attempt to convert Blue Clay; and, most pressing at the moment, shackled by a confining feeling, an unrelenting one, he groped for answers. For a while, quiet worship and soft chanting in front of his handmade cross, close to the summerhouse, had brought a modicum of satisfaction.

Despite the prospect that the elusive visitor portended, his confined living arrangement cramped and constrained expression. Yes, the enigmatic woman with the blue-feathered headdress darted here and there and foreshadowed as at least one promising conversion candidate. If he could just celebrate mass and chant with jubilation and be himself. Instead, he kept his religious fervor subdued, submitting to restrictive compromise for the sake of keeping peace with Genesis and the Creek. Abiding faith would somehow spawn more favorable circumstances, especially the hope for celebrating the Eucharist.

Would his precious chanting ability diminish or just become mediocre? A sudden panic and unreasoning fear possessed him, followed by an urge to flee. But he'd experienced firsthand the awesome wilderness. The fine education of his priesthood had not provided wilderness survival techniques acquired by the heathens. Everyday, everywhere, everybody spoke Creek. Their strange talk, their pagan beliefs, their alien ways of living confronted him at every step. There was not a soul with whom he could share a cerebral conversation, nor to appreciate his fine intellect. Pent-up feelings grew tighter and tighter, so tight he would really just like to jump out of his skin.

He took a deep breath, gathered his wits, and decided he must swallow his pride and take the risk of calling on the formidable Shaman Skytalker. First, he needed a plan. An initial complimentary comment would be in order, not as a manipulative device but as a good opener.

Padre approached the shaman with a most respectful nod and said, "This is a beautiful summer day. People are happily buzzing like bees getting their work done."

The shaman returned a silent nod.

Though Padre felt none too comfortable in the shaman's presence, he said, "I've been wanting to ask your opinion on a matter."

Shaman Skytalker waited with apparent interest.

"You see, I wondered if there is a place not too far away where I could be alone. I need to pray and sing louder for my holy Catholic religion and say my rituals louder, too. I've been worshiping quietly so as not to offend anyone. But before you consider my request, I wish to let you know that I sincerely appreciate the Owl Clan's hospitality. In no way would I do anything that would jeopardize my visit here." Something ancient seemed embodied in the shaman. Would he fathom any understanding?

The shaman puffed on his pipe and meditated. He would not let the missionary know how pleased he was to hear this, nor how much he had wanted to get him away from Owl Clan members. From the beginning, he had not liked the idea that the missionary might tempt his people with White God foolery. Only because of forefathers' teachings had he agreed to share and help the missionary, so no evil spirits would visit the Owl Clan. Finally he said, "You might like the Mother Earth over by the blue pond."

"Oh, I don't want to displace your people from a nice area. The blue pond sounds so ideal."

"Our people like best the flowing water at the creeks."

Padre heaved a great sigh of relief. "The blue pond sounds like a wonderful place. I can't tell you how thankful I am. Will you tell me how to get there?"

"I'll ask one of Owl Claw's sons to show you the way tomorrow."

"It's one of the most beautiful areas I have ever seen," Padre said the following day, though he knew the "pond" was a "lake." Stone-faced, Owl Claw's son merely observed; but that did not diminish Padre's reawakening energy. The place not only abounded with tremendous natural beauty, but it also offered great potential for chanting and meditating with complete freedom. It would revitalize his spirit and bring solace. He visualized planting the cross and constructing an altar of sapling poles on the sandy shore.

The next day he put his plans into action. And though the altar was as primitive as the cross, it, too, reawakened pride in his soul when he genuflected in reverence. The spot he chose for his worship, alongside the pond, was a veritable paradise, pristine and surely like the Garden of Eden. Blue-shadowed hills of massive pines walled the northern side, and to the south an immense vista extended beyond the water, providing both space and seclusion. Here, he even forgot the indignity of not having his cassock. But another concern took its place. Had he sacrificed the only potential candidate for conversion, he had found so far, by changing his worship place to the blue pond?

Before praying at the cross, he always filled a small clay vessel, which he brought from the village, with spring water and blessed it. Blessing himself with this holy water added another important symbolic dimension, while at the same time another was sorely missed. He had no wafers or wine to consecrate for the Eucharist.

Only a few days had passed when the vastness of the blue pond area created a feeling of insignificance. In his loneliness he decided that marking off a space would cozily encapsulate him, create the semblance of an outdoors chapel. At the edge of the woods he found thick sticks for marking the four corners. He stepped off a rectangular area, about six by eight feet. Then as he began collecting stones, selecting only the deepest-blue-colored limestones to enclose his outdoor sanctuary, he caught a glimpse of another bluishness, a familiar bluishness. It was she all right—a grace. By the grace of God his potential candidate for conversion to the Holy Word had found the sanctuary. His heart raced.

With a spring in his step he outlined the chapel in no time at all with the most beautifully shaped blue stones he could find. While he was laying out these carefully chosen limestone chunks, he imagined the nuggets on the princess's necklace had come from similar stones. He left an open space, which faced the blue pond, for entering and exiting. There he placed the vessel of holy water. This scaled-down, open-air chapel comforted him. In addition to his elusive visitor, birds aplenty surrounded the chapel serenading. He rested and watched their dramatic interludes of gliding dives, sudden upturns, and streaks into oblivion. Unfamiliar slate-colored birds turned blue whenever they flew in the sun's glinting rays. At ground level, the sweet shrub's dull, deep-red flowerettes, the huge glossy-white magnolia blossoms, and mixed-hued honeysuckles dotted the greenery and scented the air.

As Padre freely communed with God, his chanting, thin at first, began reverberating with the robustness of earlier days. His masses resonated without inhibition. The sanctuary truly seemed like a bit of heaven on earth.

Now exhilarated, he would somehow influence the princess to come forth from her hiding. He felt ever so ready to teach her.

Perhaps he would see her again today. He looked out over the lush, waist-high fronds of ferns fanning the breeze and wild apple trees, which stood higher than the ferns, then to the taller trees. The young woman usually hid behind mammoth trunks of long-leaf yellow pines in the background and sometimes slipped closer to the apple trees, but she was nowhere to be seen amongst them. So while meditating, Padre studied the giant pines. Their steadfastness emanated an air of strength, the sort of strength he sought for administering his mission work.

From her hideout, the princess frowned. When she had first started watching him, she could hide behind trees and bushes as naturally as a doe. Little by little the white missionary magic gripped her heart and clouded her mind. Now, at times so gladdened with his ways, she sometimes forgot her usual attention to shrewdness.

The next morning, on her way to the sacred, red-clay hole for practice in the shamanic ways, she said over and over in her mind, *I must be more careful, much more careful.* She must not forget again and almost stand upright. He might see her. And foremost, the shaman and the elders must not discover that she is interested in the white missionary's spirit ways. She would have to answer to them. Her father and mother would feel disgraced.

*But his strange ways unfold faster than I can make sense of them. Shaman Skytalker says I show signs of having spirit gifts, but I cannot understand the strange, new ways of the white missionary. He points to four places on his chest. I like that. Four is our sacred number, but he does not move in a circle. I must try harder to figure it out. Surely, these are gifted ways of the white man. Surely they would help me in my vision quests.*

Down in the circular, red clay hole, she whispered a prayer, "Breath Maker, the missionary's graceful bowing, before the table and cross is the most beautiful movement. It is a most honorable-looking movement. I think I can do it. But, am I practicing it the right way? I will try again. I must lower the right knee all the way to the ground and bow my head in the most respectful way so the wonders will work. I think I am doing it the right way. If only I could trust speaking with the shaman about this. It is too soon. I am sure he would not understand until the missionary has proved himself." She stopped, looked around, and listened to make sure she had not alerted her secret finding, for he probably still lingered, sick, where she had first seen him, beyond the red hole. Maybe river noises were loud enough to keep him from hearing.

She continued in a softer tone, "Should I mark off a space with blue limestones for my vision quests? I could—on the other side of the pond near the blue herons' nests. Hmm. No." She shook her head. "Someone from the village might find it and say I am following the ways of the missionary and bring me before the elders. I cannot risk that. Father and mother would say that I dishonor the Owl Clan. I call to you, Breath Maker. It would be easier if I were not the daughter of the chief.

"The white man should be told that when he points four times on his chest, he should move in a circle and not point like a jumping rabbit. Please, Breath Maker, how can I ever bring myself to speak with the strange, white missionary and tell him about my newest secret, so he can help me? Maybe I should call on ancestors' help. And I have to tell you. I despise his white skin." Her voice rose stronger. "I am sure he's like that of the strange whites who killed my husband at Horseshoe Bend. I hate every bit of his white skin," she screamed and muffled the sound with her palms.

Softly crying, she hoisted herself onto the lip of the hole. No. No, she must not weaken. Quickly she wiped her eyes. She plucked a white daisy and angrily snatched off a petal. She yanked the rest off one by one until she had plucked the daisy clean. She scraped up the discarded white petals, crushed them with all her force, and pounded all their whiteness into the red dust. "I can never, never forget that whites made me a widow. No, nooo. I cannot tell the white missionary about my new secret. I will just watch the curious things he does. I will learn."

Padre now pictured himself as coping valiantly with his frustrations at the blue pond sanctuary. The truth, dozens of times he had wondered what damage General Jackson may have done to Pensacola, albeit Dominicans do not whine. Duty here must be met. Maybe he would catch a glimpse of a settler's shack one day, then another one, and another one. He should not agonize about all the changes that might have or might not have occurred at the garrison. Yet, Genesis' raft trip to Pensacola for *Senor* Colabro could not come any too soon, for he longed to hear the news.

On this June day, images of his holy items and best clerical robe lingered in his mind. When would the elders ever see fit to return his shoulder bag of possessions? Though he had been without them about six weeks, it seemed much longer. Would he ever find an appropriate occasion to don his best priestly robe again even if he had it in his possession? When would he ever be able to celebrate the Eucharist again? And how he missed Genesis' companionship. While praying, he tried ever so hard to purge his resentment. His once-lofty thoughts had plunged to the point where he even anguished over the loss of security, which Genesis had provided.

His trepidation transported him back to *Andalucia's* Moorish history. Was his bloodline linked to a Moor? Had the wandering lust of a Moor scattered hereditary seeds all the way to the village where his ancestors lived? He squinted into the sunset. The questionable future shadowed full enjoyment of the ponded woodland. He searched for the blue-feathered headdress among the tawny trunks and tangled growths of honeysuckle and laurel vines that webbed the trees together. His mind seemed just as tangled. In this muse, his line of vision lowered to the bushes and shrubs and razor-sharp wiregrass blades that claimed every spot where they could possibly eke out existence. Surely his rigorous religious training could reflect at least some of that rugged determination.

On each visit, Padre cherished the approach to his sanctuary. The cross, a symbol that touched him deepest, made its statement, simply but boldly, as if its reflection belonged on the horizon. Today, as always, he walked by the lower end of the stream, which fed into the pond. He stopped and splashed his face and neck with the refreshing water. On these long summer evenings at the blue pond, he sometimes talked to himself. Today, he said, aloud, "I can't wait for that icy-blue spring water." Near the bubbling spring he cupped his hands and sipped and sipped. Limestone at the spring's base reflected their beautiful blueness into the water.

Onward he walked through patches of velvety moss and grass and small ferns bordering the pond, but he must not look into the water and chance seeing his reflection. It would awaken memories. He could not bear to think about that departing day in the Cadiz port when, though he had seen his crippled shadow in the water, he still had hopes of helping to build a new church for St. Michael's Mission. His head now hung lower; his feet undulated in the warm white sand as he made his way to the holy water. It had not completely evaporated, so he blessed himself and stepped to the altar. There he genuflected and prayed and prayed.

Later, he straightened his back and walked along the pond's edge again, meditating. Different parishioners at St. Michael's Mission and Padre de Galvez, Father Mulvaney, too, came to mind. Farther, the spring stream seemed to gurgle louder and ripple harmoniously over the downstream rocks, sounds he lived for while in this mood, so vital with life. He wished to hold onto some of this vitality, let it seep inside. He deemed it best not to chant until he had absorbed all the energy that the spring area released. Then he would practice his finest Gregorian-style chants, which were nothing like those heathen chants in the village. He vowed to maintain the high level of mastery for which he had long been respected. The archbishop had said his chanting was the best he'd heard since Padre Sierra passed away, and he would never forget that exquisite compliment. He nodded his head in affirmation.

The following day at the sanctuary, fresh bouquets of water lilies awaited, one at each side of the altar, the most delicate of blue hues Padre had ever seen. The first thought that came to his mind was that the princess must have placed them there. Her essence always gave him a feeling of importance, the importance he deserved. Whenever he knew she was hidden among the trees, he'd perform his chanting with greater feeling, with much more drama and meaning. It was delicious, delicious as Captain Zamora's *tapas* tray of anchovies, olives, cuttlefish, and dried figs must have been, the one, which the captain had passed to him on that first night aboard ship. His mouth now watered for those savories, the smell of which had turned foul with his seasickness on his first day at sea. At present he would settle for a piece of dry wheat bread.

How desperately he needed to reach the young woman and convince her to come forth. These flowers sufficiently indicated her caring. Still he worried that even if she came forward, would he be able suppress his humiliation over not having a cassock? Of greater importance, could he suppress his abomination of the native woman's half-nakedness?

Fresh bouquets of blue water lilies again greeted Padre on the following day at the blue pond chapel. Now his missionary zeal overcame all other concerns. It surfaced just as naturally as it had that second day in the village when he had engaged in the ill-fated controversy with Blue Clay about the difference between the true God and Breath Maker, the idol. Genesis had gotten angrier with him than he had ever experienced.

This time Padre thoughtfully channeled his zeal into an altogether different approach. Though a humble and modest priest, he at last decided to use his Gregorian-chanting talent to help the young woman reveal her presence. After all, she undoubtedly wanted to speak with him. There must be something she needed to discuss. And then, perhaps, he would find an appropriate opportunity to tell her about the Holy Word. She could be saved.

He knew she hid nearby today. She had moved in even closer than usual, for he had heard her muffled sneeze. He must seize this favorable chance. In his best Gregorian form he chanted: "Blue Feathers, Blue Feathers, where are you? Where are you? God has true love for you. And I would like to speak with you."

She did not come forth. He looked up at the sky, raised his arms, and chanted, "Lord, Lord, help the young woman reveal her presence. Lord God Almighty, by the power of the Holy Spirit, strengthen her faint heart, so I may teach her the Truth."

He looked around. The blue feathers were nowhere to be seen. He stood dumbfounded, stroked his beard, and prayed softly: "Blessed Mary, ever virgin, most holy of all the angels and saints, you know this young woman's heathen beliefs are sinful. Blessed Mary, I ask you to intercede with the Lord our God. Ask our Lord to bring her to the realization that she needs to hear my teachings." He crossed himself.

He searched though the twilight's blueness for the four blue feathers. But everything looked the same, save for the amber sun, now only a sliver of a disk visible on the horizon. Daunting demons of defeat echoed in the stillness. He had poured out all the warm goodness from his heart until it felt empty, utterly empty. His entire body felt empty, though at the same time heavy, too heavy to set in motion. With greatest effort he set forth toward the village.

In suffering perplexity he lumbered to the village, yet in some indefinable way he sensed the time had come to take some other action. He'd done everything he knew to do about the young woman's enigmatic behavior. He had given his best effort.

That evening, the worst of all times, Genesis told Padre everything Willow Trap Weaver and Princess Blue Heron had revealed to him about Brave Thrower, Tupelo, and how the princess feels about whites.

Padre winced at each daunting detail. He said, "I'd like to talk with her, tell her whites are not all alike, any more than Whistling Acorn represents all Muscogee men." Padre lifted his arm and examined its color and said, "There's nothing I can do about this color of skin, but I surely can explain how peoples' souls differ. I must find a way to prove to the princess that all white men are not warmongers. Far from it. If I could only find a way to explain that I have twice traveled great distances to escape war." Meanwhile Genesis fell asleep.

Somehow, Padre had thought this new day at the sanctuary would be different. Not so. However, as soon as he was about ready to leave the blue pond area, the blue heron feathers arose above the fern fronds, ever so slowly. He stood, stunned, as Princess Blue Heron eased closer and closer. Then she stopped. The familiar headdress with the four blue feathers melted into the sky. At first he noticed her reticent, birdlike grace. His glance was followed by a more significant look. Closer, she looked beautiful, aglow in earthy shades of umber, ocher, and bronze against the fiery setting sun. Yet she wore a shy expression.

When he found his voice he said, "Come, Princess Blue Heron," and motioned with an outstretched arm. "Please come talk to me. Tell me what you are thinking. It's all right to talk with me. I want to be your friend."

She took a step toward him, then hesitated. As soon as he advanced toward her, with both arms outstretched, she stepped backwards. He paused realizing he should not act so forward.

"How does the white missionary know my name?"

"I wanted to know who you were. Since the first time ever I saw you, I wanted to know your..."

"Why does the white missionary want to know?" she interrupted.

"Uh…something about you interests me. Deeply. That's why I chanted for you to come out of the woods and talk. I worried about you. I talked with Genesis about you."

"You talked with Genesis about me?"

"Yes. I wanted to learn about you. He told me about you. He said that you are the daughter of Chief Wahoo Rope Maker and Golden Maize Grower."

"Did he tell you more about me?" she asked cutting her eyes obliquely at him.

"As a matter of fact, he did. He told me you are the widow of Brave Thrower. I have been waiting for a chance to let you know how saddened I feel that whites killed your husband. I have very deep feelings about wars and people getting killed. You see, my parents and my brother were killed in a war in Spain before I went to Pensacola. They were killed by white people, too. But not all whites are alike. I do not believe in killing. And I am truly sorry your husband was killed."

"Did he tell you about my son?"

"Yes, he told me the sad news. I deeply regret that you suffered yet another loss." He looked down momentarily, his voice changed to heartfelt compassion. "It is always tragic to learn of a young person's death. Genesis told me just yesterday that it had happened only weeks before we arrived at the village."

"Genesis told you all?"

"Well, I don't know about that, but he did say Brave Thrower had been killed before his son learned to walk. That must be heartbreaking." Tremors punctuated his sympathetic voice.

"But now…now," he said, focusing directly on her dark, solemn eyes, "I believe you have something to say. Please," he said in his most encouraging voice. "I listen."

She looked at him, her face filled with indecisiveness.

Finally she stroked her chin and said, "I, uh, it's a…something I saw. Villagers must not know." She paused but instantly knew she must not wait another day to tell her secret. Death may be near.

"Don't worry, I will honor your wish. I will not tell the villagers. I keep secrets. People tell me secrets. Many times I can help them."

"Uh, um…" She stepped backwards and stopped, hung her head and turned slowly away. Would she forget and reveal her long-kept secret of studying his powers to increase her shamanic abilities? She might, so she must not take the risk of telling him what she had recently seen.

"Princess Blue Heron," Padre exclaimed. "I can't let you go like this." He gently took her arm. She stopped and gazed at his white fingers wrapped around her bronze arm. She shook her head but did not attempt to move.

196

"I'll help, I promise with all my heart I'll do whatever I can to help you," Padre pled. Then he felt a spasm of inhibition, amazed at his forward-acting behavior. It struck his conscience as so out of character. What had come over him? Embarrassed, he quickly released his hold.

To his surprise, she replied quietly, "I, I guess I have to tell you...I must tell someone. There is no one else." Suddenly her expression turned dour, and she recanted, "No. I must not."

"I hope you will change your mind. I will not tell *anyone* your secrets."

Something about the way he'd just squinted his eyes in earnestness appealed to her. It was the way her husband always looked when he was most serious-minded and honest. Yes, she saw truthfulness. She would let the white man prove his honor. She turned her head toward the padre, and said, "I must trust you." Then she stammered, "I saw...it's a...a black sk..." Abruptly, she turned, ran away, and disappeared into the woods.

# THE BURIAL GROUND

"I know the trail markings to the burial ground," Willow Trap Weaver said to Genesis in her usual soft manner of speaking. "Before we go, I must ask something of you. You must keep very quiet while we are there. The burial ground is sacred, very sacred."

"I understand. I will make you proud of me. I have a question, but I will ask it before we leave."

"What do you ask?"

"Well, I was wondering why Tupelo has a grave? Princess Blue Heron said that he drowned and washed away with the river."

"For the other life he needs his play things, and as the grandson of the chief, he must have his special loincloth. Most small children have no loincloths. Other things for his journey to the other world I remember: a spirit blue limestone from his mother's necklace and a basket of bur oak acorn caps that he liked very much to play with, all are there for him. Princess Blue Heron could tell us more."

On their way to the burial ground, Willow Trap Weaver plucked a honeysuckle garland, sniffed it adoringly, and draped it around her neck. "I take one piece only, I waste not. For the hummingbirds, I leave the rest. See near the vines, spinning, spinning, spinning are their tiny wings. Up. Look. There," she pointed. "Look inside the nest. Two eggs like little beans."

Genesis smiled. Sometimes she drew him like a magnet. He would like to grab her and squeeze her whenever she explained things so sweet-like. How could he continue resisting her?

They walked in silence. Ahead, as they approached a long crossing log, Genesis' footsteps faltered. He had had precious little practice in walking on logs, and never had he walked on one stretching over such a wide, deep gully. Willow Trap Weaver stepped onto it as if it were an extension of the path and in no time at all stood watching him from the other side. He molded his feet onto the slick, rounded wood, then stepped cautiously. About midway he wavered and stopped. What to do? His face flushed hot. A sickening feeling came over him. He couldn't bear to look into her eyes. She came, took his hand, and held it until they walked the rest of the way. Silence was a blessing.

At the burial ground, Genesis stood before the small mound. It was the freshest looking one for as far as he could see. Respectfully, he tried to picture the little loincloth and play things, which were buried there in eternal stillness.

Willow Trap Weaver looked down peacefully at the part of Mother Earth holding Tupelo's loincloth and play things in safekeeping, ready for the activities of his other life. She laid the vine of fragrant honeysuckles on the mound. In no time at all, bees buzzed through the quietness and lit upon the tubular blossoms, partaking of their bulging rich nectar. She watched the bees flying to and from all four sacred directions, honoring Mother Earth. They were part of the burial ground. They would be part of the afterlife, too. She looked around feeling the spirits of the dead. And then, as if ancestors planned it, a mocking bird sang. She looked in the direction of the sweet sounds with satisfaction. Ancestors had surely sent spirit guides to bless this visit.

After departing the burial ground, they remained silent. Genesis would wait for her to speak first. When they came near the honeysuckle vines again, she sighed, "The smell, how sweet."

"Uh hm. It is so nice here. Let's take a rest." He took her hand and with his other one, opened the thickly trailing vines. They ducked their heads, entered, and sat underneath the fragrant blossoms. From their positions, near the edge of the vines, they faced a small clearing of snags. The lowering sun cast rosy rays that filtered through the snags' airy openings and onto Willow's face. These rays deepened the pink tint of her lips as they always had done by the river. This warm color brought out their fullness, set Genesis aflame. He squirmed. His eyes jumped to her breasts, her full-rounded nipples now wrinkling, as they always had done after she had been in the river. But now it happened as her eyes met his. He slid his arm around her waist and gently drew her closer, so close her soft breasts and hardened nipples projected against his chest. Their lips met; her eyes closed. Then he settled her snugly into the grass. He started to scratch a fuzzy feeling on his arm. There, a striped caterpillar lifted its head as if welcoming them. It quickly humped its way toward his hand.

Like the caterpillar they tilted their heads, but to each other. They exchanged smiles and then playfully passed the fuzzy little creature back and forth, letting it connect from his arm to hers, her arm to his, as they breathed lightly in rhythm. Soon, they breathed heavily. Their warm breaths merged. The caterpillar humped away. One moment was enough to know the greatest thing, the moment of extraordinary recognition, the moment their souls united.

Later, Genesis roused from the reverie and nestled his face to Willow's cheek. "Thank you for showing the burial ground and explaining all about Tupelo," he said and patted her bronzed shoulder. Her skin felt so soft, softer than the caterpillar.

She smiled and said, "For a long time, we have been here." Her eyes swept around, then widened. Her expression turned worried. If she had been using her spirit senses, she would have been aware of changes taking place, the signs of a brewing storm. Surely, she would have noticed the darkening sky and the differences in animal behavior. Those signs were second nature to her from early training, but she had been completely unmindful that squirrels and rabbits had run for cover. The birds began swooping about madly, barely visible in the growing darkness. "We must go," she said. Now."

Aghast, Genesis took her hand, made a mad dash, but it was too late. Eerie purple air already alternated with daylight lightning. The storm had preempted any escape. Black clouds were billowing in, hanging deathly low as if to smother them. Slanted lightning slit the sky and was followed by close thundering crashes. All of a sudden wind gusts kicked up sand, pelting their faces. Slanted sheets of rain whacked their bodies.

"We must stay in the vines," she said, her arms turning to gooseflesh.

Genesis extended his hand to her and led the way, deep into the vines, to an old deadfall. They sat. Thunder blasted. Limbs cracked and snapped. They huddled. When lightning again struck nearby—for sure it hit a huge tree—Willow Trap Weaver straddled the log and faced Genesis. She rocked back and forth quietly chanting.

There was no way of knowing how much time had passed, but night had come upon them, and moments grew longer. Somewhere nearby another tree was struck, for pungent whiffs of scorching, green timber filled the air. Raindrops fell from their ears and noses. Water sluiced from their garments. Rivulets tickled their spines.

When the thunder and lightning subsided, Genesis said, "Look at my teeth. They surefire must be dripping, too."

Willow Trap Weaver merely wiped her face and arms and wrung out her hair. "Ancestors heard my chants. Guided evil spirits away. But listen, a wolf's howl." She knew the difference between an animal's howl and a villager's howl, which sent a message; she would explain it to Genesis at another time. The rain had slackened to slow drips. "Now we go," she said.

Unmindfully, they walked through puddles and stepped over downed limbs in their haste to return to the village. They were also unaware of two figures following them. Owl Claw and his son had gotten caught in the quickly brewed storm while hunting and were now on their way home. Owl Claw's suspicion of Genesis' untoward behavior now turned to rage and grew hot as he followed them, grew even hotter as they approached the village. He would not wait for the sun to rise. Tonight he would set Genesis straight.

After Genesis had accompanied Willow Trap Weaver to her house and turned to go to his house, a strong arm suddenly grabbed him, forced him underneath a tree, and slammed him against the trunk. At once Genesis recognized Owl Claw. He was under Owl Claw's siege again. The old terror returned. Yet he wanted to be the only one who knew that he was scared to death.

"You must never lie with a woman in Owl Clan unless you marry," Owl Claw snarled through clenched teeth. If you are ever caught lying with a woman before marriage, I will make sure everything under that loincloth is cut off, *everything.*" He shoved Genesis' head against the tree trunk with such a force, a clunk resounded in the night's stillness.

"I never want to break Owl Clan rules. Never. But I need to tell you that I want to marry Willow Trap Weaver. I want to live with her the rest of my life and have children with her. I need to know how to make marriage."

Owl Claw heaved a great sigh. He studied for a few moments and said, "To be honorable, you must roll a stone to her. If she rolls it back to you, she will marry you."

"I can do that. I can do that tomorrow. Oh, thank you, thank you. I surefire thank you, Owl Claw. I think she will roll the stone back to me. Tomorrow, we see." He rubbed the rising knot on the back of his head.

Padre missed Genesis' companionship, lately speaking with him at length only on rare occasions. On this particular morning when Genesis left to work on his dugout, he took the basket of fox bones that he had dried and honed into fine scrapers, hole punchers, and needles. So lonely, Padre decided, though uninvited, he would nevertheless observe Genesis using the tools and check on the progress of the dugout. He had noticed, in his careful observations of the few times he had seen Genesis recently, subtle changes of behavior.

Lo and behold, he came upon Genesis in the midst of working on a basket. To his questioning look, Genesis said, "When my arms ache from hollowing out the log, I work on gathering baskets. I make them from the bark of my log and the handles are grape vines."

"You did a fine job on the baskets," Padre said as he picked up one and admired it. "But mostly women make baskets around here."

"Now Padre," Genesis said as he slapped a mosquito from his arm, "you surefire know how to insult. That's as bad as a mosquito taking a bite on your pecker when you try to take a piss. Just open your eyes wider. Can't you see them baskets are different? They're surefire not woven like women's baskets. See how I laced two pieces of bark together for the front and back and laced wooden bottoms on. They're kinda like a tall bucket. Need them for gathering grapes, berries, and mushrooms—persimmons, too. Creek call them gathering baskets. I made them for...well, you see, I will marry Willow Trap Weaver during the Green Corn Celebration."

Pow! Padre felt as if he had been hit by a cannonball. He cleared his throat and said, "Congratu...," and then drew in a breath and started again. "Congratulations. When did this all come about?"

"I surefire don't know what you was up to lately, but I've been up to my hocks in work. Willow Trap Weaver has been watching me work on the dugout every day on her way to check on the fish traps in the river. I helped her with the fish baskets, and we talked many times. Not a whole lot at first, but I started liking her. She is different, very different from any woman I ever knew in Pensacola. Has the sweetest voice I ever heard, so sweet I don't even hear the birds singing when she talks." He smiled. "I like the way she talks, too, nice and slow. And I like the way she looks. Very much, but I really started liking her when I found out how smart she is." He paused.

Padre stared at the mischievous look in his eyes and said, "You never told me much about her."

"*Humph*, I might as well tell you the rest. Things around here surefire ain't like in Pensacola. Owl Claw caught us coming in late after the storm the other night and warned me that I better not try to lie with her unless we get married."

"Yes, he is so right. Besides, you could lose an ear."

"Hell! Not no ear. He'd be after cutting off my pecker and everything else." Genesis grabbed at his genital area as if in pain and said, "Nearly scared me to death."

"I could have told you how to crush the desires of the flesh. Priests learn to do it by fasting, self-denial, or even physical pain. Three times a week at the monastery, we closed the doors of our cells, and to a haunting chant, we disrobed and scourged our flesh to bring it into submission."

202

"Uggh, you really did that? How'd you do that?"

"Each cell in the monastery, where we slept, had a whip of heavy cord, knotted at the end. The Superior walked the hall to make sure we complied."

"I damn sure rather beat myself like you priests did than get castrated. But all I needed to know was how to make plans to marry. Owl Claw told me how, and I done it just like he told me, except I didn't roll no plain stone to Willow Trap Weaver. I used my lucky one, and, sure enough, she rolled it back."

"What on earth are you talking about? You never told me any of this."

"Well, that's the right way to do it. It happened so fast, I got plumb dizzy. The world was just a'spinning. Padre, you know I don't tell you everything. Never did." Genesis slapped his hands onto his hips, akimbo, and widened the width of his leg stance. "Padre," he scoffed, "don't forget. I'm nineteen years old. *Humph* I mustered at the garrison ever since I was fourteen, while you was praying or whatever you were doing at St. Michael's. Shoot, I could have been married already. I'm surefire a long shot from that twelve-year-old you met when you landed in Pensacola."

Padre was well aware that Genesis now stood inches taller than he, but for the first time, it seemed to make a demeaning difference. Worse, the former wharf-like waif now flaunted a cock-a-hoop attitude. He felt like asking if the possibility of marriage would have been to one of the fifty-eight women listed on the census as laundresses and seamstresses. Everyone knew that was not their true occupation.

"I see you're not wearing your shell crucifix."

"Uh hm. I gave it to Willow Trap Weaver. I um…well, when you gave me the crucifix, our agreement was to reach the Montezuma Trading Post. We done that already." He clamped his mouth shut and whisked his forehead. "I honored the agreement."

"I must concede that you fulfilled the pact. And I do think Willow Trap Weaver will make a good wife for you. Her weaving skill is highly valued. I've watched her weaving, side by side with her mother. And she's very caring and patient with her little sister."

"You are right about that," Genesis said. "I watched her set the willow traps in the river and tie the ends to the cypress roots. Many times. The Weaver family catches lots of bluegills. They dry them for the villagers. And I went for a ride with Willow on *Grandeza*. She likes him very much. Sings sweetly to him, very sweetly. I've started calling her by just her first name—Willow. Every time, every single time I see her, she looks like a pretty willow sapling with easy-moving limbs that's filled with fresh leaves."

Still shocked, Padre knew all too well that he should not be. It was Genesis' rightful destiny to marry whenever he saw fit. Considering the stripling's rising status in the village, he could have chosen any young woman here. But while yet reeling from utter disappointment of the Montezuma Trading Post, this last blow struck him more profoundly. He would be alone now.

The building of Genesis' marriage house piqued Padre's curiosity, so he paid a visit. It was located next to the Weaver family's housing. All the Weaver men had helped Genesis, in one way or another, with gathering materials and planning the traditional structure, while Willow and her mother engaged in their weaving. Padre marveled at the construction progress. The poles were now ready for layers of bark.

"I want to learn exactly how much goose dung to put in the mud," Genesis said to the oldest Weaver brother. Before Genesis realized it, he had curled up his lips and said, "Whew! It's not so much the smell. Just the idea of working with shit in the mortar." The Weaver men snickered.

"I don't really care about the stinkiness," Genesis said to Padre. "It's the stickiness that's important to me." He rubbed the tips of his thumb and forefinger together. "What I surefire care about is getting it good and sticky. It must be just right so the bark stays on the poles for a long, long time."

While blending the batch of the mud, dung, and water mixture to a smooth, shiny consistency, Genesis retched, not once, but several times. Still, he refused to give in. With each retch, he grabbed the handle of the bone mixing paddle with a tighter grip and firmed his mouth in determination, hoping no one had noticed his cowardly retching. By the time they started to mortar bark pieces onto the poles, he had begun adjusting to using the concoction. The flat bone tool, with which he meticulously buttered the mixture, had once been a shoulder blade of the fox he'd killed earlier for making his bow. Though rather small for spreading, he had insisted on using this tool he'd so proudly made. As soon as they completed the east side of the hut, Genesis stood back, cupped his hands in back, and rotated his head from left to right, admiring his handiwork.

Padre walked around the corner to observe the weaving process. He marveled at how well the Weaver women kept the gauges of their baskets true, but at the same time he was bothered by a pang of guilt. He felt a certain bitterness toward Willow for her part in taking Genesis away from him. Wishing to redeem his soul, he said, "All the baskets stand straight. Not one is floppy, not even that big one you are weaving."

"This big one is special. It will be four hands high and four hands wide," Singing Basket Weaver said. Then she continued with her weaving, alternately humming and chanting.

For good measure Padre would go a notch further with the compliments, this time to Willow. "Most amazing is your patience in weaving the pine needle basket. It is so small and delicate."

"Yes, we use them for the tiniest sacred objects," Willow said, "like hummingbird feathers and eagle talons."

The fish, racks of them sun-drying nearby, filled the air with their telltale odor. Padre observed them with a curious expression.

"When the sun makes the bluegills very dry, we store in calabashes," the elderly Singing Basket Weaver said, wiggling her fingers so as to show her long weaver's fingernails, thicker than raccoon claws. "In winter we cook bluegill chowder."

Honey Cloverleaf touched three fish, one by one, with her forefinger, counting, "*Humken, Hokkolen, Osten.*"

"No, no," Willow said. "It is *Humken, Hokkolen, Tutcenen, Osten,* one, two, three, four—not one, two, four." Then she walked over and hugged the child.

Padre silently admired Willow, not only for her skill in using her long, pliant fingers, but also for an inner quality that radiated calmness and confidence, compassion, too. He would love to try to convert her to the Holy Catholic faith but dared not risk Genesis' reaction. He bade the Weavers farewell and set out to seek solace at the blue pond sanctuary.

Without breaking gait, Padre descended the bluff overlooking the blue heron rookery and cast his vision neither upward nor downward. Instead, he looked straight ahead, directly in line with the cross at the other side of the blue pond. Before his eyes met the cross, they fixed on the largest brown and blue fowl he had ever seen. Could it be? Closer, yes? No? *No, it was not a bird.* It was the princess sitting amidst the herons as if spellbound. Something else had caught his attention, also, and he must warn her about it right away. He eased toward her ever so carefully. The birds moved toward the pond, though not a whit did she move. He said softly, "Princess Blue Heron, it is I, the padre. There is something I must tell you." Still, she remained stoic. He gently sat near her. "I do not wish to startle you, but I must tell you something important. There is great danger nearby. There's a blue snake, a big blue snake over yonder on that bump of a hill. There, by that hole," he pointed.

Without turning her head, she said, "I know. Indigo snakes are sacred. It will go into the rattlesnake hole and eat the rattler."

"Rattlesnakes are poisonous."

"Not for sacred indigo. They eat the rattlers and then live in their holes."

Her poise and confidence settled him somewhat. The explanation seemed unbelievable, though on second thought, he felt she knew whereof she spoke. The snake slithered into the burrow.

The time had come at last when Padre had a chance to study Blue Heron's profile. Her face, with high cheekbones and smooth bronze skin, was framed by her long, black hair—straight and shiny. A tortoise shell comb, beneath the back of her headdress, stilled the shimmering strands from the southern breeze.

She finally turned to face him. Large, elliptical eyes, centered with onyx orbs, windowed the look that had haunted him ever since the day she had handed him the raffia wash mat. More recently, she had almost confided a secret to him near the sanctuary but had run away. Today, maybe, she would divulge it.

# A NEW *ANDALUCIA*

Hundreds of tiny, bright blue blossoms spangled on the background bushes like jewels. Sweetly scented, they helped neutralize the fetidness of fresh heron dung, its odor having been accentuated by sun-baked sand. Mosquitoes buzzed. Padre, without thinking, slapped at a fiercely biting one. The princess did not even blink. With ambivalence, he went ahead and dared—he must take the chance—to move a little closer so as to be within a more comfortable speaking range. Her herbal rubbings wafted. No wonder the mosquitoes chose not to feast upon her.

In a spiritual gaze Princess Blue Heron cut her eyes obliquely for a moment, her only movement. *The missionary's hump—today it is on the side closest to me—it covers part of his face from my sight. Surely the large thing is sacred, filled with spirits which other people do not have. Even with special spirits in his hump, there is so much he would not understand.*

Blue Heron had revered shamanic gifts since childhood, many times choosing to practice healing with her basket of spiritual objects rather than play with a doll. The missionary knew nothing about the care Shaman Skytalker and her mother and father had always given so that she could develop shaman's ways. Not even these dear people knew how she longed more than ever to possess true shamanic powers since the deaths of Brave Thrower and Tupelo. Lately she had beseeched ancestors for guidance more and more and would make greater, painstaking efforts in future spirit quests.

Though Shaman Skytalker had warned the villagers against taking on the white missionary's religion, she pondered whether ancestors might have sent the padre to show her the white god magic. The white man's strange ways might help the Creek in these changing times, especially since Sharp

Knife had defeated northern Creek clans, and many of the people had moved to the Florida Territory. As long as she could keep it secret from the elders and other villagers, search for white man's powers might be all right, might bring better vision quests. Her father and mother and the Owl Clan would honor her. One day she would earn a shaman's name.

Princess Blue Heron gently straightened her posture and rotated her head as she permitted her dreamlike vision to leave her body. She studied the feather-like clouds. They looked like owl feathers, surely lucky since they floated overhead in a protective way. Never would this type of clouds touch the ground with an unlucky warning. Now she felt brave, braver than when she had talked with the missionary and had run away. The time now felt right, so she looked toward the missionary and asked, "When you bend your knee and lower it to the ground and bow your head before the high table, what does that mean?"

"The high table is an altar where I offer praise and prayers to God," the enthralled padre said. "When I bend my knee and bow, it is called genuflecting. That means I am showing respect and honor to God. It comes as natural to me as breathing." A voice in his head cried *show restraint*. He must use utmost care and not bungle his chance to convert her to the Holy Word. He said, "I never saw so many blue herons in one place."

Princess Blue Heron, her hypnotic expression now fully replaced by naturalness, said, "Through the canebrakes, the great birds go wading, searching for the right meal. Today I learned that herons make no ripple when they step in water. Without warning, their beaks stab the water, and they swallow. Sometimes I do not even see their catch."

Padre pointed upward and said, "There goes one flying away, legs and feet still extended." He glanced back and forth between her and the bird. "And look at that wing span." He stretched both arms out, sideways, as far as possible and said, "The wings are wider than both my arms can stretch, at least six feet."

She nodded.

"Except for that wide wing span, you are most aptly named." He paused when he noticed her position poised against a backdrop of wild apple trees. Why was he taking note of the apple trees? He wasn't exactly sure. Though a bit startled for some vague reason, he felt obligated to continue what he had started. "You have the same graceful walk…and if you don't think I am invading your privacy, I would like to add that you have a long, graceful neck, and the long legs, too, like herons, though you have only four feathers."

She half smiled and caught herself. "Creek are good at studying their members and giving the right names. I liked my name very much till my husband was killed. I now wish to earn a new name." She would not tell him that she yearned for a name worthy of a shaman, for he would not understand the ways of Breath Maker.

"You were so absorbed in watching the herons when I arrived, you did not notice my presence."

"I knew you were there. I felt your spirit in the ground as you walked nearer. But I must keep my mind only on the herons while I study them with my heart. I wish to receive their spirits inside my bones for the bird dance. This dance is very important, a gift from ancestors' teachings."

"Where will you dance?"

"I always dance the Blue Heron Dance at the *Poskita*. Whites call it Green Corn Ceremony."

"I would like to see your special dance. May I?"

"Yes, all the villagers come. Soon the maize gets ripe. Then we fast and make ready for the celebration. The bird dance comes in the evening after the feast and games."

She picked up a stick and said, "A stick like this has much meaning for herons and for my dance."

"I would like to hear more about the stick's meaning."

"Sticks are important to herons when they look for mates. About a moon, or maybe two moons ago, herons looked for mates. The man heron brings a stick to the woman heron. The woman is perched on last year's nest and if she likes him, she will take the stick and add it to the nest."

"What happens if she does not like him?"

"If he does not fit her liking, she drops the stick and sends him away."

Padre started to smile and thought better of it when Whistling Acorn's banishment came to his mind. "Their nests must be very big," he said. "Where are they?"

"Yes. Very big." She stretched her arms out from each side as far as they would extend and said, "They are this big. At the top of tall trees."

"I never knew a stick could be of such importance to herons."

"Yes. When the ways of the stick are settled, they get together. The woman heron lays three or four eggs, maybe even six. Both herons take turns keeping the eggs warm."

"That's a nice story. When do the eggs hatch?"

"Heron babies not long ago shook off their shells. May Song Moon time—about the time you and Genesis came to the village. You seemed new to me, new as new baby herons."

"You know very much about your namesake."

"I try very hard to learn about herons' spirits. To understand, you must be quiet and still. Wait very, very long time to see everything about herons' lives, to feel inside your bones, your flesh, and your heart every time they move their legs, their heads and necks, and wings and every sound they make. You have to live their life. It makes my heart happy. I like herons very much." She hesitated.

Padre forced silent forbearance. And he reaped more than he had ever expected.

"There's something else I like very much," she said. Again, she hesitated as if gathering courage, then began anew. "I like very much the word I heard the braves talking and laughing about when they found you in the forest swamp."

In contemplation, Padre stroked his beard. It was strange how those fearsome moments now brought ecstasy to him. Endurance, blessedly, had brought rewards linking him to a potential candidate for conversion, conversion from the nonsense of shamanic powers. He smiled. "I think you are speaking about *Andalucia*, the region from whence I came."

She smiled and nodded.

"An-da-lu-cee-a is in Spain. The beautiful area here reminds me of it. The rivers here run about the same distance to the sea as the one on which my home village is located. The warm weather is also much like my homeland."

She tried saying the strange word, making several attempts. She finally came close to the correct pronunciation with, "Analoosa." She covered her mouth for a moment and then shyly said, "I like the word."

"I like it too, and the land it names. I like it so much, I've given that name to this area around the blue pond. I call it New *Andalucia*. It is so much like our *Andalucia*, Spain, except there are no mountains."

"What are mountains?"

Again, he stoked his beard in contemplation. "The best way to describe mountains, I think, is to call them very large hills, very large ones."

"Higher than our tallest trees?"

"Some mountains are."

"I think I would fear them."

"Some are fearsome."

Padre would wait no longer to broach the subject of their last meeting when she had finally come out of her hiding and had begun to tell him a secret but had run away. "I would like very much," he said, "to hear the secret you almost told me over by the cross."

Princess Blue Heron covered her mouth with both hands and froze in place, save for uncertainty rising in her eyes. She hoped the buckskin pouch dangling from her hands, though small, would help distract his attention from her expression. No fear should ever show, for it was a sign of weakness. Under the cover of her hands, her mouth spoke before her heart was ready, mumbling, "I know not what to do about something I saw."

"Tell me about it. Maybe I can help you."

Suddenly, she lost faith in her decision to talk, clasped her hands behind her back, and sought the spirit rock in her pouch. It felt smooth and cool and calming, strong, too, as she rubbed it, careful not to let her motions become known.

"I...I saw a man, a black man hiding nearby the river," she sighed. "I think he needs help, but if I tell my father about him...," Her voice had faded. She rubbed the rock, her hands now clammy and not gliding easily.

Padre said, "The black man must be a slave...a runaway slave."

She nodded. "Some tribes capture runaway slaves to do their work or to sell them. But I...but I. No, no one should ever know this. I do not think it's right to capture slaves. Or buy them either, or sell them."

"I agree with you with all my heart."

She caught a deep breath. "I...I have been watching you in your spirit ceremonies. That is why I thought you could help me do something for the man. He looks sick, may be dying. I would like to help him. I hope this does not displease you." She must be careful not to let him know that she also watched him because she wanted to learn how to make better vision quests. The Owl Clan Council knows that whites' religion is not good for tribe.

Padre would hold onto the thought of the black man and first seize the chance to address the more pressing matter of conversion. If this plan did not work, he would redouble his efforts to the issue of the black man, an urgent matter, also, but one which he felt confident in handling. He would begin his plan in a casual manner. "As I have told you in my chants, I knew you were there. I caught glimpses of the four blue feathers from time to time. And it had to be you who sometimes placed fresh bouquets of blue water lilies by the altar."

She hung her head in shyness.

"Their beauty stirred my heart. But I couldn't understand why you always hid from me, and in the village, you always vanished from my sight."

With her head still lowered Princess Blue Heron said, "I do not like whites. They killed my husband." Then she looked up and said, "But you carry no weapons. And I like your spirit ceremonies. The honorable bowing is best."

"It is called genuflecting." Again he said the word, but slowly, "Gen-u-flect-ing."

"The word seems so strange," she said.

"It will not be so hard for you to say when you get accustomed to it. It is a part of worship." He would use his best effort to control his strong emotions, and not refute her false feelings about white skin until he had a chance to build rapport with her.

"You make strange signs on your chest," she said. "And I like the way you touch yourself with the water before you start ceremonies and when you finish. When you do those sacred-looking things, your ways look much like the shaman's spirit ways. And your singing..." Her voice faded again. Speechless, she could not tell him that the sounds sometimes made her insides quiver. It was a thing she could not accept to expect that which had come to her in her loneliness might be shared with a near stranger. She cleared her throat and said, "You must never, never tell anyone the things I say."

"No. Never. I will never tell anyone. Your talk fills my heart with gladness. I would love to teach you all about God's holy symbols. They are not spiritual in the way you think, but yes, they are most sacred."

She clamped her lips together, rapid thoughts racing. No, no. Not his God. Never. Only his holy symbols that she could use in vision quests. This was what she needed to learn about. "The water in the bowl you touch it to your face," she said, knowing that was something she could do. "I watch you every time with my best eyesight and best listening, but I cannot understand what you do to the water."

She adjusted her posture. It was better to suffer than show weakness. Then she said, "But now I need other help. I need to know what to do about the black man. I have made vision quests to find an answer. Ancestors did not guide me to anyone else for help. There is no one, no other person I can tell about him. My mind knows no rest," she said, her voice wavering. She had *almost* given away her secret yearning for shamanic powers, but perhaps he did not notice. She must be more careful.

"Tell me more about why you hesitate to trust me."

"You look so strange with your beard, and I fear you, too. Your skin is white."

His time had finally come to change her mind about whites. "Not all white people are alike." He pinched the skin on his arm. "Our skins are different only in color. Underneath the skin, my heart is filled with goodness," he said proudly. "I think yours is, too. That's what counts." His eyes narrowed as he tried to ensure his sincerity.

Once again, the expression reminded Blue Heron of her husband who had died bravely. That was the way he had always looked whenever he wanted to prove his most heartfelt truthfulness. "Yes," she said. "But you see, I...I heard elders arguing many times. Some said tribe should capture runaway slaves if they see one. Many of our braves were killed at Horseshoe Bend. Then many Creek ran away to Florida Territory. Owl Clan needs slaves. They could even barter a slave for tools, maybe a gun. Other elders say Breath Maker sends evil spirits to those who keep slaves...I prayed many times for a vision dream...for truth. My vision dreams tell me it's not right to have slaves. I think the black man needs help," she said and shuddered. Not only had she shuddered for the black man, but also because she had almost slipped yet another time with her other secret of practicing the missionary's ways in the red hole.

"I understand." Padre said. "I know some tribes have slaves. But I think you will feel better to learn that at the Pensacola mission, we befriended runaway slaves. We called them maroons. Part of my mission work was to help them. One maroon I'd counseled, I saw the very evening Genesis and I left Pensacola. That maroon and his Creek wife were catching crabs there on the water's edge."

"Did you know Creek women, like Genesis' mother, before you came here?"

"I knew a number of them, but I never saw his mother after she left Pensacola and joined a band of Seminole. But yes. I knew of other Creek women, some very wonderful people like Angel Roundtree. The mission assisted them whenever possible. Come," Padre extended a hand, "We will get a drink of water at the spring. You will feel better. It's the iciest, bluest water I ever saw, the best I ever tasted." He would not tell her how his leg tingled as he arose. He was unaware that it had gone numb from sitting in a cramped position.

"I know. I know. I always drink there."

"Well," he said shifting his weight from his tingling leg, "if you do not wish a drink of water, will you please tell me more about this black man?"

"I do not know...except he is hiding, but I heard him moan. He looks sick...scared, and I think he is hungry. He carries a strange thing like a gourd drum with a handle. It hangs by a rope from over his shoulder. The strange thing has a long handle with strings stretched across the top. The strings...they are long as the whole thing, about this long." She held up her hands about three feet apart.

"Will you show me where he's hiding?"

She cast her eyes downward. Could she tell the white man? She squeezed the spirit rock, running her thumb around its edge. "No, I don't know if I should. I worry if...if villagers find out. He is hiding in a secret place, beyond the river trail, close to where I sometimes go on...," Her voice faded. She must not mention the sacred red-clay hole.

"But you see," Padre said, "perhaps I can help him, maybe tell him how to get to a priest I know in Pensacola. This priest could help him."

The princess studied the padre's face.

"Only if you promise to keep the secret."

"I promise; God is my witness," and he crossed himself. The princess looked as vulnerable as the softest feathers on the vanes of her feathered headdress, the wispy ones closest to the quill. "The man must be starving. I can take my evening bowl of stew to him." He stroked his beard. "Maybe if we give him food, he will talk with us." Padre paused, his eyes blinking rapidly. Then he said, "I have a plan. I'll meet you at the river trail with food for the man. You," he pointed to her, "stay in the forest near the edge of the trail. I can walk the path and follow your blue feathers as you lead. As soon as it is safe, you can motion for me to join you."

She nodded. "I must return to the village. I will leave now. I will go fast."

With greatest pleasure, Padre watched her lilt away. Then he walked toward the spring. He was making progress with a potential convert. He nodded his head in confirmation. He helped himself to the icy-blue spring water.

Walking onward, he felt his steps springing in the sandy shoal with utmost ease. He shed his boots for greater enjoyment of this feeling and moved along the pond's edge, meditating. He reflected on the different parishioners at St. Michael's Mission and Padre de Galvez, Father Mulvaney, as well. To celebrate his progress in reaching Princess Blue Heron with the first lesson of the Holy Catholic Word, he would practice his finest Gregorian chants.

Without usual careful attention to her surroundings, Princess Blue Heron hastened along by instinct, disheartened that she could have been wrong in entrusting the white missionary with so much. Would he keep the promise? She also worried that since Owl Nose knew her scent so well, he may have followed her. Her father had always trusted Owl Nose's spirit sense of smell. In times of worry about whether she was fasting too long after her husband was killed, he had sometimes sent Owl Nose to follow her for protection. A stray villager could have seen her, too. In past visits to and from the blue pond, a part of her had always kept mindful of this possibility. She had always taken notice of the way every blade of grass stood or laid, whether the movements of leaves and branches were caused by a breeze or an animal, or a villager. More important, she had frequently sniffed the air for any odor of bear grease. But today she was unmindful. Yet, who in the village would be interested in coming here to see the missionary's ceremony except her. The only other member of the Owl Clan interested in vision quests was the shaman, and Shaman Skytalker wanted no part of the missionary's ways.

In her most heartfelt way she needed to make sure of the missionary's honesty as well as make sure her visits to the blue pond to watch his spirit ways would bring no evil. She must go to the red-clay hole in Mother Earth and ask ancestors to send spirit guides. She could not risk stirring their anger and suffering their punishment by evil spirits.

At the sacred red hole, she stopped and bowed to Breath Maker before entering it. Then, very carefully, she would try the genuflecting action just one more time. First, she bent her right knee and lowered it all the way to the red clay ground. Maybe she had done it correctly this time. But today, worries still tormented. Had she told the missionary too much? She waited, more anxious than ever, to see if there would be any reaction from evil spirits. When none came, except red dust on her knee, she tried to look full of dignity upon arising, just as the padre had always done. After she had gone through the ritual several times, with no ill effects, her heart began filling with contentment. She may have mastered it this time. It would certainly be beneficial in her spirit quests. Yet she could not make a vision quest today. She did not have her basket of spiritual objects with her. And she decided not to look for the black man now. There was not enough time. Hurriedly she climbed out of the red hole and made her way to the village.

The shaman, the chief, her mother, the villagers—none of them should learn about her practicing the strange ways, nor that she would take the missionary to meet the slave this evening. Search for white man's powers and help for the black man might not bring evil spirits, as long as these matters were kept secret.

Caution gave way to joy.

*White missionary's ways may help me earn a shaman's name. My father and mother and the Owl Clan will be proud of me.*

After returning home, she stashed maize cakes in a small basket and hurried to meet the missionary.

As the sun was close to setting, Padre and Blue Heron advanced closer and closer to the black man's hideout. The wide-eyed padre stepped stealthily as a hunter stalking prey. To his amazement, he had followed at Princess Blue Heron's pace as she glided effortlessly on her tiptoes. They proceeded in utter silence, Padre holding the bowl of stew upright, weaving in and out of the trees, and avoiding dense palmettoes as furtively as she.

All of a sudden, Princess Blue Heron held up her hand and stopped. "Listen, smell," she whispered, "he's snoring." Then she pointed, "Look. The black man. He's sweating."

The man's nearness, when they discovered him, startled both of them, for he was lying down, and they came near him before they realized it. At once, the man opened his eyes, and when he glimpsed Padre and Princess Blue Heron, he struggled to his feet, snuck around a swag of palmettoes, and hid behind a tree.

They continued their approach tentatively. Meanwhile, Padre talked in the gentlest tone he could find from within himself.

"We come as friends," he said. "We have food for you. We want to help you. See," he beckoned with the clay bowl of stew stretched forth in his hand. "And when you eat we will leave you alone. We are not here to capture or hurt you."

The man did not come forth. He just darted glances from behind the tree, his nostrils seeking scent of the food.

"If we go closer, he may run away," Padre said softly. "Let's just wait a while and try again."

Padre would not give up. He must succeed in order to gain Princess Blue Heron's trust. But his repeated pleas brought only disappointment. Minute by minute his expectations, once so high, dwindled. Shadows in the forest made his skin crawl. Sudden fear overwhelmed him momentarily. He squared his shoulders, got hold of himself and said, "We'll try again tomorrow."

Princess Blue Heron nodded. Padre saw only her nod, not her grieved face. He raked a mound of brown pine needles with his hand and placed the bowl of stew on top. Princess Blue Heron fanned the flies from the stew and placed two maize cakes over it.

"We will return tomorrow evening with more food," Padre said loud enough for the man to hear. "We want you to get your strength back. And I promise, as God is our witness, not to tell anyone that you are here. Enjoy your food. Eat it before the ants and animals get it. We will see you tomorrow."

# THE *BANZA*

Before falling asleep that evening, Padre prayed that the Negro man would still be there the next day. Performing benevolent deeds for the man presented a golden opportunity to impress Princess Blue Heron, for she wanted so much to help the sojourner.

But when they approached his hiding place the next evening, he was nowhere in sight. Had he left? They crept closer. The clay bowl they had brought the previous evening lay on its side, empty, blowflies still scavenging residual nothingness. Had an animal eaten the stew? Not only was the bowl empty but also the spot where they had first found him asleep. Both of their faces registered bitter disappointment as they stared at the tree, that same tree, where they'd left him the previous evening.

Padre whispered, "Did you see a movement behind the farther tree?"

"He is there!" Princess Blue Heron exclaimed in her softest voice.

"Yes, yes," Padre said in a low voice. "He's peeking again."

Though awestruck, Padre sensed already that they might have better luck talking with him this time, for even in the dusk of the forest, the man had appeared more vital in his fleeting motion today. Perhaps he had, indeed, eaten the food.

And predictable as the oncoming night, odors of today's food brought longer glances from the man. His nostrils flared. Finally, he came creeping forth with caution. The crude instrument that he carried resembled a banjo, which Padre had seen in Pensacola. A rope tied to each end of it was hitched upon his shoulder like the strap of a shoulder pouch. Wariness suddenly seemed to overcome him. He stopped. Barefoot, he wore only loose, ragged pants, short ones, held up with a single rope gallus, which slanted on the bias from his waist, then over his chest and shoulder. From the side view, you could see that it again slanted diagonally across his back to the opposite side and was attached at his waist. Punctures for the gallus added two additional holes in his pants.

Padre gasped, for now as he came closer, marks on the man's body looked like welts and wounds. Dark, crusted blood covered some. Others looked as if they had been recently reinjured. Padre winced as though he had just been inflicted with a similar wound. He swallowed hard and swallowed another time to recover his composure. Then he lifted his shell crucifix from his chest with his clammy hands and held it forward, saying, "This cross symbolizes God. I wear it to show people I do God's work. I help people and tell them about God."

The man gave a slight nod in a knowing manner.

Since the man seemed to understand, Padre extended the bowl with his other hand, and said, "More stew for you. Here, smell it. It smells good." At that very moment Padre reached in his carrying basket for the maize cakes to go along with the stew, and the man dodged behind a tree again. "Don't be afraid, I reached only for these maize cakes. See. Smell. I have no weapon. He turned the basket sideways. There's nothing with which to hurt you. I promise not to hurt you." With the food in his hands, Padre stretched his arms forward as far as he could extend them.

The man took another furtive glance at the bowl, thrust a hand as if to fetch the bowl, then backed away with a suspicious expression. One maize cake fell to the ground. Anon, the bread blackened with ants. The man bent down and scooped it up with his large hand, all the while his line of vision remaining steadfast on the padre and Princess Blue Heron. He blew the ants from the bread and devoured it. Then he lurched forward and grabbed the bowl.

"Let's sit," Padre said, motioning to a log about four feet uphill. Padre and the princess sat on one end. At last, the black man took guarded steps toward it and, with greatest caution, eased down on the far end of the log. He maintained a fixed stare at them as he relished the food, downing it in no time at all.

Princess Blue Heron swung one leg over and straddled the log, facing the black man. Her swift action had nothing to do with modesty nor the absence of undergarments. Instead, she was merely moving with her instinctive quickness, and surprisingly the action did not frighten the fugitive. Padre straddled the log, also, though not with her agility.

"I promise," Padre said looking directly at the black man, "not to tell anyone that you are hiding here." He crossed himself and raised his right hand. After a brief pause, he added, "I promise you more. I'll bring food to you each day till you are strong enough to continue your journey."

The man stared, wordless.

"I am Padre Juan Adamio Morales. My friend here," he touched her shoulder, "is Princess Blue Heron, from the nearby Indian village. She found you resting here and wanted to help you. Will you tell us your name?"

"Don't make no difference."

"Oh yes, it does make a difference. I want to know. I'm interested in your welfare. My friend, Princess Blue Heron," Padre said as he touched her shoulder again, "wants to make a difference, too, a big difference in your life." The mere feel of Blue Heron's soft skin throbbed through him. Waves of guilt followed close behind. He had not intended to be so forward by touching her. He cleared his throat. It gave no relief. In the stillness, forest sounds echoed eerily. Strange territory and darkness made all the difference. Mosquitoes buzzed louder. Then a startling splash vibrated from the direction of the river. A hungry alligator or snake? Maybe just a huge fish or turtle?

Meanwhile, all three studied one other.

At last, the man answered, "They calls me Chad."

"Good name. All right, Chad," Padre said as he stroked his beard. Should he direct this man to Pensacola so that Padre de Galvez might help him? Would Chad get snared by American soldiers? It was terribly risky but still the best of existing evils. He decided he must say it. "I will give you my best advice. I think you should walk the Indian Ridge Trail going south. It borders the river to Pensacola."

"Heard tell of a trail."

"Good. I know where you should be able get help in Pensacola, because if I'm right you've run away from a master. Uh, is that right?" Then he quickly added, "Now don't be afraid to tell the truth. It will be kept a secret. I just want to help you."

Chad kept silent for a spell. He cut his eyes away, nodded, and held his head as if it were heavy as a cannonball. He said, "I run and walked...climbed trees if'n I heard somethin'. I run and walked...for days...maybe three days...stayin' close by the rivers, till the world turned black. I woke up here."

Padre asked, "Did you find any food on the way?"

"Found nuts and acorns, left over from last year. And berries. I et so many I got the scours."

"That's too bad. But I'll tell you, Chad, the trail to Pensacola is not too hard to follow, though in some places of heavy growth, you have to be careful that you stay on it. I traveled that very trail all the way from Pensacola, only about two months ago. And when you get to Pensacola, go to Padre de Galvez. Everyone knows him. He's an old man, very kindly old man. Been a missionary there a long, long time."

Padre started to pick up a rock but stopped. He said, "I will take a rock to scratch Father de Galvez's name on a stick. I will also scribe his helper's name—Father Mulvaney. Either one of them can give you help. Carry the stick with you. Now don't be afraid of the rock. I won't hurt you."

Padre pounded the smallest rock he could find with a larger one to get a sharp edge. While he scratched the names on the stick, Chad appeared ready to make a fast getaway at a moment's notice. Though the etching rock was small, Chad's eyes darted from it to the direction of the river, back and forth.

"Padre de Galvez and Father Mulvaney will do what they can to help you. And if you wait and look long enough, you're bound to run into a maroon—that's an escaped slave who has become a free man in the Spanish territory. A maroon will show you the way. But you must not, and I emphasize you must *not*, be seen by any American soldiers. They'll capture you for sure. Do you understand?"

Blue Heron had hung onto Padre's every word as if reading his every intonation, every gesture.

While they waited for Chad's response, the croaking of the river frogs reverberated through the trees, their hoarse cries resounding with much greater gusto than usual. Dusk had already brought on the hooting of owls in the background.

Chad nodded, though even in the twilight his face reflected suspected danger. Finally, his expression eased, but it was only after Padre had thrown away the etching stone.

Padre handed him the scribed stick and said, "Tell us about the wounds and welts on your body. We can bring you some resin to cover them."

Chad did not answer. Deepened twilight had descended upon them.

"I think you've been beaten," Padre said. "Was it your master?"

Chad shook his head. Eventually he said, "Masser pulled out his pistol and chunked bullwhip to Big Boy. Ordered, 'Draw blood.'" Chad paused. Then with a grave expression he said, "Big Boy hoed cotton with me. When Big Boy didn't want to whip me, Masser hollered, 'Crack that whip, you blockhead before I kill both you niggers.'" Chad had held up his hand to show how the master had drawn the pistol. Then he swiped his forehead.

In the distance a wolf howled plaintively, just like the howls Padre had heard when he and Genesis had been escorted from the swamp by the Creek. As he looked in the direction of the haunting howl, luminous fungus on a rotted log caught his eye. It glowed more eerily than any fox fire he had ever seen.

Nausea gripped Padre. His flesh crawled. He grabbed his stomach with one hand and his mouth with the other, fearing he might retch. Though he did not vomit, Chad's whiplash wounds stung and pained as if his own nerve endings were completely naked. It was one thing to hear of Napoleon's atrocities in Spain, but oh so different to come face to face with similar ones in American woods. At once, he worried that the princess had seen his reaction.

No. Thank God. Princess Blue Heron had cupped her hands over her gaping mouth, her moist eyes still anchored on the wounds.

"The whip lash snapped, curled around me, throwed me down. Snapped and snapped till I couldn't see Masser's pistol pointin' at us no more. My soul left the world till next day."

Padre at last thawed sufficiently to utter, "Inhumane. It's unbelievable the torture one human being is capable of inflicting on another." He shook his head woefully.

"When I come back to life, I knowed I had to run away, try to find my wife at a sugar plantation in Florida. Even if I die."

"Why did that devil have you beaten?"

"My heart was sick for my wife. She be sold to sugar plantation owner in Florida." He brushed some maize cake crumbs from his lips. "Couldn't hoe fast as I used to."

With great difficulty, Padre swallowed and said, "I extend to you my heartfelt sympathy." When he looked around, he blurted in astonishment, "Angels above, it's getting awfully late." He noticed Blue Heron's worried expression. "Chad, wait here for us tomorrow. Near sundown we will come. Now don't leave. We will bring ointment, resin ointment, for your sores, uh, whiplashes, so you don't get an infection. More food, too, and some extra for your journey."

Padre and Princess Blue Heron stood. In silence, all three seemingly sorting through all they'd learned from each other. Princess Blue Heron picked up the bowls, and she and Padre began walking away. No sooner had they started than Padre turned around and said, "Now remember. I ask that you wait for us tomorrow."

Chad shrugged, then haltingly nodded.

The sojourner's lack of commitment aroused skepticism in Padre. He wanted with all his heart for Princess Blue Heron to be satisfied with the outcome of this undertaking. Success of this mission was important, not only for Chad's benefit, but also, it offered the promise of an introductory step in gaining Princess Blue Heron's favor. Not just for converting her, rather, her influence might benefit his stay in the village. She could possibly speak in his behalf to regain his shoulder bag with his holy possessions. This venture mustn't fail.

The following evening, Padre waited at the river trail. He worried when he did not see the blue-feathered headdress in the edge of the forest. What had happened to Princess Blue Heron? He hoped no one would smell the food in his carrying basket. He sauntered about the entrance of the river trail and tried to appear as if meditating while waiting around.

Desperately, he wanted this mission of mercy to be fulfilled without detection by any villager, most of all, by Owl Nose. Part of Padre's *Caritas* training had included providing alms. While waiting he reflected on the beloved Latin word, for it meant more than love, more than caring. He tipped his head to sanction this. Still, the blue feathers had not shown up. Meanwhile he worried, too, about whether General Jackson had invaded Pensacola. Would American soldiers find and capture Chad? Had he made the right decision in his advice to Chad? Was Padre de Galvez still alive...or well enough to help the escapee?

Out of the corner of his eye, he saw movement among tree limbs. His heart beat faster. His eyes widened. On the second look, it was just a pair of rival squirrels in a territorial skirmish or some other antic. Another time, motion in the woods caught his attention. No blue feathers emerged. Nay, nay. The gentle action turned out to be nothing other than a browsing deer. His shoulders slumped. Then squirrels scampered again, perhaps the same pair he'd seen previously. The sun hung low now, dark shadows lengthened. Only a few birdsongs and the occasional, gentle rustling of palmettoes sounded.

After he'd waited as long as he could tolerate, he reluctantly left, walking in the direction of the river. He felt ever so leery about finding his way to Chad's exact spot. Try, try. He must try to find that hiding spot.

A few yards down the path, he looked back and blessedly caught sight of the blue-feathered headdress. His heart pounded with gladness. Never before was he so happy to see the four blue feathers as this time. As Blue Heron approached, he sighed, *"Whew,"* and caught a deep breath. "What happened? Did some one get suspicious? Is anything wrong?"

"Shhh. Owl Nose saw me with this," she said under her breath and pointed to the buckskin cache of food. "If Owl Nose smelled the food, he might follow. He might know something already. I fear," she whispered through the sultry air. "He might be worried about me. Maybe my mother asked him again to keep evil away from me. He has the sharpest sense for smell, sharper than anyone else in Owl Clan."

The thought of Owl Nose possibly following them struck Padre like an impaling scythe. To the devil with him. Padre flung his hand downward and swung it backwards in dismissal. By the grace of God, he must prevail with Princess Blue Heron. He mustn't allow the likes of that meddling savage to besiege him with yet another crisis in this wilderness.

Padre kept glancing toward the white daisies edging the path. Their brightness reassured his steps. Princess Blue Heron had said, "They are the last to give up light in the evenings and the first to bring forth light in the mornings." But would Chad give up on them? No. By the grace of God, he had waited, though he stood looking anxious to leave. Also, by the grace of God, they had not been nabbed by the hook of Owl Nose. Yet, could he be lurking nearby?

"*Deo gratias*," Padre whispered, "Chad's still here." So relieved, he even became conscious of the ever-present, ever-biting mosquitoes. He swatted them and marveled at the fact that they never seemed to bother Princess Blue Heron. He couldn't decide which was the lesser of the evils, the herbal odors or biting mosquitoes.

Chad swallowed at the sight of the food. While he ate the squirrel stew and acorn cakes, Padre kept vigil for any sign of Owl Nose. Assuaged and confident that they now were probably safe from Owl Nose's potential interference, Padre asked Chad if he could hold the musical instrument. Surely it must be a crude banjo. After looking it over, he said, "We would like to hear what it sounds like."

Chad handed him the empty clay bowl and said, "I play for you. Then I go to find my wife." When he stood to strum the instrument, he held his shoulders higher than on the previous day. Though his expression remained sorrowful, he no longer cowered like a mistreated human.

The sight of the whiplash welts again grappled the pit of Padre's stomach. Never would he forget this atrocity. He lifted his own shoulders upward and said, "I saw an instrument in Pensacola that resembled this one." Padre cleared his throat in an effort to find a more cheerful speaking tone. Then he said, "Did you make this one?"

Chad shook his head. "Old man made it. Masser took our drums. Said he heard slaves at other plantation sending messages with drums. Said messages help slaves escape. An old man in our hut had good idea. He remembered the Kimbundu *mbanza* in Africa, so he cut out the top of a gourd and put a long stick in one end where he cut a hole. Then he cut out another top for the gourd after we et a groundhog."

"I know, I know," Princess Blue Heron interrupted. "He saved the groundhog skin and stretched it over the open-faced gourd, but first he scraped and cured it," she smiled. "Then he pulled gut string around to hold the skin on. And I say more." She pointed, "I can see he used groundhog guts for strings."

"Zactly right," Chad said.

"What do you call this?" Padre asked.

"We calls it a *banza.*"

Chad strummed the strings and surprisingly sang rhythmically to percussive plucks, "I'm just a poor way-far-ing stran-ger a-trav-lin' through this world of woe." He stopped and said, "We learn't this from some travlin' folks. Masser let them camp close to our quarters with their two covered wagons, and we listened to 'em singing by the fire after they cooked and et. In a few days they left, said they was heading west."

"Now I be on my way south to find my wife." Surprisingly he then sang another line: "I'm go-in there to see my Maud-ie." His eyes shone with welling tears as he added, "If I can find the sugar plantation in Florida where she be sold."

"Wait, Chad," Padre said. "We brought food for your trip, and Princess Blue Heron has resin ointment to put on your wounds."

"I already smelt somethin' good in the buckskin." Chad smiled wryly.

The waning daylight was barely adequate for them to apply the ointment to Chad's wounds. He sat not uttering a word, nor a single sound, not even squirming. As they worked ever so closely, Padre smelled Princess Blue Heron's herbal odor, unaware that this time she'd rubbed her arms and shoulders with sage for luck. Though this was not the first time he had smelled the same herbal wafts, this evening her scent seemed different, much more intimate.

Then they combined their offerings of smoked venison and maize cakes, as well as parched maize. Princess Blue Heron retied the four corners of the buckskin cache and handed it to Chad with a smile.

"Remember to follow the trail," Padre said. "It's never very far from the river. If you wander away from it, you could easily get lost in the forest. I hope you find Padre de Galvez, for he can help direct you to the sugar plantations. And I hope, with all my heart, you find your wife. God be with you. I will pray for you," he said as he patted Chad's bundle of food and then crossed himself, hoping that Chad would be able to persevere through the primeval forest and swamp.

After he and Princess Blue Heron had walked a few steps, Padre stopped. He turned toward Chad and said, "I must warn you. Don't grab any vines until you make sure they're not coachwhip snakes. And another thing, don't step on any logs until you make sure they're not alligators." The moon had now risen to a point so as to shine on Chad. What Padre saw bothered him. Chad's skin shone with the luster of a satiny ribbon, like an eerie, black-satin funeral ribbon.

Before they slipped off in the darkness of night, Chad turned his head back long enough to answer, "I do my best to keep my stick safe and look out for snakes and 'gators, so I can find sugar cane plantation where my wife be sold. Free my wife. Or die trying."

Triumph graced Padre's steps. He was getting closer and closer to his goal of conversion. Somehow it seemed Blue Heron had discovered that they shared common experiences of losing their dearest loved ones and of deep spiritual strivings to help others. These were natural bridges. However, other obstacles in their contrasting cultures still stood. Could these be surmounted?

All the while, Blue Heron silently thanked Breath Maker for revealing the white missionary's spiritual gifts. She hoped with all her heart that these would add to her shamanic gifts. But no one in the Owl Clan should find out about her interest in the missionary's powers nor of the help, which she and the padre had given Chad.

Padre had trouble staying in step with the princess. Something about this acquaintance, this unconventional relationship with Princess Blue Heron, the likes of which he never before experienced, tantalized and perplexed him, deeply, all at the same time. His only intention had been just to ennoble himself to her in a priestly way. Though this mission had been shrewdly planned and turned out intensely intriguing, it was not at all devious of heart—well all right, maybe, just a little.

Saying evening prayers was worrisome for Padre. In their benevolence, had he and Princess Blue Heron, before they realized it, acquired more than just a staunch camaraderie in carrying out their secretly plotted scheme? He dug his fingertips into his furrowed forehead. Menacing recall of an incident inched bit by bit through his memory, budging with the same difficulty as a stubbornly-stuck boat being kedged from a sand bar: The Pope had yielded to Napoleon's request and granted dispensation to hundreds of French priests who had contracted civil marriages during the revolution. Circumstances of war, albeit still inexcusable, had precipitated the priests' inevitable involvements with women. They were reduced to the state of laymen, unable to perform any religious ceremony or to fill any ecclesiastical office, a most woeful, though justifiable, outcome. *God forfend. I shall not become involved like those priests.*

Although Princess Blue Heron was, indeed, the most beautiful, gentlest woman he had ever known, Padre had staunchly overcome the worldly luxury of telling her so. Why then, Lord have mercy, had he caught her on an occasion or two reveling in her womanhood as if she may have been exploring the possibility of lying with him? He had seen that look, that carnal look, from women in the past and met with no trouble in putting it out of his mind and going about his priestly duties. Now he would not worry. It was Princess Blue Heron's womanly birthright. Years at the monastery had prepared him well for worldly temptations. Yes, he had always sloughed off evil passions with the alacrity of his intellect and substituted divine supplication; but this insular place, this unspoiled paradise of the wilderness, had made such a difference.  Why, dear God?

# OF ONE FIRE

Three full moons had passed since Genesis Zamora and Padre Juan Adamio Morales had arrived at the Creek village. On this early summer morning, Genesis slept with the intensity that only he was capable of. Suddenly he sat up and held himself in place as still as a rabbit that had been paralyzed in a standoff with a predator.

"You must have been dreaming," Padre said.

"I was in a hell of a lacrosse game at the *Poskita*," Genesis said as he stretched and arose. "I dreamed Fish Wrestler got both his arms broke."

"That sounds like a nightmare. There would be no more fish wrestling for him for a while, if that had happened."

"Uh hm. But let me tell you, when I watch him practice lacrosse, I get all worked up. Every evening he gets braver and wilder. All the players say they will win over the other clans at the *Poskita* this year and bring honor to the Owl Clan. Shoot, if I had been practicing since I was knee-high to a brown pelican, I'd be as tough as any of them and help them win."

"The game is too harsh for me," Padre said.

"It may be for you, but I surefire belong to everything here, belong just as much as the moon and the stars belong in the sky. Willow talks so nice about the *Poskita*. She said that it's like a good dream that comes back every year."

"Villagers' passion for the big event seems to be intensifying. I have noticed excitement building in their faces and movements."

"I don't pay no attention. I only know what I heard Willow's family say about the *Poskita* while we built the marriage house. And I guess I've been too busy to listen to or look at anybody except Willow."

227

"I suppose you are anxious to get back to work on your dugout."

"Um hm. But first, I'll work on my chunkey stone," Genesis said and left.

Underneath a live oak tree, Genesis worked on a stone, which he had selected with great care. He honed out the center and then whetted the outer edge until it matched the size of Fish Wrestler's favorite chunkey stone. It looked fine. Fine enough to win? He was unsure. Before sundown each day he practiced the Owl Clan's way of playing the game. Genesis felt good about his ability in throwing the stone, yet he needed more skill in other parts of the game. Before throwing the cane pole to where he guessed his lucky stone would glide, he practiced just sliding the crooked end of the pole behind the rolling stone as he trotted. Next, he started the guessing part of the game—throwing the cane to where he thought the chunkey stone would end its roll. He was learning how to guess well. He would surefire try to win at the *Poskita* games.

The nearly ripened maize signaled that it was time to prepare for the *Poskita*, the most important Creek celebration. Some whites called it the "Busk," others called it the Green Corn Ceremony. This festival of thanksgiving also marked the beginning of a new year.

Chief Wahoo sent Wingfoot, Falcon, and Lightfoot, the newly designated runner, to invite the Alligator, Eagle, and Raccoon Clans to the celebration. The messengers carried bundles of sticks for each of these outlying villages. The runners gave directions for village leaders to break a stick each day. It would be time for the *Poskita* when all the sticks had been broken.

On the evening after the messengers had left with their bundles of sticks, Padre asked Genesis, "Has the Weaver family been discussing the Green Corn Festival? I'd like to know what they say about it from a family's point of view." He tipped his head, proud that he had disguised his craving to hear harmless gossip concerning the Weaver family.

"Willow Trap Weaver and her family surefire told me all about it. That's mostly all they've been talking about lately. I'll tell you. I'll tell you everything."

Genesis and Padre sat against stumps near the summerhouse. Genesis picked up a brown pine needle and idly picked at his teeth while collecting his thoughts.

"The Owl Clan's *Poskita* celebration is a big one," Genesis said. "Lasts for eight days. Notice now, that's double the sacred number of four. In smaller villages they celebrate only four days. One of the most important things," he slapped his thigh for emphasis, "is the fasting. *Poskita* means to fast."

"I uh, I don't understand. You say *Poskita* means to fast, yet this is a celebration?"

"Just let me explain. Creek have both. The first three days are for making ready and cleansing and fasting. Then comes the celebrating. That's when," he said, with triumph rising in his voice, "I will declare my marriage to Willow."

"Oh yes," Padre said and looked down. He knew all too well that after Genesis' marriage, he'd be totally on his own. Besides, it was finally sinking in that the Creek did not want to hear about God and the Catholic Church and Spain. *Senor* Colabro had said that there were so few white settlers and that one needs gunpowder and guts to survive in the Alabama wilderness. Padre had no gunpowder and alas doubted whether he had the guts. Had he escaped the potential trap in Pensacola, only to step into another one here? Yet, he had obeyed his superior's orders. He would fight against feeling embittered, for bitterness carried the taint of a craven.

"I will cleanse my body, my mind too," Genesis said proudly, "with the black drink that Willow's brother gave to me. And I will fast for two days and two nights just like all the braves. I must prepare just right to announce my marriage and start the new year."

"What kind of marriage ceremony will you have?"

"You will see. Owl Claw told me what to do. Hell, it ain't nothing much to it. Nothing to be scared of."

"You seem to enjoy getting settled into the Creek customs. I'll fast at that time also, but it will be for the Holy Day of the Assumption. I'll spend my two days of fasting at my outdoor chapel by the blue pond." How he wished he could celebrate the Eucharist.

The villagers, in preparation for the *Poskita*, started purifying themselves. They drank a strong brew of the vine *Ilex Cassine* in water. This black drink was not only a purgative, cleansing their bowels, but its emetic quality also sent them vomiting. And it contained enough caffeine to keep them stimulated.

When Padre arrived at the blue pond, he righted the cross and altar, wind-blown from the previous day's thunderstorm. Righting his feelings was not as easy. A solitary lily drooped, among charred ones, in one clay vessel. The other vessel lay on its side, empty, its once-beautiful contents now strewn about and rotten. Without fresh, blue, water lily bouquets, the sanctuary boded of emptiness, a grave starkness. What had happened to Princess Blue Heron? He had not talked with her since they bade farewell to Chad. Each time he had caught sight of her in the village she vanished, sometimes as if into air, just as she had done when he first came to the village. More than elusiveness, she obviously disappeared out of sheer avoidance. Understanding…was it ever to be? He chose not to dwell on it.

Instead, he began his first set of prayers, submitting that he had ofttimes accepted changes, setbacks, and never-ending adjustments in daily life. Yet, were these reasonings as objective as he had thought or were they mere absurdities that had deceived his conscience? Staring at the heavens, he lapsed into a reverie. Holy God, would life here forever be a capricious cloud—constant, then inconstant, inchoately forming and reforming cryptic messages, leaving him like a muse in a mass of foolish fodder?

At the blue spring Padre splashed his face over and over, regained his earthly footing by willing himself to reset his feet on the bedrock of his holy training. He centered on the important Holy Day of Assumption and began another series of prayers. It was sublime, spending the afternoon in selfless supplication for the sick, bereaved, and helpless people of the entire world. Yet, how would he get through two nights, alone, here at the blue pond?

As evening settled in at the blue pond, introspections brought such a different perspective. How would the Creek princess fit into his missionary endeavors? Recently, he had missed her curiosity and laughter, her need to learn, not to mention her mystique. Their talks had returned him to elemental rudiments of childhood memories, the simplest pleasures that lay buried in his past. One rumination after another blurred his association with her into a nebulous cloud again, far too complex to be reduced to a passing friendship like the nearby ants that kissed and scurried away from each other in the last light of day.

Despite her heathenism, the princess had proven her integrity to humanity by helping Chad and saving him from recapture into slavery by her clan. Besides, she deserved merit for the way she dealt with the adversity of her husband's death and her son's drowning. This undaunted spirit, Padre admired deeply. The natural forces of her womanhood, the kind that nature's determination sent coursing through her veins, the kind written in procreative eternity, the kind she'd already experienced before widowhood, were neither good nor bad. They were just there.

But had he unintentionally sown any seeds of misunderstanding? His relationship with Princess Blue Heron had rested on a purely divine level. He had suppressed any flashing carnal thought. Flesh! That was it, earthly flesh nourished by blood carrying nature's destined intricate interworkings. Why, it could have claimed its carnal will, but his indomitable iron clad character that was ingrained at the monastery had triumphed over any infinitesimal earthy fancy. That same character training would get him through these two nights, being all alone, and then the time might yet come when he could convince her of the Godly, Catholic way.

Seeking to fathom the truth, Padre pinched the flesh on his arm, brought it closer to study its color in the twilight. He had never felt superior because of his white skin. Nay. Nay. The demon he needed to pray about was war.

The baffling circumstances dictated by warmongers had channeled the detritus of war into his life, displacing his mission, compromising his goals, diverting him to this wilderness. His diligent probing into the farthest depth of his conscience, followed by prayers, sustained him through the darkest hours till he finally fell into sleep.

The following day, the day of fasting for the Assumption Holy Day, Padre sought redemption from all transgressions, even the most inconsequential ones, and particularly for time spent in self-indulgence. He prayed for God to mete penance. In deepest humility, he beseeched God for guidance in his strivings for conversions. Lo and behold, in the blessed light of sunshine, he spontaneously burst forth chanting the "Creed of Nicea":

> "We believe in one God,
>     the Father, the Almighty,
>     maker of heaven and earth,
>     of all that is seen and unseen.
> We believe in one Lord Jesus Christ,
>     the only Son of God,
>     eternally begotten of the Father,
>     God from God, Light from Light,
>     true God from true God,
>     begotten, not made, one in Being with the Father.
> Through Him all things were made,
> For us men and for our salvation
>     He came down from heaven:
>     by the power of the Holy Spirit
>     He was born of the Virgin Mary and became man.
> For our sake He was crucified under Pontius Pilate;
> He suffered, died, and was buried.
> On the third day He rose again
>     in fulfillment of the Scriptures;
> He ascended into heaven
>     and is seated at the right hand of the Father.
> He will come again in glory to judge the living and the dead,
>     and his kingdom will have no end.
> We believe in the Holy Spirit, the Lord, the giver of life.
> Who proceeds from the Father and the Son.
> With the Father and the Son He is worshiped and glorified.
> He has spoken through the prophets.
> We believe in one holy, catholic, and apostolic Church.
> We acknowledge one baptism for the forgiveness of sins.

We look for the resurrection of the dead and the life of the world to come. Amen."

Then Padre marveled that this prayer was promulgated at the Councils of Nicea and Constantinople in the year 325. Though one of the oldest prayers in Christianity, it was one he treasured and turned to for awakening deep spiritual worship.

A whit of insight germinated, instantly grew, and struck him with a crushing blow. Half bent, he grabbed his abdomen. "Work?" Good Lord, it was such an alien notion for an educated priest. He had done only a pittance of hard labor since being ordained. Shackles of peasantry again? The priesthood had sweetly, ever so sweetly, long ago liberated him from the life of a peasant. After all, he had spent years studying at the monastery, so he could impart the sacred teachings of his beloved Catholic Church and perform other missions. Would he now have to admit that he should contribute menial labor to Owl Clan's communal welfare? Children pick insects from garden plants and carry water, grandmothers shoo birds away from crops, grandfathers teach the ancestral ways. What work could he perform? If truth must be known, he probably could help the Creek with felling trees and clearing land for gardens.

He turned his palms up and grimaced at their tenderness. A Dominican would never allow flesh in any form, neither tender nor divinely blessed, to hinder being God's servant for the good of all people.

"Come," Genesis said, after Padre had returned to the village. "We can watch some of the men catch fish in the creek with black powder. We need many fish, very big ones, for the celebration. Besides, we'll see what else the villagers are doing to prepare for the *Poskita*. One thing I already know. Today, women harvest maize and other crops and clean. And they pitch all cracked or chipped pottery vessels onto the shard pile and bury worn out buckskin and feathered clothes. They give it back to Mother Earth."

Padre, assuming he would find out soon enough, didn't bother asking Genesis how he had coped with the black drink. Meantime, as Padre traipsed through the village alongside Genesis, his line of vision flitted from one activity to another. Some women busily swept out the houses with brooms made from the plentiful broomsage. Others raked around the buildings with deer antler rakes. Young women carried vessels of white sand and sprinkled it in and around the houses. Men repaired buildings or sorted worn-out tools. One group of women shucked and shelled maize. An elderly winnower handled the kernels with great care.

"Everything that's worn out," Genesis said, "is buried. The men give back to the earth old worn-out tools. Replace them with new tools. For the new year, they start with everything clean and pure." Genesis stuck out his arm, swept it horizontally, and reiterated, "Start *everything* new. Debts of forgiveness have to be taken care of, too. Willow said that her mother spoke to her oldest brother, you know, Fish Wrestler. Well, she said that he must ask forgiveness for scratching Honey Cloverleaf too hard with bone needles."

"Did the child do something real bad?"

"Fish Wrestler thought it was. She had taken his arrows, a whole quiver full of them, dumped them out, pulled out all the fletchings, and was blowing and throwing the feathers away in the air."

"That does not seem to be such a terrible offense."

"You don't understand. Them was owl feathers, sacred owl feathers."

Soon they joined the fishing group that was led by Shaman Skytalker and followed them along to the creek. Some of the men toted empty baskets for storing their expected catch, also willow switches on which to string fish.

Padre asked Fish Wrestler, who walked alongside, "What does the shaman carry? It looks important the way he holds it with both hands."

"Shaman Skytalker carries the clay pot of special black powder," Fish Wrestler answered. "It's already blessed. At the *chafoka*, we had a meeting. After the helpers pounded the leaves and stems of the devil's shoestring into powder, the shaman asked Breath Maker's blessings on it, so Owl Clan catches many fish for the *Poskita*. You will see."

"Is it the same as the black drink they used for cleansing their innards?"

"No, no. This black powder is special for catching fish."

Suddenly the group became silent as they walked along the riverbank, reverently silent, while Shaman Skytalker selected a calm, half-moon-shaped inlet of the creek, waded in, and sprinkled the devil's shoestring powder on the water's surface. Although the black powder was not harmful to humans, it always stunned the fish. The Creek men understood the next step without being prompted. They waded into the water and splashed, mixing the powder into the water.

"I go in too," Genesis whispered. "What about you, Padre?"

"I'll just watch."

As the stunned fish floated to the surface, the men caught them with their hands. Genesis participated wholeheartedly, harvesting fish as fast as he could. Though it was not much of a feat to catch stunned fish, he, nevertheless, had a look of full enjoyment. Two elders strung the fish on willow switches and placed them in baskets.

Padre took a second look at the wiggling baskets. As the catch flipped and thrashed, he felt a stronger and stronger commonality with every fish out of water. Though not strung on a willow switch, other constraints held him in check.

After the days of cleansing and preparation were finished, the ritual of extinguishing the old fire and making a new one, the most sacred part of the *Poskita*, would begin. Early that morning Genesis bounded up, bright-eyed. "This day," he said, "I declare my marriage to Willow. I feel like I've been riding the tail of that shooting star I saw while we was traveling on the trail from Pensacola. And when I'm with Willow, I feel like I can conquer the world, Sharp Knife, too." Then he held his head between both palms and said, "My head needs to be bigger today, needs to be big around as my dugout. There's so much to think about on this day."

"For one thing, anticipation of the chunkey game competition must have gripped you during the night. You heaved and hurled, probably the chunkey stick, with your flailing arms, and you were grinding your teeth."

Padre's voice faded as Genesis went to check his chunkey stone. It looked lucky. He had polished the stone to a glistening finish. For good measure he dipped it into white sand, spat on it, and whisked it with soft buckskin one more time. The new moon had grown round since the day he had found this shinier stone and given the first one back to the riverbank.

As Padre watched, Genesis said, "Today, all the old fires at the family houses must be put out, even the sacred one in the center of the square ground."

"That's the fire, the first one we saw when we arrived here. That reminds me of my infamous discussion with Blue Clay on our second day in the village when he had said that fire was the symbol on earth of Breath Maker. I will never forget that conversation when I told him the sun is not God, and he got so angry."

"Remember though, ole man Carrier was right. Fire reminds people of Breath Maker here on earth."

Though he'd like to set Genesis straight for all time, Padre parried with the frustration only within his mind. He could bide dealing with Genesis until more appropriate circumstances developed.

On this promising day of the *Poskita*, everyone went to the square ground, where the sacred fire had to be extinguished. The shaman performed the ritual of starting another sacred fire for the new year. He wore the albino deer headdress that flowed into a cape, the same one he'd worn at the council meeting when Genesis and Padre first arrived. The *Poskita* was a festive occasion, for he also wore albino moccasins on this day.

All the villagers and visitors from surrounding clans watched in reverence as Shaman Skytalker wiggled his gnarly, four thumbs and poured sand on the existing fire. Then with a most solemn expression, he knelt and prayed to the Great Spirit, Maker of Breath. Next, after strewing dry wood chips, rich in cured resin, from a small basket, the shaman—revered for his ability to start a fire on the third spin—twirled his fire drill into the sand amidst the chips. One, two, three spins—smoke appeared as if by magic. He blew a hefty breath onto the smoking chips. In seconds a tiny flame ignited the chips. Then he heaped finely-cut kindling onto the small flame, followed by the heaping of logs. The flames grew into tall, wavering orange tongues.

Council members, Arrowhead Maker, Tall Cane Walker, and Turtle Shell Dancer placed ears of ripe maize on logs, one at each of the four sacred directions, and pushed the logs toward the fire. Finally, Shaman Skytalker offered the maize to Breath Maker by giving one ear at a time to the fire. Thus, the annual thanksgiving offering had been completed. Council members piled on more logs. The new sacred fire, from which the villagers would light torches to start new fires at their home sites, signaled the beginning of the new year.

Padre sighed in anticipation of what would happen next.

# UNITED BY AN EAR OF MAIZE

Chief Wahoo, wearing his huge headdress of owl feathers, stepped forward with dignity and grace. Villagers and visitors, their eyes filled with respect, watched each step of the chief's slow, deliberate approach toward them. Before he began his annual inspiratory speech for the *Poskita*, his line of vision swept unhurriedly over the people. He cherished this duty of building confidence in the Owl Clan. He began: "We have received many blessings from Breath Maker. We must follow the customs of our ancestors and honor our Breath Maker in the coming new year." He paused and started afresh. "The welfare of our people depends on the maize crop. We celebrate the *Poskita* to offer thanks for Breath Maker's gift of a good maize harvest. To give up our ancestors' teachings would split our people apart. We must not trust white missionaries."

Genesis nodded and sought contact with Padre's eyes, to no avail. Padre's vision focused in disbelief on the chief.

"The Owl Clan is bound together by sharing the same sacred fire," the chief said with great eloquence. "Fire is our Breath Maker on Mother Earth." Then he looked upward to the sky and said, "We give thanks, and we share with visitors."

An ominous ring, like the ring of the death knell's somber, slow peals, tolled in Padre's heart, announcing deathly doom for his mission hopes. Despite all his expectations, he now had no choice but to adhere the chief's dictums. He must accept with finality that there would be no conversions in the Owl Clan. Another voice, a stronger one, at once pealed, *Yea though I walk through the valley of the shadow of death, I will fear no evil, for thy rod and thy staff are with me.* No one could take away his abiding faith, nor the power of silent prayer. Never. The chief's announcement would not be the end of the world.

After the speech, each family representative took a kindling torch, ignited it at the sacred fire, and left to start a new fire at the family house.

"I will light my torch and make a fire at the new marriage home," Genesis told Padre. "Willow will help me with it before the feast."

Loneliness had never struck with such piercing poignancy as now. Yes. The chief had quashed his mission, quenched all hope, quelled any progress. But, more white settlers could come along, even as early as tomorrow. What about this very evening?

After lighting new fires at their homes, villagers as well as guests, would commence celebrating and continue for the remaining days of the *Poskita*. Scents of roasted venison, smoked turkey, and blackening fish wafted in the air, along with pungent odors of hickory and fruit wood embers. Women streamed back and forth bringing food to the square ground for the feast. Rows and rows of squash, beans, potatoes, and a thick, creamy mixture with maize kernels, which looked like pudding, rested on the grass.

Acorn cakes and, especially, maize cakes tempted Padre. Blended odors of the different foods smelled so delicious, and partially veiled the hurt of chief's warning to the people about white missionaries. Large round vessels held sassafras tea. Everyone drank from communal gourds.

Though Padre's mouth watered and his stomach felt ever so empty from fasting, he wished to verify Princess Blue Heron's attendance more than to eat. People filled their clay bowls with chosen foods and delighted in the feast. Smoke, from the cooking area, spiraled straight up to the cloudless blue sky. Then thankfully, gentle southern breezes occasionally puffed plumes sideways, a welcomed sight, for this kept the mosquitoes at bay.

Padre wove through the celebrating crowd, continuing his search. Visitors exchanged whoops gaily among themselves as well as with the villagers. Stomping usually accompanied the whoops, stirring inevitable clouds of dust. Stooped elders milled amongst the crowd. Many children blew flute-like reed instruments, and in the background, spirited drumbeats never ceased. One young man proudly carried a lopsided lacrosse ball.

In the elbow-to-elbow sea of people, Padre never once thought to look to the right of his own elbow. Suddenly, a basket jolted against his arm. He smelled a familiar herb. The odor mixed with that of fresh fruit. Lo and behold, Blue Heron loomed alongside carrying a basket overflowing with scuppernongs, crab apples, and berries. A sprinkling of assorted nuts topped the fruit.

She smiled mischievously, "I'm sorry I bumped your arm."

He detected the fragrance of wine on her breath. Legitimate mistake or not, when she jolted the basket against his arm, he tried to conceal his momentary thrill of surprise and pleasure.

She adjusted the basket's position on her hip and asked, "Would you like some fruit and nuts?"

"Uhm, yes, thank you. But I've been fasting—I need, uh I need..."

"I know. You need some solid food first. Come. You can taste my mother's blue ash dumplings."

"Blue dumplings?" A smile escaped despite his will. "I never heard of them."

"Of course," she cut her eyes obliquely at him. "My mother makes blue ash dumplings."

"Thank you, I'd like very much to taste them." He willed to erase the smile from his face.

With a crudely carved wooden ladle, Blue Heron scooped up dumplings from a large pot and nearly filled the small clay bowl. She handed the bowl to him, jutting her hip provocatively.

"Good. Good," Padre said nodding his head. "They taste very good. But what makes them blue?"

"It's very simple. No secret. Just roast some purple pea hulls and pound them into powder. Put only a pinch of the powder in the maize meal. That makes the dumplings blue. It's good for you."

"Why's that? Why is the pinch of pea hull powder good for us?"

"The shaman said we need to use the powder in cooking sometimes. Our bodies need a little bit of ash. Helps make us stronger. Makes us feel better."

Still reeling from Blue Heron's sudden friendliness, Padre said, "You're in very good spirits. It's such a pleasure to see you and talk with you."

"Persimmon wine makes my spirit stronger. I drank persimmon wine with my father and mother. We drank it in honor of the *Poskita.* Remember my father is the chief."

"Why of course. The tradition is very appropriate for the chief's family."

"I will leave now," Blue Heron said. "I will dress in dancing regalia. And I must make special spirit preparations. Meditate for spirit vision dreams. Tonight I will dance in the very important Bird Dance."

"Yes, I remember. Your dance is for your namesake."

Padre reconciled that there was no impropriety in the fact that the festive occasion and wine had led Blue Heron to approach him with flirtatious behavior. He valued any moments with her, even tenuous ones. Also, realization that her friendship would be an inside connection to the village elders had heightened his awareness that it would be prudent to maintain a relationship with her.

After the feast, games began. Those who wished to engage in safe physical competitions like footracing or target shooting would have to wait until after the chunkey and lacrosse games or find a place away from the ball field. Others who sought less strenuous activities retired to edges of the field and engaged in rivalry of mental skills and chance. These games, some similar to dice games, were played with marked sticks or pebbles. Wagers bantered back and forth.

Anticipation of the chunkey game competition gripped Genesis. While awaiting his turn, he visualized his practiced moves, his arm muscles throbbing with excitement. Now, he would prove his skills. He heard Willow chanting a sacred melody for him as he entered the field. During the games she whooped and clapped, as he hurled the cane pole and glided his lucky stone, but the other players had guessed more accurately in every game so far. Why wasn't he winning? In Pensacola he had cued an occasional carom with the best billiards players. Now he needed to defeat at least one of Willow's brothers. How he intensely wanted Willow to be proud of her soon-to-be husband.

Fortune defied. Both Weaver brothers, Fish Wrestler and Mad River Swimmer, had outguessed Genesis every time. As he left the field, he looked aghast at Willow's reaction. She displayed no smile for him, only a questioning face. He must practice a hell of a lot harder for the next *Poskita*, because only half of his blood flowed with Creek ancestry. He had been a winner in billiards in Pensacola, and he damn sure could be a winner in chunkey next year. But now he had to figure out how to make it up to Willow on this, their marriage day. She stood as stiff as the lacrosse stick with which she braced herself, watching the lacrosse players. They bounded onto the field as if athirst for blood.

Days before the *Poskita*, Mad River Swimmer, one of the fiercest lacrosse competitors, had boasted to Genesis and Padre, "This year, the Owl Clan will win the lacrosse games. I'll make Chief Wahoo proud. The visitors will leave defeated and disgraced. I swam and swam to make sure we lose no more. I swam every time the river was mad, so my arms and legs are very strong for lacrosse. You'll see, we surely will win."

For good measure Genesis had brought his lacrosse stick, which Willow held, but with unfeigned reluctance, he had decided to be a spectator. He had watched the Owl Clan's rough-and-tumble practice and heard their hair-raising tales of past games. Padre's words about some games in the past having been gory, even lethal, stuck in his mind. He'd been so busy working on his dugout and the marriage house and then with practicing chunkey that he'd not taken time to practice lacrosse often enough to pride himself in the sport.

Now, a last minute pang struck him. Unable to face a reputation for cowardice in not joining the lacrosse game, in addition to his defeat in chunkey, he must enter the field. Yes. He surefire would not sit on the edge and pick his nose. He jumped up and grabbed his lacrosse stick from Willow's hands and entered the field as if he were a practiced warrior. Willow had been hanging onto the stick with all her heart, her eyes radiating some strange and potent force.

The game started slowly. As more contestants entered, momentum built. Here at the Owl Clan, the players carried two stick racquets, instead of a single one like the northern tribes. A woven pocket, attached with bent branches at the end of each racquet, was just deep enough to scoop up the small buckskin-covered ball. Filled with animal hair, the ball was fairly lightweight.

Since he had only one stick, Genesis stayed near the periphery. Thoughts about announcing his marriage to Willow filled his head while he surefire tried to help win the lacrosse game. Excitement escalated into a frenzy. The spectators, men, women, young people, and elders, whooped, chanted, and clapped.

"Ahh," Padre sighed incredulously and then said to Willow, "Look at Mad River Swimmer's break out. Does he have the ball? Yesss, he's got it. Watch him move! Such spirit and fire! He's hurled it straight between the goal posts." These bright moments obscured the chief's death knell speech.

Anon, an exuberant opponent overjumped and slammed head-to-head against Mad River Swimmer. A *crrrack* startled Padre! Neither player moved. The game stopped. Mad River Swimmer and his opponent were placed on drags and removed.

Meanwhile, Willow had gone forth and leaned toward Genesis, who looked worried as he stood on the edge of the playing field. She cupped her hand to the side of her mouth and whispered, "Getting hurt is part of proving bravery."

Genesis nodded. Then the game resumed. Whether he had proven to be helpful in winning, he was unsure. One thing *was* sure. His participation lent some relief to his disappointing chunkey performance. And another thing, he would carve an owl on the handle of his lacrosse stick like Willow's brothers had done. Then he could feel the owl's fierceness and speed when he played next time.

At dusk, the gourd drums changed from a thumping rhythm to a tumultuous crescendo. The dancers appeared. Then the drummers returned to the rhythmic pattern. Padre could see that the simple directness of the drumbeats aroused a basic feeling in the people. Dancers, many in faraway trances, picked up on the beats, tapping their feet and clapping their hands from their positions on the sidelines. Most participants had pieced moss capes together with vines, using only bird feathers for decoration. Some added lucky stones, animal bones, and coloring from materials, which had been derived from their Mother Earth. On their buckskin skirts, some of the dancers had etched birds and animals and different designs representing nature, many of which appeared primitive enough to have been passed on from ancestors.

Regalia plumage especially attracted Padre's attention. Several dancers had woven feathers from different birds into the moss, creating capes with a mosaic effect, like beautiful Spanish-mosaic-tile artwork. Others covered their colorful capes in feathers from a single bird species, like the one of spectacularly bright yellow. Another outstanding one was covered with red feathers, the most brilliant ones.

It came as no surprise to Padre that Princess Blue Heron stood out from the group, extraordinarily exotic. He moved close enough to observe details. Lush, blue heron feathers completely covered her moss cape, the sharp ends having been embedded into a base of woven Spanish moss. He grimaced. Why was he noticing every minute detail, even the most subtle? Yet he gleaned for more details. Ringlets of blue limestone nuggets, which matched her necklace, ornamented her ankles and wrists. The usual four, blue heron feathers, fresher looking ones, distinguished her headdress. And finer fringe adorned her new skirt.

What was the new scent? Aha. Tanbark. Her freshly tanned skirt gave off the unusual, tangy odor. Above her ankles and wrists she wore buckskin bands festooned with rows of deer hooves that rattled with the least movement. They were very small hooves, sewn on at their fleshy ends with sinew. This evening her aura was most mystic. Her eyes had the faraway gaze of being in a trance, truly not of this world. Padre struggled to keep from staring and tried to purposely cast glances at the other dancers.

The drum beat tempo compounded. The intensity pierced the air, proclaiming the dancers' entry into the open field. Each dancer interpreted his or her dance in terms of the bird species represented. Dancers decorated with mixed-type feathers moved as they felt inclined to do so.

In the beginning Princess Blue Heron simulated preening to get each feather in exact position, followed by slow wading into the imaginary pond, her head hunched into her shoulders.

Padre unabashedly partook of this unprecedented experience. After all, he had witnessed her sensitivity to the herons and her endeavor to portray these birds with integrity. He felt entitled to lighten up on his reserve and delight in her valiant efforts. Little by little, before he knew what was happening, he had indulged wholeheartedly in the pageantry and its passion, unaware of his surroundings.

Blue Heron ducked her head, her nose almost touching the ground, and followed up with a graceful leap into the air, her chin pointing upwards as if taking the flight of the wild ones. At intervals, she switched to staccato stomping and shivering. Perhaps this part was her interpretation of the birds' mating activities. Her chanting varied from soft to loud, in smoothly blended increments.

Padre grasped the message as soon as she took some sticks from the sideline, caressed them, and built a nest in the center of the field. With her nose, she nestled imaginary eggs to the center of the nest. Then she sat, bowed her head, and rocked back and forth, silently, to the beat of the drums. With sudden abruptness, she jumped up, ran away, and returned, pretending to feed newly hatched babies.

In a slow stepping dance, she mimed the coaxing of the baby birds to follow, for she glanced back at least three times, directing the imaginary fledglings with the flapping of her "wings." By fluttering her tongue against the roof of her mouth, she embellished this somewhat subdued part of the presentation with stimulating vibrato trills.

Sounds of *Andalucian* Gypsies came to Padre's mind. Endearing nostalgia set him at ease, loosening constraints of priestly demeanor. Another vibrato trill sounded, and his warmed heart titilated. Pleasure rushed, beyond that which a priest should experience. Embarrassed by his protuberance, he bent over, his chin to his chest, and snuck away like a craven from a battlefield. Meekly, he looked around. Anguish cooled his ardor. Should he return to the summerhouse? He started in that direction but did not want to leave. Instead, he decided to ease back into the crowd. He crept among the people with the caution of a spy. No one bothered looking at him, for each person seemed deeply involved in the spirit dances.

The other dancers, as energy waned, left the field one by one. In the end, Princess Blue Heron danced alone. She, truly, had been the favorite performer. Over and over she repeated her routines. Beauty of each move and each sound continued to evoke the worldly phenomenon of gooseflesh. Attracted and repelled, the ambivalent padre still stayed.

She truly looked the part of a blue heron, as she portrayed its life cycle, even after she had flung off her feathered cape and tossed it to her mother on the sideline. Her face went serene as she lilted away on her long, bird-like legs, her feathery lightness an embodiment of the majestic creature's grace. When she returned, she drifted into another trance. Then she danced the scene of the bird's death. Alas, she lay with her limbs and head drawn up into an egg-like shape.

After the drums ceased Blue Heron sat on the grass, untying the rattlers from her arms and legs, completely spent. Padre dared to move to her side as soon as her mother and father joined the visiting chiefs and their wives near the sacred fire. Blue Heron panted and dabbed the perspiration trickles, not acknowledging him.

"Do you mind," Padre said, "if I look at your rattlers? I enjoyed watching your dancing performance. You portrayed blue herons' life cycle so realistically and at the same time stayed in rhythm with the drumbeats."

"I've danced all my life," she said and took a deep breath. "My dancing spirit comes from our ancestors."

"The rattlers look like deer toes," he said in an effort to start a conversation.

"Yes, yes," she said breathlessly. "Deer hooves. I sewed them onto buckskin with sinew. I have more rattlers than any other dancer." Without looking up, she continued, "Our people give many deer hooves to my father."

"You have many good fortunes."

"At times evil spirits have visited me, too." She frowned.

"I'm sorry. I realize you have had more misfortunes than most people." He wished to stretch the time with her. His mind went blank. A trifling topic surfaced. "I'd like to know what Genesis' marriage ceremony will be like."

"Soon you will see. Genesis will break an ear of maize to celebrate life, health, and happiness with Willow."

"Oh, that is very different from the Catholic marriage ceremony," Padre said. Then in desperation, he asked, "Will Genesis take the Weaver name as Creek tradition dictates?

"Yes, he must."

"His children won't even bear his name?"

"That is our way," she sighed as if uninterested but added, "and he must honor the will of his mother-in-law. Singing Basket Weaver and Willow's brothers will be heads of the family."

"Just exactly what are their duties as the heads of the family?"

"Willow's brothers will teach the children and scratch them when they do wrong."

"Oh, I remember hearing about Tupelo's having been scratched by your brothers whenever he did something wrong. And I've seen some children around the village with scratch marks."

"Other children tease when they see scratches. That helps. Shames more."

"Uh, I've been wondering, exactly what do they scratch the children with?"

She folded the rattler bands into a neat stack. "Depends on what the child has done. Sometimes we just scratch with prickly balls from sweet gum trees, like we use for cleaning clay bowls. Other times, we may need to use hawthorn stickers or even bone picks." Her voice had begun trailing.

"I see," Padre said. He lowered his head, disappointed at his insipid attempts to merely chat.

When he looked up, the nearly full moon illuminated Blue Heron's face. Her bronze skin glimmered with perspiration. But again, pain showed in her eyes, the pain he'd detected from the beginning.

Padre cleared his throat. "How can a Creek father feel sure that his children will grow up the right way when he cannot even teach them right from wrong?"

"Creek men like the women to be heads of the family. They say it brings about good things."

"I'd like to understand that better."

"It is very easy to understand. A Creek man carries the name of his wife's family. Makes him try harder to prove himself."

Padre felt better. His drivel, trite as that of his unenlightened youth, had been productive after all, for she continued, "Creek men feel good when they prove themselves strong and brave. Willow is very happy that Genesis will fit in with the Weaver family. She showed me all the new things in their marriage house, all the things they will need: deerskin rugs to sit on, a winter bed cover of woven moss that is filled with very fine goose feathers, and best of all, new pottery. Willow asked the pottery makers to inscribe an eye on one vessel, a sacred owl's eye. She has a lid for it, too, so she will keep herbs in it. The eye is colored brown, the rich brown of hickory nut coloring and has a nice yellow dot in the middle. The other clay vessel is colored with lines of bloodroot, from top to bottom, the richest, red bloodroot. Very, very pretty pottery." Blue Heron would be careful not to let the white missionary know how much she had wished for a happy marriage like Willow and Genesis'.

"Their marriage house sounds comfortable, well-equipped for their needs."

"Yes. They have many baskets and new water gourds, too."

At that moment, Padre heard Genesis' voice rise above the din of the crowd. Then Genesis broke an ear of maize and gave one-half to Willow, symbolizing their marriage. Everyone whooped.

Willow's irises fired with passion and glistened like orbs of obsidian as she reverently held the half ear of maize, which Genesis had shared—the food of life. Life with Genesis would be good, like the maize. She had heard it snap; she beheld its beauty; she smelled its fragrance; she felt its wonder; she would taste its flavor. Genesis took Willow's hand. They dashed away smiling, holding the half ears of maize in their other hands. Thus, the celebration had ended for the evening, and the people had begun leaving.

Padre felt empty, empty as the ball field.

Blue Heron picked up her belongings; and, to Padre's utter amazement, asked, "After the *Poskita*, would you help me make a *banza* like Chad's?"

At first, Padre stood stunned. Finally finding his voice, he said, "I will certainly try."

Before turning to leave Blue Heron said, "Making a *banza* must be kept secret. No one should know. I'll bring a gourd, a nice one, to the blue pond, and the other things for making it," she said as her voice faded.

Soon, all Padre saw of her was the blue heron headdress moving down the path, in the light of a villager's lightwood torch. The headdress and torch quickly became invisible in the disappearing trail. Padre shunted toward his abode, groping not only with the darkened night—the moon was now covered with clouds—but also with the death knell speech by none other than Blue Heron's father. Perhaps helping Blue Heron make a *banza* would, in turn, bring about glad tidings. Hundreds of cheerful lightning bugs, darting in all directions—up to the chin circling around and down to the ground in figure eights—would not allow Padre to lapse into whining within himself. The lightning bugs' on-off flickerings furnished a sense of bearing. Were they harbingers, as well?

# FEVERS

The Owl Clan had not allowed the threat of rain, portended by a red sunrise, to diminish enjoyment of the celebratory part of the *Poskita*. True to the elders' teachings about weather, rain came. By fate's fortune it had started late into the night, without great consequence; however, the skies had continued pouring forth nonstop for two days, ceasing celebration.

Within her heart Willow had wished for rain, days of rain, hoping for it to come *after* the first celebration day of the *Poskita* and her marriage. She had wanted the wind to howl through the trees, lightning to reveal Genesis' face in the dark of their house, just as it had when they had been caught in the storm and had hidden in the honeysuckle vines after visiting the burial ground. Inside the marriage house she could hold her cheek close to Genesis, feel his warmth, and wiggle into his strong arms without the fear she had felt in their honeysuckle hideout. Her fulfilled wish was delicious. There would be many *Poskitas* in the future, which would last for the usual eight days.

Padre needed to confer with the shaman about the revelation, concerning work, that he had received while fasting for the Holy Day of Mary's Assumption. While waiting for the rain to slacken sufficiently, he looked down at his left arm and traced the long, ropy scars with his forefinger, scars that had been with him since childhood. Half aloud he said, "Jumping in the midst of hay pitching was merely impulsive, childish behavior on my part." His older brother, wearing an oversized, handed-down hat, had unintentionally thrust the pitchfork's iron tines into Padre's

246

arm, gouging it, all because the big tattered-straw hat had hindered his brother's vision.

He touched the scars again, which, even in their thickness, were vulnerable to insect bites. There was no getting away from the evidence of his peasant childhood. The scars attested to that lowly position. Alas, he could not forever evade the hard work he had known in his early life. He, too, should contribute menial labor in this wilderness. So through the misty rain, Padre hurriedly walked to consult the shaman. Under the pretense of inquiring about Mad River Swimmer's condition, Padre made his entrance.

"Mad River Swimmer will heal, but Racoon Runner died the day after the lacrosse game," the shaman said in a matter-of-fact manner.

"He did? I am very sorry to hear about his death."

"Yah, Racoon Runner died honorably, proving Muscogees' bravery in the lacrosse game. Owl Clan respects his spirit. He proved the teachings from our brave Muscogee ancestors."

Padre willed against showing his disdain of young men being venerated for dying in such a barbaric manner. Instead, he said, "Head injuries are dangerous, but I am sure villagers are proud of all the players' bravery. Their power in the lacrosse game thrilled the villagers, and I found myself getting caught up in the excitement, too. I am still concerned about Mad River Swimmer's condition. Was he seriously injured?"

"He is better now. His earth spirit returned to his body on the day after the game. And when the rains slowed down, Racoon Runner's family took his body on a drag back to the Raccoon Village."

Padre mustered his courage and quickly readied the wording of his sacrificial offering. "I've been thinking." He paused, while the shaman waited inquisitively. "I, I should give of myself in common work with the villagers. Each person helps for the good of the village. I feel I need to help, also. I would not be good at hunting." He let his deformed back sag a trifle more, reinforcing his incompetence. "Still I could help with cutting the trees and clearing and tending the land. I did some of that work when I was growing up but look at my hands." He held up his opened palms. "I will have to toughen them."

The shaman clasped his hands and studied his four sacred thumbs as he wiggled them, creating an air of mystical communion. Then he said, "I will talk with council members about this." As he spun his double thumbs, Owl Claw blustered into their midst, with the breathless River Raven following.

"*Senor* sends River Raven to request the white missionary to come to Montezuma Trading Post," Owl Claw said. "A white worker is sick with the fever. He needs missionary's help to meet his white God in other world. And the *senor* would like to speak with Genesis."

247

The shaman and chief met with council members and decided that Owl Claw and his son could accompany Padre and Genesis to the trading post. To perform his priestly duties for the sick man, Padre explained his need for his holy belongings in the shoulder bag. Surprisingly, the elders agreed to permit Padre to wear his cassock, as well as take along his prayer book and healing oil in the shoulder bag.

Awed by his newly found mission, Padre felt it came as a direct blessing, for he had just offered his greatest, most personal sacrifice to the Owl Clan—work. He was the quintessential sacrificer. He had even sacrificed beyond the expectations of his capabilities.

Upon entering the Montezuma Trading Post, Padre recognized the sick man, his round face sweated and yellowed with fever. Closer, Padre grimaced. The worker's spongy face was filled with pock marks holding enough grime to grow mustard seeds. His clothing reeked of malodorous body filth. Though he had been too sick for several days to use snuff, the stale stains still lined each side of his mouth and chin, just as they had the first day Padre had seen him. He lay upon a pile of pine straw. Irregular wet markings in the sandy floor, underneath his hips, divulged telltale signs of urine. Hot fever, the kind followed by death, radiated from his body. Yet, he shivered with a chill.

Padre placed a fur skin over the man's shivering body and fetched the small bottle of anointing oil. Even though the man lay deathly ill, Padre couldn't help feeling exhilarated that the shaman had returned the shoulder bag, which had been confiscated before the tribunal. It felt so righteous to once again handle his precious holy possessions, though he would have them only for this particular occasion.

As the man lay gasping and wheezing for breath, Padre anointed him, tracing a cross on his hot forehead. Then he held an arm forth and prayed: "Lord Jesus Christ, you shared in our human nature to heal the sick and save all mankind. Mercifully listen to our prayers for the physical and spiritual health of our sick brother whom we have anointed in your name. May Your protection console him and Your strength make him well again. Help him find hope in suffering, for You have given him a share in Your passion. You are Lord forever and ever, Amen."

The sick man said, "Need," then he gasped a short breath, "to make a confession," he whispered.

Padre asked Genesis, Owl Claw and his son, *Senor* Colabro, and the workers, who had looked on with timid uncertainty, to step outside the trading post. Unable to bear the stench of death in the place, Padre covered his nose and mouth with a piece of old homespun which he took from the shoulder bag, the homespun on which *Herr* Gunter had, only weeks ago, parceled out parched corn. Padre had known that this piece of fabric would come in handy sometime, never dreaming it would be needed in a situation like this particular one.

After a brief, though belabored confession, the dying man slowly reached his tremulous hand into his pocket, pulled out a worn pouch, and handed it to Padre. "Use this for...mission wor...," His voice faded. Padre solemnly administered the Sacrament of Extreme Unction. After he intoned another prayer and crossed himself, he rubbed his sweaty palm down the side of his cassock, having momentarily forgotten he had worn the good one for this holy mission. At last the chance had come to administer for the Church, although the ritual of the Extreme Unction was a sorrowful experience.

The man's fevered eyes froze in a faraway gaze. Padre went to the door and quietly informed the men that they could return. Scents of rum and snuff infiltrated along with them. In a matter of minutes, the sick man's heaving abdomen slowly came to rest as he exhaled a stone-shattering death rattle, which pelletized the silence and subdued the once-boisterous group. It even unnerved Padre. Alas, the rowdies bowed their heads in a semblance of compassion. The young one with missing front teeth hurriedly swiped a tumbled teardrop. Padre reached over and closed the deceased man's eyelids and covered his face.

Outside, before the party mounted the horses, *Senor* Colabro said, "The mosquitoes have been much worse this year. More mosquitoes always bring more fever. Yet rumors are that more white settlers will be moving into the territory now. A drifter from northern Alabama told me that General Jackson has promised white settlers protection against any Indian attack."

Owl Claw and his son exchanged perplexed looks.

"That sounds just like the old Sharp Knife," Genesis said.

*Senor* Colabro continued, "The drifter said that Jackson claimed the whole Creek Nation, Seminole, too, are under his control now. Many changes are sure to come."

Padre turned on his heel toward the *senor* and asked, "Did the drifter have any news about Pensacola? If the general, indeed, has control over the Seminole, it does not bode well for Pensacola."

"Sorry to say, I didn't ask him. But maybe I can help you out with some news soon. You see, the rains have raised the river high enough to take a raft of logs and skins to Pensacola. We will bury the worker and get ready for the trip. And Genesis, you come back tomorrow. We will be ready to go."

As Padre left the Montezuma Trading Post, he wondered just how he could best use the gold coins for mission work? He had already put the money in one of his boots and would not mention it at the Owl Clan. His heart hung heavy as a cannon ball.

Darkness began descending with the same heaviness as Padre's heart. Neither Padre nor Genesis nor Owl Claw and his son talked very much as they rode back to the village. Owl Claw seemed to need calling upon all his senses to help him in leading the way.

The sultriness, which followed the rainy spell, still weighted the late afternoon air. Padre had failed to show up at the blue pond. Princess Blue Heron gathered nearby rushes, and nonchalantly began weaving them into a mat. Blue butterflies swirled and looped, occasionally lit on blossoms, and sipped nectar. She smiled at the reflection of a blue butterfly alighting on her hair momentarily. Special gray birds (Indigo buntings) swooped back and forth. Their magical gray feathers always turned blue in the sunlight and at all other times turned back to gray. She gathered more rushes and continued weaving. The mat grew to the size for a sleeping pad, yet Padre had not shown up. Dragonflies, which were diving and soaring at the pond's edge, caught her attention, the many colors of their delicate wings brightening her spirits for a while.

When the large sun slid down to half-size beyond the blue pond, Princess Blue Heron worried about the white missionary's whereabouts. She retrieved the gourd, which she had placed in the pond to soak, so that the top could be cut off for the *banza* without breakage. Then she gathered her other belongings and, along with the gourd, placed them on the mat. Reluctantly she picked up the mat and left, looking back once at the blue water lilies she had placed on each side of the altar. On the way back to the village, she hid the gourd, the bobcat guts, and groundhog hide, tools, too, in the hollow of a tree, the one she had chosen for storing her *banza* whenever she and the padre would complete it, for the *banza* must be kept secret.

First, upon returning to the village, she checked for the white missionary, but he was nowhere in sight. Where was he? Why she checked on the horses, she was not sure, but they were missing, also. She needed to find out what had happened to them; so through the darkening twilight, she sauntered, ever so watchfully, about the village. No one should find out what she was up to. She stayed in the cover of darkness, when she found Skytalker and the elders sitting in a circle under the sacred oak. Something very important had taken place or soon would happen. They had held many important meetings there, for the size and strength of the old tree always shed its wisdom upon them. Did this meeting in some way concern the white missionary?

At once, her heart beat faster. Was she in trouble? Had her secrets been found out? Breathing ever so shallowly, she sat and listened, rubbing her fingers over a lucky piece of limestone, which she had found near the blue pond. Bullfrogs, repetitiously croaking from the creek area, comforted her momentarily. She had always liked their sound, the rising and falling of it as the breezes blew and faded; but now fear clouded the full joy like a heavy fog. In rhythm with the frogs, she massaged the stone. Surely it was lucky, for it was shaped somewhat like a heron and had the same bluish color. It would be a good addition for her pine needle basket of spiritual charms.

Soon Owl Nose joined the circle of elders, and Shaman Skytalker said, "I will tell you everything from the beginning. River Raven ran to village with the message that the white missionary should go to Montezuma Trading Post right away. The white, moon-faced worker there has the killer fever. He will die soon. He wants Padre to help him get rid of his sins, so the white God accepts him. The killer fever has attacked our village, also. Five of our people are sick with hot fever, chills, and aches. Sick ones have kept me very busy. Jumper's spirit is already lost from Mother Earth. He may soon go to the other world."

The next afternoon Padre and Princess Blue Heron sat near the edge of the blue pond, while he explained about his missionary sojourn to the Montezuma Trading Post the previous day. She listened intently to his account of the moon-faced man's fever while she gazed at the searing sun, mesmerized by its extraordinary outthrust of fire. She would not reveal how she wished to get an opportunity to help heal the fevered villagers as soon as they completed the *banza*. They must get started making it right away, so she quickly plucked the gourd from the edge of the lake. "I looked at every gourd in the storehouse and picked out one best suited for the *banza*."

"It is very nice, quite large, much larger than the ones dangling from the tall, crossed poles near your mother's garden. The way the limbs are crossed near the top of those poles reminds me of my holy cross."

"Yes," she smiled. "Those gourds are nesting places for purple spirit birds. Creek people like purple spirit birds. They are sacred. They eat insects so we have good gardens. Do not forget. My mother is Golden Maize Grower. She grows many gourds for these birds to nest in. For water jugs and seed keepers, too."

"The birds do not look really purple."

"Oh, when Breath Maker shines on their wings and heads, they look purple. And they sing like this." She imitated the low-pitched, rolling twitter sound and then smiled.

Padre's carving skills and Blue Heron's firsthand experience with cured skin and guts lent confidence as they started construction of the *banza*. Padre chose a stout cane from a nearby canebrake and sized it for the fingerboard. Blue Heron had once again soaked the brittle gourd, which prevented breakage during the cutting, and she lent practiced hands for stretching the groundhog-skin top and bobcat guts. Without undue trouble

251

the nearly finished instrument had thus far met with their satisfaction, though in Padre's head a dull ache had begun pounding.

While assembling the parts, Padre had reveled in the way the surrounding area reminded him of his *Andalucian* homeland. The name of New *Andalucia* rolled over and over and over in his aching head. Perhaps the worker who had just died at the Montezuma Trading Post might have, also, come from the *Andalucian* Region.

After securing the strings, Padre tested them and decided to tighten all three. Then he felt satisfied with the mellow thumping sound. Despite the fact that he had started to feel slightly weak, he laughed at himself trying to imitate Chad's "Wayfaring Stranger" song. He handed the *banza* to Blue Heron and asked, "Where will you keep it?"

"In a hollow tree. That's where I hid the things for making it. The hollow in the tree is big, big enough for me to get inside if I lower my head. I will cover the opening with brush." She began picking the strings tentatively but soon lost herself in a soulful chant to her rhythmic accompaniment. She lifted herself and danced, unabashedly, as she picked the percussive beats.

Chills ran down Padre's spine. Hallelujah! He had reestablished harmony with Blue Heron just by helping her make the crude instrument. He looked upwards and beheld the waxing moon. It was one of those days when it had already risen, adding its small amount of luminosity to full daylight. He wondered if he had he been drawn under the spell of some lunar-like magic? No. Never. Think straight. Teach her! Teach her! The time is right. A few samples of his scholarly training at the monastery might impress her. Then he could bargain for the exchange of her stories, as he had done with Genesis in Pensacola.

Abruptly, the insularity of this environment closed in on him. In Pensacola, he had often looked out at the massive body of water, on which his ship had sailed when he had traveled from Spain, and felt its connection to his past. That bond had been severed. The alien wilderness now encompassed him. He had felt somewhat achy since morning but attributed it to his horseback ride to the Montezuma Trading Post. He ached even worse now. And though he felt much warmer than usual, a chill came over him, then sheer weakness. A voice in his head told him he must excuse himself and return to the summerhouse, the worst of times to feel incapacitated, since he had just reestablished a favorable rapport with Blue Heron. Fading sounds of her thumping and accompanying chants followed as his laggard footsteps groped toward the village.

On her return to the village, Princess Blue Heron stopped when she heard moans and coughing. Quietly, she crept into the moon blossom vines. In her hideout, while readying herself to run in a blink, she, at the same time, visually searched the surroundings. There, around the bend and at the edge of the path, the missionary lay motionless. She eased near him. Then closer, she felt the heat of his body, ablaze with fever, but he did not speak. Had he lost contact with this world? He shivered with a chill. He must be suffering from the terrible killer fever that had claimed the life of the moon-faced man at the Montezuma Trading Post and had attacked so many Owl Clan members already. She had seen her people struggle with the fevers in the past and knew of the fever's evil spirits.

She ran to her house for a gourdful of cool water and a supple wahoo mat and soon began wiping his forehead, gently. Thankfully, she had had the presence of mind to also bring a fur skin wrap from her house, for the missionary shivered with another chill. He remained silent except for moans and coughs, his body still hot. She tried to get him to sip water from a drinking gourd. Though he tolerated very little of it, she persisted, knowing he must take water.

When he began babbling about his mother and the smell of warm baked bread spread with olive oil, Blue Heron knew he needed spirit care; but she must first have him moved to his house. She would move her dream catcher there, also. Not many of the villagers knew about it, since it was not a custom of the southern tribes to use this kind of sacred object. Her husband had brought it to her from the northern Creek. They had traded with a faraway tribe for the dream catcher and had given it to her husband in exchange for his promise to fight in the coming battles.

No one was in sight to help move Padre. More villagers must have been stricken with the fever. Shaman Skytalker would be busily performing rituals for the sick, using his medicine wheel and spiritual articles. So, she had no choice. She must use her own medicine wheel and basket of sacred objects, though they had not yet been proven.

She fled to the storehouse and grabbed a drag, rushed to Padre's side, and rolled him onto the drag. Then came the hard part, dragging him to his dwelling. She alternately dragged and rested, frantically checking on his breathing before taking each rest. She continued dragging and resting and checking on him until she finally reached his house.

Fatigued and deeply disturbed about her hasty decision to help the white missionary, she now worried about what her mother and father and the elders might think. Should she have given more thought before she moved him? What evil might befall her? Yet, she needed her mother's help in getting him to the sleeping area. Though doubtful and distraught, she still must ask for her mother's help. She trembled inside when Padre moaned. She *had* to tell her mother. Now.

"Daughter, I ask you not to spend so much time helping the white missionary," Golden Maize Grower said in a demanding tone rather than an asking one. "Many villagers are sick. They might need our help." She puffed on her corncob pipe, her face growing grim. "You have had so much sadness in your life, and yet you take on the care of this sick man." Her tone rang of despair. "This terrible sickness is too much for you to handle now." She slammed her pipe down, firmly placed her hands on her hips, stomped a foot forward, and declared, "I do not approve, Daughter."

"But Mother." Blue Heron's line of vision swept over her mother's face, wrinkled with her years of wisdom, like other wise elders. "The missionary is so sick. There's no one else. Villagers have help from one another. Please help me. He is on a drag by his house now."

"You take on too much, Daughter." Golden Maize Grower shook her fist at Blue Heron so hard that the gray frizzed hair, circling her round face, danced wildly like Spanish moss blowing in a storm.

"I, I must help the padre," Blue Heron said, lowering her eyes to the dream catcher in her hands and turning to leave. "He has no one else." She clamped her lips in exasperation while walking out.

Golden Maize Grower waddled like a goose behind Blue Heron. Until she saw the padre, she had squawked complaints like a nurturing mother goose affectionately training a gosling, although she had turned and respectfully nodded to the owl's feather over the door of her house. Without another word, she helped her daughter place Padre on the bed of straw and moss, positioning him on his back. Afterwards she heaved her hands tightly on her hips and sighed in utmost disgust. This stance forced her to turn sideways as she approached the doorway. She cast a menacing look back, then proceeded outside without uttering a word.

Blue Heron held the dream catcher. She touched the pliant tree branch, which gave it a circular shape and the buckskin, which was wound all the way around. She ran her fingers along the intricately woven bobcat entrails, from the fiercest of bobcats, which webbed the center. Her husband had told her that the fine weaving was a magical sieve. No evil spirits could enter. Good spirits were smart enough to stay on top of the weaving and not get caught in the web.

She rubbed the fetish which adorned the dream catcher, a front-right bobcat's paw, the most trusted one for warding off evil. Then she touched each bead and feather attached to buckskin strips hanging from the circle; they were of the most sacred kind, having been blessed by the shaman of the faraway tribe. The dream catcher would capture any new evil spirits the fevers might bring. Finally, she placed the sacred object beyond the padre's head.

Sensing that he could not hear her, she looked at him and whispered frantically, "I must call on the Master of Breath for healing help." She stood still remembering: Father has told me many times that I have shown signs of having spiritual gifts. My will, he often said, is strong for holding my attention on meditating and seeking until far away thoughts come. Father's eyes squinted with truth when he said that these signs are good for making vision quests. "Yet I do not know if I have the *true* gifts of the shaman," she murmured. "But I must try to prove myself. I must do it now." She ran to fetch her basket of spiritual charms.

# THE BUBBLING STICK

"The missionary's spirit is not long for this world," Golden Maize Grower said when she returned to check on her daughter. "Come home with me and get some rest."

For Princess Blue Heron, abandoning the sick padre was not an option. She had listened to her mother with honor showing in her eyes, yet she turned toward the sick man and silently remained steadfast in her vigil. Golden Maize Grower slapped her thighs in exasperation and departed. Throughout the night Blue Heron applied cool, wet wahoo mats to Padre's hot forehead. Whenever she tried to coax him to swallow small amounts of water, most of it drooled from the side of his mouth. If she tried to force it, he would start coughing and choking until she held his head upwards.

Alas, she slumped down on her knees, her palm to her forehead. The bullfrogs and owls and alligators had quieted. Padre's gasping was so scary her stomach quivered, but fear was a sign of weakness. She must stay strong. Would his soul leave Mother Earth before she had a chance to make a vision quest for ancestors' help? She must wait for dawn of Breath Maker to go to the sacred, red clay hole. Though both gourds of cool water were running low, she urgently needed to concentrate on making the vision quest. She crept to a deerskin and sat with her legs folded, rocking back and forth in the darkness and chanting, in her softest voice, a healing melody.

Between chants she dwelled on the spiritual quest. It must be her best effort yet, a chance to prove she really possessed shamanic powers. Against her wishes, she dozed in the earliest morning hours, although she soon awakened and fitfully awaited the dawning. Before leaving, Breath Maker's presence must rise in the east so ancestors could see how to guide her. She pictured in her mind the red clay hole that had been hollowed out in Mother Earth by a fallen, burning star. There, ancestors would guide her in bringing down Breath Maker's healing powers. Her stomach felt empty, very fitting for clear visions. "Only by fasting," Skytalker had told her many times, "can one receive best visions." No thought of food would even tempt her.

Before the first sliver of light beamed above the horizon, Blue Heron had gathered her medicine wheel, basket of sacred objects, and pouch of spiritual herbs, which she had brought to Padre's house the previous evening. She put them down and once more wiped Padre's face with a freshly dampened mat. She poured the last drops of cool water from both gourd vessels, replaced the maize cob stoppers, and then put the small drinking gourd to Padre's mouth. "Drink Padre, drink cool water. Your body needs cool water," she said ever so gently. Unable to get any response, her heart pounded. Previously, she had been able to arouse him for at least a few moments. In terror, she shrank back murmuring, "Evil fevers have claimed his spirit. I must hurry before evil fevers take his breath." She snatched her basket with one hand and the medicine wheel with the other and backed away, thrusting another hopeful glance at the dream catcher, then at the two empty water gourds. Maybe her mother would bring another gourd of cool water. Surely, her mother would want to visit the padre this morning to find out about his condition.

Initially, Blue Heron dashed through the edge of the forest, catching glimpses of the luminous, white daisies that marked the nearby trail. Soon out of breath she ran slower while praying that no one would stop her, especially that Owl Nose would not be on her trail. There was no time to waste. Fresh morning air sharpened her senses after the feverishly hot night. Dew drops on the grass and weeds enlivened the soles of her feet. Song sparrows soothed frantic spurts of doubt plaguing her. Would she be able to make her spiritual quest in time to save the missionary from the fever?

Over the knoll, her pace slowed. Yes, thankfully, the circular, red clay pit was still in place. The opening looked like a huge clay bowl, carved into the earth's belly. In her head she heard her mother's voice: *Daughter, why did you worry? The pit would not grow wings and fly away.* Blue Heron unleashed a halfhearted smile.

The meteorite had not only left remnants of charred snags standing near the hole, but also had burned some trees to mere stumps. A narrow clearing all around the edge of the hole bore testimony to the weather's destruction. Daisies had taken up residence near the rim; and thirsty, great-white butterflies were already flitting amongst them, lighting upon them, and partaking of their nectar.

Down into the clay pit, Blue Heron's feet deftly claimed their way, carrying her to the center. The medicine wheel must center the hole. She whirled to face the rising of Breath Maker and turned the wheel so that the red quadrant, which she had colored with the darkest bloodroot sap, faced the east. She deliberated on that section, allowing the entire meaning of the color to settle in her mind. Red symbolized Breath Maker, the great God of all. It also symbolized fire, Breath Maker's presence on earth, and blood, the nature of life.

She looked at the opposite wedge, the moon segment, which was colored black and represented death and the region of the souls of the dead. She paused and sought her ancestors' help.

Next, her vision turned to the northern quadrant, the direction of cold, from which hung blue heron feathers. She shivered as a voice in her head rang out: *Blue stands for trouble and defeat.* This had bothered her ever since the American general had defeated the northern Creek, and it bothered her even more with rumors now circulating that the same general would protect white settlers moving in on her people's hunting grounds. Perhaps that is another reason why she painstakingly sought shamanic powers, for she needed to earn a shaman's name and help protect her people from whites. But she would not dwell on it today. There was not enough time today.

Finally she turned to the white goose feathers adorning the southern wedge. The color of white meant peace and happiness. Lately, she had begun questioning this quadrant's meaning in a different way. She wanted to spend more time with the meaning of "white," but forced herself to move on. Most important now, the missionary needed spiritual care. She would get back to the blue and white quadrants at another time.

Blue Heron faced Breath Maker, sat, and placed the medicine wheel toward the bright rays. This clay hole in Mother Earth gave spiritual renewal. She let it seep into her flesh and bones. Surely this opening was like the one in Mother Earth from which her people had emerged in the beginning of time. Here, the spirits of ancestors would hear her and guide her to heal the padre, if she properly prepared her thoughts for a vision dream.

She must hasten to her task, waste no time. Time was precious. So, she folded her legs and gazed toward Breath Maker. She chanted while rocking back and forth, the same chant that Shaman Skytalker had used. She continued until her mind felt cleansed and ready to receive visions of ancestors. Slowly, she raised her arms. Her chin lifted upwards. Bright, warm rays filtered into her eyes, and she felt their power flowing throughout her body. At the same time she admired the great white butterflies that sky danced across her line of vision with the greatest of ease, honoring Breath Maker. She aimed to also honor Breath Maker by moving like the butterflies in her quest.

Her stomach felt more empty and flatter. "Best for vision quests," the shaman had said.

*My body is becoming light, soft as butterfly wings. I feel peace. Now my body is starting to float. I go up and down. I flutter my arms like butterfly wings. I am drifting. I listen for ancestor spirits to show me how to bring Breath Maker's breath and healing power to the padre, rid the evil spirits.*

Soon her tongue vibrated. The vibrato produced a different intonation from any in previous times. It felt so fitting. She cherished the nuance, caressing her heart in an endearing manner. Then she lifted her hair up and let it fly outwards as she circled, making wide arcs inside the red hole. Each time she came in front of the medicine wheel and rising Breath Maker she bowed four times, making one bow to each sacred direction and praying special chants for ancestors to listen.

The chants brought forth spiritual forces, which sent her body trembling and even stranger sounds into her chants. The highs went higher and the lows sank lower, the soulful sounds coming from a place inside which she never knew existed. Never had her body trembled with such spirit. Little by little she felt her mind leaving this world. She had no control over it, nor did she wish to control it. Panting, she finally wilted into an egg-shaped lump, her cheek to the clay.

After recovering she looked around as she wiped perspiration from her face and body. The feeling of fluttering like a butterfly was in harmony with Mother Earth, but a *white* butterfly? Something about that bothered her. It had some strange or hidden meaning. On the other hand, she felt deeply thankful for the strong force that had sent new sounds for her chants and spiritual tremors in her body. But would her vision quest help the padre? Had she sufficiently prepared for it, or had she been too hasty and dishonored the ancestors? Had Breath Maker heard her prayers to send the evil spirits of the fever away? She tried to swallow the choking, mixed feelings.

The sacred objects in the basket had not been used, nor had the pouch of spiritual herbs. Suddenly, her head bent down. Terrible doubts raced through her mind. If she had not made a successful vision quest, would the padre go to meet his God? Would Breath Maker be angry with her? She quickly gathered her belongings and climbed on her hands and knees up to the lip of the clay bowl as fast as she could climb. When she tried to stand upright, blackness came over her. Her knees went to the ground.

After sensing the light, she felt her arms and legs tingle. As soon as she regained sufficient strength, she stood, steadied her feet against the ground, and asked for forgiveness for being so senseless as to rush into the spiritual quest. Why, she'd even forgotten to genuflect! It might have helped.

On the way back to the village, she imagined that her mother had looked in on Padre. Breath Maker's warmth had now heightened the smell of sweet clover from all directions. Bees worked clover blossoms and swarmed around wild grapevines in a small clearing, which she passed. She swallowed at the thought of fresh honeycomb. It would be so wonderful to suck on a fresh, sweet honeycomb, but she must not take the time to search for it. She needed to check on the padre.

"Padre is yellow as a squash, and he doesn't move," Golden Maize Grower said, "except when he has a chill, he shivers. I opened one of his eyes, and the white part is yellow as his skin." She studied Blue Heron's expression. "Here." She removed the maize cob stopper and handed Blue Heron a gourd, which contained water.

Blue Heron sighed with relief. The padre was still alive. Then she said, "Thank you, Mother dear, for bringing the water." Blue Heron accepted it, turned from her mother's wondering gaze, and wiped Padre's face. She held his chin up, forced his lips open, and let water drip between his parted, parched lips. Then, caressing the gourd, she turned toward her mother and thanked her again, this time with her eyes and a nod, a language understood only between the two of them.

"So you have been on a vision quest, Daughter. And you are fasting. I see in your eyes, you are weak."

"I had to make a vision quest, dear Mother. The padre's spirit left his body. I fear evil fever will soon take his breath, too."

"My daughter, there are already thirteen sick people in the village. I ask you not to fast any longer. You will get sick if you weaken yourself." She took a bowl from a basket and in a commanding voice said, "Here, eat the *sofkee* I brought."

Blue Heron tipped the gourd to her lips, took a mouthful, and chewed the larger maize bits before swallowing the gruel.

For the next two days, she felt tired, barely able to care for Padre. During this time Golden Maize Grower continued visiting with her protests, though she still brought food and cool water.

Upon her arrival the second day, Golden Maize Grower lifted a reed, about two feet long, from her basket. "Here." She handed it to Blue Heron. "I brought this bubbling stick to you. River Raven told Shaman Skytalker that Seminole use bubbling sticks like this to blow breath into water. It gives more breath for sick ones. When the water is full of breath bubbles, the sick should drink it."

"Thank you. Thank you dear Mother, Seminole have found another way to share breath. I will blow my breath into the water for the padre."

Golden Maize Grower met Blue Heron's eyes and said, "I will go to Shaman Skytalker for help. Maybe he will come and pray for healing

260

blessings for the padre." Suddenly she heaved her hands onto her hips and exclaimed, "Daughter, you need rest." She let her hands fall to her sides, and she sighed, her shoulders slumping to roundness. Then she picked up her empty basket and had already turned to leave when she said, "I will come back later."

After bowing, in a slow, solemn manner, in each of the four sacred directions, Blue Heron blew through the reed and bubbled the water, over and over. Then she administered the water droplets by again forcing open Padre's lips. "Drink my breath," she quietly pleaded. "It will help you breathe."

But Blue Heron realized she must do more. Outside, she filled a clay vessel with white sand. On top of the sand she sprinkled cedar chips which she had taken from her basket of herbs. She lit them with a kindling stick that she had ignited at the closest family fire and then brought the vessel inside. As the cedar chips smoldered, she added sacred sage. Surely, the two aromas would rid the house of the evil spirits' stench that had caused the fever. Comforting cedar-sage odors filled the air and lingered while she paced back and forth on the sandy floor.

When Padre suffered a severe chill, she covered him with a deerskin and rubbed her hands together, waiting anxiously for the shaman. The sick villagers might be keeping him busy. No doubt, her mother's influence would bring him soon.

After Breath Maker had moved overhead, the air thickened with dampness, the day grew steamy hot and oppressive with heavy humidity. Padre began gasping for breath. This time she must not wait to make bubbles. Blue Heron blew her breath close to his steamy face and said, "I give you my breath, take my breath, it will help you to breathe." Seeing no change, she shrank in disbelief.

Soon frantic, she ran outside, stood behind a large pine tree, and chanted wildly into her cupped hands. Unable, to hold back dissatisfaction with her efforts any longer, her face cringed with defeat. Her shoulders curled onto the pine trunk.

She felt a moan coming, then a scream. Bravely she tried to restrain it. She could not. From the depths of her belly, a scream burst forth with heretofore unknown force. She squeezed her palms over her mouth with all her might to stifle it. Another one sprang forth, draining the last bit of the maddening force. No sound was left. Tears rolled. Her throat felt raw. She swiped her cheeks and grabbed around the tree for support.

What else in the world was she to do? Empty and ashamed, she lifted her head and timidly turned toward Breath Maker. She snugged her back against the tree's rough bark, seeking security. Soon, Breath Maker drew her unquestioning attention. Her arms limply lifted and stretched toward the sky without her willing them to do so. She gazed in a trance-like state. With energy dissipated, her soft voice intoned a simple chant: "Ancestors, I know you are with Breath Maker. I wait for your spirits to awaken and help me heal the sick man."

Spellbound, her eyes remained fixed upon Breath Maker. Deeper and deeper she drifted, imperceptibly, into a reverie in which she sensed the clouds parting, her arms becoming longer and longer.

Her quivering lips moved wordlessly.

*Through the clouds my arms are rrr...reaching toward...reaching toward Breath Maker for breath. My arms now reach you, my long arms will take your breath to the missionary. Thank you, Breath Maker.*

A southerly breeze had swept over her. Humbly, she peeked at her outstretched arms. They were now their usual size. Quickly she folded them to her breast, protecting the sacred breath, and darted furtive looks around. No one was watching. Perhaps all the villagers who felt well were helping the sick. With meek steps she found her way inside and opened her arms, in a way as to encircle his head, and released the sacred breath.

Passage of time became only a blur. Alas, one morning, Padre's wan face filled with bewilderment as his sickly eyes met a woman's hand grasping his arm. Then his eyes met her face. She looked familiar. "Where am I?" he asked with the temerity of a lost soul. Lacking strength to probe farther, his eyes closed, and he murmured, "Ugg, bear grease." With a curious and tremulous hand, he touched the grease that covered his parched, cracked lips. Other faint smells like cedar and sage mingled with the bear grease and provoked a slight retch. He shakily grabbed his stomach. He felt weak and ached all over. He must have been ill. Very ill? For how long? One thing was sure. A woman was near, for he felt her presence.

He didn't have to wonder very long about the identity of the person nearby or his own whereabouts. He recognized the familiar, soft chant as a shadowy form approached. He blinked. Blurs materialized into the form of Princess Blue Heron carrying a bowl. Steaming tendrils from the bowl spiraled into the air, enlarged, and formed another blur.

Padre's jaundiced eyes fluttered until his vision focused clearly again. She had knelt beside him and started to speak but held back, as if waiting for permission. She clasped his arm until his eyes met hers. "Your soul is back," she said, "Breath Maker brought your soul back to Mother Earth."

Padre gazed in awe at Princess Blue Heron. Had he died...and come back to life? Foolish thought. No one, except Jesus, had done that. Yet the shadow of death veiled his being. Death?...Yes, he knew a lot about death, but his own? No. Not yet. Perhaps it could have occurred in war, but he was ill-prepared to die of a sickness, for he was too young.

"The evil fever took away your spirit for a while," Blue Heron said. "Fever almost took all your breath away."

He tried to raise his head but instantly fell backwards. "What? What happened?"

"You have already passed through the tight crossing of paths that the hot fever brings. Breath Maker gave breath for you to squeeze through to the path of this world. The evil fever almost took you on the other world path."

Padre had no strength to correct her.

"I brought *sofkee* for you. Eat. It will bring your strength back."

With her precious wooden spoon, which she had always kept in her basket of spiritual objects, she scooped a small amount. "Here, I pounded the maize so the *sofkee* is very soft and I added water to make it thin, the way our people make it for the sick."

His head hurt terribly when he swallowed. He grimaced. The gruel tasted bitter like the taste in his mouth. After the second spoonful, his lips refused to open. With his body aching, he was completely spent. How it hurt to swallow, but afterwards he still nodded trying to show his gratefulness. Blue Heron reminded him so much of his mother. She seemed to know what was good for a sick person. She tried to help him feel better. She had an air of instinctive confidence.

Often, Blue Heron repeated the feeding process. By nightfall, with her persistence, he had consumed all the gruel in the small bowl and nearly a gourdful of water. She basked in the merits of her efforts. She would refill the gourd with cool water and quickly gather more rushes on the same trip to the creek.

While watching over the padre, she had woven rushes into mats so that she could replace the soiled ones underneath his body. Now she had begun weaving more mats. The padre was feeling better on this fine day. She had proven her shamanic skills, well, at least so far. Suddenly she dropped to her knees, wrapped her hand around his arm. A strange feeling pervaded when she looked at her hand clasping the padre's arm—bronze skin against white, though the white still showed some yellowishness. She stiffened. Something had changed. She tried to go back in time, get hold of the old feeling of hating white skin, the white skin that had reminded her not only of her husband's death but also the white padre's religion, against which the shaman had warned them. But try as she might, she couldn't get hold of the old feeling. She tried harder. What had happened to it? It would return soon. It must.

The next morning Padre, dry-mouthed and achy, rubbed his eyes and partially sat up, propping himself up on his elbow. In only seconds, he flopped down. Later he tried again and sat up a few moments. By sheer determination, he sat up longer on each successive attempt. Blue Heron chanted soothingly as she prodded him with fresh water. When she left to get food, he staggered up, needing to relieve himself. His legs refused to work. Things blurred. He collapsed. Blue Heron returned, found him lying, shamed, in a pool of urine. What could he do but accept her mercy?

"Today I dug sassafras roots and boiled tea to make you strong," Blue Heron said, smiling. "And I brought stew, thin stew."

In slow, awkward stages, Padre sat upright. Every joint and muscle ached. He felt tired and brittle. Though his mouth still tasted foul, he accepted a spoonful of stew and chewed on it, ever so slowly, for a long time. It had no flavor to his palate. Finally he swallowed it. While Blue Heron waited patiently for him to finish eating, she talked about the dreams he had had during the raging fevers.

"It's getting easier," Padre said, "to distinguish reality from dreams. I must have been on the edge of death. Now I realize I was dreaming about being at my mother's house and that she was baking bread. I was right there with her, looking at her caring face, watching, listening to her pound the dough. I could just smell her bread baking, like when I was a child." A ghost of a smile appeared on his haggared face.

Blue Heron returned a heartfelt smile. He was on the path to recovery. She had helped his healing.

"I know I lost consciousness of the world. How long did the fever last?" he asked, his voice still higher pitched than usual.

"It lasted for days. Evil spirits haunted me with fear. I tried to make a vision quest, but hurried too much. My mother brought a Seminole bubbling stick, so I blew water full of bubbles, big bubbles that held my breath. Then I gave you the water, but you did not have the strength to drink very much. So I blew my breath in your face. Still, you needed more.

"I waited and waited for Shaman Skytalker to come here, but he was healing the villagers. So many suffered the fever. I could wait no longer when you started gasping for breath. So I went outside and prayed. That's when Breath Maker sent a breeze of sacred wind. My arms brought it to you, and your breathing improved, right way."

Feeling in no condition to challenge her beliefs, Padre closed his eyes and drifted into sleep. In only minutes, a shattering, involuntary body jerk awakened him.

"Was my sickness like the same fever that the worker had at the Montezuma Trading Post?"

"That is the same evil spirit." she answered. "It attacked many people in the Owl Clan."

"I'm sorry to hear that the fever attacked the villagers. I am so indebted to you for all you've done. How many people in the village came down with the fever?"

"Many. That's why Shaman Skytalker could not come here. He said it was the most evil kind of fever. People sweated, shook with chills. Their teeth rattled. They heaved, vomited...green and black like mold. Their bowels gushed with scours, slimy and green and black. Eleven people died so far."

# WILDERNESS WITS

An ant carrying a colossal crumb scooted all the way from the summerhouse to an anthill several feet away from the doorway. Padre propped up on his elbow and marveled: *An ant, so small, so simple, the most wondrous ant I ever saw.*

He delighted in the tiny minion carrying its load, hundreds of times its own weight, dutifully just as nature had predetermined. In his lifetime he'd seen streams of ants, colonies of ants, and different species of ants; but this little creature created rapture beyond belief. Soon tired, he sank back on his bed. Then, eager to see everything within sight, he again propped up on his elbow. Heretofore insignificant things—a brown leaf blown against the door opening, his pale yellow fingers, the curvature of the anthill and of all things, more ants!—all these amazed, astonished, and astounded him.

*What has come over me?*

Nevertheless, he would allow himself to cherish the invigorating infusions that these commonplace creatures and details brought to his soul. It helped to distract his attention from residual pains, overall aches, and tiredness of his illness that made him feel as if he'd been on a long, strenuous journey. Still, just being alive felt...well, it was beautiful, miraculous, more beautiful and miraculous than he had ever known. Life truly was a God given gift. With this rediscovered gift, he would strive to be a better person. He had always been an exemplary priest; he would strive to be an even better person, also. To begin with, the crumb-carrying ants heartened him, regardless of his tender hands, to make good on his offer to help with the felling of trees for the Owl Clan, if only he had more energy. He eased back on his bed.

266

Other things he had taken for granted in the past, he now esteemed, like excellent vision. Thank God, his sight had not been impaired, for it had enabled him to see that first ant when he had felt better. One by one, an entire army had joined the solitary critter, stopping head-on, passing information, some climbing their hill with food, others going off in the opposite direction in search of an almighty crumb. The tiny workers' simplicity of cooperation and complexity of power had mystified him as never before, earning their place in life's great circle of miracles.

Though still confined inside the summer house, Padre's attention turned from the tiniest animate life to larger phenomena within sight of the door: glossy green needles on huge pine trees, squirrels skittering along tawny limbs, feathery clouds floating on the blue stream of sky. Renewed appreciation of mystifying beauty continued each day with slow, ever so slow, recovery. And truth told, that included Blue Heron. She was not so heathen after all. He felt he might have died here in the wilderness without her.

He knew, firsthand, that Blue Heron was truly good-hearted, not only to Chad but also to himself and probably would be to anyone seriously in need. He looked down at his old, tattered riding britches, thankful she had washed out the urine and waste and perspiration. How many times, he wondered, had she replaced soiled rush pads—on which he had lain semiconscious or too weak to move—with fresh ones. She'd bathed him. She had even seen him naked. He could not bear the thoughts. But, that was history and just as he had told Genesis, history couldn't be changed any more than the growth rings in a tree.

More and more Padre felt that he, indeed, owed his life to Princess Blue Heron's diligence and tender care. Her voice had held both soft music and solemn authority as she cared for him. She had been patient, kind, gentle, an angel of mercy, and for this he would forever be grateful. He willed, for the present, to avoid any controversial confrontation with her. He would do nothing to diminish Blue Heron's beliefs in spiritual quests. Though unable to relinquish completely his desire to convert her to the Holy Word, he still appreciated her deeply. After all, she had no control over the teachings that had been instilled in her from childhood. Below all these thoughts he continued being bothered that her Creek beliefs countered Truth. He weighed that matter against another matter that remained at stake—his life. Yes, his very life depended *still* upon the goodwill of the villagers, including Blue Heron.

Days later, the sallow-skinned Padre ventured outside the house for the first airing since the fever had attacked. Blue Heron held his arm, steadying his unsure steps. His knees still wobbled, his legs barely worked. Recovery had been a long time in coming. He and Blue Heron sat on a log near the anthill. The air was fragrant with dried grass of fall. In the quietness, a squirrel nibbled a thieved nubbin, then scratchily clawed his way to the end of a limb and made a flying jump to the next tree like a fuzzy gray line at once washed away. Another squirrel skimmed softly across a limb. Padre's soul brimmed with the outdoors freshness of autumn and the wild beauty of one squirrel's flight and another's quiet movement. His eyes moistened. He caught hold of himself and asked, "Have you heard anything from Genesis lately? It is my fervent wish that he and Willow are well."

"Every day while you were sick, I told you the Weaver family did not suffer the fever. But, I did not wish to tell you that Genesis had rafted logs and skins to Pensacola, for the *senor*, along with his workers."

The mere sound of Pensacola sent Padre's heart pounding. At last he would get news about the invasion. "When will he...?" In his excitement, he sucked in a gnat and nearly choked. After a coughing spell he said, "When is he expected to return?"

"Willow might know. She comes this way nearly every day. She usually...oh look down the trail. I think that is Willow with the fish baskets. Yes. She sometimes stops to rest and ask about you. Maybe she will talk with us when she gets closer. She is very happy that the elders have asked Genesis to come to the meeting when they talk about the burning."

With an inquisitive look Padre asked, "What burning?"

"Well, about every three or four years, they burn a section of land, so new growth comes."

"New growth? There seems to be enough of everything around here. Why do they need new growth?"

"Deer come only where there is tender browse they can reach. And quail. Quail must have cover for their winter coveys and spring nesting areas."

"So, Genesis is going to help with the burning?"

"Yes. Decisions must be made where to burn and how much and when. And beforehand, the trenches have to be dug to stop the fire. Willow is very pleased Genesis will have a chance to prove himself. He wants a Creek name very badly, and he wants the council to return the bow and arrows he made. The elders still study him."

Willow placed her basket on the ground and fanned the flies from the fish She looked distressed in the dark blue shadows of the oaks and pines. Blue Heron jumped up and ran for a gourd of cool water. Willow drank, then dashed behind a tree, gagged, and vomited. When she returned, Blue Heron insisted that Willow sit and rest for a while.

Padre said, "I am pleased to see you, Willow. You are probably anxious for Genesis' return from Pensacola. When do you expect him?"

"Any time now, we could see him coming. I will be very happy. He will bring me presents and presents for all the Weaver family."

"Genesis seems to be a good husband," Padre said, still delighted with the news of Genesis' expected return.

"Yes, but there is sadness, too. Fish Wrestler says we need to talk with Genesis about helping Big Brother. Big Brother brings trouble for Owl Clan. He's been visiting the new store near the trading post. Mr. uh...Mc something. How do you say it?"

"McAlister," Blue Heron said. "Since the padre is feeling better now, I was planning to tell him about this white man. My father has told me all about him. The McAlister man opened a trading store close to the Montezuma Trading Post—not for just hides and logs. This new trading place is where you can buy things, like in Pensacola. This storekeeper told Father that many people are moving here and will buy goods. Father is worried about the greed of whites, about the way they crave our hunting grounds. Mr. McAlister called it Alabama fever. Our people know it is not the evil fever that makes you yellow. This one is worse, far worse. It is fever that hurts the heart—it is whites' fever for taking over Mother Earth."

"Yes. Mr. McAl...whatever his name is, talked to Big Brother," Willow said. "He told Big Brother that white people need many things. Whites cannot wait for goods to come from Mobile or Pensacola."

"Other big changes are coming," Blue Heron said. "Alabama Territory will be changed to a state in a few months. My father told me. Whites will make rules for our Creek people. Elders have been holding council meetings under the sacred oak, talking about the evil news. Elders fear whites will take over Mother Earth, like Tecumseh and the other prophets had said would happen."

"I think that's what the American general had in mind with his invasions," Padre said. "The Sharp Knife General wants to carve states out of all the land. It does not sound good for the Creek." On the other hand, it held promise of possible converts for him, promise he would not speak about now.

Blue Heron and Willow looked grave during a lengthy silence.

Finally Willow said, "The storekeeper lets Big Brother drink rum, plenty of it. All the villagers can get goods and gamble if they mark 'X' on paper." She covered her mouth as if in fear and said, "I must go." She fled.

Padre's jaws clamped, his mouth stiffened. Sharp Knife had indirectly inflicted deeper lacerations with his invasions. The handwriting was etched with undoubted clarity in Padre's mind. He knew the ploy of the storekeeper. Surely Big Brother understood it, too, but just got fogged up with the rum. A strong conviction to enlighten and protect the villagers

269

from debt and save Creek land possessed Padre. He needed more strength and could hardly wait to regain it.

So much had changed since he had been sick—the bittersweet joy and agony of Genesis' expected return with news about Pensacola, the bittersweetness of the store opening and new settlers arriving. Yet, converting the settlers to the Word would be pitted against the possible loss of Creek land. And this land sustained Creek who had befriended him and helped save his life. The simultaneous attraction and repulsion of these contradictory feelings gnawed at him beyond belief. He needed spiritual guidance.

"Tomorrow evening," Padre said, "I would like to visit the sanctuary area. It seems so long ago since I was there. I would really like to pray for direction and chant thankfulness for my healing. It's been a long time since I've chanted. I hope I can still remember how." He smiled weakly.

The strangest of all sensations came over Blue Heron. The sky between the clouds had reopened to her, not with breath this time but with new understanding. Though she could not read books nor write, she could read nature, the nature of all living things. She possessed natural abilities handed down by ancestors. This new understanding fed her spirit like food when she was hungry. The Owl Clan needed Padre. An elder had said that they needed someone with book learning, who could read the papers that the whites are asking the people to sign. Why, Padre was even wiser in book learning than Genesis and could help protect Mother Earth from settlers coming in. And she had helped save his life. Surely, he felt indebted. Her feelings for him had been changing. Yes, she already held a place in her heart for him. She needed to find a way for Padre's talents to fit in with the Owl Clan.

She closed her eyes and rocked, serenely, from side to side. Thoughts of the wise women's teachings that she had heard in the birthing house came to her. In addition to when Tupelo was born, she had been there many times awaiting and assisting births. She had heard the wise old ones, always with twinkles in their eyes and confident smiles, explain a certain spirit that women have within themselves. If women get in touch with this spirit and use it in its natural way, it can work like magic to lead the men in fulfilling secret wishes for them. Blue Heron thought she now understood the meaning of this special spirit. She especially remembered that words of this special spirit must never, never fall upon the ears of men. Now that everything good was coming true in her healing efforts, she just might have the cleverness to try using the wise ones' advice. Though she never had any practice, she could hardly wait for the undertaking.

Finally, she sat still and met Padre's eyes. "Very well," she said, "but I must go with you to the blue pond and make sure you will be all right, that you really are strong again. And another thing, the missionary robe you wore to the Montezuma Trading Post to perform rituals for the worker with the fever..."

He nodded and turned slowly toward her but not slowly enough; it made his head ache.

"Well," she said, "it must be washed."

"Yes, indeed, you are right."

"But you should not wash it," she said, "I'll take care of it."

"I appreciate that. And I've been wondering. How could you be close to me and take such good care of me and still not get the fever?"

"Some of our people do not suffer from the evil spirit of the fever." She shrugged. "I am blessed by our ancestors' spirits."

"Other things must be taken care of in your house," she said with a serious expression, "since the fever had already taken hold of you the night you returned from the trading post. Your bed padding must be burned and replaced with new straw or a rush mat. Your dishes must be cracked and thrown in a special place by Shaman Skytalker. He will pray that the evil spirits leave along with everything that he throws in the pyre pit. And your body must be cleansed."

"First, there's something I would like to ask of you," Padre said. "I would like to carve '*Andalucia*' on the *banza* gourd if it meets with your approval. While we were making the *banza*, I kept thinking about how that area reminded me of *Andalucia* in Spain. But on that afternoon, I started feeling so achy and feverish that I had to leave early. When we go to the blue pond, will you take an etching stone along, so I can carve the words? I hope this is acceptable to you."

"Yes, I like that name. I would like it carved on the *banza*. And while we are there, I will help you wash your hair and beard. Afterwards, I can pluck the *banza* and chant and dance to celebrate your healing." She felt excitement in her eyes as her spirits lifted like the sudden flight of a great blue heron headed happily for her nest. Without shame, her confident smile met his eyes.

271

# NOTCH

# 111

# PENSACOLA NEWS

At last, Genesis returned from Pensacola. Word passed quickly throughout the village. Padre's hurried gait toward the Weaver site contrasted sharply with the lethargic movements of his recuperation and his recent strollings. To Genesis, who sat in the midst of the Weaver family gathering, Padre hailed, "*Deo gratias,* you're back." In one continuous movement he clapped his hands and rubbed his palms together with an unmistakable aura of enthusiasm. The percussive resonance floated through the sudden silence of his breaking into cherished family moments. Unheedful, he fired questions: "How's my beloved St. Michael's Mission? Did, did General Jackson...well I need to ask, did he attack the garrison this time?" Too fast for answers to be given and with the air of being the most significant person around, he lobbed yet another question. "And Padre de Galvez and Father Mulvaney, are they all right?" How he craved news, like a thirsty man craves water. How he itched to ask if Padre de Galvez had helped Chad, but knew he must restrain himself until he could speak privately with Genesis. Even in privacy, there would be no discreet way to question about Chad.

Abruptly, Padre realized he was being ignored. Taken aback, as if all his breath had been knocked out of his lungs, his spirits plummeted faster than a felled fowl. Slowly, he looked around. Perhaps he was not the most important person with the most pressing need for tidings, after all.

Genesis was about to show off his recently purchased gunpowder but stopped dead still, held his oblique look at Padre, and thought: *If you want a staring contest, I'll surefire win.* As soon as he felt victorious he continued attending to the interests of Willow and the Weaver family, dismissing Padre with a mere wave of his hand.

Padre's malformed shoulders slumped at the thoughtlessness of Genesis' gesture, a mere pittance of recognition. Holy Mary, Mother of Jesus, how could Genesis act so full of his own self worth, completely overlook his plea for even an iota of Pensacola news? Padre had lived for it, waited long hours and days. As fast as he choked back the hurt it raced ahead of his efforts, piercing the pit of his belly like the pitchfork that had impaled his arm in childhood. With all his might he tried to stem a forming tear. He bit into his cheek, then harder; and though no one noticed, Padre wept. He turned his head sideways, flicked one cheek, then the other, hoping it appeared as if he had whisked mosquitoes.

Padre stood transfixed while Willow affectionately rubbed the bright cooking pot Genesis had brought to her. And Willow's mother jingled her presents in cupped palms, two shiny thimbles. She opened her hands every few seconds, looked at the thimbles, and smiled widely, the rotting snags of her front teeth fully displayed. Certainly the thimbles would become just beloved trinkets to be sewn onto her *Poskita* regalia, for she would never be able to slip them over her long, thick fingernails which she used as weaving tools.

Genesis put aside the newly purchased gunpowder and foot-long knife that he had been showing to the Weaver men. He lifted a jug, filled a drinking gourd, and passed it around.

Padre smelled the wafting rum before the gourd reached him. For the first time in his life he bolstered his sagging spirit with a drink, a generous one, then another after the gourd had been refilled.

Genesis watched in utter surprise when Padre took a third swallow. Genesis said sternly, "I'll meet you at the summer house tomorrow. I was asked to deliver something to you. I'll bring it to you." He returned his attention to the Weaver family.

Padre squared his shoulders, cloaking his piquedness as best he could, and said, "Of course, of course. Thank you. I, uh," he sighed impatiently, "I'll be waiting for you." He lowered his head in shame. After all, Genesis had been simply fulfilling his role as a family man. Questions of monumental importance, vital to his own life, still stirred in Padre's mind, but lasted mere moments. The rum suddenly veiled all concerns. Haphazardly as a blind man he blundered away. *Dear God, how I had wished for the Pensacola news. I am thankful, (hiccup) for the rum. It helps. But, Dear God, (hiccccup) how I wonder what on earth Genesis brought from Pensacola?*

As soon as Genesis walked inside the summerhouse on the following day, Padre sensed some ominous news forthcoming. In a most solemn manner, Genesis reached inside his large buckskin shoulder bag and pulled out a scuffed satchel. What an odd item to be in his possession, for Padre recognized at once that it belonged to Padre de Galvez.

"This satchel was left with a message that it should be passed on to you. There was...uh, there was lots of damage done in Pensacola on the night of the big storm."

Shocked, Padre gazed. He forgot about his aching rum-head.

"You know the storm, the one that near about blowed us away right here. Well, it blew a hell of a lot harder in Pensacola before it roared through here."

"How well I remember that storm; it blew down my cross and altar at the blue pond."

Slowly, with his most heartfelt expression, Genesis handed the satchel to him and said, "Padre de Galvez, he uh...died the night of the storm." He paused for a reaction.

Padre gasped, said a prayer, and made the sign of the cross. He had wanted to admonish Genesis for being inconsiderate yesterday. Instead, he tenuously accepted the satchel, examining it as if it were a strange object. Then he ran his hand caringly around the edges.

Appearing ill at ease, Genesis said, "That storm ripped up palm trees and snapped off lots o' oak limbs in Pensacola. Blew off roofs. Blew sand everywhere, piles of it in some places." He sat and raked his fingers through his auburn hair, which was slicked down with bear grease. Afterwards he examined and rubbed his greasy hands together. Padre remembered how Genesis used to fretfully rake his fingers through his hair when he worried. Back then, his hair had been a bushy mess.

"I hate to tell you, but everything's different down there now. No more Spanish power. Governor Masot surrendered. Sharp Knife's officers are in charge."

"What happened to the Spanish officers?"

"Had to give up, like worms surrendering to a robin. Guns and gunpowder, rank medals too. At the Emerald Saloon, I heard a dandy say that the Spanish surrendered to the 'Napoleon of the Woods.'"

Padre grimaced. "That is a fitting description of the tyrant. I escaped one Napoleon only to face another one."

"Spain's surefire got no power now, no more power than one of them sunk ships in the harbor." Genesis shook his head and exhaled a heafty breath. "Pensacola's still got plenty of rum and gambling and dancing and billiards, but it ain't the same now."

"What will the Spanish army do now?"

"Oh hell, everybody got loaded into a ship and sent to Cuba."

Padre laid the satchel down and grabbed his anguished face, covering it with both hands, and moaned. Then he made the sign of the cross.

Genesis said, "Rumors floated around town that even if the garrisoned men had money to book passage back to Spain, most of 'em surefire didn't want to go back. And I'll tell you something else. I heard that them new people from Carolinas have started coming in already, applying for homestead land all around Pensacola. Most people said ole Sharp Knife invaded only 'cause he was land hungry. First thing he got done after driving the Spanish army out was, guess what? He put the land office in. People said he's put in for land for him and all his friends. New people'll be lucky to get a chance at squatter's rights up in the woods."

Padre eased down on a deerskin, still hanging onto Genesis' every word and mumbled, "It hurts. I can't tell you how painful it is. Glorious Spain, no more power." He shook his head remorsefully. "St. Michael's Mission, what will happen to it?"

Genesis shrugged, his eyes filled with compassion.

After a brief silence, Padre asked, "How did Padre de Galvez die?"

Genesis shrugged again. "The old Creek widow, the one that helped out at the dining hall, you remember her. Everyone called her Angel, Angel Roundtree."

Padre nodded knowingly, his eyes seeking the rest of the story.

"Well, she'd been looking after him now and then. Found him dead in his bed the morning after the storm. He'd told Angel and Father Mulvaney, before that day, to try to get the satchel to you if anyone ever heard from you. The workers at the tanning yard, and the log yard, too, was on the lookout for us."

Padre shook his head in disbelief as he picked up the old satchel and studied it. It looked so strange yet was so very familiar. How Padre de Galvez had treasured its rich cordovan color and its fine Spanish leather in the days when it was newer.

Finally he said a short prayer, opened the small, scuffed leather bag, and pulled out a small. well-worn book, Padre de Galvez's prayer book. Next, he found the elderly man's crucifix. Closing his eyes, Padre reverently embraced the bequeathed holy objects. Along with a "Thanks be to God," he crossed himself, opened his eyes, and pulled the last items from the bottom—two notes. First, he read, silently, the one written in familiar penmanship. For a while, he studied the shaky handwriting scribed by the hands he'd known so well, he could pick them out in any crowd. At last, he read the note aloud for Genesis:

*June 8, 1818*

"*Padre Morales, my dear brother of the Holy Catholic Church, Spain and the Church have suffered terrible losses here. I pray wherever you are that you are safe and will live long. My time on earth is nearing the end. I submit to you my crucifix. My memory still serves me well how you unselfishly gave your own to the mission altar when it was left bereft after General Jackson's first invasion. This is in no way to diminish the fine shell cross you later carved for yourself. The Church's few gold coins are in Father Mulvaney's care to help serve what is left of our faithful St. Michael's parishioners.*

*I have requested Father Mulvaney to pen the vital facts concerning the takeover of Pensacola. This is a follow-up to your diligent pursuit of the events leading to the first invasion and your persistence in seeking full information of subsequent threats. Presently, General Jackson has not only seized this city, but also, according to my understanding, has control over the entire Creek and Seminole nations. Many white settlers will now move into the Florida Territory.*

*It is my fervent prayer that my order for you to leave harm's way in Pensacola has kept you safe. My brother in Christ, I command you once again, perhaps the final time. I order you to return to Pensacola and assist with the Church's Holy mission under the supervision of Father Mulvaney.*

*May the blessed Mother ever intercede for your welfare and the angels eternally watch over you.*

*God bless and keep you always.*

*Padre de Galvez"*


Padre paused in deep reflection before reading the second note aloud:

"JUNE 9, 1818

NOTES ON THE SECOND INVASION FOR PADRE MORALES: ACCORDING TO RELIABLE REPORTS, GENERAL JACKSON CAME WITHIN SIGHT OF PENSACOLA ON MAY 22. GOVERNOR MASOT RETIRED TO SAN CARLOS ON MAY 23, LEAVING LUIS PIERNAS IN COMMAND. WITH THE GARRISON TROOPS BEING OUTNUMBERED FOUR TO ONE, JACKSON OCCUPIED THE REMAINS OF FORT SAN MIGUEL WITHOUT BLOODSHED. HOWEVER, PIERNAS WAS POWERLESS TO SURRENDER OFFICIALLY. AFTER JACKSON'S THIRD SUMMONS FOR THE GOVERNOR TO SURRENDER, FORT BARRANCAS WAS INVESTED.

AMERICAN BATTERIES WERE INSTALLED WITHIN FOUR HUNDRED YARDS OF IT, ONE NINE-POUND GUN AND FIVE EIGHT-INCH HOWITZERS. OUR MEN OPENED FIRE, AND THE AMERICANS RETURNED IT VIGOROUSLY. ACCORDING TO THE PEOPLE WITH WHOM I SPOKE, THE GOVERNOR FELT THAT BOTH HIS HONOR AND THAT OF THE KING HAD THUS BEEN PRESERVED. HE ORDERED A WHITE FLAG FLOWN AND SIGNED A TRUCE WHICH GUARANTEED THE SPANISH GARRISON WOULD MARCH OUT WITH FULL HONORS OF WAR AND BE TRANSPORTED TO CUBA.

I PRAY THAT YOU FOUND SAFETY. UNTOLD MISSION WORK AWAITS HERE IN PENSACOLA.

IN GOD'S HOLY NAME I HAVE OBEDIENTLY RECORDED THIS MESSAGE AS DIRECTED BY PADRE DE GALVEZ.

FATHER MULVANEY"

"Oh Lord, I am thankful the men did not fall like a line of dominoes," Padre said and closed his eyes in prayer.

After Genesis had remained respectfully quiet for a while, he said, "Uh hm, I was afraid they'd get slaughtered like shoats. I been thinking, if you decide to go back, surefire don't leave alone. We'll be rafting again before long. And I have to tell you, the *senor* makes me the leader now." Genesis' face brightened. "He lets River Raven take it easy, just lets him stand up front. River Raven tells me where every bend and sandbar in the river is. I already nearly about know it by heart, like him. Makes me feel important, a hell of a lot more important than even when I got the interpreting job at the garrison. Only thing, Maypearl ain't around to stick out her tongue at me and get her hair yanked out when I talk about it. But I surefire wouldn't think of yanking her hair now. Things are mighty different. I've been meaning to tell you that Willow will give us our first child soon."

"God bless you and Willow and the expected child. I had noticed the signs already."

"When I think about the baby coming, my chest feels like it swells way out, bigger than the biggest bullfrog in the whole Alabama Territory." For a moment, Genesis picked at a thumb cuticle. He looked up and said, "When I was in Pensacola I was hoping I wouldn't even see Cleo. I don't miss her a bit now. Didn't want to have a damn thing to do with her."

Padre stared stoically in space.

"Now, don't leave till *Senor* Colabro makes another trip," Genesis said. "It should be soon. The moon is growing. Logs and smoked meat sell good in Pensacola. The new people need them things."

"These people who are moving in, are they by any chance Catholic?"

"The head man at the tanning yard said Father Mulvaney told him that they have their own religions, all different kinds of religions. *Humph*, that high-minded Mulvaney's got the top job at the mission now. The Spanish soldiers, the ones that was in the garrison when I was there—the ones that had a little fire in them—used to say he suffered from some kind of Irish lunacy. Wonder how he'll face the new people?" Without waiting for an answer, Genesis turned to leave. As he approached the doorway, he turned his head back and said, "I didn't ask why the priest didn't go to Cuba with the soldiers."

After Genesis left, Padre removed his shell crucifix and placed the bequeathed crucifix around his neck. He thought that as soon as the elders return his possessions, the shell crucifix, which he'd carved in Pensacola, would be stored in the metal box in his shoulder bag. That beloved, little oval box had held his crucifix from the monastery, the crucifix which was long-lost after Jackson's first invasion. How he had cherished looking at the inscription on the inside lid of that box, proof that he had come from the *Andalucian* province. His thoughts reimmersed in how he had come to be here in this Creek village and about the identical shell crucifix he'd carved and given to Genesis. It had symbolized the pact that they would reach the Montezuma Trading Post together, but it was now being worn by Willow. Changes, changes, changes. Why had he been so proud, so brave, so defiant of the archbishop's warnings back in Spain?

Padre prayed to the Archangel St. Michael to grant blessings at his namesake mission. Then, for Padre de Galvez's soul, he implored St. Dominic, praying raptly for his former superior. Prayers spawned memories of their mission work together. The elderly priest had truly been charitable, when he, the younger one, had confided about possibly leaving the garrison with Genesis. The superior priest had not only forgiven those sinful thoughts but had also *ordered* him to leave. Padre de Galvez's decision, though made with the wisdom of his years and his love for perpetuating the Spanish tradition of the Church, had come as such a shock. And now another shock riveted the subordinate priest, the order to return to Pensacola. Padre would obey. He had always been true to his vows of obedience to his beloved Dominican Order. Yet, his thoughts wavered. Could he fulfill the obligation this time? Return on a raft?

Padre lay wakeful.

*Can't sleep. Howitzers keep on booming inside my head. My throat feels like a twelve-pounder's stuck in it...at least a nine-pounder.*

He had imagined the outcome of Pensacola a thousand different ways. The truth faced him head on and reopened the bleak chasm of despair.

*So, Andrew, Andrew, Andrew Jackson, are you sleeping peacefully tonight? Do you feel victorious? Have you felt the people's pain? Have you seen the tears? Do you realize this is the utter end of His Majesty's colony? Do you even have the faculty to care? If you are gloating, Mr. General, Napoleon of the Woods, go ahead. Oh God, no...No more of this. I loathe wallowing in pity. Somehow I must find faith to overcome my bitterness.*

Padre flung an arm forth as if jettisoning the spell of despair. Of greatest importance now was fulfilling his latest orders. "Good Lord," he said aloud, "my strength has not fully rebounded since the fever. Contemplation of returning by raft is enough to set a saint reeling."

In her most subdued manner, Princess Blue Heron chanted and strummed the *banza,* remembering Chad and awaiting a possible appearance by Padre this first day after Genesis' return. Thoughts of all that had happened with Padre's cleansing here at the blue pond were not of first importance. Today she had not even thought about further plans on how to fit the padre into the Owl Clan. Presently, her mind was filled with remembrances of Chad and hope of hearing something about him.

Stunned by the weightiness of his new order and fear of the rafting trip to Pensacola, Padre, on his way to the blue pond, maintained the steadiest walking gait that he had experienced since before his illness. Unknowingly, he had submerged all memories of the cleansing tryst in the blue pond. On this day, prayer and meditation at the outdoor chapel were foremost concerns.

Blue Heron was in the throes of wondering whether Genesis had heard anything about Chad when she saw the padre approaching. She did not wish for him to know how anxious she was for news, yet soon found herself saying, "I have been thinking about Chad. It makes evil spirits tear up my mind. Sometimes I do not wish to hear about him. It could bring trouble for me, helping a runaway slave, if the villagers learn about it." She put the *banza* down and timidly said, "But I must ask. Did Genesis bring back any news about Chad?" All the while, her eyes kept seeking Padre's new necklace.

Padre reluctantly compromised his wishes for worship, sat on the sand, propped himself with his hands, and said, "I have not been able to trace Chad yet. Padre de Galvez, maybe you remember he is the priest I sent him to. Well, Genesis brought back word that this elderly priest died the night of the big storm." Padre rubbed his palms together, whisking off the sandy granules. "The dear old man made arrangements to have this crucifix sent to me." Padre lifted it from his chest. "This one."

"I saw right away that you wear a different necklace." Could she dare get the nerve to ask him what happened to his shell necklace, the identical one like Genesis gave to Willow? No. It was a point of honor not to speak of one's hurt. Padre should never know how she feels about Willow prancing around like a doe, showing off the beautiful colors in the shell necklace, which Genesis had given to her. Blue Heron bit her lower lip. *Spirits bring other women all the good luck.*

"I suppose you could call this a kind of necklace, but remember, it is a holy one," he said, touching the crucifix. "Getting back to Chad. I do not know if he even found his way to Pensacola, or if he got there before Padre de Galvez died."

"I've thought many times about his sad face, the way he cowered like a...a beaten dog when we first saw him," Blue Heron said. "Have you told the secret that we helped him?"

"Angels above, no, not at all, not to Genesis, nor to anyone. I would not violate that trust, not ever. And another thing, certainly if Chad did get to Padre de Galvez and the priest was unable to help, I am sure he sent the needy man to someone who could give assistance. I have prayed for Chad every day, prayed that he found the sugar plantation, the one to which his wife had been sold. But most sugar plantations are well east of Pensacola."

"When I strummed the *banza today*, I thought of him, his terrible wounds. The way his sores looked still tear my mind, like someone ripping a shiny magnolia leaf into pieces."

"Perhaps you should also think about the good side. Remember, we gave our best to him, and he gave his best to us. There is something else I must tell you. You should know that in addition to the crucifix, Genesis brought other things, among which was a letter from Padre de Galvez. In the letter, he ordered me to return to Pensacola. Sharp Knife now controls the town. He sent the Spanish soldiers to Cuba, but another priest and I will serve the people who are left and the newcomers, too. Genesis has already told me that I can return with the rafting crew on their next trip. It should be soon."

Blue Heron's eyes widened. She protested, "You have not yet gained all your strength back. Sometimes evil spirits of the fever return to people and makes them sicker than ever before. You take a big chance if you leave too soon." She covered her mouth with both hands. Never could she tell him that she had planned for him to...she could not bear to think how she had hoped he would use his book learning to help her people in their dealings with the settlers. Embarrassed, she released her hands from her mouth. His whiteness...his strangeness aroused anger she had never before known. She had a fitful urge to scratch him...scratch him with a sharp bone needle...scratch him until blood covered his white skin. He should feel her sting...and deeply. *How could I have wanted his strange ways to be part of the Owl Clan?* After that thought, her insides withered. She shrank, feeling helpless as a wounded fawn. Then without warning, she snatched the *banza* and ran away, unmindful of the padre's baffled expression.

Padre rose and resolutely went to the outdoor chapel. He prayed and meditated with the clearness of mind that he had been accustomed to at St. Michael's Mission. Thoughts of fever and deliriums had fled and had hidden in shadowy recesses of his mind. Determination for absolute obedience to his orders overshadowed any residuals of his sickness. No notion of Blue Heron entered into this searing singleness of purpose. An excitement reminiscent of his sailing day back in Cadiz, excitement, which he thought had been forever lost, now revisited and roused his energies. Inward sparks singed the edges off worries of mind-numbing cottonmouths and alligators as well as sand bars, logjams, and tricky river currents.

At the very next full moon, Genesis and Padre would depart from the Montezuma Trading Post with the rafting crew, Genesis leading the way. It seemed fair to leave Captain with the Owl Clan in return for the hospitality, though he actually had no choice. But there would never be another *Andalucian* icon in Pensacola to take *Grandeza*'s place, nor a blue pond sanctuary. On his last visit to the blue pond, Padre offered the Blessing of St. Francis, a most befitting benediction for this New *Andalucia* area. And Blue Heron had accepted the shell crucifix, or necklace as she called it. It was the only appropriate, tangible token of appreciation he could offer for all the tender care she had provided.

In the pain of separation, Blue Heron still had the presence of mind to hide the beautiful shell necklace inside the gourd of the *banza* where it would stay until she felt comfortable about explaining the gift to the elders. For the time being, the *banza* and necklace would be safely stored in the hollow tree. True, Willow wore Genesis' necklace, but there was a big difference. Genesis was no dreaded missionary.

The night before departure from the village, Padre took time for resting in the mercy of God. He reread well-loved pages of Padre de Galvez's prayer book. He turned the tattered pages, reverently remembering how his superior had sought wisdom, comfort, and possibly hope, in them. There was something encouraging and settling about just touching Padre de Galvez's prayer book.

Alas, daylight arrived. Padre and Genesis would go to the Montezuma Trading Post, from whence the raft would depart the following morning. Before leaving, Padre thanked the Owl Clan elders again and again and bade farewell while diligently looking for Princess Blue Heron amongst the gathered villagers. Finally, at the rear of the crowd, the blue-feathered headdress towered above the people. To Padre's chagrin, Blue Heron's eyes again held silent sorrow. Yet, how grateful he felt for her patience and care.

*I take with me more tolerance and understanding of diversity in people than I ever dreamed there was to comprehend, more sensitivity, more appreciation for animals and nature, as well. I am forever changed.*

Even in the face of bidding goodbye, even in the face of potential death during the looming raft trip, Padre felt God's presence drawing nearer to him.

# THE DREAM

Early the next morning, at the Montezuma Trading Post, the rafting crew and Padre walked downstream to a protective cove. Sight of the raft sent Padre's mind spinning. No more than bound logs would be between him and the swollen, swift river. He figured the only way he could handle traveling in such a formidable fashion was to keep his head down and follow Genesis' directions. Genesis treated him as respectfully as one of the Creek elders, for which Padre felt grateful in this extraordinary instance.

With the first step onto the raft, the undulating movement sent Padre's heart pounding. Worse, the roaring river would soon envelop them. He must not look into the water and see his shadow, as he had done just before departing Cadiz. It would be too much to bear. Even in the cool fall air, he broke out in a sweat. From his sideward vision he glimpsed the rowdy crew hooking trees at the fore. Then he meekly turned his head to sneak a look at the men jamming the river bottom in the aft. Soon, the raft was out of the cove and underway. How his stomach churned when they entered the rushing river of the great forest. The smell reeked of the same terror as when he and Genesis had encountered it in May. Albeit, at last, he knew he must lift his head. The cursing crew had settled down. They had not harassed him at all. They seemed to have an entirely different attitude toward him than they had displayed on the day he first had seen them at the Montezuma Trading Post. Had the sanctimonious way in which he cared for the sick and dying worker effected the change? Only God knew.

Padre admired the crimson-tinged dogwood leaves. Other trees along the shore also bore smatterings of autumn colors. Thus, he fathomed that this frightening trip had not robbed all his senses, at least not the esthetic ones. He trusted he had passed through the most unbearable part of his river-rafting crisis. But sunrise to sunset the river rushed on, stubborn and strong. He dared not test the strength of the logs' bindings. He wondered if they would hold fast for four days of these undulating currents.

Reality of night changed everything on this river of cane. Its eternity began early with the workers tying the rafts to the hefty trees on the banks. Unable to see a foot ahead in some places, he looked upward. Against the background of bright stars, swarms of big-eared bats fed on insects over the river. Death rang in every echo of the owls' and alligators' calls. Miles of curling currents and careening sharp turns, yet to be faced tomorrow, set his stomach tossing and churning again and rendered him barely able to partake of evening sustenance. While trying his best to sleep, he still endured restless hours, which every now and then mixed with anticipation of returning to Pensacola.

On the fourth dark morning, Padre restlessly hungered for dawn. Daylight would come. He would watch the light strengthen and the shapes emerge. Still, it mattered not whether it was daylight or dark, the river's menacing overhangs never cautioned him to think of their danger. And mere walking over slippery, rounded logs required practice, which he would not need after today. Rafting was for the quick and young. Thank God, the four-day maelstrom would end this morning. On this last day on the river, he must keep himself safe. Blessedly, the crew got underway earlier than usual.

After they had begun twisting and drifting the last meandering leg of the journey, Padre confidently dozed. A terrible dream snapped him into wakefulness. Could this nigh unthinkable dream become a reality—Blue Heron bearing a white infant, then being banished by the Creek council for having a child without marriage. In the cool morning mist, Padre shivered and wrapped his arms over his chest. Had the treacherous quicksand of war driven him into moral quicksand.? It *had* driven him to drink too much rum at Genesis' homecoming. Worse, he could use another hefty ration of rum this very moment. It had seemed so easy to make light of sorrow by going numb with rum. For the first time in his life, he felt that it was not so unreasonable for people of untainted character to encounter circumstances, which could cause them to succumb to the evils of libation in relieving pain.

Tender sentiments for Princess Blue Heron rekindled, deep and everlasting as this river of cane, sentiments too intimate to ever share with laity. Her eternal mysticism, her soft soothing voice, and the times when her eyelids closed and she hummed her healing chants, had dispelled his preordained postulations. No, she was not heathen, rather, she was endearing…ethereal.

287

War! Why, the very roots of evils that befell him had truly been imbedded below the quicksand of war. Setbacks. Fevers. Loneliness. Pain. How could he not ease his pain with rum? And how could he not show gratitude for Blue Heron's care and go along with her desire to help with his cleansing at the blue pond? *Damnable War possesses power greater than a priest's will.*

Suddenly, someone yelled, "We're in spitting distance." There was no more time to grieve about war or anything else.

Into the dark blue sky of the predawn salty air, Padre gazed toward the vanquished town of Pensacola. Without Spanish rule, the town was a mere vassal, as empty as the locust shells hanging onto limbs in a narrow, fogless, section of the river, only a stone's throw away. Soon, earliest morning sunbeams brightened a portentuously prominent one. This particular empty locust shell seemed to depict a likeness to his innards. He still wondered in utter panic if there was any truth in his horrific, purgatorial dream. He shivered again. The men grabbed the ropes for a landing. Almost imperceptibly, he realized he would leave his empty shell, as the locusts had done, with new life. He would be filled to overflowing with masses, Eucharist celebrations, baptisms, marriages, and funerals. A saying he had heard came to mind: "Lo, many yesterdays, only one today." Somewhere in the distance, dogs barked forlornly. He stroked his bequeathed crucifix.

The homecoming both satisfied and daunted, daunted like the heaviest fog they had encountered upstream. Upon landing, Padre eased into a back stretch and tentatively tested his land legs. Then he dropped to his knees, kissed the ground, and offered a thankful prayer. Through the milkiness, he hobbled on sore legs toward a stout palm tree and, despite his sore back, he hugged the palm. Alas, he was back and on level land. The palm seemed to be more than an ordinary tree on this redeeming return. It symbolized the familiar place where he would now start anew to accomplish his longtime goal of building a church for St. Michael's Mission. The church would have missals, chalices, and altar linen.

After thanking and bidding the men farewell, he singled out Genesis and said, "Be sure to visit the mission on your next trip. We will probably have a great deal of news to tell each other."

"Surefire, Padre." He patted the priest's humpback and added, "Don't be taking no trips into the wilderness by yourself."

Padre cut an oblique glance at him and released a partial smile, despite his aching back and body. Seriousness returned. He wished to find Father Mulvaney. Padre desperately needed to make confessions so that he could receive the comfort of absolution. He studied his bearings, turned and waved to Genesis, and sallied his sore bones forth in anticipation of celebrating mass with consecrated Host today and sleeping in a bed this night.    Return to civilization would clarify his unsure future, a future without Spanish rule, as predictably as the sun would dissipate morning fog. But the bizarre dream and its questionable portentousness…?  He shuddered but continued walking.

# MIRACLES

The following spring Genesis could hardly wait for a rafting trip to Pensacola. Upon arrival in Pensacola he could hardly wait until the smoked venison and turkeys and cured skins were unloaded; but, of course, afterwards, he helped the men untie the raft of logs. Further waiting, while the overseer tallied the account, brought another payoff, different and unexpected. Genesis heard extraordinary news. After quickly distributing wages to the workers, he set forth to find Padre. He had expected Padre to be somewhere along the beach, for early afternoon would be the time for Padre's meditative walk; however, before Genesis approached the sandy beach, he saw Padre sitting on a bench underneath a tree in Ferdinand Plaza.

"Spanish rule again! What a surprise," Genesis shouted to Padre, "I surefire didn't think this could ever happen again. I found out about it right after we unloaded the raft."

"No one was more amazed nor prouder than I," Padre said as he sprang to his feet, smiled, and extended an arm in a welcoming gesture. "It is absolutely miraculous that for the *second* time, the American government has returned Pensacola to Spain. And it is somewhat of a miracle on this fine day to see you in the real flesh and blood."

Padre hung his head.

"You're surefire acting strange," Genesis said. "What's wrong? I thought you'd be acting so high and mighty about Spanish rule again that you'd be spitting out your big words, faster than hot grease popping out of a frying pan."

Without raising his head, Padre said, "Well you did catch me off guard; and yes, I guess several things have been preying on my mind." He hesitated. At the spur of the moment he could not formulate an answer that was entirely satisfactory to him. Instead, he centered on Genesis' point about big words and expanded on that subject. "For years I was so proud of my education and priesthood that I did have a tendency to show off. It has come to pass that I can now accept, with some difficulty, that this shortcoming was an effort to hide my peasant background."

Genesis listened intently. The intonation, in Padre's voice, rang familiar. It had returned almost the same as it had been in the early years.

"Well, other matters have, also, concerned me lately."

"Padre, is there something wrong with you?"

"Oh no. It's just that I've thought a lot about Princess Blue Heron and how she cared for me during my sickness." He cleared his throat. "Is she...is she still living in the village?"

"She surefire is. Where else do you think she'd be?"

Without answering, Padre asked another question, "Does she still look the same?"

"She's looks about the same as she did when you saw her last fall. Chief Wahoo and Golden Maize Grower watch over her like a hawk."

"Have there been any changes in her life?"

"Not that I know of. Now Padre, what kind of changes do you think there would be? You must really be pining for her, and you're ashamed to admit it."

Padre caught a deep, relieving breath. Since last fall, unbidden thoughts of the blue lake cleansing episode with Princess Blue Heron had taken their toll on his spiritual well-being, shook his very faith in himself. Now, quite relieved of worries, he sighed and said, "That's not exactly the crux of the matter, but you are close." He could not tell Genesis that the awful nightmare of Princess Blue Heron, bearing a white child and being banished from the tribe for having a child outside of marriage, had at times haunted sleepless nights as well as daylight hours. Genesis would be a good listener but Padre still would not bare his soul. Padre still was not even absolutely sure just what had happened at the blue pond when Princess Blue Heron had taken him for the cleansing after the fevers. Parts of what had happened were now just a blur. He was not sure of anything other than how he had felt indebted to the princess for her care during his bout with the fevers.

Padre took a deep breath and said afresh, in his most ecclesiastical mien, "Let's get back to the good news here. No one was more amazed nor prouder than I when the U.S. president made this rightful turnabout of Pensacola to the motherland again." He put his hands together in prayerful form and thought: Perhaps prayers have wrought this miracle. Or perhaps this was the miracle portended years ago when he had landed in Pensacola.

Perhaps this miracle was his reward for dedication to the Holy Catholic Church and God.

"Old Sharp Knife cut his own self out by seizing Pensacola again without authority from his government," Genesis said with feigned laughter as if to break the serious mood. "The Spanish ought to give him some of his own medicine, bad medicine like the firing squad. He was always mighty quick to use it on others."

"Genesis, I would never go so far as to sanction a firing squad. I was aware that Foreign Minister Onis had been negotiating, not only for the rightful restitution of Pensacola to Spain, but also punishment of General Jackson. It was not always easy for me to keep staunch faith during those negotiations. I regret that." Reference to faith halted Padre's words, yet he now realized there was no need to worry about keeping faith in concerns over Blue Heron. He might never have to suffer from the tortuous nightmare about her, another miracle, a very personal one. Still, he must not allow Genesis to become suspicious of the flood of relief which he had begun experiencing, so he said in his priestly, caring way, "Genesis, you are looking healthy."

"Uh hm, and it looks like you finally got over the fever."

"Yes. It seemed like a long time in coming. It took days and days to recuperate from the devastation of the fevers as well and reconcile myself to American domination, which thankfully was short-lived. My health never has really been the same since the fever, though Pensacola sunshine and sea breezes have contributed a great deal to restoring my strength. Just watching a glorious coastal sunset and walking on the warm sandy beaches makes a person feel better. I had barely brought myself to accept Jackson's government when Onis pulled off this diplomatic feat for Spain. He is the greatest negotiator that one could imagine. You probably have not heard the details."

"I didn't wait for no details about the turnover. After we unloaded the trading goods and separated the logs and got paid, I hurried over here to see you."

"We owe it all to Foreign Minister Onis, his mettle, his Spanish sensibility. When no results were forthcoming in his negotiations, he approached a Washington official in the middle of the night and demanded the return of Pensacola to Spain and punishment of Jackson. Onis achieved a compromise and more, too. The government in Washington didn't punish Jackson, didn't even touch him; but two weeks ago, *marical de camp Juan Maria Echevarrial* brought Pensacola's new governor, Lt. Colonel Jose de Callava, from Havana. February of 1819 will forever be memorable. What a beautiful sight when Callava's garrison disembarked—24 officers and 483 men from several Spanish line regiments, following him. Comforting memories returned as I watched them. Why I thought I could even smell my mother's freshly baked bread brushed with warm olive oil, the essence of Spain itself. Yes, Jackson's tactical triumphs turned into empty victories."

"That's good, that's good. Things are going to be good for me, too, at the Owl Clan Village. Our first baby will come any day, and Willow thinks that before the next *Poskita*, the elders will give me my new name and return my bow and arrows."

"That's fine to earn a Creek name. Just don't ever forget your first name. Your mother gave you that worthy bibical name. Hmm," Padre cleared his throat. "It was one of the first words she had learned in the white man's language at the mission."

Genesis listened attentively to the comforting words.

"Your strong name, so caringly bestowed, may foreshadow the genesis of some great feat. I mean a, uh..." Padre turned his palms up with fanned fingers as if groping for a morsel of wisdom. "I hope your bibical name is actually a prophecy that will be fulfilled for you in a significant way."

"I appreciate what you're talking about, Padre, 'cause I think I understand what you're trying to say. Don't worry. I'll still appreciate my old name, even while I'm appreciating my new one when I get it." Genesis stood to leave and said, "I have to meet the workers and get them on the trail back to the village before Log Dancer drinks too much rum." He heaved out his chest and asked, "Padre, do you ever think of the rest of the Owl Clan?"

"I do, I do as many times as there are leaves on a live oak, the largest of live oaks. How are Shaman Skytalker and the elders and everyone? It's been about, let's see, about six months since I last saw them."

"Everybody's about the same since you left."

"I regret that I was so caught up in the accreting changes here in Pensacola that I did not inquire about all the villagers earlier. My visit with the Owl Clan was life-altering. It opened my heart wider, wider than I could have ever imagined. I care about the Creek more than I ever realized was possible. I am especially fond of and grateful to Princess Blue Heron. Truth told, I am fond of and grateful to all members of the Owl Clan."

# FLORIDA'S FATE

The moon cycle increased to fullness and decreased again and again, until another year had rolled on. And more years passed. Meanwhile, Genesis made occasional rafting runs to Pensacola.

On his most recent trip to Pensacola, Genesis asked a Seville Square dandy, "Where are the Spanish officers and soldiers garrisoned now? I haven't seen nary one of them."

"Haven't you heard?"

"When I unloaded the raft, nobody said anything about them."

"Well, probably because the news is somewhat stale now. They were sent back to Cuba in March. Florida is now a territory of the U.S. To be exact, I penned in my record book that it happened in March of 1822, a fine year, a lucky year. My dry goods business will flourish now."

Genesis thanked the dandy for passing on the information and quickly set out to find if Padre was still in Pensacola. Sure enough, Genesis found him returning from a visit to hospitalized parishioners. After they exchanged greetings, Genesis repeated the dandy's gossip and asked, "Padre, how did this happen?"

"It was another twist in the convoluted, yet inevitable fate of Florida. Yes, this one is final. The U. S. government paid Spain $5,000,000 for the Florida Territory, but it took General Jackson a while to make the deal official, which is another whole story unto itself. Looking back, when Pensacola surrendered to Jackson—in the second unauthorized invasion— May 29, 1818, he then right away seized the royal archives, appointed one of his colonels in charge, and posthaste departed for Tennessee on the 30th. Of course, I was living with the Owl Clan back then. You will recall, after that, I had rafted back to Pensacola. Shortly thereafter Onis negotiated for the *second* return of Pensacola to Spain. But now, this changeover is altogether different—*final*. It is a purchase. I experienced the changeover firsthand. After both parties signed the purchase agreement, the United States president sent Jackson here as Governor of the new territory, and I actually saw him."

"If I had seen him, I would have kicked him in the ass and then smashed in his skinny face." Genesis windmilled his arm and said, "I woulda punched hell outta 'em, bare-handed, too, just like I done that coachwhip back when we was on the trail."

"His guards would have nabbed you as if you were no more than a gnat and jailed you."

"I ain't never been in jail, but that would surefire be worth it. And don't make no mistake about gnats. They're mighty small, but they have a way of fighting for their place in this world."

Rather than addressing that statement, Padre said, "After the exchange of flags, both parties celebrated with a big ball in the evening. Everyone of distinction attended, both Spanish and American—Colonel Callava, Rachel Jackson, Father Mulvaney, and can you believe it? I was there, too. Delicacy of food and wine and the splendor of the plate graced the tables under fragrant smoke plumes of Cuban cigars."

"To hell with the fancy stuff, what did you do when you saw Sharp Knife?"

"The instant I laid eyes on him was an unbelievably defining moment. I kept thinking, Andrew, Andrew, Andrew Jackson, how merciless can you be? Scarcely tolerant, I watched his every move. The jubilant Jackson drummed his fingers on the table. Each move was sure to mean something, something vital to him, like his infinite avarice. Then when he was alone, while others danced and mixed, his other side showed through—finitely simple, sickly, and weather-worn. Still, when he made his way through the crowd, hands reached out extending a welcome."

"Padre, how'd you feel about all that welcoming? I woulda raised hell."

"Something about him seemed formidable, but in hindsight I can't help thinking his mind must have been fraught with torturous thoughts of guilt. I overheard one official say that Jackson's one regret was that he did not hang Governor Masot. By the grace of God, Father Mulvaney and I endured the occasion, finally speaking charitably of him as a human being as we walked home."

Time came all too soon for Genesis' departure. With the efficacy of a mature cleric, Padre intoned blessings for him as well as the entire Owl Clan.

"Padre, you're outdoin' yourself, gettin' to be more than a match for the way Padre de Galvez used to be."

For few moments, Padre luxuriated in the praise of his former student. Then his thoughts leapt into a more priestly vein. Extending sacerdotal blessings, even to a wilderness dweller, lent levity to Padre's pressing concerns about his future under American domination.

# A GIFT FOR PATSALIGA

Indeed, Genesis had fared well at the Owl Village most of the time, but the elders still had not approved him for membership in the Owl Clan. During the many full moons that had come and gone, he thought that he had proven himself worthy of the Own Clan in countless ways and surefire deserving of a Creek name. Yet, it was not until he had helped with the last land burnings that the elders ceremoniously accepted him into the Owl Clan and bestowed the fitting name of Golden Gopher. While helping to mark the land to be burned, Genesis had found the largest gopher ever seen by any of the clansmen. The elders declared that the burrow would be kept secret, for they would kill and eat the gopher only if hard rains, or the lack of rain, ever ruined the maize crop, thereby causing winter starvation. Genesis was proud, very proud of his Creek name; but it had come when times had begun changing, diminishing the importance of tribal names. Whites' names were becoming desirable, so he continued to be known as Genesis. In his heart, he treasured his original name for at least two reasons: In the first place, the name had been given to him by his mother and secondly, Padre always thought it might have a special meaning. Padre had done a little preaching in that regard.

One fall afternoon, Genesis plodded along the main river trail toward the village using both hands to tote a special rock, which he had just harvested from the riverbank. The wedge-shaped rock looked just right to steady the wobbly crossing log at the bathing creek. To rest his arms, he placed the heavy rock on the ground. Then he slowly stood erect, looked upwards, and watched a flock of geese flying south in notch formation. As he lowered his eyes he caught sight of a familiar figure, Big Brother, moving toward him in the sad but familiar straggling gait, zigzagging from one side of the path to the other. Spellbound by heartfelt hurt, Genesis watched each step of Big Brother's approach. As he came within spitting distance, Genesis noticed that Big Brother's hairline had receded on both sides of his head into two paths, which issued from his forehead for a distance half way to the crown. Big Brother's face was ladened with disgust. Hate in his eyes blazed wilder than that of a snapping fox that had been roused from a lair.

Genesis' first impulse was to try to be helpful. But before he spoke, Big Brother, in a slurred voice that had also grown much lower in pitch, preemptively shouted, "Genesis, I feel like blassssting an arrow right through your hard heart. Scouting for whites in the land oooffice. Oooverseeing sale of our Mother Earth. You have the bloooood of our people in your veins, yet you never understood we are part of this land. I wwwish I had gone out West already. Patsaliga (Creek for sitting pigeon) even said it would be best for our cccchildren. You don't even remember that I treated you most like family when you first came here."

Genesis caught a whiff that strongly reeked of rum. He kicked the fine rock that he had carefully harvested, felt pain, then kicked a patch of ground until dust flew. Laboring though uncontrollable, heart-thumping anger, he managed to say, "Easy. Calm down, calm down, Big Brother," and gestured to a nearby log. How well Genesis understood the problem. Big Brother's compassion had betrayed him, again and again, setting him up as an easy target for deceitful land grabbers with rum.

Big Brother flopped down on the log, sighed, and flung his hands over his face. In a muffled voice he said, "Nothing is the sssame since whites with Alabama land fever started cccoming in. But I never, never thought you would gooo against ancestors' teachings and sell us."

"And you ain't never, never been the same since you started drinking rum and gambling at the trading store. You never, never listened to good advice about that so-called free rum. It's easy for you to make your 'X,' but its surefire not going to be easy for you to pay up."

Big Brother pointed a finger, "Don't yyyou tell me. I'm tired of lllistening to your Pensacola talk. Every day there's more greedy whites coming in. Eeevery time I go hunting more trees have been cut. Deer are scarce. Lllucky if I see a turkey. You think you're bbbetter'n the rest of us 'cause you can read and write your name?"

Genesis decided not to argue with the "rum." He kept quiet while picking his teeth with a brown pine needle. Big Brother slid off the log and flattened out on the ground. As soon as he hit the ground, his eyelids closed, his mouth flew open, and he snored like a bear with a bellyful of honeycomb.

Meanwhile, Genesis sought a solution as he picked up a twig and slowly scratched his head with it. When he thought Big Brother had napped long enough, he tickled his nose with a yellow flower. Big Brother awakened and sneezed. In a heartfelt tone, Genesis said, "There ain't no sense in raising a fuss over the past, 'specially about something we can't bring back. I've been through that. You can't change the past no more than you can change the growth rings in trees."

"Genesis, one thing's nnnot for sale. Our spirits. Sacred from ancestors. We are ppppart of the land."

"My mother told me that. I have been knowing that since I was knee-high to a brown pelican. That's not going to stop our people from selling the land, 'cause they like to have goods just like whites. You know how our people get fooled by whites. Nearly every Creek wants whatever money can buy. No stopping it. I know by scouting for land for whites, I can stand up for what's true and honest for our people when they start to sell. I protect our people."

"*Humph*, I'm the one that stands up for what's true and honest. I forbid Patsaliga to learn how to spin. I will not allow her to learn evil white ways. If it was left up to me, I'd burn all them spinning wheels and looms. Willow's and Blue Heron's, too. And all the plows," he said with disgust.

"Hold up. Don't touch my belongings. I worked for them. The Owl Clan has taught me many things. Chief Wahoo showed me how to make wahoo rope, and I worked damned hard when I first came here, making it and bartering it." Big Brother seemed to be growing calm, and his slurred speech had already improved. Genesis said, "Life was hard at times, but running the rafts to Pensacola helped a lot, and now that I got the land-scouting job—that's how I got Willow a spinning wheel and loom. That's how I got the plow, too. These things are good for my family and *don't touch* them. Maybe you should..." Genesis' voice faded as he noticed that Big Brother had dozed again.

Late one evening, Willow approached Genesis, with unmistakable purpose in her footsteps, as he honed an arrowhead near the storehouse. From her carrying basket, she selected a well-ripened persimmon and tossed it to Genesis.

Genesis gently pressed the fruit, testing its tenderness, then twirled it around as if admiring the deep orange color before relishing a bite.

"While I gathered persimmons with Patsaliga, she told something important," Willow said.

Genesis' attention heightened. His shoulders shivered gently from a gusting autumn breeze.

"Patsaliga said that she and Big Brother would move to the West when the weather turns warm, when dogwood blossoms open. Mr. McAlister told them their land here would pay off the debts at his store."

The chilling effect of autumn air deepened when Genesis heard Willow's sad news. Still, he said, "I ain't surprised," shielding how the news ripped into the pit of his stomach. He asked, "What does Patsaliga say about leaving?"

"She said they could live with ways of the ancestors on land promised out West. Big Brother wants to go there and make a new start."

"Have you talked with Blue Heron about their move?"

"Yes. She opened her heart to me." Then, Willow told Genesis all about their conversation: "Blue Heron said that with all the changes coming about, she had been thinking about her dear mother's teachings before her mother went to the next world. Blue Heron said that all her life she had heard these teachings, but they seemed different when her mother lay weak and tired, barely able to puff on her favorite corncob pipe. Her mother had told her that as an elder, it was her duty to make sure Blue Heron understood that life does not end with death; that life is a circle, forever and ever endless; that when we leave this world, we go peacefully to the next one; that Creek are not afraid of the dark, or the forest, or death like whites; that whites are the only ones who call our Mother Earth the wilderness."

Genesis interrupted, "With great respect for Golden Maize Grower, I'd like to add one word—*most*—we are not afraid of the dark like *most* whites."

Willow nodded. "Blue Heron said that she knelt and touched her mother's forehead. Like many other times, her mother repeated that Mother Earth is the mother of all living things. Then Blue Heron's mother told her, very carefully, that she must pass the teachings on; that we are akin to everything that lives—every grain of sand, every pine needle, and every rock; that we must respect all of Mother Earth; that if you break a tree branch or clean a partridge for eating, do it with respect; that we must remember the ways of our ancestors...and when she sees the purple spirit birds keeping watch over the gardens, to think of her. Blue Heron said she had stayed with her mother as darkness fell around them. Sacred owls, large-sounding ones, called hoo-hooo-aw, four times."

Genesis felt the hairs on the back of his neck rise when Willow mimicked the haunting owl calls. At times like this, she was as one with nature. She was just the same as she had been when he first talked with her and visited her secret space, the little cave filled with sacred bones at the river's twin oxbows.

Willow brushed a wisp of hair from her cheek and continued the story. "Blue Heron told me how echoes through the woods had doubled the number of the owl calls, blessing her mother as she journeyed into the next world. Then Blue Heron just sat quietly for a while. I waited patiently. Then she said that this was the moment when she had promised the guardian spirits she would go to the sacred red clay hole and meditate. She said she would make visits to the red hole for as long as she lived to keep her mother's memories alive, so they could be passed on."

Genesis had listened intently. After Willow had finished repeating this conversation, she eased closer to Genesis. His body heat and persimmon-tinged breath comforted her. The cool air felt right for leaning closely to his strong shoulders.

Demon shadows followed Genesis throughout the winter months after he had learned that Big Brother, who had befriended him when he first came to the Owl Clan, planned to move to the West. Now, in this renewal cycle of the earth, he watched with mixed feelings as the dogwood buds swelled larger each day.

The fateful spring day arrived when Big Brother's family would leave. At the break of dawn remaining members of the Owl Clan gathered, faces fixed in sadness, bodies motionless in grief, and stood under the sacred oak tree's tenting branches from which hung thick, gray moss. The pendant tufts pointed to the gray, gloomy expressions of the people. Under this tree, important councils had been held in past years, but now the villagers had assembled to bid Big Brother's family a safe journey. Genesis witnessed firsthand the pained faces, not only of Big Brother's family relinquishing their homes and leaving the burial ground of their fathers, but also the villagers' who would remain. Willow carried their second son, wrapped in bobcat fur and strapped to a cradleboard, which hung on her back. Their first son stood nearby. Singing Basket Weaver, now a withered woman, placed her hand on the first son's shoulder. Neither the sweet call of the warblers nor the deep-purple beauty of nearby violet blossoms appeared to give any relief to the stark-faced members of the Owl Clan.

Shaman Skytalker, wearing his albino skin regalia, could barely lift his feeble arms or wiggle his four thumbs, now distorted with arthritis. He looked to Blue Heron Healer, who recently had begun performing most of the shamanic duties, and nodded for her to give the farewell blessing. Solemnly, she said, as her hand outstretched to Big Brother's family, "In my vision dreams, ancestors brought messages that we must find new paths. There will come more whites than there are trees in the forest. We cannot reach fullest blessings if we carry hearts full of hate. The old ways do not help now. Better it is to keep our hearts filled with the old ways. We must keep the old ways safe in our hearts and pass on the teachings, lest we forget our forefathers when we walk new paths. We have many memories of Big Brother's family here, and we must promise to ever keep the burial grounds of their ancestors sacred." Blue Heron Healer lowered her arm and bowed. The shaman nodded his bowed head and said, "It is so."

Newly elected Chief Owl Claw stood beside the elder Wahoo. Chief Owl Claw wore the former chief's huge headdress, its owl feathers now tattered. This regalia had already begun swallowing Wahoo's aged, shriveled body even before he relinquished it to the new chief, who looked into the sky and prayed, "Breath Maker, we ask that you keep the evil spirits from our Brother's family as they walk the paths to a free part of Mother Earth. We pray for your blessings on them in the faraway land." He bowed his head for a few moments, and when he raised it, the villagers whispered among themselves.

Genesis felt a warm hand on his shoulder. To his amazement, Big Brother had approached as quietly as a hunter, leaned over, and begun speaking softly in his brotherly, caring way of the past. Big Brother said, "I will begin a new life with my family."

At once, Genesis again noticed the two paths issuing from each side of Big Brother's forehead and reaching near the crown of his head. Astonished, Genesis noted that only since last fall, one path had grown noticeably wider. A great rush of relief coursed through Genesis' heart. What if...what if the broadened path had opened wider as a good omen, beckoning Big Brother for a second beginning out West? He said, "Big Brother, it just came to my mind that we are alike in yet another way."

A questioning look came over Big Brother's face.

"I got a new start here in the Owl Village," Genesis said. "Now you have a chance for a new start. You learned much here. I hope you will find goodness out West like I found here."

Big Brother nodded, and they shared a long look, as if each wondered if it would be a final one.

With a sort of reverence, Genesis watched Blue Heron Healer and Willow as they exchanged farewells with Patsaliga, who still looked as gentle and peaceful as a sitting pigeon, her namesake. Genesis understood how care pressed on the women's hearts this spring morning, care that stirred, care that they shielded as each had shielded her unborn children. Blue Heron Healer and Willow wore shell crucifixes over their hearts that had been given to them by Padre and Genesis. These were the same crucifixes that Padre had carved in Pensacola to seal the pact with Genesis for reaching the Montezuma Trading Post. Willow removed her crucifix and carefully placed it around Patsaliga's neck. Then Blue Heron Healer extended an open palm toward Breath Maker and uttered another blessing, a very short one. Now one crucifix would travel out West.

Genesis worried: *I've seen things, been through things here in Alabama that I never ever thought could happen.  What will become of the crucifix going out West?*

# CALEB

Two days after Big Brother and his family had left the Owl Clan to go out West, the man in charge of the Sparta Land Office, Moses Thomason, and a companion reined up their horses at the village, both looking terribly serious. Genesis had always liked working for Mr. Thomason, though today the boss seemed awfully different. The long, lean bodies of Mr. Thomason and his companion, clothed in dark clothes and black hats, at once reminded Genesis of the coachwhip snake that he had fought in the great forest. The men startled him, stirring up the same sort of scare as when that coachwhip snake had whipped itself onto one leg, then the other until he whacked it away. He was really scared because yesterday the storekeeper, Mr. McAlister, had been found dead, an arrow through his neck. A customer had discovered McAlister lying face down in a pool of blood, inside the store where Big Brother signed an "X" relinquishing his land. Genesis rubbed his furrowed brow as he observed the formidable visitors. Would they accuse him of killing McAlister? Would he lose his job with the land office, the most powerful position for helping the Creek while at the same time scouting for land prospectors?

Mr. Thomason assured Genesis that they had come in peace. Then he asked if he and his companion, Caleb Lange, could meet with the village council to offer a proposal for reopening the McAlister store.

At Genesis' urging, Chief Owl Claw reluctantly agreed to grant the request with the stipulation that the visitors would have to wait for the council to make preparations. The council members no longer prepared themselves with the black drink, but the chief had to gather all the members, adorn regalia, and go through sacred chants before meeting with the white

304

men. After council members had gone through their rituals, they stood in a line in front of the old *chakofa* and faced the two whites, who had patiently waited.

Chief Owl Claw said, "The visitors may speak."

"Before I tell you about the man I have brought here," Mr. Thomason said, "I want to make sure you know that I feel Mr. McAlister committed wrongs against the Creek at the store. He should not have encouraged drinking and gambling in return for Creek land. But a native has also committed a wrong by murdering him. If any members of Mr. McAlister's family had lived nearby, they would have demanded that the state government investigate the murder. An investigation could have brought untold trouble here. You already know Indians have no rights in court." He straightened himself to his tallest countenance and said, "The man accompanying me is of an altogether different character from Mr. McAlister." Mr. Thomason placed his hand on his companion's shoulder and said, "Now, I want to make it *very* clear he is a man whom I believe is as good and honest as the day is long." Then he introduced the new man, Caleb Lange, and added, "Caleb is from Virginia. He inherited money from an uncle who had a large tobacco farm there. I will let Caleb explain his purpose here."

"First," Caleb said, "I wish to thank the council for giving me the chance to explain how I am different from the store owner who was killed. Most importantly, I want to make sure you understand that I am not here to fool the tribe members with rum or rob the tribe members' land like the deceased store owner. I most definitely will not do anything to deserve an arrow shot into my back."

Caleb shifted his feet and straightened his shoulders. "I want to make sure you understand what happened back at my home in Virginia and the reason I am here: My brother and I did not see eye to eye on running the farm we inherited in Virginia. He is more of a farmer at heart than I am. After a whole lot of arguing and grief, we agreed that he would pay me for my share of the farm. While we were signing the papers in the bank of a nearby town, I talked with a prospector who had just returned from the Alabama Territory. He said that this land here in Alabama is very rich in timber, some of the largest trees he had ever seen. I thought that this area might be where I would want to settle. I have discovered in the short time I have been here that the prospector was right. I like the place even better than I ever imagined. I like it so much I wish to stay and reopen the trading store. The land officer has told me of Mr. McAlister's evil way of dealing with natives when they traded at his store." Caleb cleared his throat noticeably and said, "I *promise* to deal fairly and honestly with the Creek.

When you have council meetings, I ask that I may attend them and work out problems, if any arise."

Mr. Thomason had told Caleb Lange that many new settlers would need supplies, thereby making the store very profitable, but kept silent about the possibility of huge sales of vast land and timber, which he anticipated making at the Sparta Land Office.

Caleb Lange continued, "And there's one other thing. I wish to start a church with white members who are willing to share their knowledge and goodwill with the Creek. Perhaps some of the Owl Clan members will want to attend the church and learn new ways. Now I will answer any questions you may have, so there will be no doubt in your minds about me."

The council members reconvened inside the weather-worn *chakofa*. Chief Owl Claw said, "I do not trust white men who run stores and talk about Mother Earth's trees."

Blue Heron Healer, now officially the shaman, encouraged the council to work with Caleb Lange. In her heart, she had already respected the way Caleb had squinted his eyes, as if truly promising he would deal honestly with the tribe. It was the same look she had seen in her husband's eyes and the white missionary's eyes when they had vowed themselves truthful. Besides, she warned the other council members that with all the changes coming about, it would be worse if some other white man, mean as McAlister, came along and reopened the store.

Genesis, who had been elected council member in Tall Cane Walker's place when the Walker became disabled, approved of Caleb, too. The idea of starting a church sounded beneficial for the clan, especially in these changing times. Willow could use some extra help from church-going whites with the loom and spinning wheel. There might be other good things she could learn from the church people. After all, he had learned from whites in Pensacola and especially from Padre.

The other members joined with the decisions of Genesis and Blue Heron. As the new owner of the trading store, Caleb Lange would be allowed to prove himself to the Owl Clan, since Creek tradition had always decreed that the majority ruled.

Like many endings in nature, Blue Heron was unaware of exact times when she and other members of the Owl Clan had given up certain old ways and assumed new ones. Not only was blue "pond" at times referred to as blue "lake"—and officially recognized as Blue Lake—and "maize" as "corn"; but also changes of heart had blended slowly and willingly into new behavior that felt right. But she remembered vividly the exact instance of one change—when Caleb Lange stood before the council to explain how he wished to reopen the trading store. Her arms had instinctively folded over her bare breasts and remained in that position for the entire meeting.

In the days ahead, Caleb Lange's image, his light brown hair and greenish eyes, pleasant face, fine clothes, startled Blue Heron's mind anew again and again. Secretly she thought he was the best looking white man she had ever seen, and at the same time she felt he had shown plenty of goodwill, even cunning ways. No matter how she tried going about her usual ways, he constantly appeared in her thoughts with a force she could not resist, nor did she want to.

Caleb Lange would surely visit the Owl village again. How Blue Heron looked forward to seeing him again, but she knew she must appear pleasing to him. As the days passed, she more and more accepted the notion that she would have to start wearing more clothing. The buckskin skirt simply was not sufficient. She would like to look as nice as the white women settlers.

Blue Heron confided about her changing heart to Willow and finally asked, "Would you be willing to join me in bartering baskets and seeds or maybe fur hides at the trading store for material to make dresses like the white women wear?"

"Genesis might not like it if I give up my buckskin skirt, but I'll help you make some baskets to trade." Indeed. Willow set right to work helping Blue Heron weave a variety of baskets.

For the trip to the Caleb Lange's store Blue Heron wore her cape of blue heron feathers. Inside the store she kept her head down and held the cape together tightly with her fingers, thinking she might look like a squirrel clutching a prize acorn so she let up. After she unstrung the assortment of baskets from the raffia rope hanging from her shoulders, she glanced at Caleb. Magically, ripples of pleasure flowed through her like a sweet stream. Her fingers then gripped the cape tighter as she was getting her breath.

Slowly, she looked up again at Caleb. At once her heart knew he was a man without meanness or impatience.

"Are your baskets for barter?" Caleb asked, sensing he should coax out her shyly held feelings.

She nodded.

"You have a fine collection. Settlers like different sizes for eggs and seed and picking berries." He studied them. "The weaving is very good. What would you like in exchange?"

Blue Heron swallowed hard and looked around. She pointed to the yard goods and then followed Caleb with his scissors in hand.

"This bolt of sturdy, white material is muslin and the patterned one is calico."

Blue Heron's heart raced as she looked longingly at the calico. She wondered if she were good enough to wear the precious blue-flowered material, so she directed her attention to the plain muslin. Surmising the reason for her reticence Caleb said, "You may have a piece of each bolt. And you can color the muslin with pokeberries."

Blue Heron pressed her knuckles against her lips in awe as Caleb unfolded the blue-flowered bolt. He placed the fabric from her shoulder to mid-calf. "Is that about the right length?"

Blue Heron nodded wide-eyed.

Caleb cut double lengths of each fabric. "You will need some thread and needles. The needles that you use for buckskin are too large."

So overcome with joy, Blue Heron's buckling knees would hardly hold her up. So overcome, she had no idea yet that Caleb was carried away with her natural beauty and unassuming attitude. So overcome, she was at a loss as to her next move.

Caleb wrapped the fabric and notions in brown paper, and as he was putting the scissors away, he took a second, long look studying them. "Since today is Saturday and it's getting late, and I'll be closed tomorrow, you can borrow my scissors if you promise to return them Monday morning."

Blue Heron's face lit up. She smiled and nodded.

At the dawning of Monday morning, having worked fervently making the dresses, Blue Heron ran her fingers along the calico dress, up and down, over and over, admiring the beautiful blue-flowered fabric. Finally she put the dress on, shivering at its softness. Then she slung the cape over her shoulders, though she would wear the cape only until she was out of sight of the village. She was not yet ready to give any explanations to the villagers about her new dress. In return for Caleb's favor of lending the scissors, Blue Heron had selected a precious piece of hickory-smoked venison to take to him. After lining a basket with succulent live-oak leaves, she nestled the venison in the fresh leaves, topped it with more leaves, and then placed the scissors in yet another layer of leaves. She headed for the trading store.

In the following days, whenever alone, Blue Heron joyfully chanted: "From little seeds good things grew; from little deeds dreams are coming true."

# THREE NOTCH ROAD

In the following months Genesis aspired more and more to fulfill a dream. Since private ownership of movable objects had become acceptable for tribe members, he had been saving some of his earnings for the very special purpose of buying a mare. As soon as he felt assured that he had accumulated sufficient money, he resolved to buy not just any ordinary mare. Rather, he willed to find one worthy of breeding with *Grandeza*, none other than one of pure *Andalucian* bloodline. There would be offspring for the children to train and ride, and with more mares and stallions, over time, there would be foals for the grandchildren. The *Andalucian* bloodline could be passed on. How he hankered to get started with the next rafting trip to Pensacola so that he could search for the mate that *Grandeza* deserved. He also had news to tell Padre, for many changes had taken place in Montezuma, particularly during the past months of his scouting for the land office. Before leaving for Pensacola, Genesis gathered his family around him and said, "I'll be looking for the right mate for *Grandeza*, and I want you to know I'll work as hard at my searching as a bur oak root looking for water." Every set of eyes lit up.

In his heart, Padre exulted in the surprise of Genesis' warm handshake and greeting. Enthralled, Padre took a step back. Yes, Genesis had shown promise, even as a youngster. Padre stroked his beard and thought that before this visit's end he must find a way, an adroit way, to seek out his former student and determine just how he had learned the new courtesy of a handshake.

More than on any other visit in the past, the two men studied each other: Padre's hair and beard had grown grayer, and his malformed shoulders were further stooped. Genesis' hair had thinned and receded, and the lower pitch of his voice was noticeable. Deeper lines now edged the eyes of both men and lined both of their foreheads, though the lines were more distinct in Padre's face.

Genesis burst out, "Padre, you should see Montezuma now. We just got a courthouse and jail. They carved the year, 1824, in the log right over the courthouse door."

"I am pleased to hear the trading post community has grown large enough for a courthouse. With human imperfections, the need for a jail is sure to follow. The Montezuma Trading Post must be the county seat."

"You're right about the jail and the county seat, but the place surefire ain't just a trading post no more. It's a village now, so you're supposed to just call it Montezuma."

"Fine. I'll be careful to use the correct name in the future. How is Willow?"

"She gave us a daughter since I last saw you. She's happy. Our two sons are still growing like pine saplings, surefire learning to be brave. Willow wrapped them in bobcat fur when they was babies. The bobcat's fierceness came inside both my sons from that fur. They already practice spear throwing and footracing with their Weaver cousins. And there's something they want very much—a colt from *Grandeza*. I hope to buy a mare to mate with *Grandeza* while I am here. Not just any mare. I want to find a silver, *Andalucian* beauty."

"I am very pleased to hear about your plans for continuing the *Andalucian* bloodline. You have many blessings, Genesis. I think of you very often and of Princess Blue Heron. How is she?"

"I already told you when I was here on one of my rafting trips that she had earned the name of Blue Heron Healer and how good things kept on happening for her, especially after she was elected shaman. And ever since she married that new storekeeper—you probably heard that his name is Lange, Caleb Lange to be exact—lots more good things happened for her."

"Of course, I heard that she had married. I was told that she had been wooed and won by a prosperous storekeeper, and I might add that I was quite shocked that she married a white man."

"That's right, and a lot more's happened, lots of changes. There's something I need to tell you about the first store owner by the name of McAlister. I've been putting it off. Well, I'll just tell you later 'cause it ain't good news. First, I want you to know that Blue Heron and Caleb have a baby daughter named Sehoy and Willow said Blue Heron will give another child."

"Sehoy is a beautiful name for her daughter," Padre said, his voice involuntarily weakening with each word. At once, the image of Blue Heron's tender face emerged from a shadowy alcove of his mind, tenderness that he had become dependent upon in his sickness. Imperceptibly, he cupped a hand over his mouth. Suddenly he realized that any residual feelings for Blue Heron must not become visible, so he lowered his hand and nonchalantly tipped his head sanctioning his good reasoning. And though he was able to conceal it, he tacitly rejoiced that Genesis seemed oblivious to his having been taken aback.

Genesis continued, "Willow told me that 'Sehoy' means daughter of the wind in Creek. Wind is sacred to Creek. Willow likes Blue Heron's new house, a very nice house. A board house."

"Where did they get the boards?"

"From the sawmill. I guess you didn't hear about Montezuma's sawmill. A man that I scouted timbered land for, by the name of Morgan, had a creek dammed up, so the water pushes a wheel to make the saw cut. It's nearly the same as the first sawmills in Pensacola. Most people still use a froe to split logs for their houses around Montezuma, but Caleb wanted a board house for Blue Heron. It's real boards. And you should see how many goods Shaman Healer has, even a fancy parasol and shoes that button, and they go to church a lot. Willow says Caleb told her that Blue Heron went from buckskin to batiste and is still as sweet as when he first met her, still his shining star."

"What is this batiste?"

"Willow said it's some kind of fancy cloth. Caleb and Blue Heron talked me and Willow into going to church, too."

"Do other villagers attend church?"

"Some do."

"Well, that is an astounding change, compared to when I was there. How did that come about?"

"When Caleb first found a preacher man and started the meetings, they didn't have no church house. The people sat on split log benches out in the open, and we stood midst the trees and watched their church doings. When they put up a palmetto roof, we could still see. We figured there wasn't nothing to be afraid of, so when they built the church house, we went inside for the meeting and just stood in the back. Most of the church people were nice to us and asked us to sit down."

"Apparently the Owl Clan members enjoyed the church meetings."

"Creek learn things from the church people. And we really like it when they sing their special song—'Rock of Ages.' I told the preacher that I like to hear them sing it, but that them words don't make no sense. He explained that a preacher in England wrote the words when he was taking shelter from a storm on a rocky cliff. The preacher didn't have anything to write on but a six-of-diamonds he found in his pocket. The strange part is that most preachers think playing cards sends people to hell, but if he had not had that six-of-diamonds card we might not have the song."

In a stronger voice Genesis continued, "I told him I still didn't understand the words, and he said he hadn't finished yet—that the rock of ages was a very old rock and the cleft was a split in the rock large enough to shelter a person. And that's why the next line is 'Let me hide myself in thee.' But the preacher said the rock really stands for Jesus. Them people sing their hearts out on that one, nearly blow the roof off. I wouldn't tell anybody else except you, Padre—sometimes the way they sing that one gives me chill bumps. And you should see how they baptize people. Nothing like in your church. They go down to the river and the preacher man stands in the river and holds a piece of cloth over the nose of whoever's getting baptized. Then the preacher braces the back of the person with his other hand and lowers the person backwards till the person is below the water. It's a sight to see."

"Yes, I've heard of that type of baptism by different churches around Pensacola."

"What I really like is when the preaching man reads from the Bible, the first part where my name came from. He said that nearly anything you need to know, you can find it in *Genesis*. It made me think about my mother, and I told Willow all about her again and more about how she and my sister went south to live with the Seminole."

"I have thought about your mother, too, and Maypearl. You probably know that there are many problems between the settlers and Seminole here in the Florida Territory. Most of the Seminole have retreated even farther to southern swamps. I trust their tribal members are safe."

"I surefire think they are. Seminole know how to live in swamps where whites can't even get to them. But Padre, I didn't finish telling you everything. My firstborn son learned to sing a white children's song. Learned it from a boy he played with after church. It's about 'The Sow Took the Measles.' That song makes you laugh and cry. But it's not no church song. They just sing it when they play outside."

In light of the knowledge that Blue Heron had undergone transformations in addition to attending church, Padre felt safe in asking, "Did you ever see Blue Heron's *banza?* I helped her make one."

"Shoot, she's got that thing hanging on the wall in their store. A fiddling man saw it and was interested in it. And before I forget, I want to tell you that while he was there, he fiddled a tune that he called 'The Eighth of January,' all about Jackson's battle in New Orleans. He sure could fiddle that tune, but I don't think he understands a thing about how evil and greedy old Sharp Knife is."

"Some people have just never been told the entire story about the general while others plainly agree with Jackson's sentiment of expansion."

"Uh huh, but about that *banza*, everybody that trades at the store sees it. It's right in back of the scale. You can't miss it and the '*Andalucia*' word carved on the side of the gourd. New people are always curious about that word, so Blue Heron tells them all about when you was here and how you and *Grandeza* come from that place in Spain and how you said that Montezuma looked so much like that place. Sometimes I tell people that my father came from Andalusia, too."

Padre smiled.

"Andalusia! That reminds me I can't talk all day. I want to find that Andalusian mare I got my mind set on. I gotta find just the right mate for *Grandeza*. Our sons wish for a colt very much."

"I notice that you are now pronouncing my homeland name a little differently from the Spanish way. The correct way is *Andalucia*."

"Aw shucks, I say Andalusia same as everybody around Montezuma says it now. They don't have time to say it fancy like the Spanish."

"I still like the Spanish way. Albeit, I trust that you will find a special mare, one that will beget progeny worthy of the *Andalucian* blood line. You'll have the honor of riding your mare back on the new Three Notch Road. I was amazed when I read that General Jesup had ordered the army to construct the road all the way from Pensacola to Ft. Mitchell, Alabama. Even more amazing, I learned that the feat was accomplished swiftly by only twenty-nine men. But most amazing of all, there was only one casualty and that was to an unfortunate snake bite."

"Padre, if I could get a bet out of you, I'd bet one of them rattlesnakes that we saw stacked up on that ridge bit him. That was the damnedest pile of rattlers I ever saw. Never run into anything like it again. Never."

"Yes, that was one of the scariest sights we experienced while traveling the trail to the Montezuma area. I wouldn't be surprised if that was the place where the soldier's unfortunate fatal encounter with the snake occurred. But the fortunate part is that the army just finished the road in August, just in time for you to take your mare back to Montezuma."

If Genesis had been privileged to an understanding of clockwork, Padre thought he would have told him how the inspecting officer had described the Three Notch Road: "The notches engage a traveler and move him onward like pawls progressively engaging and interlocking the notches of ratchet wheels." Instead, Padre said, "Travel on the road will be entirely different in comparison to when we rode the narrow Indian Ridge Trail. Remember how we looked and looked that evening we got in the forest, trying to keep our bearings and stay on the trail?"

"Uh hm. And you've made your speech about that road. Now, there's some things I want to tell *you* about it. I found out that the army just widened the old Indian Ridge Trail wide enough so two wagons that meet can pass one another without one having to stop. I'll tell you what I really like. The road comes right by Montezuma. And you should see them notches in the trees that mark it. They ain't no little notches. Them things is gashes. The army cut them in sets. Three to a set. And they sit on top of each other like a column. Shoot, them things are wide as I can stretch my arms, more than three feet. Gashes are deep, too. Betcha there're every bit a foot deep."

"It is my understanding that they did not cut those mighty gashes in a whole lot of trees. After all, that is a long route."

"Oh hell no, not in a lot of them—only about every 100-200 yards or more, depending on the lay of the land. You remember how you can see pretty far in the forest, 'cause there's not much undergrowth at your eye level. They just cut enough of 'em to mark the road."

"I, indeed, look forward to viewing the esteemed Three Notch Road. A storekeeper offered to let me accompany him on his next delivery beyond the first markings. With great anticipation, I waited. Then, unfortunately, I could not go. Instead, without a hint of malice, I performed my priestly duty. You see, a funeral mass took priority. God willing, another chance for me to see the notches will materialize."

Suddenly silenced, Genesis looked down and rubbed his hand across what remained of his slicked-back hair, studying. He had spouted all the good news. With a serious expression, he said, "There's bad stuff happening in Montezuma, too. Before I leave, I have to tell you that besides Big Brother and his family, other Creek gave up land to pay their debts at the old McAlister trading store and moved out West. Some others just outright sold their land and moved to the West. And another thing, I have to tell you, not all the whites that came in are churchgoing people. Some of them ain't nothing but greedy land grabbers, not fit for hell, like that McAlister man, the first owner of the trading store. Remember, I told you I had some bad news. Well, somebody put an arrow through McAlister's neck. It could have been big trouble for the tribe. But then Caleb come along and reopened the trading store."

"Yes, I remember," Padre said. He had already heard of problems in Montezuma but listened to and empathized with Genesis' woe. "I realize you want to get on with your business, but before you leave, Genesis, I would like to show you around the new church."

"New church?"

"Yes, indeed. With my renewed effort and Father Mulvaney's efficacy, my longtime goal has been fulfilled. I wish Padre de Galvez were alive, so he could see it."

When Genesis' eyes swept the inside of the church, he said, "This surefire beats the warehouse chapel by a long shot."

"The parishioners are pleased, too. Back in Spain, this is what I had dreamed of accomplishing, a church for St. Michael's Mission, St. Michael *Church*." Padre's voice wavered with pride. "Father Mulvaney worked very hard helping to raise the money and getting the church built. Of course, I assisted in every way that I could. I contributed money bequeathed by the Montezuma Trading Post worker who died of the fever. I never mentioned the money to anyone, since he had intended it to be used for mission work."

"Betcha you don't like working under Father Mulvaney like you did for Padre de Galvez. I'd put money on it."

"Oh, things change. Over time, Father Mulvaney has become a shining example of tolerance and has developed into an admirable superior. I have garnered great respect for him, or maybe I should say that he has earned my respect. After all, I never told you, but he was educated at the Irish College of the University of Salamanca in Spain."

Padre's accomplishments moved Genesis to eye him with greater respect. "Padre, you got everything going like you want it now. No more problems."

"I disagree. Life *is* good, bountiful in many ways, but there are always problems, always new ones to address. In addition to the warring between Seminole and settlers, political conflicts boil in anticipation of Florida's potential statehood."

"What's this political trouble about?"

"The most heated issue is slavery. Monied plantation owners are pro-slavery and to others, the practice is despicable."

"Shoot, we have all kinds of arguments about slavery in Alabama. Some get downright ugly. C'mon Padre. Have some fish with me. I need to eat before I go looking at horses. I can't wait to get a belly full of them red snappers from the Pensacola Bay."

After the meal, Padre warned Genesis to be careful in scouting for land and timber buyers. He said, "From what I hear around town, there could be more killings among the Creek and whites in Alabama."

"Padre, I surefire ain't going to be like no bay oyster, hiding in a shell. No, siree. I can be feisty as a bobcat." He smiled and continued, "Anyway, if they ever do take me down, they surefire can't take my spirit."

"How true," Padre said, "and in comparison, worse times have existed for both of us."

As Genesis departed in search of an ideal mare, Padre extended his arm forth and said, "May the blessings of God go with you." Genesis walked away as stalwart as a conqueror, once again reminding Padre how, way back on the Indian Ridge Trail, he had compared Genesis with the likes of Alexander the Great. Indeed, Genesis was a conqueror of sorts, in everyday life. A long-gone, sympathetic question strangely bled anew. Was Genesis destined to fight fierce battles as the great Greek had done?

Padre went for a walk on the beach. In his prayers, he would forever continue including Genesis and Blue Heron and the Creek in his petitions. And, as in recent weeks, he purposely looked for his reflection in the bay water, for now he wore his hump more like a badge of honor rather than as a reminder of a priest ill-suited for pursuit of a mission dream. He had begun looking with ease at his reflection in the water ever since St. Michael's Church had been completed. And he had been blessed with the courage and wisdom to overcome, most of the time, the arrogant superiority of his earlier years. Repetition of that venial sin had blessedly decreased, for lately he no longer suffered from the pain of peasantry and the accompanying need to be overly proud of his education and priesthood.

# GYPSY

The stable owner who sold the perfect *Andalucian* mare to Genesis had been exactly right about her. Before the trader introduced Genesis to the prized animal, he had said, "I have just the right mare for you. She's as lively as a Spanish gypsy, pretty as a pearl, and perfect of body."

At first sight, Genesis' head swam with delight, for in addition to her good-looking appearance, he sensed that the mare took to him right away. Not only was she worth the price, but she also deserved a top-quality harness and new bridle, too. And he'd surefire continue calling her Gypsy. *Grandeza* would be as proud of Gypsy as he'd been of Willow.

Returning to Montezuma, Genesis sat tall on the fine saddle, hoping he would meet someone along the new Three Notch Road who would recognize Gypsy's outstanding bloodline. Maybe he could catch up to the workers who had accompanied him on the raft. They would be so impressed, their eyeballs would jump out. If he had not been in such a rush in leaving Pensacola, he could have shown off Gypsy to Padre. Padre would have praised her fine qualities, for he knew a hell of a lot about Andalusian horses' bloodline.

And Padre should surefire feast his eyes on the Three Notch Road. What a difference from the old Indian Ridge Trail! The notched trees hastened progress with the steadiness of a ticking clock, engaging Genesis' senses and moving him forward to his special mission in Montezuma. His dream was coming true.

Yet, on the night Genesis arrived home, it was too late to introduce Gypsy to her intended mate or to the children. To Willow, he said, "My father was always traveling the seas and didn't help me train *Grandeza*.

317

And since your brothers was never around a horse much, I'll surefire stay close by our sons, show them how to take care of and train the colt we hope for, from our perfect pearl. Training looks easy, but it's not. It takes a long time to train a horse to know the rider's orders. I want Gypsy's offspring to learn what the rider's shift of weight or a push of the leg means. And if the horse gets scared, the rider needs to learn to read the signs and find a way to settle it. Our sons will learn this."

The following morning, when Genesis introduced the two "Andalucians," *Grandeza* sniffed Gypsy, but she squealed and quickly turned away. Genesis said, "It must not be the right time."

# *PRESIDENT* JACKSON

During 1818, while Padre and Genesis were getting accustomed to living with the Owl Clan near the Montezuma Trading Post, Andrew Jackson had returned to squiring his estate in Tennessee. Suffering the ravages of chronic dysentery, the enfeebled Jackson had left Pensacola only two days after he had seized the town for the second time. Then he returned to his home. Diplomats could disentangle details and clean up the dregs.

He had hardly become reacquainted with the humble Hermitage's silvered logs, for which he felt a tenderness, when he decided that his remaining days would not be many and that Rachel deserved a better home. He set about selecting an appropriate site nearby and building a grand, new Hermitage complete with splendid landscaping. The slaves would be permitted to occupy the original buildings.

Jackson also spent time with his farming ventures and getting reacquainted with the boys who were being cared for by him and Rachel. And since he had been away from home for extended periods, unable to provide the standard of care demanded by the eye of the master, he sold his racing horses.

During this time, the United States was in negotiations with Spain to purchase Florida. Jackson received news that Spain had hesitated to ratify the treaty for the acquisition of Florida. Government officials in Washington thus concluded that the Spanish were acting in bad faith. Jackson wrote to President Monroe, "…Sir, you know my services is my countries (sic) as long as the country should need." Then he prayed for peace and sent for the children and grandchildren of the old slave Peter. Expenses of locating and reuniting the slave family at the Hermitage increased his debt; but it was worth every penny, for Peter had pined for them.

Meanwhile, the Washington government received an ultimatum from Madrid demanding suitable punishment of Andrew Jackson, or negotiations for the sale of Florida were at an end. Jackson struck out for Washington to defend himself, threatening to cane a senator as well as cut off the ears of critical congressmen. However, Congress voted to vindicate Jackson's actions in Florida. This was his greatest triumph since the Battle of New Orleans. Before he returned home, he visited his "sons" at West Point. His "sons" were Rachel's two nephews whom they had raised. Lincoyer, their adopted, full-blooded Creek son—whom Andrew had found suckling his dead mother's breast after the battle of Horseshoe Bend—had been apprenticed to a harness maker and later died of tuberculosis.

Had America congratulated itself too soon on the acquisition of Florida? Would there be yet a *third* invasion of Florida, this time *authorized* by Washington? Jackson received confidential instructions to prepare a military movement for the purpose of awing the Spanish. Instantly he replied that his health was very precarious, but that with the smiles of heaven he would endeavor to place once more the American flag in Pensacola and then beg to retire if he survived. On a separate sheet of paper, as if not to embarrass the government, he asked if he should seize Cuba also?

President Monroe had learned his lesson about Jackson's habit of acting militarily without authority. The president halted the calling of the army and consulted Congress before granting free rein to Jackson on Spanish soil again. As an alternative, the president considered appointing Jackson as ambassador to Russia but dismissed that thought when Thomas Jefferson threw up his hands and said, "Good God, he would breed you a quarrel before he had been there a month!" He made this remark despite the fact that Jackson had become an early convert to the idea first proposed by Thomas Jefferson that Indian removal be linked to an exchange of land.

Finally in February, 1821, Spanish Minister Francisco Dionisio Vives delivered the ratified treaty, consummating official purchase of Florida by the U.S. Forthwith, President Monroe offered governorship to Jackson. Jackson would not hear of it. At once he wrote a letter declining the offer. But now with peaceful conditions existing, Congress reduced the army, which, in turn, eliminated Jackson's position as Commanding General of the Southern Division. In light of this momentous change, President Monroe convinced Jackson to accept governorship of Florida. Jackson accepted on the condition that his resignation become effective as soon as the Government was organized.

Rachel accompanied her husband to Pensacola. She stayed in town while the general camped with an army on the outskirts, waiting for Spanish Governor Callava to set a date for the transfer of government. Rachel's first reaction to Pensacola's rainy spell was one of amazement. The vertical rain, according to her account, compressed the Pride of China trees, yet caused no flooding. Absorption by the porous sand and runoff into the bay took care of the downpours. The view of the bay was the most beautiful water she had ever seen. She further observed: The languorously-moving inhabitants spoke Spanish and French, some even spoke four or five languages. There were fewer white people by far than any other. Never could she have imagined the mixed multitude of people in their vividly-colored garb and with their varying complexions. Seamen strolled with knives in their belts and coins burning their pockets; "absurd little" Spanish soldiers were everywhere; "yellow women with well-turned limbs darted insinuating glances; Jamaican blacks bore prodigious burdens on their heads; a fish peddler filled the street with incomprehensible cries; a Seminole Indian presented a set expression of unfriendliness; a grandee proudly rode in his fine carriage." She thought the worst people must be the cast-off Americans.

Rachel Jackson felt that the Sabbath was profanely kept. A great deal of noise and swearing filled the streets; shops were kept open; trading, in the broad sense of the word, took place, more than on any other day.

Betty, Mrs. Jackson's mulatto maid, became so mesmerized by the Pensacola scenes that Rachel reported her delinquencies. Mrs. Jackson said that she would request fifty lashes if she did not behave herself. She even considered ordering public lashing as soon as they, the Jacksons, got possession of her.

Neither the general nor his wife yet *possessed* anything in Pensacola. Just as Thomas Jefferson presaged to President Monroe regarding Jackson's possible appointment as ambassador to Russia, Jackson had, indeed, ever since he returned to the Pensacola area, quarreled with the Spanish Governor Callava. Callava, while waiting for transport vessels for his men, expressed his intention to remove and confiscate all cannon from the fortifications by explicit instructions from the King. After hearing this news at his campsite, Jackson became infuriated. He stormed into Pensacola with his Fourth Infantry. Callava proposed a compromise but still clung to postponement by using subtle tactics. Finally, they negotiated a compromise, and a smiling Callava met the stern-faced Jackson for exchange of flags, ending almost three centuries of Spain's colonization in Florida. Callava received rations for his men's return trip to Cuba. Jackson got the cannon.

While Rachel enjoyed the sunshine and gulf breezes, the most healthful she had ever known, Andrew, in no mood for relaxation, demolished gambling houses and closed shops and bazaars on Sundays. Rachel said that in one week's time, she heard no more fiddling and dancing, nor cursing. Jackson had altered Pensacola's lively social life but had not obliterated it. Among those active in social circles were officers of the Fourth Infantry and President Monroe's civil appointees as well as John Innerarity, a prominent member of the Cabildo or town council of Pensacola. Royal governors, British soldiers, international adventurers came and departed, but, according to local opinion, John Innerarity and his Forbes Trading Company remained the actual rulers of Florida. The company had covertly assisted Andrew Jackson in removing Englishman Alexander Arbuthnot as a troublesome commercial competitor. It was gossiped that like a white shadow, John Innerarity glided through the weaving labyrinth, never on the losing side.

But Andrew Jackson, before leaving Pensacola, had a confrontation with John Innerarity over a disputed land estate, which involved a mulatto. Innerarity claimed the records of this estate were part of the archives, which Callava intended to take to Spain. After all efforts had failed in obtaining these archives, Jackson resorted to no less than ordering his military to rouse Callava from bed one night. If Spanish Diplomat Onis could rouse the Americans during the night in Washington, he could certainly return the favor to Spain here in Pensacola. Jackson's men learned upon arrival at Callava's home that he was in bed but fully clothed, playing "possum." They wrenched him from his home.

In settling the matter at the nighttime hearing, Jackson took his usual short cuts to justice, justice according to his perception. When Callava still adamantly refused to turn over the records, and Innerarity would not or could not coax him to do so, Jackson signed an order for slamming Callava into the lowly *calabozo* where the meanest of criminals were incarcerated. At last, the two sides came to an amicable solution, and the mulatto received at least part, if not all, of the estate of her land-owning, Spanish father.

On October 5, 1821, Jackson informed President Monroe that he had organized the government in Pensacola and was going home. Albeit, before that letter reached the president, Jackson had already seen, in his view ahead, a copse of redbud trees gracing the Hermitage. Back in Tennessee again, he wished to find enjoyment in his later years. Among a huge assortment of items, he ordered: seven cases of furniture, silver for the dining room, brandy, cigars, and even a keg of almonds, for which he had a fondness even though they had no place in the diet of a man plagued with dysentery. Jackson spent a great deal of time reading the twenty newspapers to which he subscribed and which usually covered his red-carpeted study.

Andrew Jackson stood poised on the plinth of popularity as America's hero. Wheels of expansionist sentiment had already rolled, were still rolling, would roll farther in later decades of Manifest Destiny. Jackson had subdued the Creek, defeated the British in the battles of Mobile and New Orleans, seized Pensacola twice, and had now witnessed the American acquisition of Florida, in its entirety, from the Spanish. Cries came from all parts of the country, "Jackson for president."

Rachel said that she hoped they would now leave her husband alone and address him as Mister again, not General. She knew he was not a well man and never would be unless they allowed him to rest. She felt that he had done his share for the country. In the thirty years of their wedded life, he had not spent one-fourth of his days under his own roof. Most of his time had been spent traveling or fighting the Indians. She had felt it was his work to do while she watched, waited, and prayed most of the time alone. Now they were talking about his being President. Major Eaton, General Carroll, Mr. Campbell, the doctor, and even the parson talked everlastingly about his being President. In resignation, she asked that the Lord's will be done.

Though a reluctant and losing candidate in 1824, Jackson ran in the next campaign and was elected president of the United States in 1828. What did Sharp Knife's election portend for the remainder of the Creek nation?

# SILVER SON

L ooking back, after Andrew Jackson had relinquished governorship of Florida and was becoming reacquainted with Tennessee life, the Owl Clan Village in Alabama was struggling with and adapting to changes, some for better and many for worse. Gypsy had dropped a finely formed foal sired by *Grandeza*. As soon as the newborn's coat dried, Genesis boasted to Willow, "He's our Silver Son. I'll surefire stay close by our blood sons, show them how to care for the foal and how to train him." The colt grew large and strong, fit for any task. And Genesis kept his word.

The following four years flowed by like the river of cane after a rainstorm and turned out to be just as unpredictable. Silver Son had now grown to over sixteen hands in height at his withers, displayed a spirit as lively as Gypsy's, and looked as fine of bone and sinew as *Grandeza*.

Paralleling the growth of this wonderful Andalusian stallion, there evolved the heretofore unthinkable discussions regarding the education of Genesis' children, as well as Caleb and Blue Heron's children. After Caleb had finally persuaded Blue Heron to send their precious Sehoy to a distinguished boarding school in Mobile to receive the fine education that she deserved, Genesis longed to provide equally for his two sons. Caleb had already said, "We will send Abel, also, when he is old enough." Finally, Genesis prevailed upon Willow to send their sons to the Creek Missionary School in Eufala. If the teaching-learning way of the school worked out to their satisfaction, they would consider sending the younger children.

Other momentous, and sometimes tumultuous, changes rocked the Creek Nation. President Jackson had his way. Two years after his election, the Indian Removal Act was passed. Changes of heart at the Owl Clan

Village from peacefulness to preservation and retaliation moved in tandem with material and physical changes enveloping the Creek inhabitants. Silver Son came to be known as "Silver Warrior," exemplifying Genesis' sentiments that he would fight to save Creek land, if necessary. Need for warriors, both man and beast, became apparent to Genesis after the emerging Creek leader Opothle Yoholo and his delegation returned from Washington with a renegotiated treaty and spate of promises that were soon broken. Within only days of signing the treaty, hordes of white speculators swarmed into Creek country, some with wagonloads of whiskey with which to victimize the natives for their land. Sometimes they also inveigled them with gambling games. White citizens and state authorities defied federal marshals who were sent to protect the Indians. When Yoholo's delegation returned to Washington for redress, the national leaders deferred blame to the state government. The Creek were told that they should move to allotted land in the West if they did not like the Alabama law.

Tribal government had already begun collapsing, even before Chief Owl Claw became enfeebled. State laws prevailed. The Creek had few, if any, rights in the courts. Shaman Blue Heron Healer, now known to the white population as Mrs. Lange, pined for her people and, somehow, at the same time triumphed in her family life as wife of the prosperous Caleb Lange and as mother of their privileged children.

One day while on a fateful visit to the post office, the Montezuma postmaster said to Mrs. Lange, "The stagecoach driver just dropped off a letter with news of significant magnitude. I am sure that Caleb would want to be informed."

"Yes. I can take the message to him."

"I must warn you. Brace yourself. Andrew Jackson was reelected as president."

"President again? This is terrible news," Blue Heron said with a frown forming. "How well you know that Creek still speak of him only as Sharp Knife. We have known the pain of his slashes in Alabama long before you arrived—ever since Horseshoe Bend Battle." She paused, looking as if her thoughts were of some faraway place, then asked softly, "And now, the next cut? Just what will it be?" Not waiting for an answer, she turned and quickly departed.

Memories flashed in Blue Heron's mind like a flood. Four years ago, Caleb had discussed Sharp Knife's first Inaugural Address with her, as well as his first State of the Union message. In as gentle way as possible, he had wanted her to know that though Jackson was urging removal of the Indians, she would be protected, as the wife of a white citizen, from moving. Today, toward the sun she gazed. Without conscious intention, she stopped, searched for Breath Maker with the same intent of her younger years. As her eyes moved upward, sunlight lit the gray-feathered, full-winged birds and momentarily turned them bluish before they hid in the trees. Farther up, hawks flitted fitfully writing messages, surely warnings, on the cottony clouds, which floated against the blue sky. Into the corner of her heart, where she wished not to knowingly visit, an indefinable force nudged until she relented.

There, in that space, she reluctantly recognized a huge change, a huge and horrible change coming. She could see it as plainly as one could see a canoe floating down the river. She understood that with Sharp Knife's reelection, something awful was going to happen, something far worse than had ever happened before. She understood it just the same way that she understood life and death. Never had the future looked so bleak for her people.

Jackson's performance as President in his first term had apparently impressed the rest of the population with great favor. His place on the plinth of popularity had now earned not just reelection but an overwhelming victory. Nevertheless, in answer to dissenting minorities, religious groups, and those who criticized overzealous states righters, Jackson sought compromise between state and federal officials by sending Francis Scott Key to investigate the infinitely troubled Alabama Creek. Mr. Key had already made a favorable reputation for himself with his famous poem about the 1812 War.

In making every effort to assuage Blue Heron's increasing fears, Caleb kept abreast of developments by reading and discussing the Nashville newspaper with the Montezuma postmaster. Then he passed the news to Blue Heron. He said, "Mr. Key reported that it was too late to reassert federal authority. Exercising force now would threaten a civil war. But Mr. Key was so disturbed by wild talk of a mob attack on Ft. Mitchell that he worked, and they say that he worked feverishly, through many conferences with state authorities for a compromise, just as President Jackson had ordered." Caleb hesitated and then said, "Now, I know the first part of what I must further tell you will not sound promising. Still, I must tell you." He swallowed hard. "Mr. Key said that he finally agreed that the federal government would overlook the 10,000 whites already lodged on Indian lands and refrain from evicting trespassers except in the most obnoxious cases."

Blue Heron grasped her forehead in disbelief.

Caleb walked over, placed his hand on her shoulder and said, "This second part you'll like, at least a little bit. In return, the state government has agreed to take more earnest steps in maintaining order and preventing excesses against Indians."

For Blue Heron, this so-called compromise destroyed her last lingering hope for federal authorities to really relieve Creek suffering—debts, loss of land, stolen livestock. All the failed Creek uprisings now took on new meaning. Unable to endure the continuing injustices, Blue Heron felt compelled to meet and discuss these pressing matters with Genesis and the Weaver brothers. Was it too late?

They met with her and listened but did not share commiserations. The divisiveness of the Owl Clan was never more poignant. Blue Heron had too long been removed, distant, and for the most part, lived the privileged life of the whites. Blue Heron left the meeting in woeful defeat. After she had departed, Genesis was the first to vent his feelings. Distraught and edgy he said, "What does it matter to her that the land is being taken, driving our people to move to the West?"

# GENESIS' NEMESIS

Crouched with his hunting party behind a huge, forest deadfall, Genesis' heart tightened at the thought that though his Golden Gopher name was not his most important means of identification, he wished a Creek name could have been bestowed for bravery rather than heroism. Many times he had wondered why it was his destiny that he had begun earning a reputation as a brave only days after bestowal of the Golden Gopher name. If only the storm had thundered though the village a week earlier.

From his doorway Genesis had been watching the blackening sky when a powerful bolt of lightning blazed down. Thunder blasted. A terrible crash brought screams. *My heart was beating fast as the raindrops and my knees were trembling, but I just had to check if I could help the villagers.* Without a thought for his own safety, he ran in the direction of the crash.

The deadfall, behind which he sat, now reminded him of how the lighting bolt had struck down a pine tree, chasing its taproot, and upheaving a two-foot mound of dirt. He would never forget the crashing noise, nor the fallen tree as it lay across the crushed corner of Blue Clay's house. The lightning had traveled underground several feet to the Carrier house. As if his actions had been controlled by an unknown force, Genesis scurried through the scattered rubble dimmed by smoke and heated by flames. Quickly he pried a smoldering, fallen timber and released the elders. He scooped up the badly burned body of Blue Clay's wife and motioned for Blue Clay to follow. In stunned silence, Blue Clay limped as he trailed behind.

Willow tenderly attended the elderly woman. In no time, she had to tell the sad news: "Blue Clay's wife has already left this life to meet their

328

ancestors." Blue Clay, in a wounded and defeated voice that trembled and broke intermittently, said, "The ball of fire from the fallen pine came through the house and struck my wife. I must seek the wisdom of the council to find out how we angered Breath Maker."

Genesis cautiously shifted his crouched position behind the deadfall when a faraway gunshot shook his thoughts, transporting his sentiments to an incident, which came soon after the storm. It was another incident, which could have merited a Creek name of bravery for him. While he had been paddling his canoe along the river of cane, he had heard nearby gunshots. Another canoe—a larger one transporting Creek from the Alligator Clan—had been riding the slow current downstream. Its occupants paddled faster to avoid the firing shots. Before the larger canoe passed Genesis, shots sprayed closer, one downing the brave in the large canoe.

Genesis overtook the large canoe, women now paddling it. As soon as they rounded the first bend, Genesis paddled onto a sand shoal and directed the women to pull in also. After securing the canoes, he yanked off the buckskin band that had encircled his head. He tied it upwards from the man's blood-spurting wound on his upper arm and said, "Take him to your shaman quickly." Several days later, council members from the Alligator Clan appeared at the Owl Clan with gifts of blackberry wine and salt pork. After members of both councils drank wine, Genesis said, "Them shots surefire came from state militia. Nobody else would be out wasting gunfire like that. It's a sorry thing when men get their fun from scaring and nearly killing one of our brothers." The tribesmen soothed their hurt with more wine.

As Genesis crouched behind the deadfall reminiscing, he was completely unaware that his bravest act was yet to come.

The Owl Clan, like the rest of the Creek Domain, had continued shrinking, the lives of the remaining members forever altered; yet it was not until 1836 that an unexpected circumstance set off Owl clansmen to undertake drastic steps for preservation of the Creek. While on a hunting trip, Genesis and the three Weaver brothers discovered a group of wretched wayfarers, mere dirt-caked skeletons except for their bloated bellies, hiding in the woods. The strangers gazed like men of stone lost in a cave. Genesis and the other hunters observed them until Genesis felt assured that the starving strangers were displaced Creek. Gripped with brotherly feelings, the hunting party then approached the sojourners in friendship. Genesis soon learned that they were, indeed, Creek who were plagued with grief, grief so severe that it was nigh incommunicable.

Genesis explained to them that extra care must be taken to keep them hidden. Only two days ago, a band of Creek, riled up about the state government's treatment of their brothers' rights, had attacked both the Smith and Holloway farms, murdered the parents in both families, and smashed the children's heads to death at both homes. Genesis said, "They stole everything they wanted, including livestock, and left the buildings in ashes, just like the whites had done to them. The sheriff has sent out a posse looking for these braves. We must wait for night. Then we will hide you in our homes and give you food."

Later, in darkness, the hunters escorted the wayfarers to the village. After the hungry men had eaten as much as their long-starved bellies could tolerate, they began telling of atrocities to Creek: public whippings of men, rape of women, and wrongful accusations which they had witnessed in and near their village on Alabama-Georgia line.

Genesis and the Weaver brothers rallied together, vowing a renewed effort to assist the Creek on the state border. As they talked, the sacred solidarity of brotherhood gleamed in their eyes. Genesis clenched his fists tighter and tighter and gritted his teeth in an effort to stall his outrage. His hunger for risk rebounded full force. News of wrongdoings, the whites to the Creek and the Creek to the whites, had been widespread; but never had he heard the like of the firsthand stories, which these wandering men told. This was too much to bear. Far more than seeking thrilling adventures of his youth, he now felt ready to fight, willing to die.

The urge of fiery retaliation streaked through Genesis' veins like a bolt of lightning setting a tree aflame. It took hold of his spirit. He whisked his sweated forehead. Damn, damn, damn the whole bunch, the greedy whites, the state militia, and the Washington force, too. Yes, he had thought of fighting back many times. Now he *must* become a warrior, take up arms and fight them, every one of them. He and the Weaver brothers must start now, not wait to enlist braves from the Alligator or Raccoon Clans, nor even the fierce warriors of the Eagle Village. He felt too much like his people now, too much one of them as they were to one another, too much a part of their everlastingness, not to fight.

Willow saw into his mind as if looking through an open door, his darker spirit moving into action, ready to spill over any instant. Rage, hot as fire, clearly shone in his eyes. She listened to him as if not surprised, as if she were ready to handle any decision, which came forth.

As Genesis prepared to go to battle, an intense feeling that he was doing what was right pervaded every thought and action. He would even go through cleansing, the old way, with the black drink to bring out his fierceness. For the first time in his life, he felt ready for war paint. Catching the spirit, he scraped more powder from the red rock and mixed it with grease. He streaked layers of this extra red paint on his face, even dabbed streaks on his arms, for his mind was fully bearing on the land grabbers, the evil doers. Suddenly, it came to him that he would have to do something else that he had never done before. He must sound a warhoop, a strong warhoop, surefire not a cowardly one.

Willow watched as Genesis and her brothers galloped away bravely on their horses. The chilling sound of their war cries reverberated through the dampness of heavy dew. Would a sheriff's posse hear and capture or kill them? Not wholly pleased about Genesis' departure, Willow suffered a terrible splitting sensation, a sort of breakage between them as if a log were being split, one piece going one way, the other waiting on the ground with uncertainty. But she must not dwell on those thoughts. Genesis and the entire Weaver family had joined in the spirit of helping fellow Creek by defending, not taking. The Weaver family no longer merely suspected, at some level of understanding, complicity of the federal and state governments against Creek, rather, they now felt blatantly betrayed.

Albeit, neither Genesis nor the Weaver brothers envisioned the strength and breadth of the forces which they undertook to resist. The trouble with their own way of guerilla-styled warfare was that they could not avoid a head-on confrontation with state militia bastions, which outnumbered them by far in manpower and weaponry. These Creek warriors not only lacked experience, but also were totally unpracticed against the military. In the face of impossible odds, their willingness to rally for the common cause could set them up as easy targets, even though they felt they were among the chariest of Creek defenders. Amidst the last to take up the cause, would zeal for their preservation actually overcome reasoning and destroy them? Nevertheless, nothing else really mattered now.

Farther along, as the Owl Clan warriors rode east, close to the Georgia line, Genesis said, "I don't know what I was thinking; but I surefire know what I was feeling when them starving brothers told their stories about how they had been treated."

Later, Genesis and the Weaver brothers eased their mounts down a cliff on the Chattahoochee River, keenly aware that fighting had already been taking place; for on their approach, the horses had tossed their heads from side to side each time a shot was fired. Smell of smoke still floated in the air. Yet, Genesis' party was unaware of the enormity of what had just taken place only an hour and some odd minutes previously and within sight of their present position at the Alabama-Georgia boundary.

A group of Creek, after enduring four years of brutal harassment, had attacked Georgians, who were supposedly on their way to Alabama for looting. Immediately following that attack, the Creek warriors boarded and burned a steamboat that was plying upriver to Columbus, Georgia. Then shortly, they set fire to a bridge over the Chattahoochee River. The Weaver party arrived only in time to witness the fire smoldering, the smoke still billowing in shroud-like plumes.

Fish Wrestler said, "Looks like the battle is already over. Maybe we can still help."

"Um hm," Genesis said. "I feel dead right we can."

Before the Weavers and their mounts reached level terrain, a flock of blackbirds, alight on wild pea vines, which covered the steep bank, suddenly let go with a feathery thunder and endless cloud of blackness. The commotion unsettled Silver Warrior. He misstepped onto a sharp stone and lost balance. Like most horses, Silver Warrior's natural tendency to flee from danger thrust him into panic. He slipped on the slope and fell while trying to steady his footing. The fall cast him between hefty pines, his head now facing uphill. He was also blocked by dense thicket undergrowth. Worse, he landed with his front legs doubled up under his shoulders.

As Genesis was tossed, he had instinctively put out an arm to save himself, and instead of flopping over safely on his side, his wrist was trapped under the partial weight of Silver Warrior as the horse's body broke into the thicket and Genesis was slammed against a huge pine. Despite the crunching of branches, Genesis heard his wrist crack. His was a hard fall and Silver Warrior's was even harder. The Weaver brothers jumped down to help, but their horses reared in agitation. Genesis, still wedged, said, "Go before your horses get stuck, too."

When Fish Wrestler looked back questioningly, Genesis waved him on, with his uninjured arm, without taking time to reason, without even a thought for his own safety. He could take care of Silver Warrior as soon as he unwedged himself. Though never one to shrink from trouble, he soon discovered that the horse's large, well-developed body was impossible to budge with one arm, especially with the blockading undergrowth. Ignoring his own pain, lacerations and abrasions, Genesis valiantly endeavored to cut through the thicket, knowing the stallion, even with the fieriness of his blood, could not rise as long as his front legs were underneath his shoulders.

"Come on, Son," Genesis said encouragingly, as if still ignoring his injured arm, and stroked Silver Warrior's head with the fealty that only the most caring master could have for a wonderful horse. Silver Warrior struggled when Genesis, with one arm, tried to pull out first one front leg, then the other. Unaware of close by enemies, Genesis had unknowingly given them sufficient time to advance even nearer.

Positioned in front of Silver Warrior, eyeball to eyeball, Genesis knew by the change in the horse's eyes, something amiss had entered within view. Genesis turned in time to see three mounted soldiers and at once, the soldier in the middle with round, beady eyes and a drawn gun. The black eyes of the forest coachwhip flashed in his mind the instant he heard the gun fire and felt his neck spew blood.

The men fled without firing at Silver Warrior or even looking back at the victim of their vicious assault. When the Weaver brothers heard a gunshot, Fish Wrestler stealthily came out of hiding to investigate. By the time he reported to the others and they reached Genesis, it was too late.

Genesis said, "Take me bac..." then the harshness of his anguished moan softened.

The Weaver brothers hurriedly set about rescuing Silver Warrior. It was hot and getting hotter. It took the strength of both men to lift the horse's shoulders sufficiently to free his legs. They placed Genesis' body over his faithful stallion's back. Fish Wrestler took Silver Warrior's reins and led him alongside his own horse as they trudged up the cliff and hastily departed through the forest.

At a distance, which they deemed safer, the Weaver brothers laid Genesis' body on a bed of pine needles. Fish Wrestler picked crust from Genesis' neck wound, dabbed his finger into Genesis' brave blood, and soaked its deep, red richness into his sweated buckskin headband. Mad River Swimmer also smeared his headband. With pride, they would wear this symbol of bravery back to the Owl Village. Quickly, they cobbled a scrub pine drag for transporting Genesis' body before his body stiffened.

# RED OF THE RAINBOW

On the burial day, late in May, Willow gazed at the rainbow arching high into the sky. It made all the difference to her. She had always known that rainbows were bridges, which made it easier for warriors' souls to reach Breath Maker. She knew it was true for the red band of the rainbow, the color of warriors' blood, was always, always closest to Breath Maker. The whites had not the heart to believe truth. She would make no excuses to anyone for believing in the old teachings.

At the burial ground, Willow looked longingly at Genesis' lacrosse stick, with the owl carved on the handle, and his first bow and quiver of arrows being placed with his body, along with his chunkey stick and stone. How Genesis had liked playing chunkey, and though he later made better bows and arrows, he always cherished the first ones he had made when he came to the Owl Clan Village. The freshly dug earth smelled mellow. Secretly, Willow wished she could go to the other life with Genesis.

Before the whites streamed in; before the killing and looting started—whites killing and looting Creek, Creek killing and looting whites—before the tribe weakened; before Genesis was killed, life was sweeter, easier to foretell. She wondered when the horrors and the changes would end.

In unified gazes of awe at the rainbow, her children and grandchild stood amidst saplings growing along the boundary of the burial ground, their heights varying like the young trees. For a moment, Willow thought she understood that it was all right that they were just as open to change and growth as the tender pine saplings, their roots just as shallow. Life lay ahead for the children and grandchild, just as it did for the growing trees, though her tree of life had fallen.

334

When she turned to leave the burial ground, a dizzy spell came over her. In this saddest of moments, she must hide her weakness, her uneasiness, too, and set a worthy example. She would not give in to the dizziness. Instead of giving it a chance to take hold, she looked at each of her children, one by one, then at her grandchild. What were their thoughts? The two older sons stood brave with their wives. The youngest son, as always, carried the mischief of his father in his sparkling eyes. The girls—both of them had been playful as squirrels when they were younger—had a faint tinge of Genesis' red hair in their own. Willow had noted many times their way of basket weaving, their taking to the tiresome dullness, the over and over sameness of it as a part of their womanliness, as she had always done. Something odd about the way she now saw her offspring cleared her mind, gave her strength to shed sorrow for herself. She took a deep breath, breathing in the smell of the freshly dug Mother Earth so as to never let its memory go.

Willow led the way from the burial ground, the Weaver family following her. Next came Blue Heron leading the remnants of the Owl Clan.

Blue Heron watched Willow with sisterly compassion. She remembered the same journey that Willow's moccasins now walked. Widowhood would not be easy. Back when she had been a widow, the chief and the elders and the tribe had stood strong. The shaman had been very important. The earth had been full of trees and animals. The *Poskita* had been a joy. Now…

As they walked onward, honeysuckle fragrance wafted toward Willow from the thicket where she and Genesis had waited through the thunderstorm before they joined in marriage. Like a storyteller spinning a tale, memories of their life together unfolded as if it were the greatest story ever told. The sweetness in the air touched Willow in a way both distant to her heart and near, so near, as had been the warm, fuzzy feeling of the caterpillar, which she and Genesis had playfully passed back and forth. Yet the distance between her and Genesis' body at the burial ground grew with each step. Creek mothers must stay strong. She had only to look at one of the children to see something of Genesis, living and growing within the spirit circle, a circle never to be broken.

335

# MESSAGE IN THE SKY

Genesis had not lived long enough to experience the heinous banishment of the Owl Clan. He had been saved from experiencing the most egregious act to befall the Creek people, the final surrender of their Mother Earth. The battle between the Creek and the whites on the Alabama-Georgia line, in which Genesis met his death, was sufficient evidence of Indian savagery to justify Sharp Knife's next slash. President Jackson forthwith ordered the army to round up all the Creek for forced removal to the West, at bayonet point if necessary.

Arrowhead Maker, so tortured, unable to accept leaving his beloved Mother Earth, took a different path. With wrinkled, feeble, and gnarled hands, he honed his flint cutter to its sharpest edge. This time he would not make a fine arrow or arrowhead. This time he had a more important matter to finish. This time he would show the whites that he would not be taken from this part of Mother Earth. After darkness came and unbeknownst to others, he went to the burial ground. There, he dug and rested and dug and rested, most of the night, until he had hollowed a shallow grave. Before daybreak, he lay in his Mother Earth and by the strength of his will, as unmistakably unbendable as his trusty flint, he slit a long, deep cut across the side of his neck. Relief began with the spurt of blood. Peace settled in slowly as he raked his beloved Mother Earth over his body. His arms moved slower and slower. They stopped. Like a layer of dead leaves, frayed and faded brown, he lay in his grave, his fine flint, his spilled blood, and his bones to rest forever with his ancestors in Mother Earth.

Perhaps querying doubts came into Blue Heron's mind when, in the final months of the year 1836, she tenuously watched the vultures write an ever-moving black line across the western sky. Certainly, the message in the sky followed the path of the chained Creek on their march. Certainly she knew the message they were writing on the clouds. Certainly she knew how the people felt about leaving the land, their burial grounds, their possessions. As Caleb's wife Blue Heron certainly knew she was protected from banishment, but Caleb had forbidden her to leave the house during the roundup of the Creek, for fear she might be seized by the federal marshals through mistaken identity. Caleb had explained that militia, strangers in the area, might feel she was lying if she told them she was married to a white man. Time passed slowly as Blue Heron watched the message in the sky and painfully pondered alone. She knew so many things and felt so many things that Caleb did not understand about the Creek and never would, including her deep spirit feelings for her first marriage—how her husband, Brave Thrower had been killed by Sharp Knife's army at Horseshoe Bend and how her four-year-old son, Tupelo, had downed in the river of cane.

Many memories of Willow came to mind. One of the oldest and best was how well Willow had remembered Tupelo and Brave Thrower. When Blue Heron and Willow would meet for heart-to-heart talks, Willow would sometimes speak of Brave Thrower's long, brave chin with the deep crease in the middle and how the ancestral blood passed on to Tupelo had given him the same brave chin with a crease just like his father's. Blue Heron now wondered where Willow and the children and the grandchild fit into the line heading toward the west. She wondered if Honey Cloverleaf could withstand the trip. She wondered about the rest of the Weaver family and Owl Claw's children, and grandchildren, and whether they were hungry. Blue Heron grabbed her aching stomach wondering if she would ever have the heart to eat again.

So many other questions came to mind. Two she dealt with in her mind immediately and with ease and clarity: Would the beloved banished ones see Big Brother and his family out West? Would children of Genesis and Big Brother's families intermarry? Would they see the shell crucifix necklace, the one that Genesis had worn on his trip from Pensacola and had then given to Willow, who had later given it to Patsaliga when she and Big Brother had gone out West?

That evening, Caleb showed Blue Heron an article in a Montgomery newspaper, which termed the final battle on the Alabama-Georgia boundary as "humbug." The article declared that the fear of a Creek war was a base and diabolical scheme, devised by interested men, to keep an ignorant race of people from maintaining their just rights.

Caleb said, "But to the opportunists in Washington it was a justifiable way of disposing of the Creek problem."

Weeks later, Caleb and Blue Heron heard of the many horrors facing the Creek on the way to the West, the cold winter, lack of food, moccasins worn out to bare feet, disease, the pain of leaving their dead along the paths. Caleb and Blue Heron also endured the news in a Montgomery newspaper article telling about all the land that was bought after the Creek removal. More than six thousand acres changed hands in one week, land covered with mammoth pines. Gigantic logs rolled and burned endlessly, making way for king cotton.

# SEHOY'S HOMECOMING

When Sehoy returned from boarding school at Christmastime, Blue Heron marveled that though her daughter displayed a much greater air of confidence, she had maintained her graceful manner. Then Blue Heron's attention transfixed upon the shell crucifix, which Sehoy wore. It still hung from the buckskin strap, and the colors were lively as ever. Blue Heron had given the crucifix necklace to Sehoy on the first day she had gone away to school. This same necklace, which Padre had given to Blue Heron when he departed for Pensacola, held wonderful memories, for he had given it to her after she had helped heal his fever. In turn, she had earned the "Healer" name. It came to Blue Heron's mind that she should share with Sehoy the complete story of the cherished crucifix.

Of even greater importance, Blue Heron felt that Sehoy should understand the part of her ancestry that runs rich with Creek blood and learn the ways well enough to pass them on. Of greatest importance, Sehoy should be taught about the sorrow and grief suffered by the Creek when they were banished and forced out West. Blue Heron seriously doubted whether white teachers could tell her daughter the truth of the entire story of the Creek. Blue Heron knew it would not be easy revisiting the painful times, but the years now passed as quickly as the seasons used to. A driving force urged her to fulfill her duty, so she began by retelling the story of the crucifix to Sehoy in greater detail and then progressed to the plight of the Creek. She had hardly begun the tragedies suffered by the Creek when she noticed Sehoy's pouting face.

"Sehoy, what is wrong?"

"Mother, you sound so old-fashioned. You live too much in the past."

Blue Heron cringed. At any moment she might expose lack of assurance in herself. She wanted so much for Sehoy to be proud of her as a mother, yet Blue Heron feared that she might act in a way that would disappoint Sehoy. But no, Blue Heron thought. Suddenly seized by the feeling that she might show weakness, anger raged. At any moment she just might tell her educated daughter that she had been born with the torturing streak of a quarrelsome young swan. Then Blue Heron recoiled. Never would she say those terrible words. She dismissed the swan portrayal as too harsh. A hush fell over them momentarily.

With reenergized animation, Sehoy said, "Mother, I'm thinking of only yesterday and Josiah Morgan. But you don't seem interested in what's important to me. You did not seem impressed when I told you that after Josiah boarded the stagecoach, he sat across from me and we talked all the way home. He will finish his school in May. And I could tell by the way he looked at me and my fine frock and velvet trimmed coat and hat that he liked me. Don't be surprised if you see him come in his father's carriage this summer and take me to the church picnic."

"Sehoy, my daughter, do not set your heart on Josiah. You know half of your blood is Creek. You should abide by your nature and follow its paths. The Morgans, from what I have seen of them, are rich with land and all sorts of fancy furniture and many books. They are high and mighty and seem the most unlikely to tolerate people who are the least bit different, most especially anyone of Creek blood. I once heard Mrs. Morgan tell another customer in your father's store that she did not wish her son to marry beneath the family."

"Mother, Josiah spoke in a way that I am sure, very sure, he likes me." Sehoy would not tell her mother that his piercing eyes had set her heart aquiver, even as she endured the discomfort of the bumpy ride. Rather, she said, "When he finishes school, he will run his father's sawmill. He will not work with the sawyers or common men who lead the oxen that drag the logs. Nor will he do any of the millwork. A foreman oversees the workers and operation of the mill. He will mostly keep the books, sell logs and lumber, and then sell the clear-cut land to farmers. Mother, do not look so doubtful. Over and over, Josiah's eyes kept returning to my velvet trimmed coat and hat. After all, I am the only young woman in Montezuma wearing such fine clothing and getting an education, the best kind of education. And you know as well as I that when I finish school, I can even be a teacher. Teachers get the highest respect. And I want you to know another thing. He was very gentle when he helped me off and on the stagecoach when we made a stop in Sparta."

Blue Heron tried to put a pleasant look on her careworn face. She must not reveal that part of her heart understood her daughter's feelings, that even *she* had drifted from the old ways, enjoying goods as the wife of a well-to-do white. Perhaps this was the wrong time to approach Sehoy about her Creek background, even through the protective caul of motherhood.

As Sehoy spoke, Blue Heron studied, caringly, her daughter's pretty face: skin fairer than her own, cheeks rosier, eyes lighter and larger, and cheekbones wider and higher. How would she ever reach Sehoy's innermost feelings and pass on the ways of the Creek? Had she waited too long, enjoying privileges of a white storekeeper's wife, to enlighten her daughter? Though unclear about those matters, she saw with great clarity that Sehoy's world was much different from the one she had known. Still, her strong motherly feelings would never, never change. Might she be gazing at her Sehoy the way her own mother, Golden Maize Grower, had gazed at her, the way mothers do till their dying days?

# THE FLOOD

The number of canoes being paddled along the river of cane had dwindled. Flatboats now transported many supplies and goods to and from Montezuma. At one time seventeen of them plied the Conecuh River. Their operators often yearned for freshets, which would raise the water level. Every freshet, even the mild ones, made the hook and jam propelling easier. Otherwise, it would be a more difficult trip for a boat loaded with heavy cargo like guano. Deeper water lightened the work of the men in the bow, who reached out long poles with steel hooks to hook onto trees flanking the banks as well as for the men in the stern who simultaneously pushed against the river bottom. These very freshets, so coveted, sometimes urgently coveted, by the flatboat operators eventually brought utter destruction to the little town of Montezuma.

A rainy spell came. One Monday night, the rains poured until the ground could hold no more, and on Tuesday, torrents cascaded throughout the day. The Conecuh River, Blue Lake, and all other lakes and creeks overflowed. By the middle of Tuesday night, Montezuma was inundated. By morning, Montezumans wondered how much more they could take? Wednesday's torrential downpours answered their question. They must seek higher ground. It was already too late to save floating livestock and possessions from this massive deluge. Sudden surging water of the devastating nightmare came so fast there simply was not enough time to salvage much. When waters rose past the windows, the inhabitants were unable to deal with anything except preserving their own lives.

Blue Heron felt ever so thankful that her beloved son, Abel, was still away at school. He might have been lost to the river, like Tupelo, but for a

342

different reason. Abel was now much older than her Tupelo had been when he was swept away in the river; but Abel, she most certainly knew, would have struggled to rescue livestock from the rushing waters. He was just that kind of a boy, as full of goodness as the finest ear of corn. If she had known the sad Bible story of Abel before he was named, she would have held out for a different name. She could not bear the thought of losing another son, especially not to the river.

In the wake of the flood disaster, people came together. Everyone suffered and worked side by side. Even the high and mighty Morgans worked with lowly whites, half bloods, and officials in cleaning up dead wild animals, livestock, and debris deposited everywhere. A young, mixed-blood Creek laughed harshly after he told the story of "...that Morgan man knocking a dead snake from a tree, with his shovel, and burying it and other critters with his lily-white hands full of blisters." Primitive roads and bridges that had been damaged or wiped out needed repair or rebuilding. The stagecoach driver could not deliver mail to the post office for weeks.

# FROM THE PATHS OF MONTEZUMA

Montezumans had not yet recovered from the flood when another disaster struck, a malaria epidemic. Every low spot in the terrain had provided a home for residual floodwater. Every pool of water provided a home for breeding mosquitos. And unfortunately, every person became a potential home for malaria begat by the mosquitos. Typhoid fever, also, afflicted many inhabitants. Some died. The local doctor rode on horseback alongside the county judge surveying flood damage in the area. The doctor offered the judge his best guess as to the cause of the fevers. He speculated that the stream running below the burial ground had become polluted by the burials and caused the malaria and typhoid outbreaks.

At the end of the day, after the doctor and judge had assessed the area for any other possible causes of the epidemics, these two important citizens entered Caleb's store, sat by the fireplace, and discussed the doctor's theory while drinking coffee. The highly esteemed postmaster soon came into the store on the pretense of buying feed for his horse. Caleb watched for the postmaster's reaction when the judge spoke.

The judge said, "The 1830 census for the county listed 1,522 people, and now, only fourteen years later, many of that number have succumbed to the fevers."

Caleb had often sought and taken direction from the postmaster, an older, important citizen who was always available. The postmaster, also a storekeeper, had set up the post office inside his nearby store. Neither storekeeper worried about business competition, since the postmaster's store dealt strictly in dry goods.

"Doc, your idea about the drainage from the burial ground and the cemetery to the river being the cause of the fevers sounds plausible enough to me," the postmaster said. "We *must* save our town from this condition, maybe move it to higher ground. Being the county seat, Montezuma is very important. The town must be saved." The postmaster's conviction was so strong he set about preparing to move his store and the post office to higher ground the following day. Thus, he led what later became an exodus.

The reasoning about the cause of typhoid and malaria and the need for inhabitants to move to higher ground struck Caleb as quite believable and ratcheted him into action as well.

Blue Heron lamented, "I have always lived close by the river. And I worry about our wonderful clapboard house. I do not wish to leave this fine house."

"Do not worry," Caleb said. "We will move the house, move it board by board. And we'll move the store log by log, and set it up on higher ground. When the store is rebuilt, we will have more logs cut to enlarge it. Then we will be high and dry, the store will be high and dry, and you still won't be too awfully far away from your beloved creek and river of cane."

So, from the paths of Montezuma, the log courthouse, stagecoach inn, and stores were moved to the crest of a knoll near the post office, log by log. Even the pine-pole jail was disassembled and moved. In addition to Caleb, all the other inhabitants followed the postmaster's lead until each house had been moved to the crest of that beautiful knoll, about three miles from the original settlement. Drainage ran off in four directions.

From the beginning, people referred to the new settlement as Newsite. Albeit, the Newsite name would not last. The postmaster had his own idea. *Ah yes, the high ground of the beautiful knoll—I will name Andalusia. I've admired the rhythmic beauty of this name every time I looked at the banza in Caleb's store. But it must be spelled and pronounced Andalusia, the way the settlers and I like rather than the Spanish way of Andalucia that is carved on the banza.*

# HUMKEN, HOKKOLEN, TUTCENEN

With the ravages of the flood behind Andalusians, alas, 1844 brought rich blessings for Blue Heron. One fine day, Josiah reined up at the store in a wonderful new carriage. Sehoy sat beside him cuddling Emma, their infant daughter. After greeting Caleb and Blue Heron and showing off Emma to the customers, Sehoy walked over to the primitive *banza* hanging on the wall. Blue Heron followed her daughter and granddaughter. A radius of warm, amber sunlight beamed from an opening in the pines and through the door, encircling and highlighting the old keepsake instrument.

With great pride, Blue Heron observed her daughter's actions. How quickly time had passed since the wedding. Sehoy had been the most beautiful bride she had ever seen. She had worn a white batiste wedding frock which had been specially hand sewn and embroidered with tiny dogwood blossoms by a lady from the church. Sehoy had carried a bridal bouquet of freshly blossomed dogwood. And now, on this day, Sehoy showed promise of becoming a wonderful mother.

Mother, daughter, and granddaughter enjoyed a magical moment as they took a fresh look at the old keepsake instrument which had become commonplace. Sehoy beamed happily as she looked back and forth from the baby to the *banza* and spoke. Blue Heron radiated even happier, listening to Sehoy explain the old momento to Emma, as if the infant could understand. The child flashed lopsided grins and cooed.

"Emma, my little love, this *banza* has lasting meaning, everlasting meaning for you," Sehoy said. "You will hear me tell the story many times how Genesis and Padre Morales traveled from Pensacola, on the old Ridge Trail, to the Owl Clan Village and how the padre helped your grandmother

Blue Heron make this *banza*. It's like the one that the dear slave Chad carried. I will tell you all about him, too, one day. See the big word *'Andalucia'* carved on the gourd?" Sehoy pointed. "The padre carved that word on the *banza* because this beautiful land here looked so much like *Andalucia*, Spain, where he was born."

She cuddled the baby closer and affectionately said, "My little one, you will hear these stories many times till you know them well, especially how the postmaster started calling Newsite by this name." Sehoy smiled and added, "The stagecoach driver was not very pleased. He thought the name was too long. But for you, my dear little daughter, the name surely will be important. Andalusia is your birthplace. Soon you will like saying this beautiful name. We don't worry a bit about pronouncing it the way the Spanish do."

Sehoy looked for approval and found it in her mother's proud eyes. "Mother, as we rode over here, you should have heard how I explained to her about my childhood and how I grew up here."

This was getting hold of Blue Heron. It caught her, joyously, in the heart. She marveled at Sehoy's remarkable change of attitude and growing wisdom. Now, Blue Heron felt that her granddaughter's future held promise. The Creek ways would, after all, be explained to little Emma, a miracle beyond Blue Heron's expectations. In this most glorious moment, without her having any say over it, an invisible force moved Blue Heron to intone a fluttering, guttural chant. At the same time, possessed with the spirit of bird like motion resurgent after years of disuse, she lifted her arms and bent forward at the waist. She stepped with high knees as she had done years ago in the blue heron dance. After bending her back to and fro a few times, while simultaneously moving in a circle and chanting, she gasped for breath. Then she smiled and said, "You see, my heart spills over already; but tell me, daughter, what you said to Emma on your way here, tell me everything."

Caleb gazed in admiration; the customers gazed with curiosity.

"Well, for Emma's very first outing in Andalusia," Sehoy said, "I asked Josiah to take us along the Three Notch Road and through old Montezuma. Even though the weeds and brambles have choked spots where the houses once stood, I still had such a strong urge to take Emma through the area where I was born, and played, and grew up. As we followed the long curve from Rose Hill, the climbing sun shone on the tree notches marking that part of the Three Notch Road. And just imagine, the road was once part of our people's Ridge Trail. When we rounded the longer curve to the south, I counted the set of notches in one of the huge trees for Emma—one, two, three." Sehoy would intensify her mother's happiness a step farther by saying, "Please tell Emma and me, too, how to count them in the old way."

Blue Heron smiled with pride. Then, slowly, very slowly, she said, "*Humken, Hokkolen, Tutcenen.*" She smiled unabashedly. There was so much to be amazed at, so much to be thankful for on this special morning.

Hours after Sehoy and Josiah and Emma had departed, Blue Heron realized something was amiss. A strange feeling gnawed at her heart. After one of the happiest visits with Sehoy, Blue Heron felt she just did not have complete happiness and peace after all. The wondrous feeling of knowing that Sehoy wished to pass on the ways of the people was something she had always dreamed of but thought might never happen. But no, this spiritual joy did not last. By late afternoon latent, torturous thoughts revived and pierced these cherished feelings of her daughter and granddaughter. Blue Heron silently studied. Then she knew what she had to do. But the sun had already set. She would have to wait until the next day.

Blue Heron's feet needed no reminders to find the way to the herons' nesting place at the blue lake. There, she looked all around. She looked and looked. Then she searched as if looking for a lost treasure. She *had lost* something. This place, at one time so familiar, now echoed with strangeness. There were fewer herons, and they seemed odd and distant. Then it came to her. "That's it," she whispered, "the oneness. The oneness with the herons and the blue lake and Mother Earth. I lost it. My parasol, my fine blue and white dishes, my button-up shoes—all these pleasures have taken my power to feel oneness with the earth and herons and my people." Besides, she realized that she had not studied the blue part of the medicine wheel the way she had intended. She grasped her temples with her palms. If she had given attention to the section of blue, the color of defeat, she might have better understood how to help her people before they were banished.

She released her hands thinking that it had been a long time, a very, very long time, since she had joined in the spirit with the herons. She gazed out on the lake, her lips tight together, then she eased down and sat against a tree trunk. The sun's warmth heightened the sweet scents in the air— patches of drying grass, the baking sand. For a long time, she sat watching the herons' every move. Her deep study spawned memories of Padre, his genuflecting, their talks, their deeds. The rekindling of good remembrances eventually led to the memory of the hurtful day when Padre left the Owl Clan. Despite all the goodness, which Genesis had reported about Padre after each trip to Pensacola, she still held secret grief. Yes, the padre had cut her out of their spiritual sharing. Caleb, even in all his kindness and generosity, could never understand nor replace this particular loss.

She stretched an arm and ran her fingers over soft golden blossoms atop high stems. In the stillness, a tinge of an old, almost forgotten feeling— something that she wanted very much to relive seemed to start bubbling gently like a spring in a dry spell. Was she coming together, connecting, and entering into the spirit of the herons, journeying in their ways and along their paths as she had done in the distant past? Little by little she released herself to Mother Earth vowing that worldly goods were not the most important part of life. She dozed as if in a trance.

When she opened her eyes, blue twilight filled the air and throbbed through her bones. It was the time of day when the shade of the rocks had turned a deeper blue. Curiously, the heron with a twisted beak had lingered, all alone, to laboriously harvest his meal. It struck her that the heron revealed one of Mother Earth's messages, one of the greatest truths—that there is just no way to make everything in life perfect. That heron has a place in the spirit of life as much as any other heron, she thought. Yet it could never be free of its twisted beak. Nothing was ever altogether perfect, neither Caleb nor her children and Padre. It came to her that she could never be entirely free of her past, including the imperfect parts.

On the way home, she wondered if she could she still hold onto and believe in this newly found closeness to Mother Earth, without bitterness, especially without bitterness against the white settlers and President Jackson.

For the present, she must dwell on the happiness that Caleb brings and the promising future of Abel and Sehoy and Emma. Toward a set of notches, gashed into a giant pine tree, marking the Three Notch Road, she walked. So pleased with her herself, that she had revisited the blue lake and had experienced a taste of being close to Mother Earth again, when she came to the three-notch tree, she impulsively stood on her tiptoes, stretched out her arms, and hugged the lowest notch. Her arms almost reached the full length of the roughly hewn gash. Filled with warmth, she backed away and counted the notches: "One, two, three—*Humken, Hokkolen, Tutcenen.*" Then she looked up at the twilight sky. Notches of geese, three of them, were winging southward. She counted the notches of geese the same way. Somehow, she felt that her people's spirits would live as long as the counting words of *Humken, Hokkolen, Tutcenen*—forever. She returned home as darkness was quickly descending.

That evening Blue Heron lay sleepless, bothered by the cotton patches she had noticed to and from the blue lake. The same settlers who owned cotton farms, usually owned slaves, and slavery was wrong. Years ago, she had heard the Owl Clan Council arguing about whether slavery was right. Some council members were in favor of having slaves. Arrowhead Maker had taken a very bold stand. He had said that slavery was wrong, that people should never *belong* to other people. Slaves did not belong in the cotton patches working for people who owned their bodies nor should they belong to Creek and work for them. The black people belonged to themselves. Blue Heron fully agreed with Arrowhead Maker. The slaves must be freed. They must not face defeat like her people. She must not continue overlooking serious injustices.

Genesis had long ago told her that Padre faced slavery problems in Florida. Perhaps she could even visit the padre and talk with him. Ever since Josiah and Sehoy bought the fine, new carriage, she had dreamed of riding in it along the Three Notch Road, not a short way. Rather, she fancied traveling the road all the way from Andalusia to Pensacola with, of course, overnight stays at Ft. Crawford, the halfway point. Now she wanted, more than ever, to take the trip so she could speak with Padre. Only Padre understood her true feelings about slavery and the lengths to which she had gone to help Chad. Caleb had, several times, warned her not to upset customers at the store with talk of helping slaves win freedom. Talk of freeing them almost always brought out the worst in the farmers and important townspeople. Many of the churchgoing people owned slaves. Whenever Blue Heron found someone who agreed with her stand, she would speak about it only in secret or in whispers. But with Padre, it would be different. She could ask...yes, she could ask in a forthright way just what *she* could do to help free slaves.

# MINDLESS MISSTEPS

The insular, little village of Andalusia was barely a year old when shadows of slavery had already spread all around. A few things had remained the same. The *banza* still hangs on the store wall. Blue Heron sees it, but it doesn't stand out any more than one of the logs that make up the store building. Many moons had waxed and waned since she had vowed to change her ways. She had every good intention of visiting the blue lake more often to study the herons and feel their closeness in Mother Earth's circle as she had done in her early years. She had every good intention, while there, of waiting, willing the patience of the great old trees to transmit their unhurried ways to her, though more giant trees disappeared day-by-day. But no, her good intentions had not lasted.

Before Blue Heron realized what had happened, she had slipped back into her usual habits. The happiness surrounding Abel's finishing boarding school and returning home were just more reasons for her being mindlessly swept into such satisfaction with her family life that she had forgotten about the old ways again and only occasionally thought about the banishment of her people.

It was a pleasure to have Abel home from school again. Though of a much quieter disposition than Sehoy, he enhanced exchanges with people of all backgrounds by careful listening and measured remarks. Moreover, Caleb's general store had continued prospering with more new farmers buying goods. Josiah and his father's timbering business had continued flourishing as well. No finer son and husband could Blue Heron wish for. No finer marriage than Josiah and and Sehoy's could be found. And no finer grandchild than little Emma had Blue Heron ever seen. A sense of well being and contentment had recaptured Blue Heron, leaving space for only rare thoughts of her Creek heritage.

Abel's decision to follow his talent for understanding healing remedies had not shocked his mother. What jolted her was when he had talked of seeking an apprenticeship with the apothecary in Ft. Crawford. Blue Heron's high spirits suddenly sank. She and Caleb had hoped he would go into the general store business with his father after he finished his schooling. It was not to be. Abel followed his schoolmaster's advice and, indeed, began an apprenticeship with the apothecary in Ft. Crawford, located about half way between Andalusia and Pensacola on the banks of the Conecuh River.

After Abel had left on his new venture, Blue Heron, disappointed and saddened, went to their store. She filled a piggin with water, took the cornhusk broom, and started mopping around the fireplace where snuff dippers and tobacco chewers had underestimated their thrust. During a lull in business she leaned on the mop handle and confided to Caleb, "I have always known about our son's natural gift. I could see his interest in healing remedies from his earliest years." She paused gazing into space and then said, "The first time I noticed his natural gift was when he mixed dew berries and mud in a cracked clay pot and tried to talk Sehoy into letting him rub the mixture on her sore ankle." Blue Heron smiled and continued, "It wasn't long before he wanted his own mortar and pestle. Early on, he laid claim to my basket of healing remedies and completely wore it out. I could not hold him back from his experimenting. How well I understood his deep yearning. Whatever else I did, when I was growing up, that strong force inside me to become a shaman drummed all the time. It was so powerful it just pushed its way out."

Caleb cast a devilish, oblique glance and said, "You know a leaf does not fall far from the tree."

Blue Heron returned her own version of that facial expression and said, "You could say the leaf did not fall far from the mother tree."

"Well, I couldn't hold him back either. I, too, recall what I felt I had to do when I let my brother buy out my share of the tobacco farm that our uncle left to us in Virginia. There was no way my brother and I could agree on anything. But I decided he could have the farm if he would pay me for my half of the inheritance so I could open a store. When we signed the papers that day in the bank, I heard some timber investors talking about the virgin timberland that covered this southern Alabama area, all the way to Pensacola. Said there would be lotsa settlers coming in. I had to see it for myself. The very first day I looked around this place, I knew this is where I wanted to settle and open a store. Just like when I first laid eyes on you, with those four blue feathers sticking up behind your pretty face, I knew I was going to woo you for my wife. Every now and then I think about how things were back then—the little old village of Montezuma and the flood that forced us all to move our houses and businesses up to this knoll, and how the people called the settlement New Site till the postmaster started calling it Andalusia. Sometimes it seems like just a dream."

Though Blue Heron had heard that speech many times, she smiled and nodded. "So many joyful memories and some sorrowful ones, too."

"Uh hm. Without a single doubt, I would do it all over again. I got my beautiful Creek princess. And the two of us have been blessed with two fine children and the store and the house and the church. Not to mention our son-in-law and grandbaby. We shore have much to be thankful for. And whatever Abel feels he must do, I will back him up."

Blue Heron looked at Caleb straight on and said, "Yes, what's inside must come out. It always brought me much joy talking with Abel about the remedies of my ancestors. He always soaked in every word whenever I told him anything about Creek-shaman way of healing. And I will never forget the way he smiled when I told him about toothache grass. He could hardly wait to try it out. As a child I had been just as excited about trying out the toothache grass. But everything was so different when I was young and the Owl Clan was strong and the *Poskitas* were wonderful celebrations."

At that moment, a change came over her. With her thumb and forefinger she jerked the center of her blouse and fiercely pulled it back and forth, stirring the air to cool herself while her forehead beaded with perspiration. Caleb looked shocked but had the presence of mind to lead her to a stool and fetch a palmetto-woven fan. He threw out the dirty water, and after putting the mop and piggin away, reached into the tobacco tin for a "chaw," still observing her with a questioning look.

Distressed, Blue Heron sat working her fan back and forth and gazing out the door at a large lone tree that buffered the sunset. She looked down and smoothed the hairs on the brown-spotted cowhide overlapping the seat of the stool. To her dismay she could not distinguish her fingernails from the rest of her fingers. Quickly she rubbed the ends of her fingers. What a comfort when she counted all eight fingernails and two thumbnails. She remembered that the old, wise women in the Owl Clan had said that about the time hot spells came to women, their eyes also weakened. They said that they could see things better if they held them out as far as the arms could stretch. So she stretched her arms out and was able to see her fingernails. But she still despaired over her "hot" spell. Recognition of dimmed vision intensified the despair.

Yes, she had slipped back into her usual habits. Worse yet, her hugging the notched tree, when returning from the blue pond that day, must have been the same thing that she had heard Sehoy describe about someone as "showing off." Sehoy's fine boarding school education had made such a difference in both their lives. More and more Blue Heron realized that she respected Sehoy's book learning and always tried to use new words and ideas that Sehoy used. Blue Heron would have to admit that she had come to enjoy talking and thinking more like Sehoy each day. And for sure, those thoughts of reconnecting with the herons and blue pond had been too hasty, not heartfelt enough to last as was hugging the three-notched tree. She remembered the rough, ragged gash of the first notch that she had stood on her toes to reach, but admiring it was a false show she had made just to feel good for the moment. Now it even seemed childish. Blue Heron hung her head in shame. And when she looked up, her eyes shot straight to the *banza*. Though dusty, for some reason, it stood out from the logs, reminding her of the blue pond where she and Padre had made the *banza*. She felt the urge to visit the blue lake again, and this time she surely would be more mindful of her every thought and step and that the blue *lake* is not a *pond*.

On a sunlit afternoon, much like any other recent one, Blue Heron walked unhurriedly toward the blue lake, now determined to keep her vows, especially the promise she had made to her mother that she would not forget the ways of her Creek ancestors. Between the dried weeds, dust from the dry, cracked path rose and settled over her shoes. She sneezed. Slowly she bent down and rubbed the dry granules between her thumb and forefinger as if searching through the fine particles. There, there it was. In awe she beheld the dust of her ancestors. And though she could not see it plainly, she could certainly feel the dust. She snatched open her shoe buttons and removed her shoes. The fancy shoes must not come between her and her people. She wiggled her toes into the comforting dust, then pressed the soles of her feet close to Mother Earth, feeling where her people's footsteps and the animals had tracked over the trail. She paused and looked around to get her bearings on the overgrown trail. It was troublesome with so few trees remaining. A southerly breeze, like the breath of her ancestors, blew across her face and cleared her head. She knew it would lead her to the blue lake.

As she rounded the blind bend of the cane-covered inlet, the lake came into full view. Herons, colored like the water, though fewer, squawked and stalked the same as they had always done. And as always, they wrestled with their catches, tossed them in the air, and swallowed them head first. She remembered figuring out that the herons did this so the fins would go down smoothly. After their meals, the big, beautiful, blue birds would fly away, as always, some carrying a catch back to the nests while others flew toward the lake and alighted. Despite her dim vision, she still could see the white of cottonmouth moccasins' opened jaws that gleamed whenever they crawled out to retrieve fish speared by the herons' sharp bills but which the birds found too large to handle in flight.

Now, Blue Heron set her mind to surely wait for true, unhurried feelings to fill her heart. She looked beyond the herons, out where water met the sky. They came together. Something else needed to come together. That something else was waiting somewhere for her to find, and she would be as patient as an ancient live oak to find it, no matter how many visits or how many moons it might take. So far, she had been calm since she left home, had not felt one of those terrible hot spells.

A special rock, she thought, would be comforting, one like the truest color of a blue heron, one filled with good spirits, a lucky one. She searched. All the rocks seemed to blend into one. Points and curves no longer stood out as they had when she was Princess Blue Heron, daughter of Chief Wahoo and Golden Grain Grower. She rubbed her eyes. Ah, cool water from the blue spring would clear her vision. She glided over to the spring, forever bubbling with its sweet sound, knelt, and filled her cupped hands. The blue water tasted fresh and was as cool as when she and Padre had enjoyed drinking it. A few splashes enlivened her face.

But, back at the rock piles she could see no better than before. Patience, patience...patience. She sat down to be closer to the rocks. Rock after rock, she picked up and held at arm's length, trying to assess the qualities. She turned so that the sun shone over her shoulder. Soon she found a smooth rock, thick in the center and sloping around the edge. She ran her fingers around the edge and felt a point. This was the perfect rock. It fitted in her palm with the point turned toward her thumb. Over and over she held it at extended arm's length, studying why it struck her as the perfect rock, full of good spirits. Her thoughts unfolded farther and farther back. It came to her that it looked much like the one her Creek husband, before he died bravely at Horseshoe Bend, had chosen to adorn their son's chest. Had it still hung around young Tupelo's neck when he slipped off of a rock at the falls and was swept down the river of cane?

In the stillness of late afternoon sun, Blue Heron sat and rubbed every grain of sand off the fine rock, blew on it, and stroked it again and again. But what would churchgoing farmer families think of her if they could see her now? A much stronger feeling overshadowed that question. No matter how she tried to put it out of her mind, the old nagging need to speak with the padre always loomed up. She just could not bring herself to face the matter with Caleb. The disappointing dilemma withered her earlier exhilaration into perplexity. A growl rumbled in her stomach, though she had no desire for food. Yet, Caleb would be ready to eat at sundown. When she had checked on him before her walk, he had been restacking newly arrived burlap bags of cottonseed hulls, making space for cottonseed meal.

Flourishing farmers had inquired about the highly touted meal for farm animals. Soon, she noticed that rays of the setting sun pointed toward home. Not entirely satisfied with herself, Blue Heron left the lake area, though as she returned home she rubbed, in a satisfying way, her lucky new rock.

In the following days, a spate of rains forced Blue Heron to relinquish plans to walk to the blue lake. Cloudy days worsened her eyesight. Appetite dwindled. What's more, she had no inclination to prepare food for Caleb. He simply carved away on a smoked ham he had bartered and munched on hardtack and nuts and sometimes there were tomatoes. He seemed not perturbed when she did not cook, but just went about his daily routine, not talking much to her.

The first day she felt sure Caleb had intentionally ignored her, was when she had stood at the window watching the rain still beating down on the cotton fields. Maybe the rains gave the slaves a rest. How could the churchgoing people not see the evil of making slaves of people with black skin? Of all the churchgoing people, hardly any were sympathetic to the slaves, and those few were mostly women who would speak in mere whispers. She looked at the top of her left hand and brushed it with the fingertips of her other hand. People of her color had been mistreated by the whites, too. She rubbed her hand, dwelling on its reddish-brown color. Her skin would always be reddish-brown. It would never, never change. She could never become a true white. But she had lost the old ways of her Creek people. *Who am I? Where do I belong? How do I fit into life?*

She took the lucky rock from her pocket. Yes, her appreciation for the rock and its spirit was still as heartfelt as it had been on that last trip when she had found it. And yes, her last visit to the blue lake was more heartfelt than the one several moons ago when she merely thought she had found a new beginning.

Lately she thought more and more about going to Pensacola to talk with Padre, though each time her thoughts would end in doubts. Perhaps they were foolish thoughts. Even if Caleb would approve of a trip, Pensacola would be so strange. Besides, the town might even be scary. "Whew," she sighed. She could not even imagine just what it would be like. Not only would the town be too strange, but also, what about Padre? How would he feel about talking with her after all these years? Sehoy is now nineteen years old, so it had been about twenty years since Blue Heron had last seen Padre. He might notice her failing eyesight and hot spells and advise her that at her age she could not be of much help in standing up against the practice of slavery. Her forehead beaded. Slightly dizzy, she slipped down onto a chair and fanned her hot face with her palmetto fan, not even noticing the fine job she had done in the weaving of it. The room danced in a blurry, fuzzy haze.

The rainy spell finally ended. Early morning sunshine streamed across the room toward the fireplace. With her hair pinned up in a knot, like the white women's, Blue Heron felt the sun on her back of her neck as she cooked. Fat back crackled, followed by the bubbling of scrambled eggs in one spider skillet while flour cakes browned in the other. The aroma gave the day a promising, fresh start. Caleb ate the breakfast with gusto. Still missing was Caleb's strong caring hand on her shoulder and the comforting words he used to have for her before he left to work in the store. Perhaps he had store business on his mind and tomorrow he would be back to his old self. But could Caleb's change of behavior be caused by her feelings about the evils of slavery? Caleb, for fear of losing business in the store, had recently forbidden her to speak about freeing the slaves, even to churchgoing people. They, too, were farmers and timber workers, many of whom owned chattels. Blue Heron's worry veiled her mind even as she stood in the doorway and decided that despite her problems this was a fine day, a fine day to go to the blue lake.

When she was out of sight of her home, she took off her shoes. This day was different. She smelled it in the rain-cleansed air. She felt it in the rain-soaked grass and bushes edging the path. The soles of her feet tingled, and with each breeze the rain-ladened leaves dampened her calico dress with coolness. Along a marshy stretch she moved slower, determined to be patient in these low places, as well as on the upslanted sections of the path. This walk would turn out fine. Just then she slipped on a slick-clay outcropping, lost her balance, wavered, and slammed down on her back. Sweat beaded on her face. She broke a leafy branch and fanned herself.

Sultry sun sent her groping toward the shade of a tree, one of the few trees still standing. Why had the greedy land people not chopped this one, too? Once underneath its shade she knew why. She thumped the trunk with the heel of her shoe. It was hollow. Another thing she knew. The big bump growing out of its bark was where wasps had gnawed into the wood to lay eggs. This caused the tree to grow a big, thick-skinned bump that the whites called a gall. But her people knew it was a good thing for tanning. They knew it long, long before the whites ever came here. Sitting underneath the tree brought a calming reassurance. But while she rested, the sky darkened and a sudden thundershower followed. Instead of clearing as usual, the sky turned a threatening shade of gray. She tarried for a while undecided about which way to turn. Soon the sky turned an all-over gray that tells you rain has set in. So, the rainy spell had not completely ended after all. She turned back toward home, moving with defeated spirit, not minding the gentle rain. Other things bothered her. Even though she had cooked a good breakfast, she dreaded facing Caleb. The changes she had noticed in Caleb lately worried her. Never anything outright. The coolness. The distance. The lack of attention at bedtime, which hurt worst. Struggling to understand Caleb felt almost like trying to make sense of how the church teachings differed so greatly from the way some churchgoing people treated slaves.

A curious circumstance caused Blue Heron to take a different path on her next walk. While Caleb weighed out flour from the barrel for Brother Fletcher, the preacher at the Conecuh River Church, the preacher told Blue Heron that the land next to the Creek burial ground was being clear-cut. A picture of Tupelo's mound instantly sprang into her mind. Motion of the feather duster ceased and lay limp in her hand on a store shelf, which she had been dusting. Painful pangs jabbed her memories of Tupelo and his burial mound. Though he had been washed down the river, his playthings and little loincloth had been carefully buried for his next life. Concern for her father's and her mother's burial mounds and then Genesis' and all the others' flooded her mind.

Noting her worried expression, Caleb said, "As soon as I can get Josiah to mind the store, I'll go with you to the burial ground and hopefully put your fears to rest."

"That is kind of you, Caleb. I appreciate your caring."

She looked into blurry space, studying. Suddenly, she said, "Caleb, I must go right away. This is something my heart tells me to do, and it's just as well that I go alone." Blue Heron whisked her handmade feather duster along the shelf, tossed it into an empty keg, and then with a somber expression noiselessly left the store. She needed go to the burial ground alone. There just always was that untouchable space between Caleb and her people that she could never bring together.

Waves of worries hurried her steps. She did not think to remove her shoes until she descended into the stream valley near the log crossing. As she studied the long, naked, slick log, she unbuttoned her shoes, removed them, and placed them in her carrying basket. She inhaled deeply, called up her courage, but her feet did not move forward. After another deep gasp for air, she set forth, instinctively gripping her curled toes over the rounded log's surface. Successfully across, though slower than in the past, she ascended the upslanted sandy swath and at the crest, what she saw at first glance claimed her breath. Close by, clear cutters still killed trees. Two axmen swung in perfect rhythm. Each chop of the metal axes that they heaved into the living trees pounded into her head. Then came the deathly buzz of the crosscut saw. The smell of fresh, warm pine sawdust drifting by sickened her like a corpse too long in the sun. Still, she labored onward, wide-eyed.

Never could she have foreseen this nakedness of her people's burial ground. While still some distance away from the burial ground, the wide-open space seemed disrespectful and irreverent. The burial ground had lost the spiritual protection of the giant old trees. Not only had the trees colonnaded the burial mounds, but their tops had also entwined into canopies, holding in the sacredness. Now, mostly scrub oak and saplings stood near empty places where the giant protectors had held forth. Branches no longer interlocked at the top to hold in her people's spirits. Sturdy perching limbs no longer stretched out for mockingbirds and song sparrows to alight upon. Cool shade no longer comforted visitors. Even a nearly blind person could see the deathlike difference now. Even a stranger would surely feel sorrow.

Whiteness of far off fields deepened her sorrowfulness. Each additional field of cotton meant more slavery. Slowly, she moved toward the sacred burial ground, stopping at the edge to breathe in the spirits of her Creek ancestors. She took a long look. There were some things a person could never get used to. No more protective tree arms entwined at the top, no more lower arms hung heavily with moss in deep reverence. So much had gone wrong that she needed to help make right. In earlier years, Caleb had refused to hear of her traveling the long, dangerous journey out West to visit and see what she could do for her people. If she could go backwards she would try harder to be strong and work to keep enough of Mother Earth for her Creek people to live on.

*I have allowed my marriage to mold me into the ways of the whites. My daughter also became a bride of the greedy, her husband a destroyer of the forest. Sehoy's book learning taught her to think and talk like whites. She is not alone in this. I followed in her educated footsteps. It seemed so, so—it seemed the right thing to do at the time. Caleb was so proud of both of us that I...I listened to my ancestral spirit less and less, locked out warnings. Too long I trusted in the government's false promises, willed myself to pretend, pretend that everything would be all right. I still pretend that everything is all right. I must stop now. Eyes of ancestors here at the burial ground see how the evils came about. Even with my eyes weakening, I see plainly how I enjoyed the goods of the whites so much that I let the bad things happening to my people slide into the forgetful part of my heart.*

Blue Heron wept in grief. She wept in grief for outliving other Creek. She wept in grief for sins against the forest by the timber men and farmers. She wept in grief for the slaves, real people brought here in iron shackles. She wept in grief for the banished Creek, some of whom had been taken away in similar iron shackles. She wept in grief for there was nothing but the mounds to show for all that the Creek had meant here. After a heart-wrenching sigh, she held back the next one for the sake of the dead. With extended arms and open palms, she proclaimed, "I release all my pretending. I trust the sacred wind to blow it away. There...there it goes."

She wiped the tears and unknowingly sensed her way directly to Tupelo's mound. Here, she needed her spirit rock, the one like her husband had chosen to adorn Tupelo's chest. She knelt and took the rock from her basket. It fitted her palm and brought comfort as she remembered her first child.

At the mounds of her parents, Golden Maize Grower and Chief Wahoo, Blue Heron cupped her hand over her mouth to stop the flow of regrets. How would they feel about the path their daughter had taken? How could she live with having enjoyed the beautiful parasol and calico dresses that Caleb had provided while her people were banished. How sad it felt thinking what she had looked at but had not seen in her heart. How could she live with it?

*No words can change the past. I can look away, but the pictures in my mind do not go away. I can look away but it does not change what happened. The pretending is gone. I will live with the truth.*

Blue Heron rubbed her fingers over the smooth rock. But everyone had carried out a part in the wrongdoings. Still, the faces of her people watched only one person now, wondering what she would do next. She must do something. She forced herself to take a step. That step forward meant she would not reach backward. There was something she could do for the land. The thought warmed her heart. She vowed that one day she would stand on this burial ground and say that she had helped slaves walk on Mother Earth as free people, like the whites.

*This stand I will take in memory of my people who are gone but not forgotten. But how? How? How?*

She stepped lightly toward Genesis' mound. Though only half his blood was Creek, he had learned Creek bravery and proved it by fighting for the Creek at their last battle on the Georgia line. Did he ever realize how he might have started Andalusia's name by bringing Padre to the Owl Clan when they were escaping Sharp Knife's invasion of Pensacola?

Near Genesis' mound Blue Heron noticed an unusual tree, stunted and misshaped. She gazed in awe. Why it was shaped like Padre. Of its two limbs, one was straight, the other had a hump like Padre's humpback. Surely, the ancestors had sent this tree to watch over Genesis' grave and to guide her to visit Padre for advice. If the whites knew how she felt about the tree, they might make light of it, but there was absolutely no doubt in her mind about its meaning.

Thoughts of Padre reminded Blue Heron how he had secretly helped her bring food and directions to Chad, the sick runaway slave whom she had found while on one of her spirit quests. She and Padre had learned he was on his way to the Florida to find his wife who had been sold to a sugar cane plantation. Perhaps Padre could show her how she could help the slaves around the Andalusia area. But Caleb, for fear of losing business in the store, had forbidden her to speak of freeing the slaves, not even to churchgoing people. Separate halves of her life bent toward each other like two storms converging from opposite directions. Her face stiffened. She could not delay any longer. She *must* talk with Caleb about going to Pensacola. She would like to go as soon as possible, whenever Josiah made his next trip with the carriage. Padre, alone, understood how freedom for the slaves would help free her heart from the bitterness over wrongs that had been inflicted on her people. Seeking advice from Padre seemed the right thing to do.

On the way home Blue Heron looked for the tree with the huge hollowed-out hole where she had, years ago, hidden the *banza* and the crucifix necklace. The tree was gone. She would not look for deer tracks or turkey tracks or even rabbit tracks, not because of her dimming eyesight. Rather, she knew that with so few trees, there would be none. The view in the distance was more unsettling—treeless clay hills, burnished red as blood and patches and patches of cotton, boll after boll filling flatlands with a ghostly whiteness.

Blue Heron wondered about the sacred red hole where she used to go for spiritual quests. Was it still there? She needed to know, but there was so much to do. Caleb and the children had helped her make some sense of the white God, and she enjoyed going to church. Yet, it would not hurt to visit the sacred red hole very soon and call on ancestors in the other world to send spirit guides to her people in the West. As she walked toward home her feet stirred the dust. She could not see it, but she knew it was there. It always made her sneeze. Yet, she could see shadows of her people in the blue twilight. "How I wish I could have a second chance to help my people," she lamented.

Later that evening Blue Heron walked outside into the cool air. She folded her arms over her bosom and faced the sky. Certain thoughts that had visited her at the burial ground belonged sealed in her heart. She whispered, "These thoughts belong *only* to my heart, just the same as the twinkling stars and moon belong only in the sky."

# ANOTHER VIEW OF PENSACOLA

Caleb's reaction had been a bit surprising. He said, "I can understand that you would like to make a visit to Ft. Crawford and Pensacola." He paused as if studying the matter and added, "Come to think of it, a trip to the coast might be good for you. I'm sure one of the main reasons for the trip is because you know that on the way down there Josiah puts up for the evening in Ft. Crawford, and you could visit with Abel."

"You are right. I am anxious to see how our apothecary apprentice is getting along."

"Uh hm, I've been thinking the same thing, but I just can't get away now. Farmers are still selling their crops and settling up their accounts at the store. Got a big order of supplies coming in, too. Anyways, the change for a few days might improve your appetite. I heard that Pensacola weather is good for whatever might ail a body. And to be sure, Josiah wouldn't mind having your company when he makes his next business trip there. Besides, you'll probably enjoy visiting with your old friend, the padre. Even though it has been a long time since I heard anyone around Andalusia mention him, I imagine he is still a very fine person who would pass on interesting information. I can't remember ever hearing anyone speak ill of him."

Never had a fall season felt better to Blue Heron. Planning for the trip brought renewal of spirit. Not only had Caleb been amenable to the idea of her going to Pensacola, but Sehoy was, also. She offered to lend her valise, which she had used for traveling to and from boarding school, as well as her fine, fringed shawl that Josiah had given to her. Sehoy said, "Mother, since

I am accustomed to traveling, I'll help you plan. I know the things you need to take. And you should wear the shell crucifix necklace for good luck; I think the padre would be pleased to see you wearing it."

As they rolled and bumped along The Three Notch Road, Josiah was a very caring son-in-law, even in unexpected ways. He had tried to ease Blue Heron's fears, the first being one that a store customer had raised about the road being rough in places. When they came to a deeply rutted section, the wheels bounced up and down noisily on the hard, sharp-edged clay ruts. Josiah said, "Don't worry, the most skilled wheelwright in Pensacola made these wheels, so I believe they will hold up just fine along this rutty section." In the log-lined lowlands the wheels alternately slid down and bumped up on the curved logs. Thankfully, in other sections the logs had been split and the curved side placed against the dirt or clay.

Along comfortably shaded sections of the road, Josiah had sometimes talked about Sehoy and little Emma. One of the most pleasant conversations was about his satisfying a wish of Sehoy's. He said, "Sehoy has had her heart set on a pergola for a long time. I plan to build one, a nice latticed one, and plant a scuppernong vine for shade in time for her to sit underneath and nurse our next child. And Emma can romp all around it, too. Not to mention the sweet provender, as Sehoy called it, that all of us can enjoy. I ordered workers from the mill to girdle the old sweet gum that stands in the way now, so it'll come down easier. I hate to lose the tree, but just think of the satisfaction we'll all get from Sehoy's pergola. Besides, Emma shouldn't play with the sweet gum balls. Her hands are too tender for those pincer-like spines."

Thoughts of the old ancestral ways rippled through Blue Heron. Only a generation ago, Creek women had valued those pincers for scrubbing clay pots and scratching children for misbehaving. Waging a kindly battle now to enlighten Josiah just might rile him, so she kept silent.

The sun had already hidden itself when they rolled into Ft. Crawford. It was too late to try contacting Abel. The innkeeper showed them to their beds and said that he had made a pot of chicken and dumplings for dinner. "There's enough left for two people. I'll warm it while you all wash up."

Pleased with her evening meal, Blue Heron had hardly stretched out on her bed before she fell into a deep sleep of exhaustion. She never heard Josiah when he returned from checking that the horses had been properly watered and fed.

Josiah shook her awake at daybreak and said, "There's a red sunrise. We must get started for Pensacola right away. On our return trip we can visit with Abel." Though half asleep, her concession cut deeply. In yielding she had reasoned that she stood more future chances of seeing Abel than with visiting Padre.

Nearer to Pensacola, Josiah had said, "If I have time, I'm going to look for a rifle with a walnut gunstock.  Wanted one ever since I heard of my grandpappy bragging that he shouldered walnut in the war with the British.  Not that I'd ever have a whole lots of use for the gun, but it sure would look mighty manly to have one hanging over the fireplace.  I don't think I'd ever get tired of looking at it.  That's where I want it to stay, right there over the fireplace.  And I hope to God I'll never have to 'shoulder walnut in war' like my grandpappy said he did.  But a feller never knows what he'll have to do, especially since lately people's tempers are starting to boil over when some of those officials in Washington criticize slave holders.   Heard some rumblings of folks saying the government better stay outta their business or they'd fight for their right to have slaves."

Blue Heron merely bristled and again withheld her feelings about the evils of slavery to keep peace.

As they approached Pensacola, smell of the gulf's salt air and the rustling of fronds, which gracefully flowed from atop the tall palm trees, enchanted her.  Actual arrival in the large, strange town stirred up the greatest excitement Blue Heron had felt in a long time, causing her stomach to tighten.  Though hungry, she knew she would not be able to eat a thing.  Not only did she have to excuse herself from supper, but she also lay sleepless for hours.

Having breakfast at the Gulfside Inn dining room, unlike any Blue Heron had ever known, kept her looking agog as a real, honest to goodness, waiter served the people.  Then she noticed the chairs and tables, which surely had been constructed by skilled carpenters, and patrons' garments, which were of finely woven fabrics.  Only one common-looking man wore homespun clothing.  Then Josiah ordered their breakfast.  The ham was fine-grained, and the biscuits were splendid.  Josiah said, "The biscuits were baked in a first-class oven."

After breakfast, they walked along a magical-looking street that Josiah called "Palafox Street," a name not difficult for her to pronounce.  Banana bunches, bigger than a man's head, hung at an open market stall, and at another a tethered goat bleated.  The tang of fresh oranges filled the air, then mixed and faded as they approached a man holding a string of fish.  He blew on a conch shell and cried out, "Fresh mullet for sale."  Voices of people speaking in different languages fell on her ears, overlaid the other sounds, and amused her, though she understood none of it.

Blue Heron wished to stroll, but she kept pace with Josiah along the shop-lined Palafox Street.  Midst the milling people, he pointed and said,

"There it stands, there's St. Michael's Church, Padre's church." Unbeknownst to her, he had, before breakfast, made arrangements for Blue Heron to meet with Padre. Blue Heron breathed heavily and broke into a sweat. She would soon face Padre. Now everything seemed like a dream, everything. Was she up to meeting with Padre? She dabbed her handkerchief to her face.

At first glance, Padre appeared more peaceful than when he had been a visitor at the Owl Clan Village.

"Welcome, Mrs. Lange," Padre said with a slight bow, then as if exhilarated extended his hand to Josiah.

"Thank you," Blue Heron somehow responded, but to her, the words sounded squeaky as a scared mouse. "Thank you," she said again, but this response also resounded with squeakiness to it.

Josiah quickly excused himself to take care of his business in town. As Josiah was leaving, Padre said, "As soon as our meeting is finished, I'll escort Mrs. Lange to Seville Plaza, since it is right across the street from the Gulfside Inn." Josiah nodded on his way out. Padre tilted his bearded chin at a proud angle and said to Blue Heron, "The plaza has public benches under the shade of old live oaks where one can sit and enjoy the beauty of Pensacola's bay." Then he directed her to a chair and asked, "How was your trip on the Three Notch Road?"

An unimaginable aura filled the room as the two reunited friends assessed each other, Padre in sheer calmness and Blue Heron unaware of her shallow, light breathing.

"Thanks to Josiah, the trip was fine. It was more interesting...less scary than I expected." Though more stooped and walking with the aid of a cane, the white-haired, white-bearded Padre seemed powerful in a way she had never known when he had traveled to Alabama years ago to escape Jackson's invasion of Pensacola. Unaware of her action, she had craned her head toward his face, wondering if she would be able to renew her former spiritual connection with this holy man.

Padre displayed no surprise at Blue Heron's Americanized appearance, or at her more mature face. Nor did he comment on the shell crucifix he had given to her as a parting present when he departed from the Owl Clan. But he could not refrain from calling attention to her blue outfit. "I see you still like the color of blue."

She smiled against her will.

The tinge of sadness remained in her eyes, the same kind that Padre had noticed from the very first time he had seen her at the Owl Clan. This feature had stayed sharpest in his mind. Her scent was subtler, not herbal or woodsy as he had remembered her. Of course, the heels of her palms were still pink. He said, "Tell me about your children."

Words spilled out of her and overflowed. "First I'd like you to know I have a granddaughter." Then she told him all about Emma and Abel and Sehoy.

"Thank God. Thank God your family is growing and faring well. I am delighted to hear about your granddaughter and children, but I also want you to know that your presence renews thoughts of Genesis more poignantly. His death is a loss, which is still difficult to bear. We were so different, yet understood each other so well."

She leaned forward. "I, too, feel the loss. In recent months I have suffered greatly over the loss of all my people." Blue Heron could not completely pour out her soul to the padre, but she would add, "I grieve that I cannot help my people now. But there are others I might be able to help."

As they had talked, she had maintained an air of distance about the real purpose of her visit. But she knew she must now seek Padre's advice on the slavery matter and do so with seriousness, without a trace of residual affection or attraction. First, she would ease her way toward the fiery problem by asking, "Have you heard anything about Chad, you remember the runaway slave we helped?"

"I regret to say, so far I have not but I keep the faith. He is always in my prayers, his wife, too." Padre rubbed his walking cane with the heel of his palm.

Ready, but unready, too, Blue Heron delved into the subject of her visit. "I have been wondering for some time…what do you think I might be able to do for the slaves around Andalusia? I would like very much to help them win freedom. Any help that I give to them would have to be something I can do alone. Since settlers want to own them for farm work, and my husband needs the settlers' business at the store, he fears he will lose customers, that they will stop trading at the store if I help the slaves." She held her hand over her mouth but knowing she must finish conveying her thoughts, she released it and said, "Sometimes my mind goes in circles, trying to understand both sides." She paused in a frozen gesture of appeal.

Padre lowered his head and cogitated, but only momentarily. He raised his head, looked into her eyes, and with authority said, "You have it in you. Why you have the answer, right there in your fingertips and in your heart as well as in your Creek upbringing and your quests to become a shaman, and more importantly, in the experience you acquired as Shaman Blue Heron Healer. I know from my own personal experience of your genuine care and healing knowledge when you nursed me to health at the time I came down with malaria in Alabama."

Blue Heron could not quite hide her pleasure, but she had listened intently. His way of speaking with certainty, she found convincing.

366

Padre continued with an air of triumph, "You could make your experience as a healer known to the farmers and settlers, your midwifery, too, and volunteer to provide remedies for sicknesses among the slaves."

"Padre, I appreciate that but the slaves have their own midwives."

"Yet, in the event of an outbreak of malaria, scarlet fever, flu, or the like, you could offer your healing knowledge."

"Yes, I can do that."

"After you earn the respect of the slave families, there are several ways you might aid them. For instance, the simplest thing you can do is make sure they know the northern route to freedom by guidance of the North Star. The western route is best explained by having them watch for the sunsets and after darkness head in that direction and look for open spaces, which are likely to be rivers or lakes. You are well aware of details that you can explain like those concerning flying geese at the change of seasons, and how their flights tell direction."

Suddenly Blue Heron wondered how Caleb would react if he could hear her conversation with Padre. Her throat felt dry. She broke into an embarrassing coughing spell and an accompanying sweat.

"God bless you."

Upon recovering, she said, "Thank you for the blessing and yes, Padre, you are so right. North in spring and south in the fall."

Padre tipped his head in approval. "As you already know, flying geese also give cunningly simple clues about water sources." He paused and then said, "Another small particular is for the slaves to understand that it is best for them to run before a rain storm, so tracks would be covered. Still another is to wade near the river shallows, so bloodhounds cannot pick up their scents. And you can sketch maps in sand or earth, for they can be erased quickly, if necessary, before suspicion sets in. But first of all, you must gain their trust and always, always keep encouraging and nourishing their spirits whenever possible."

"I appreciate all your advice, but it seems it would take such a long time to make any gains."

"My heart goes out to you, but the only way you can accomplish your goal is by one step or one deed at a time. One simple act at a time creates change. I realize you care deeply, but you must act. I sailed from Spain, so far away, one day at a time." With obvious difficulty he stood and said, "Come, we can walk to the plaza."

Padre pointed his walking cane to an anthill edging a pathway in Seville Plaza and said, "For some reason I have always had great admiration for those tiny creatures. My admiration deepened after one of the first things I noticed from my sick bed at the Owl Clan was an ant. Seeing that ant made me realize how wonderful it was to be alive. Now, I nearly always give pause to them."

At some point, Blue Heron relaxed as they sat facing the white-capped, emerald gulf. Not just impressed, but overwhelmed by the gulf's vast vista, she gazed first horizontally at the panorama of gentle waves, then vertically at the horizon directly ahead.

At first resting from the walk, Padre then pressed his hand to his bearded chin and basked in seeing God reflected in the swelling tide and fiery granules of sand. Then he said, "The painful practice of slavery is highly controversial here in Pensacola, too."

Even though he was not in her line of vision now, Blue Heron could catch his earnest mood, the formidable way he spoke.

"Padre, I...I had not planned to say this, but will only because I learned long ago that I could trust you. You see, I am afraid the customers will get wind of my helping the slaves and do something terrible to Caleb or his store. Josiah said some people are so mad about the government meddling in their business, they are talking about fighting over it."

"Yes. I'm not surprised. I have also heard similar rumors. I regret that slavery is the basic underpinning of the rural economy." He paused in thought, and then said, "Regardless of fears, we have to move forward and live our lives."

The sun had descended into a giant orange circle surrounded by the muted magenta and lavender-lighted sky. They stood, first Padre and then Blue Heron, facing each other. In the path of the lower sunrays, Padre noticed the vastly diminished radiance in his friend's wear-worn face. Blue Heron noticed that Padre now had a sizeable wen on his forehead, right side, which he did not have in his younger years. They both seemed to sense that their mutually enduring passion to help others had outlasted physical changes.

Before departing, Padre said, "I have duties to fulfill in the morning, but I will have time in the afternoon to visit again. If it is all right with you, I would like to show you the new church."

"I will be in Pensacola for two or three days while Josiah tends to business. My husband thought the change here would be good for me. I think he was right. Good spirits are already returning. I would like very much to visit your new church."

"You will be in my prayers." He nodded his head. "Good day and God bless you and never, never forget to appreciate your special sensitivity for justice; but you must act on it." Slowly he stood and walked in the opposite direction of the bay's beautiful sunset, using his walking cane for support.

At breakfast that day, Blue Heron had been caught up in a mixture of anticipation and worry over meeting with Padre. Now that the first meeting

368

was over, supper was much more relaxing. And it came with the thrill of surprises. First, the fancy dinning room seemed even fancier than it had at breakfast and then Josiah said, "I found out that the cook was making stew for the guests today, but I made arrangements to be served a plate of raw oysters on half shells before my stew is served."

When the oysters arrived, Josiah offered a sample to Blue Heron. Never could she have swallowed one. She could not even abide a second look, for the oysters looked like the eyes of a dying person. Instead, her line of vision followed the waiter with a big, white apron as he served other people. She slowly regained her appetite as she tasted, in small bites, her serving of corn pone and spicy stew. Soon she ate heartily wondering how much more excitement tomorrow might bring.

# A SPECIAL RISING SUN

Inside St. Michael's Church Blue Heron stood solemnly while Padre blessed himself with holy water, faced the altar, and genuflected. Then they exchanged glances, each trying to divine the other's thoughts. Blue Heron hid her perceptiveness beneath an expression of serenity. In a soft voice she said, "This brings back so many memories of the times I watched you at the blue lake."

"Yes, I also have pleasant remembrances of the primitive sanctuary. The little outdoor chapel brought much comfort back when I lived at the Owl Village."

Blue Heron touched a hand to her cheek, feeling honored and embarrassed at the same time, honored to be Padre's guest in his new Pensacola church and embarrassed at the thought of how she had tried to learn genuflecting years ago at the red hole.

"I am wondering if you have any questions about the church."

In rapt observation she answered, "Your church is so different from the one in Andalusia. You have boards, smooth ones, instead of logs. The benches are smooth and have backrests, and you have a board floor. The church in Andalusia has a sand floor. Sometimes I help bring in clean sand."

"I might have told you that we had to hold our services in an old warehouse in the past. For sure, you already knew that priests wear robes, and you have heard me speak of some Catholic teachings about the holy water, and cross, and altar."

"Yes, and I learned some things at our church about Jesus dying on the cross but who is the lady in blue in the picture?"

"That's a picture of the Virgin Mary, Mother of Jesus."

"She looks so peaceful. This church is so big and fine, different from our church in Andalusia. Do you have a different God?"

"No, indeed, but we have different ways of worshiping in the Catholic Church. I shall not try to convert you to Catholicism in one afternoon. Come with me. We will stroll along the beach; that is, if you have no objection to my slow pace."

"Not at all. I would like to walk slowly so that I can see everything. Everything. I wish to see as much of Pensacola as possible."

"Perhaps you will find some seashells that you would like to take to your granddaughter."

"That would be wonderful. Seashells from the Pensacola Beach should bring me extra notice from the little one."

Without mentioning it to Blue Heron, Padre searched diligently in the beach sand for two types of shells: One was a conch shell to show her the type of shell her hand-carved crucifix had come from. The other was for a Rising Sun for her to keep as a talisman. Though conch shells were plentiful, he turned over a few with his walking stick until he found one with the bright rose and coral colors. Before presenting it to Blue Heron, he placed it against the crucifix she wore and called her attention to the similarity of coloring. Then he explained how he had carved the crucifix.

Blue Heron clutched the shell affectionately. Soon she noted that Padre walked with utmost effort, especially near the stands of sea oats. Instinctively, she stopped so that he could rest. She turned to face the gulf water, the wide expanse of balmy waves, and set her attention on the scantily bubbled tops highlighted by afternoon sunshine.

Standing still, Padre's eyes followed the massive breadth of water; he gazed until the glittery-emerald layer melted into the horizon. Was he thinking of his homeland across the large ocean or was he thinking of the cool drinks of blue water he had enjoyed at the blue spring? Soon his eyes turned to the gentle waves nearby. He tented his hands under his chin and synchronized deep breaths with the slow rising and dying away of the small swells. Soft lapping echoed. Solace of immersing his fatigue in the unhurried undulations lasted only a brief spell.

The restful interlude was just what Padre needed for finding a Rising Sun Shell. And the timing was perfect for handing it to Blue Heron as a parting token. He told her how he had found one before leaving for Alabama with Genesis and how he had kept it as a good omen. She held the sun-warmed, friendship-warmed shell in her hand, a gift beyond any value. Though fond of her entire collection she would keep this shell separate from the others. It did look like the rising sun with its tapered streaks the color of sunrays.

Padre took in a long look at the western bay and said, "I think we will be blessed with another one of Pensacola's peerless sunsets this evening." Then he turned toward Blue Heron with an outstretched arm.

With mixed feelings, Blue Heron knew that the time for parting had come.

Padre's final blessing had tenderly touched Blue Heron. She held her Rising Sun shell as tightly as her heart held the memories of their Pensacola visits. And her eyes followed Padre's slow-moving shock of white hair for as far as she could see it. She looked down only occasionally to admire her shell collection.

# CHANCE MOSES GREENLEAF

The third day of Blue Heron's Pensacola visit arrived with brilliant fall sunshine and a tinge of gulf chill blowing in the early morning air. She and Josiah paid for their room and board, said their farewells to the innkeeper, and set forth home; but not before the innkeeper cried out, "Come back to see us." When Blue Heron looked back and responded with a smile, he said, "Once you've eaten Pensacola red snapper, you'll always return." Blue Heron waved to him.

The red snapper supper the previous evening had been delicious, although not nearly as deliciously unforgettable as the walk on the beach with Padre. The conversations they had shared gave her so much to think about. They had experienced so many common joys and sorrows. A comforting warmth enveloped her thoughts when she realized she would forever have these memories to draw from in quiet moments. She also had the collection of seashells as a reminder of the visit. Thoughts of the different shapes, sizes, shades of coloring enlivened her spirit. Each one had taken a place in her heart, especially the Rising Sun. Padre's soothing influence would forever prevail in the seashells.

Past the first set of notches marking the Three Notch Road, a series of sandy ridges cut across the road. Titi and other woody shrubs and bushes lined the road ruts. Atop the highest hill, Josiah turned his head to the south momentarily. Blue Heron looked backward and followed Josiah's pointing finger for a glance. The large town of Pensacola now looked tiny. Then in unison they faced north again with instant and mutually satisfying expressions of their coastal town visit.

Toward the north Blue Heron found many of Mother Earth's fall beauties awaiting. A panoply of orange and yellow sassafrases lined either side of the road. In some places the sassafras leaves were embedded among pine saplings, like colorful faces peeking out from frames of green pine needles. In contrast with these beautiful creations of Mother Earth which are much the same year after year, Blue Heron felt a tremendous change within herself. The visit to Pensacola had forever changed her, stretching her outlook in heretofore unbelievable directions—the advice Padre gave her, the vast gulf, the long beach, the hustle and bustle of different kinds of people, the shops, and the fishy-salty smell of the large town.

Josiah broke the silence. "I got a lot done. In fact, I have a great feeling of accomplishment. I bargained for a better price for our mill's next raft of timber. Right then I decided our next baby's name would be Andrew J. Morgan, that is if it is a boy. Sehoy had said if we have a boy, I could name him. The initial 'J.' would honor my name as well as America's hero."

Blue Heron shivered at the thought that her grandchild's name might honor Sharp Knife.

Without a pause, Josiah continued, "And I found the rifle I wanted with a walnut gunstock."

Blue Heron had already speculated that a certain long parcel contained a gun.

"I got so excited over the gun that I forgot to buy quinine and laudanum. We always keep the medicines on hand for the mill workers."

"Why don't you buy it from Abel when we stop at Ft. Crawford?"

"That's right. I can. Completely slipped my mind that the apothecary there sells real medicine now. Hasn't been hardly any time since they mostly sold herb remedies and witchcraft stuff."

The comment struck Blue Heron more forcibly than any of the hurtful ones he had made on this trip. It cut like his sawyers' blades. She tried to shut it out by pressing her hands against her eyes. Josiah had no understanding of Creek healing. But yes, Abel's apothecary apprenticeship was leading him down another path much different from what she had known as a shaman.

Blue Heron smothered her wounded feelings by reviewing in her mind the purchases she had made, each gift she had chosen for Caleb and Sehoy and Emma. A smile flowed across her face when she thought of the soft little blanket she had selected for her soon-expected second grandchild.

In the more heavily forested area of the Three Notch Road, Josiah said, "We are about as close to the river as we'll be for a few miles. Better water the horses. For the last few minutes, I could tell they need it. A little rest, too." He pulled the carriage to the side, unhitched the horses, and said, "Come along to the river so you can stretch your legs."

Though Blue Heron had a jar of drinking water, the sun had warmed it. If there was a spring feeding into the river, she would prefer to have a drink of cool spring water, so she jumped down and followed. At the river's edge one of the horses reared his head in a way that it shook a tree branch overhanging the river. A big snake flipped down on the horse's rump and slid to the riverbank. While Josiah tried to bring the horse under control, the other was going out of control simultaneously. His hands were full. Blue Heron stared motionlessly at the white-mawed monster. Of the many cotton-mouthed moccasins she had seen, this was the largest. At first, the snake looked as if it wanted to strike but with the commotion and vibrations of the horses the serpent instinctively slithered into the river. Then all that was seen of it was its head and ramrod body sticking up about two feet out of the river as the current swept it south. Blue Heron remembered Genesis' favorite snake story that he called "Rattlesnake Hill." Now she had her own snake story to tell.

Early darkening time of the year was upon them, and they barely arrived in Ft. Crawford before sunset, too late for Josiah to purchase the quinine and laudanum. Though hungry and dusty and somewhat weary, Blue Heron still wanted to visit with Abel; but it would too late to see him at the apothecary, so they washed up and ate supper first.

Nothing about the Ft. Crawford Inn seemed nearly as fine to Blue Heron as the Gulfside Inn, but that did not matter. What mattered was that she wanted to visit with Abel. After supper, she donned the fine-fringed shawl that Sehoy had lent to her, and she and Josiah set out to find the apothecary's house, where Abel boarded, at the edge of the settlement. There, in the dimmed light, Abel hoed weeds in the fall collard patch. Abel gladly put his hoe aside, and greeted his mother and Josiah. All three sat on a split log bench with Blue Heron in the middle. The apothecary, Mr. Berman, and his wife came out, welcomed the visitors, and sat on what looked like carpenter-made stools. They appeared to be in their fifties, both graying and stocky, friendly, too. Mr. Berman filled his pipe and smoked while his wife crocheted for a few minutes, seemingly by rote, not needing better light. As the sky slowly filled with stars, Blue Heron and Abel did most of the talking about the Pensacola trip and Papa's store in Andalusia. Josiah managed to include his interests—Sehoy and Emma and, of course, his prized purchase, the new gun, as well as his successful negotiation of a better price for the mill's next raft of timber to Pensacola. The conversations wound down as the night deepened and the air cooled. Josiah and Blue Heron bid all good evening. Upon their departure, Abel reminded them that he would meet them at the store early in the morning. As they walked away, Blue Heron snugged the shawl up around her neck and brushed her hand across the silky fringe, thankful Sehoy had lent the beautiful wrap to her and thankful, too, that Abel was such a fine son. When she looked up the stars hung so low and bright, their brilliance thrilled her with a sense of warmth and good spirit.

After an early breakfast Blue Heron and Josiah hastened to the apothecary store, and Abel happily sold the medications to Josiah. A sudden thought passed through Blue Heron's mind that she could use these store-bought remedies for healing the slaves. If Josiah could treat his workers with the newest medicines, there was no reason why she could not administer them to the slaves if she ever got the chance. After all, with all the other changes, why not embrace the notion of using the medicines that the whites use. Yes, of course, she would take advantage of the opportunity. As Abel readied her order he said, with all the confidence of one knowledgeable about his work, "The true apothecary's conscience makes absolutely sure that the patient always receives the right medicine, and I know my mother will use the medicines with absolute surety of conscience." Blue Heron had never been prouder of her son. The time came all too soon to give Abel a quick goodbye hug. "Come to see us as soon as you can," Blue Heron said as she and Josiah waved on their way out.

Back at the inn, while Josiah settled up expenses with the innkeeper, Blue Heron noticed a dignified man who curiously looked like a full-blooded Creek. With an official air he had spoken to the innkeeper and then took hammer, nails, and a notice from his grip. The badged man had no trouble nailing up the notice though all four fingers were missing on his left hand, leaving only his thumb. While the man nailed the notice, Blue Heron wondered why this particular Creek had not been banished. Josiah noticed her inquisitive look and quietly said, "The notice is about a reward in exchange for information on a man wanted for thievery."

When the Creek-looking man turned sideways, Blue Heron noticed a crease in his prominent chin. Immediately her attention transfixed on the stranger's face. She had always looked carefully at men with prominent chins, because they reminded her of two important people in her earlier life, her fatally wounded Creek husband and her young son who drowned.

She had been only a little surprised that she felt a Creek kinship to the officer. Another surprise loomed larger. This stranger's chin was just like the chin of her Creek husband who was killed at Horseshoe Bend. And it was also like Tupelo's, her young son who was swept down the river when he fell at the falls. Her heart pulsed faster and faster as the pull of attraction drew stronger.

The official put away his hammer and nails, said good day to the innkeeper, and left.

Blue Heron got control of herself and approached the innkeeper, who was attending to desk business while still wearing an apron that gave off a heavy odor of onions. She asked, "Do you know that official? Why he looks like a full-blooded Creek."

"Yes Missus. First, I need to excuse myself for still wearing this apron. Was chopping onions so I could put on dinner already. But gettin' back to your question, everybody knows him, Constable Greenleaf, Beat Four, if I remember correctly. He's really called by either one of his names. Some people call him by his first name—Chance, and some, mostly church folks, call him by his middle name—Moses."

An even odder twist unfolded when Blue Heron asked the innkeeper, "Do you know anything else about him? Mostly, I am wondering why he was not banished with the other Creek?"

"I sure do know, Missus. But them's long stories and they's mysterious about the way he was found in a river cove when he was just a young'un by men settin' out trot lines and so forth. What it was, was really a miracle."

Josiah shuffled his feet impatiently. "We'll have to hear the stories another time. I'm sorry. We need to get back to Andalusia."

Blue Heron threw her dignity and prudence to the wind and pleaded, "Please, Josiah, could we stay for a while? Maybe for just another day? I don't know when I can get back here again. You know, we might get rain today. The morning sunrise was red."

"Yes, but the stars were bright last night. Besides, it could rain the next day, too."

"But I abided by your wish to leave early when we had stopped in Ft. Crawford on our way down to Pensacola. You had said that we had to get started because it looked like rain was on the way. Please, would you return the favor?"

"You know I need to get back to the sawmill and Sehoy and Emma. Come now."

At the mention of Sehoy and Emma, Blue Heron said with false cheerfulness, "You are right. We must go."

While wending their way home to Andalusia on the Three Notch Road, Blue Heron took deep, relaxing breaths. The tightness in her chest loosened, and she lapsed into a daze. The joy of the trip to Pensacola was now overshadowed by a vague notion that if Tupelo had lived, he would have looked very much like the constable. Thoughts flashed. Inklings coalesced and another clue reinforced her notion of likening the officer to her first son. Tupelo had been about to celebrate his fifth Green Corn Ceremony when he was swept away in the river of cane. If he had lived, today he would be about twenty-six years old, maybe twenty-seven, about the same as the constable's apparent age. She caught a deep breath but still spent the rest of the trip home in that daze, a daze scented with onions.

Caleb grabbed Blue Heron's waist and lifted her from the carriage and hugged and rocked her back and forth in his arms. Later, while exchanging news they ate crackers from a fancy box and a can of sardines she had bought in Pensacola. Then, for most of the evening she told and retold stories of her trip as they munched on precious sweets she had brought back. Caleb said, "I wish I could have been the one who took you to Pensacola." The warmth of Caleb's capable hands stroking her shoulders, his mischievous laughs, his pleasure in listening to her stories seemed like the good old times, sending shivers of enjoyment through her being, the kind that made her see colors. But one incident she could not bring herself to talk about yet was about the Creek constable. Somehow she could not speak of it until she sorted out the strange feelings she had about the Constable's looking like what she would imagine Tupelo to have looked like, had he lived. She must let it rest inside her like a seed resting in winter.

As Blue Heron returned to her usual life in Andalusia, never a day passed without her practicing the name of "Chance Moses Greenleaf," never a day passed without her wishing to return to Ft. Crawford, and never a day passed without her yearning to ask the innkeeper to tell her all he knew about the Creek constable. Her practicing and wishing and yearning struck more poignantly whenever she smelled onions, and in her mind's eye she could see the innkeeper wearing his onion-scented apron.

Meanwhile, she still felt that she needed to start contacting slave owners and offering her healing assistance in case of an outbreak of fevers or other sicknesses. She was anxious to start using her newly purchased medicines. After all, Padre had said that she must put her thoughts into action. But, to begin with, she must get Caleb's approval.

Caleb's reply was quick, short, and right to the point. "All right, if it will make you happy but you must not do or say anything that would anger or displease the customers."

Blue Heron abided as she began by making gentle inquiries to the wives of two of the most amenable farmers, the Coopers and the Harts. Kitty Cooper was about the sweetest lady Blue Heron could think of. And Mrs. Hart, an older woman, was just about as sweet. Blue Heron explained to the ladies—first to Mrs. Hart while she waited for her husband to transact business at the store and later to Mrs. Cooper—that she had experienced success in healing and would be glad to help their slaves in the event fevers or other sicknesses should strike. She also explained that she had bought real medicines, quinine and laudanum, in Ft. Crawford. And she decided to remind the ladies that, of course, they already knew Abel is in training to become an apothecary and could send more medicines if either Mr. Cooper or Mr. Hart felt there was ever a need great enough to dispatch a rider. Both ladies had agreed to make Blue Heron's offers known to their husbands.

Nothing was heard from Blue Heron's offers until early spring planting when a team of frightened mules broke into a wild, headlong panic at the Harts' place. The mules trampled everybody and everything in sight. Three slaves, planting already plowed furrows, were in the line of the mules' flight. Overtaken by surprise, the men were knocked to the ground and stomped as the animals fled. Posthaste, Mr. Hart reined up his carriage at the store, jumped out, and summoned Blue Heron.

In the slave cabin, the women who attended the wounded men looked devastated by the tragedy. Without even looking at the victims, Mr. Hart, a powerfully imposing man, spoke to the woman who seemed to be in charge. Not a tinge of evil appeared in his gentle voice. "Cassie, I've brought Mrs. Lange here to help you. She knows a lot about healing." Then he turned toward Blue Heron and said, "Mrs. Lange, Slim, the one you hear a'groaning over there, said he heard a bone snap in his leg when the mule hoofed him. Do what you think's best for him before you look at Jimbo. I should also tell you that Rooster didn't bleed any, so you can look at him last. Now, I must leave. I have business to attend to. I will check with you later."

Blue Heron inhaled the pleasant odor of greens cooking at the fireplace, put her carrying basket down, and went directly, her hat still on her head, to the moaning man lying on a straw mattress in a dark corner. In the dimness she still could see blood seeping though rag-covered swelling on his leg. She lightly touched the bloodiest area and felt two raggedly sharp points of the broken bone, whereupon the man let out a chilling moan. Right away, she administered a generous dose of laudanum. While taking a moment to think out the sequence she should follow, she found herself staring at Cassie's triangular-shaped head bandanna. Blue Heron's plan set off a chain of action. "Cassie, we'll need a sapling, that's been split down the middle and two men to hold down Slim, so we can try to press the two ends of the bone back together and bind it up. The sapling pieces don't have to be very long, no longer than his leg. And send to the kitchen at the big house for all the empty flour sacks they have or old sheets and pillowcases they can spare to bind up the sapling boards. And we need an old quilt or part of one for padding."

While Cassie gave orders to her people, Blue Heron looked at Jimbo. In addition to the gash on his cheek, he had a swollen wrist. She quickly gave him a small dose of laudanum, cleaned the blood away from his cheek, and applied resin. Later, she would cover the cut with clean flour-sack strips as well as bind up his sore wrist.

While waiting for the supplies, Cassie stirred the pot of greens cooking at the fireplace and then stood beside Blue Heron as Rooster told of the pain in his chest.

"Hurts too much to talk," Rooster said.

"I understand," Blue Heron said and dabbed her sweated forehead, "but I must say that you don't look anything like a rooster."

Cassie answered for the young man. "But, Missus, he shore can sound like one. Sometimes he be up before the real roosters and he be a'crowing for our peoples to wake up and all the hens be a'comin' runnin'. Lord have mercy if'n he don't crow just like a rooster."

"We'll have to get you well, Rooster, so I can hear your crowing," Blue Heron said. "Sounds as if you might have some broken ribs. Take this medicine so we can bind up your chest after we take care of Slim and Jimbo."

Exhaustion set in as Blue Heron and Cassie finished binding up Slim's leg. The male helpers had left. Blue Heron sat and drank a gourd of water. It had been a long, long time since she drank from a gourd. And it had been a long, long time since she had felt so tired. As she arose to take care of Jimbo and Rooster, in came Mr. Hart.

"When you're finished, Miz Lange, come up to the big house. The Missus and I would be pleased to have you take supper with us before I fetch you back home." Then he left.

Blue Heron could not conceal her disappointment that Mr. Hart had not inquired about the condition of Slim and Jimbo and Rooster. And how could she go to the big house and enjoy a fancy supper while here in the slave cabin they had only turnip green pot liquor and corn pone?

Though totally exhausted, Blue Heron gave Cassie a slight hug before leaving, and Cassie said, "We thank you, Missus."

"Well, I thank you, too, Cassie. I couldn't have done it without all your help. I hope to come back tomorrow and check on the men." She paused, then thoughtfully said, "Maybe it won't be long before we can trust one another with some of our heartfelt feelings." Blue Heron went back to the table, shook some laudanum into an empty snuff can she had taken from her basket, handed the can to Cassie, and said, "Slim will surely need some of this medicine for pain before I return. Give him only one half of it at a time. He can have part of it during the night and the other part in the morning. And remember I have a medicine called quinine that is good for malaria if anyone ever needs it."

"Yessum. And we'll be a'lookin' for you. It's too bad we didn't have a big rattlesnake to dangle over Slim while we wus fixin' up his leg, but I hafta say yore mediicine worked good anyways."

Blue Heron released a small smile on her tired face.

# THE LIGHT OF WISDOM

"Since Sunday's church service word is spreading that you are helping the slaves," Caleb, with a look of disapproval, said to Blue Heron. "That alone wouldn't be so harmful, but there's more; and if truth be told, something that Obed Owlsey has been talking about is not fit for your ears. Still I must tell you, because you should know what's on our customers' minds. Obed said he heard that when you were tending to the slaves over at the Hart's farm, you acted like a slave lover. He said he really hated to pass this on, since I put as much in the collection plate at the church as the richest land owners."

"Caleb, all I did was help the injured slaves to the best of my ability." Blue Heron had not even yet told the slaves that they should keep in close contact with the slave who is the blacksmith, since he hears most of the news about when wagons are leaving and the directions they will take.

"I believe you but you know Obed is well thought of by all the farmers. Nearly all of them take their corn to his gristmill for grinding. Another thing. When he passes the collection plate he sees exactly who gives how much to the church and counts it and keeps track of it."

In only three days matters worsened for Blue Heron. Caleb said, "The foreman at Josiah's lumber mill stopped by the store and said that he heard from one of the workers that Obed Owsley is telling everybody that he's found out you have been a slave lover for a long time. Seems some women at the church, some of the most honorable wives, knew that you even wanted to help free the slaves, and what's more—that you've wanted for a long time to help free them. They're saying it's the same as stealing what belongs to another person."

"But Caleb, I tell you in all honesty I have always been very careful of what I said, and whatever I said was to the most trustworthy women."

"The trouble is we don't know what this is going to do to our store business. You will have to stop your talking about helping the slaves and certainly never mention a word about freeing them. And I'll have to stop you from your healing of them, too."

Blue Heron tried resigning herself to the fact that she would have to learn to live with Caleb's decision. Her despair over Caleb's orders lasted less than a week when it combined with far greater despair of a disaster, a monumental disaster affecting both of them. On an early Tuesday morning, Caleb found his store ablaze. Red tongues of fire tall as the pines already leaped from the roof. Resin-rich logs crackled and popped and in no time black smoke veiled the horrible scene.

Blue Heron and everyone within walking distance heard the screams of the first onlookers and rushed to the commotion. They gazed with tragic expressions—the postmaster, the doctor, the other storekeepers, men, women, and children of all ages. Even the dogs looked sympathetic. Suddenly a crash sounded and the chimney rocks scattered. The store quickly burned down with nothing left but the acrid smell of smoke. Before the crowd scattered, they lined up and offered handshakes and condolences to Caleb while only some of the women uttered sympathetic words to Blue Heron.

Caleb stood stunned, saddened, and seething until he tumbled down and settled like a plow behind a runaway horse. He sat staring all day as the ashes smoldered and turned gray. Blue Heron returned home and grieved alone. That evening they ate sparingly from the pot of beans and ham hocks brought over by the cook for the postmaster's family.

Josiah, not yet having heard of the calamity, dispatched a messenger the following day with two pieces of news—one good and one unpleasant. The good news was that Sehoy had given birth to a girl. Blue Heron was delighted. There would be no grandchild named "Andrew J." —not yet anyway. Blue Heron sighed with relief. The unpleasant news concerned Padre. Josiah had been informed by a Spaniard, a drifter from Pensacola, that Padre was now bedridden with arthritis, among other ailments.

Only two days after the fire an unthinkable thing happened, as if the fire were not a big enough calamity. Caleb had gone to the outhouse in the early morning as usual, but he did not return as usual. Blue Heron investigated and found him lying halfway out the flung-open door of the outhouse. A gash in his forehead gushed blood. Blue Heron bent down on her knees screaming, "Caleb." There was no answer, no movement. "No, no, nooo," she groaned. But it was true. He was not breathing. She did not have to close his eyes. They were already shut.

For Blue Heron and Abel, the funeral and memories of their dear husband and father consumed the better part of their conversations after the visitors had left on the burial day. Blue Heron kept her heartfelt sadness and deep feeling of loneliness within her heart. She longed for, more than ever, to have a greater part in Abel's life. Abel was all she had to really hold onto. Sehoy was busily fulfilled as a cherished wife and mother and did not need help, since a young widow with two children lived in her home to help care for Emma and Sarah. During the night she made a momentous decision. At breakfast the following morning, Blue Heron told Abel she would like to accompany him on his return to Ft. Crawford.

By spending time with Abel, Blue Heron thought she might, in the future, talk him into building an apothecary on the land that had been occupied by Caleb's store. Of course, a private room at the Ft. Crawford Inn would be high living, but she needed to humor herself. At this turning point in her life, she should think of herself at least for a few weeks, at least until she could gather her senses, at least until she learned to live with the tragedies and changes. And perhaps some time in the great beyond she might feel a renewed zeal to seek out the story of the Creek constable and possibly find some little thing, in addition to his chin and age, to connect him with her long-lost son, Tupelo.

Abel could not have been more amenable for his mother to accompany him to Ft. Crawford for a visit. He asked the postmaster to explain to Sehoy and Josiah—whenever they came to the post office—about Blue Heron's decision. To be sure, they would be in agreement about the visit.

The innkeeper's helper registered Blue Heron, and Abel ate supper with his mother at the inn. As they were finishing their bowls of blueberry cobbler, the innkeeper stopped by their table and asked, "How was the cobbler? My wife dried the berries last season. They were so tiny I didn't think much of them, yet they plumped up a bit and colored the cobbler like fresh ones."

Blue Heron said, "I thought I did not have a large enough appetite for dessert. I was wrong. I enjoyed the cobbler very much. The fresh cream added to the good flavor."

"I understand from my helper that you will be with us here for a while."

Abel answered, "Yes. My mother will be here for a while, and I will spend some time with her, that is after apothecary hours."

"You have a mighty fine son, Mrs. Lange. People around here took right to him."

"Thank you. I'm very proud of him."

The innkeeper pulled up a chair and said, "Since this is a Sunday, I have time to tell you the stories about the constable. I remember when you were here with your son-in-law you wanted awfully bad to hear the stories."

Before Blue Heron could explain that she was still grieving for her deceased husband, the innkeeper said, "The way the constable was found is what I call a miracle." The innkeeper wiped tobacco-stained leakages from the corners of his mouth and said, "A man by the name of Otis Henderson and his son was about to set out trot lines near where Briar Branch feeds into the Conecuh River when they noticed something strange floating into the cove. Turned out to be a Indian young'un holding onto a piece of a half-rotten log. Being a Bible-toting church man, Otis said he couldn't just walk away from the boy, so he took him home. Trouble was his wife. She asked what they would call him 'cause she wasn't of a mind to give the Henderson name to a savage."

Blue Heron quivered. The unexpectedness of the Creek boy's river rescue riveted her threadbare senses.

"Otis said they found only two clues to who boy was and neither one really told anything about him. A green leaf was stuck in his hair and he had a rock hanging from around his neck. Otis's missus said she liked the sound of the green leaf. So, Otis said since they found him by chance, they would call him Chance and Greenleaf could be his last name. They didn't give him the middle name of Moses until somebody at the church said the way he was found seemed like the Moses story in the Bible."

Abel said, "True stories are sometimes stranger than made-up ones. I had no idea about the constable's background. I only knew he had a different last name from the people who raised him."

"Speaking of raising, Otis's wife ordered the savage to sleep in the corn crib. Then a couple years later a turnabout changed everything. You see, the Hendeson boy died of what people thought was a disease of the lungs. After the Hendersons lost their son, they brought Chance inside the house and treated him like a son. They even scraped up enough money to send him off to school in Mobile. That's how he got the education to become a constable. Some people say that enforcing the law gave him an outlet for his pent up feelings of wondering about his real parents and where he came from. It was after he got orders to help the military enforce the banishment of the Creek that he got to be well known with the people. Wasn't no time till everybody thought a lot of him, 'cause they was so relieved they didn't have to worry about them Indians anymore."

The unstoppable coalescing clues rent Blue Heron's heart, finally leading her to half believe the unbelievable—could this Creek possibly in her wildest imagination be her Tupelo? But, she could not tolerate another heartrending comment from the innkeeper. She covered her open-mouthed

stare and excused herself before tears fell.  Whereupon, Abel explained to
the innkeeper about the recent fire destroying his father's store and then his
father's death and that these tragedies probably accounted for his mother's
leaving the dining room.

The next time Blue Heron saw Chance Greenleaf, she watched with
discreet pleasure as he tied reins to the hitching post fronting the inn.  She
had recognized him immediately and at once made the brazen decision to
stand in her space and shamelessly not move out of his pathway.  She just
might discover something about him, besides the missing four fingers, that
would prove she had only been dreaming that this man could be her firstborn son, Tupelo.  She just could not believe Tupelo would have ever had a
part in banishing the Creek.  Nearby a passel of crows ominously and
menacingly squawked as if treeing an owl, surely not a good sign.

The constable dropped a piece of paper and Blue Heron, without a
thought of her action, stepped on the paper to keep the wind from blowing it
away.  The constable quickly bent down to fetch the paper and as he
straightened up, Blue Heron's eyes went directly to a rock that had dangled
outside the neck of his shirt.  The rock's color contrasted vividly on his
muslin shirt.

Again without a thought to her behavior, she said, appealing with her
eyes, "Pardon me sir, I know of a rock exactly like the one you are wearing
around your neck."

With certain confidence Chance Greenleaf glared, then chuckled, and
said, "Pardon me madam, many women, when they see my badge, dream up
all kinds of excuses to start a conversation."

Her cheeks burned; her eyes flashed.  Anger streaked through Blue
Heron.  The anger raged, deep raging anger she had never known before; but
this much she knew: She had seen the crease in his prominent chin.  She had
figured his age would be the correct fit.  He had been found, as a child, in
the river of cane.  And now she had seen the rock, the rock that his blood
father had selected for him.

This much *more* she knew: The Creek constable *was* Tupelo and she
was boiling hot inside that he had treated her with such disrespect.  Why
when he was a baby she had many times put fresh spagnum moss under his
hind end and discarded the messy moss containing his waste.  And now her
high-and-mighty son was filled with "white" ways and talk.  She wished she
could scratch him with the sharpest of bones until he yelled as he had when
he was young.

A genteel-looking young woman and two bonneted little girls walked
out to meet Chance Greenleaf.  Chance picked up the older girl at the waist
and affectionately tossed her into the air while the younger girl squealed and

stamped her feet in anticipation of her turn. Then the four of them walked toward the dining room, chirping like a passel of spring squirrels.

Tears flowed down Blue Heron's cheeks; her lips quivered. Somehow she found the way to her room and, for the first time in her life, slammed the door. She tossed her shawl and, bleary-eyed, stubbed her big toe on the nearby valise. Her aching toe sent her hopping in a circle. Somehow, her actions seemed to belong to another person. She flung herself across the bed, jerking with sobs. She had no way of knowing how long she had been sobbing when she heard a knock on the door. The innkeeper's helper said, "Sorry to be of a bother Missus, but we noticed you and Abel had not appeared for supper. Is anything wrong?"

Without opening the door Blue Heron gritted her teeth and said, "Well, I don't feel very well. And as for Abel, you must have forgotten that this is his evening to do chores at the apothecary's house. If you can bring me a small portion of whatever you are serving this evening, I would be much obliged."

"Yessum, Missus. I'll do that."

Though dazed and drained, Blue Heron washed her face and then pecked at the sausage-potato hash. On any other day the flavorful-looking browned mixture would have been appealing. The onion odor, which she had always pleasantly associated with the innkeeper's promise of a story about the constable, now repulsed her.

The evening was long. Her dilemma loomed larger and larger. There was no way she could just put her son out of her mind, but how could she be patient to let their trust grow or ever get to know him; and even if she could get to know him, could she forgive him for helping to banish the Creek? Still, he had been transplanted like a young tree. He is of the forest, and the forest is good. He was uprooted from his place on Mother Earth and traveled a different path. Now, it was no longer from the vision of material things she shrank. She had a sense of deeper impoverishment, something more miserable still, the clutch of Tupelo at her heart.

The space between her and Tupelo was wider than the sky, wider than the Pensacola Gulf. She had taken long, long looks to capture in her mind forever the never-ending gulf water to the south and the stretches from east to west. She may never see it again or have the opportunity to seek Padre's advice now that he is so sick. And, of course, she no longer had Caleb's support. She was alone. It was up to her to find a way to close the huge gap between her and Tupelo. Padre had told her that she had the ability within herself to help the slaves. Well, she just might also have whatever is necessary within herself to reach out and pull in Tupelo—pull, pull, pull until the space narrowed.

*I think I know…yes, I know what needs to be done but what's missing is that I don't know how to get that pulling together accomplished. How do I get that wisdom? How can I move Tupelo to want to visit his burial mound? Would he ever want to know about the Owl Clan and his Creek heritage? Would his family ever blend with the Lange family? How would the Hendersons react to her?*

Deep inside, a kernel of hope revived when her mind returned to one of her old chants: "The earth is our mother from whence we come; the trees, streams, and animals are our brothers and sisters; the wind is the breath of our ancestors; from first sigh till we return to our mother."

When Blue Heron finally fell asleep she dreamed of Tupelo chasing lightning bugs when he was a child in the Owl Clan. Hundreds of the bugs would glow and go, glow and go with Tupelo chasing them. In the morning, loud snoring from the next room awakened her. The "glow and go" words circled around and around in her head.

Though limping on her sore toe, she went to the window. As usual, she pushed aside the curtain panel to watch the rising sun. She picked up the Rising Sun shell Padre had found for her. With her fingertips she glossed over its smooth surface and traced the sunray-like streaks from one end of the shell to the other. Then she pressed the shell to her cheek, hoping to regain good spirits. As usual, Padre's parting gift brought comfort. If it had not been for visiting Padre in Pensacola, she might never have known about how Tupelo was rescued from the river. Still clutching the Rising Sun shell, she looked out at the great space beyond in a searching way. Early light was strengthening the green beauty of spring with fresh leaves, grass, and bushes.

Blue Heron felt a faint smile trying to break across her lips as a surge of exhilaration lightened her heart. There, outside, the world was filling with light for the new day, a world also filling with new problems to be put into new light, healing light. This much more she realized. The light of Wisdom to find right answers sometimes winks and blinks like the go and glow of lightning bugs, giving a little light each time.

# LIKE THE DUST OF A MOTH

A bel anchored his spoon midst the cornmeal dumplings, tented his hands, and said, "I believe you. I really do believe you, Mother. If you had formed your conclusion only on the part about the crease in his long chin, well, a person could question that. But about the unmistakable identity of the rock hanging around his neck, that clenched it for me, especially considering how his age and the way he was found in the river would fit in the identification, too. How could anyone have a doubt with all that evidence? I can't tell you how proud I am that the constable might be my brother, even if he would just be my half brother."

Abel picked up his spoon and stirred the bowl. "I'll never forget the mouth-watering smell of these greens. Nobody likes cornmeal dumplings in turnips and pot liquor better than I, but—can you believe it—this news is so good it's just about squelching my appetite. I can't think of any other really brave man around here that's more highly respected than Chance Greenleaf. Just imagine how everyone will look up to me when they find out he's my brother. They already do, but now it would be an even more manly kind of respect."

"There's no *might* about his being your brother. Tupelo *is* my firstborn son."

"That's fine, that's fine, Mother, but I think you shouldn't call him Tupelo."

"In my heart, he's Tupelo, and the way he treated me when I noticed the rock hanging around his neck hurt me deeply."

"But that was his name a long time ago. It does not fit now. Please, just call him Mr. Constable or Mr. Greenleaf till you get to know him better. I

388

am sure he will feel sorry for the way he treated you if he gets to know you."

Abel had said the magic words. The most important issue now is for her, as well as Abel and Sehoy and her family, to get to know Tupelo—rather she should now think of him as the constable—and his family and even the Hendersons. The Hendersons most certainly had to be good people to have reared him.

The following evening was Abel's turn to do chores at Apothecary Berman's home, but since he could not wait another day to tell his mother the good news, he made a quick stop by the inn. "I just had to tell you that Mr. Berman told me today business has increased twofold since I have been apprentice there. He wants me to become a partner. Just what I dreamed of."

"I was hoping you would return to Andalusia and open your own business where your father's store had been located." A cool silence sliced between them momentarily. "Still, I know Caleb would want me to stand behind your decision. I suppose I shouldn't be surprised that the apothecary is prospering. I heard the innkeeper telling a customer only yesterday that he planned to add on rooms."

"I have to get going. I'll see you tomorrow after work. Remember to practice in your mind calling the constable by his title or real name so at church Sunday it will come natural."

Blue Heron knew his *real* name, but she had more pressing comments at the moment. "Church? I don't remember ever seeing him at church."

"They haven't been going to church for a while. The constable is hot on the trail for some bandits that stole a farmer's hogs he was driving to the Mobile market. He thinks the same rascals caused Judge Whaley's death. When they attacked the judge, his buggy slammed into a phalanx of big old live oaks. The impact killed him instantly, so they had no trouble robbing him of every cent and stealing his horses. I heard that the constable goes after bandits with a killer instinct. But he just might be at church Sunday. Sorry, I gotta run now or I'll be working outside till night time."

Blue Heron continued sitting in the corner rocker. She reasoned that she shouldn't be surprised at Abel's success. After all, she remembered how Caleb had lent her scissors to cut out her first calico dress. Abel's way with people and his business sense were just like his father's.

In her reflections she marveled at the way Abel had always brought his Bible to church services and the way he proudly carried it. Excited that she might see Chance and his family at church this coming Sunday as well as shocked by Abel's news that he would become a partner at the Apothecary, Blue Heron vaguely heard two travelers entering the inn. She forced herself to raise her head to nod to their "good day" greetings.

A growing predicament began pressing on her mind. Ft. Crawford was prospering, Andalusia was growing, but she was standing still except that her money was dwindling. Perhaps the crying spell had jarred her into realization of the way in which she was spending her time and money. She had been filling her days by constantly reliving the recent tragedies in her life—events of the horrible fire that had destroyed the store, the acrid smoke smell still stinging her nostrils; and the shocking surprise of finding her dear husband, Caleb, lying dead in the entrance to the outhouse, her stunned, saddened feelings just as real today as they had been then. Worse, she was beginning to wonder if she had, in a way, been responsible for these terrible losses. Sometimes she would go walking, not knowing where she was going, seeing but not noticing.

*At this inn, I am living mostly in the past. I must return to Andalusia soon. I must get my hands and mind busy. I must trust that my turn will come when I can get to know my long lost son and wrap my arms around his two little girls, my grandchildren. I want to hold them close, feel their breathing and the warmth of their body heat, run my fingers through their hair, and smell their scents. I must be patient.*

She imagined she could take into her Andalusia home, two or three boarders, maybe itinerant tradesmen. She imagined she could get back to healing and helping the slaves, not worrying if her house might burn. She had to move forward and live her life. She imagined she could get back to attending the church that Caleb helped build. It wouldn't be easy and was not exactly what she wanted but clearly the right thing to do now.

But most of all she would like to live in Ft. Crawford. She imagined she could get work at the inn helping in the kitchen and cleaning. She imagined Abel would build his own house in Ft. Crawford, and she could keep house for him. She imagined Sehoy and Josiah would visit Ft. Crawford with their children whenever the church had all-day meetings with dinner on the grounds. Surely Emma and Sarah would mix with Chance's two daughters. Yes, combining church and children would be a good way to start getting to know each other and blending the families. She might even learn how her son lost his four fingers.

Blue Heron had lapsed into a spiritual gaze. A white moth flitted peacefully outside the door, attracting Blue Heron's attention.

*That's what I can do. That's what I will do every time I have the opportunity. Like a moth flying around and leaving its dust on plants—for which Mother Earth must have a good reason—I will move among the Greenleaf and Henderson families at church and leave dust of goodwill, layers and layers of goodwill for everybody—my children, my grandchildren and the children of their children. The moth brought me a lesson.*

Now more than ever, Blue Heron's spirits lifted with thoughts of attending church Sunday. Now more than ever, she felt she was ready to soon return to Andalusia, at least for a while. Now more than ever, Blue Heron cherished the story of a rock—her very own "Rock of Ages" story.

# EPILOGUE

Some things never change. Andalusia is still about sixty-odd miles from Pensacola. But other things, of course, have changed. The southern part of the old Three Notch Road has been transformed into the present-day U.S. Highway 29.

In 1994, Andalusia celebrated its sesquicentennial. What has happened to the city in more than 150 years of its lifetime? The primeval forest, through which GENESIS and PADRE traveled, is now the Conecuh National Forest. It includes over 83,000 managed acres, complete with canebrakes, swamps, alligators, and snakes as well as cypress and magnolia trees, all of which were common to PADRE and GENESIS. However, new generations of long-leaf, slash, and loblolly pines have now replaced the primeval trees. Insect-eating plants can still be found in the bogs, though they bear new names like the rare, red Wherry Pitcher plant. And yes, the canes are still utilized today. Businesses in the area raise their own cane for the manufacture of fishing poles and surveying markers. Blue Spring, the large, natural spring, where PADRE and PRINCESS BLUE HERON enjoyed drinking water, still supplies clear, icy-blue water. Blue Lake, the location of PADRE'S primitive outdoor sanctuary, is now a recreation area. Blue Herons and limestone outcroppings, of a bluish hue, still abound. However, canoes seen on the Conecuh River in this decade are not always paddled by Creek. Through forest management, deer, turkeys, and fish are again plentiful. Archeological digs have revealed that both historic as well as prehistoric cultures inhabited the area.

Spanish-influenced architecture and names thread throughout Andalusia, which continues to be the seat of Covington County. What other

392

county can boast of a Rattlesnake Rodeo? Besides being a fun festival, the rodeo's main thrust is to educate people about the rattlers, which have survived well over the years. Considering PADRE AND GENESIS' experience with rattlers on the trail, they would probably sanction this rodeo's service to the people.

The original parchment deed of the 40-acre tract for the town of Andalusia, signed by President James K. Polk, can be viewed at the Three Notch Museum near the town square. At the museum one can also see the city flag. The colors and figures symbolize both the past and present: The Native American on horseback portrays the original inhabitants. Blue stands for the water of the Conecuh River. The shield and pikes represent the Spanish influence. The three-notched tree is synonymous with the area's historical journey.

Domino games, which CAPTAIN ZAMORA, GENESIS AND *SENOR COLABRO* enjoyed, have survived over time. For over twenty years, Andalusia has hosted the annual World Championship Domino Tournament.

Funeral processions command special consideration today, as in yesteryear. Be prepared to stop your vehicle or whatever you are doing, and like the local Andalusians, pause and pay respect. Men and boys, of course, remove their hats, and even little children stand solemnly.

Suppose GENESIS had not been a fictional character. Where would his grave have been located? Truth is, only the faintest indication of Creek mounds now exist. Presently, some Creek live in southern Alabama. The Poarch Creek Reservation, located south of Andalusia near Atmore, is in a different county. Each year tribal members gather on this original Creek land for the Annual Thanksgiving Homecoming and Inter-tribal Pow Wow.

Ft. Crawford is now the town of Brewton and is also located in another county.

Covington County's community of River Falls is named for the natural waterfalls that flow into the Conecuh River. This is where TUPELO was thought to have drowned. Rocks at the falls have eroded to some degree over the years.

After the Alabama legislature passed resolutions recognizing the Historic Three Notch Road, Covington County Historical Society placed street markers on Andalusia's two main thoroughfares—East Three Notch and South Three Notch Streets—commemorating the old Three Notch Road that had passed through or near the area.

Present-day Pensacola is known as the city of five flags. Of the five, the confederate flag would be a mystery to PADRE and GENESIS. On the other hand, street names, shipwreck relics, and Pensacola's famous red snapper fish would ring true to Spanish Pensacolians. Museums and reconstructed forts are filled with artifacts of British and Spanish influence as well as of the other dominions, which inhabited the area.

Archeologists' digs in the downtown Pensacola Historic Village have uncovered many important treasures, among which is the base of the well where PADRE and CAPTAIN supposedly drank water before traveling the Indian Ridge Trail. St. Michael's Church stands tall in the heart of Pensacola and St. Michael's Cemetery, with its historical funerary art, statues, and headstones is within walking distance of the church. Could the fictional Spanish St. Michael's Mission and the St. Michael's Church that PADRE helped build have had similarities to the history of the present historic church?

On the north side of Main Street, one can view the site of Panton-Leslie Trading Post, later called the Forbes Trading Company. It had been the largest Indian Trading Post in America, a truly important historic site. The octoroon's house, part of the estate which ANDREW JACKSON had helped her recover from the Innerarity nephew of the Forbes Trading Company, is one of the features of the Historic Village.

Pensacola's City Hall is located in the old Plaza Ferdinand VII, where the Spanish had drilled their troops and later delivered the Floridas to the U.S. Both East Florida and West Florida were received by ANDREW JACKSON, whose statue now graces the plaza. Across the street and to the east, one can sit on benches underneath ancient live oaks in the present Seville Square and view the eternal sugar sand beaches and coastal sunsets on the emerald bay.

HISTORICAL MARKER: In Covington County's town of Florala, near the Florida-Alabama border, an inscription on a historical marker at Lake Jackson (where Jackson rested his army after being lost in the swamps) reads:

"Andrew Jackson in Seminole War with an army of 1200 camped here in May 1818 en route westward from Fort Gadsden to subdue marauding Indians abetted by Spanish at Pensacola. Jackson determined to seize Pensacola and thus altered the course of history on this continent."

No doubt, GENESIS and PADRE, if they had been real people and were living today, would be proud to know that Spain has preserved the *Andalucian* horse bloodline. *Andalucian* traditional trainers led a spectacular performance of the horses at a Ryder Cup in Sotogrande, Spain.

# ABOUT THE AUTHOR

Annie Champa was born in Andalusia, Alabama, where she attended East Three Notch School. The city's name, the school's name, and the names of the city's two main streets—East Three Notch Street and South Three Notch Street—aroused abiding intrigue as to their origins.

The author went on to earn a BS, M.Ed., and further postgraduate credits at Kent University in Ohio and now lives with her husband in northeast Ohio.

Her career as educator presented myriad opportunities for extending development of her longtime love of reading, researching, and writing. Still, enduring magnetic pull of Andalusia's exotic Spanish name, steadfast prominence of the three notch symbol, and the accompanying legends—containing fundamentally different elements—ignited a flame for research in:

- Andalusia and its Three Notch Museum and Historical Society;
- Pensacola and its Historical Village and Historical Society;
- Atmore, Alabama, home of the Poarch Creek Indian Reservation.

Throughout the long process of researching, writing, and revising, the author's passion prevailed. Her keen appreciation for history as well as her deeply rooted heritage in storytelling inspired incarnation of the novel *Three Notches of Destiny*.